THE QUICKENING

THE QUICKENING

FRANCIS LYNDE

WILDSIDE PRESS

THE QUICKENING

This edition published 2005 by Wildside Press, LLC.
www.wildsidepress.com

I

BETHESDA

The revival in Paradise Valley, conducted by the Reverend Silas Crafts, of South Tredegar, was in the middle of its second week, and the field — to use Brother Crafts' own word — was white to the harvest.

Little Zoar, the square, weather-tinged wooden church at the head of the valley, built upon land donated to the denomination in times long past by an impenitent but generous Major Dabney, stood a little way back from the pike in a grove of young pines. By half past six of the June evening the revivalist's congregation had begun to assemble.

Those who came farthest were first on the ground; and by the time twelve-year-old Thomas Jefferson, spatting barefooted up the dusty pike, had reached the church-house with the key, there was a goodly sprinkling of unhitched teams in the grove, the horses champing their feed noisily in the wagon-boxes, and the people gathering in little neighborhood knots to discuss gravely the one topic uppermost in all minds — the present outpouring of grace on Paradise Valley and the region round-about.

"D'ye reckon the Elder'll make it this time with his brother-in-law?" asked a tall, flat-chested mountaineer from the Pine Knob uplands.

"Samantha Parkins, she allows that Caleb has done sinned away his day o' grace," said another Pine Knobber, "but I ain't goin' that far. Caleb's a sight like the iron he makes in that old furnace o' his'n — honest and even-grained, and just as good for plow-points and the like as it is for soap-kittles. But hot 'r cold, it's just the same; ye cayn't change hit, and ye cayn't change *him*."

"That's about right," said a third. "It looks to me like Caleb done sot his stakes where he's goin' to run the furrow. If livin' a dozen years and mo' with such a sancterfied woman as Martha Gordon won't make out to toll a man up to the pearly gates, I allow the' ain't no preacher goin' to do it."

"Well, now; maybe that's the reason," drawled Japheth Petti-grass, the only unmarried man in the small circle of listeners; but he was promptly put down by the tall mountaineer.

"Hold on thar, Japhe Pettigrass! I allow the' ain't no dyed-in-the-wool hawss-trader like you goin' to stand up and say anything ag'inst Marthy Gordon while I'm a-listenin'. I'm recollectin' right now the time when she sot up day and night for more'n a week with my Malviny — and me a-smashin' the whisky jug acrost the wagon tire to he'p God to forgit how no-'count and triflin' I'd been."

Thomas Jefferson had opened the church-house doors and windows and was out among the unhitched teams looking for Scrap Pendry, who had been one of a score to go forward for prayers the night before. So it happened that he overheard the flat-chested mountaineer's tribute to his mother. It warmed him generously; but there was a boyish scowl for Japheth Pettigrass. What had the horse-trader been saying to make it needful for Bill Layne to speak up as his mother's defender? Thomas Jefferson recorded a black mark against Pettigrass's name, and went on to search for Scrap.

"What you hiding for?" he demanded, when the newly-made convert was discovered skulking in the dusky shadows of the pines beyond the farthest outlying wagon.

"I ain't hidin'," was the half defiant answer.

"You're a liar," said Thomas Jefferson coolly, ducking skilfully to escape the consequences.

But there were no consequences. Young Pendry's heavy face flushed a dull red, — that could be seen even in the growing dusk, — but he made no move retaliatory. Thomas Jefferson walked slowly around him, wary as a wild creature of the wood, and to the full as curious. Then he stuck out his hand awkwardly.

"I only meant it 'over the left,' Scrap, hope to die," he said. "I allowed I'd just like to know for sure if what you done last night made any difference."

Scrap was silent, glibness of tongue not being among the gifts of the East Tennessee landward bred. But he grasped the out-thrust hand heartily and crushed it forgivingly.

"Come on out where the folks are," urged Thomas Jefferson. "Sim Cantrell and the other fellows are allowin' you're afeard."

"I ain't afeard," denied the convert.

"No; but you're sort o' 'shamed, and that's about the same thing, I reckon. Come on out; I'll go 'long with you."

Then spake the new-born love in the heart of the big, rough, country boy. "I cayn't onderstand how you can hold out, Tom-Jeff. I've come thoo', praise the Lord! but I jest natchelly *got* to have stars for my crown. You say you'll go 'long with me, Tom-Jeff: say it ag'in, and mean it."

Again the doubtful-curious look came into Thomas Jefferson's gray eyes, and he would not commit himself. Nevertheless, one point was safely established, and it was a point gained: the miraculous thing called conversion was beyond question real in Scrap's case. He turned to lead the way between the wagons. The lamps were lighted in the church and the people were filling the benches, while the choir gathered around the tuneless little cottage organ to practise the hymns.

"I — I'm studyin' about it some, Scrap," he confessed, half angry with himself that the admission sent the blood to his cheeks. "Let's go in."

It was admitted on all sides that Brother Crafts was a powerful preacher. Other men had wrestled mightily in Zoar, but none to such heart-shaking purpose. When he expatiated on the ineffable glories of Heaven and the joys of the redeemed, which was not too often, the reflection of the celestial effulgences could be seen rippling like sunshine on the sea of faces spreading away from the shore of the pulpit steps. When he spoke of hell and its terrors, which was frequently and with thrilling descriptive, even so hardened a scoffer as Japheth Pettigrass was wont to declare that you could hear the crackling of the flames and the cries of the doomed.

The opening exercises were over — the Bible reading, the long, impassioned prayer, the hymn singing — and the preacher stood up in a hush that could be felt, and stepped forward to the small desk which served for a pulpit.

He was a tall man, thin and erect, with a sallow, beardless face unrelieved by any line of mobility, but redeemed and almost glorified by the deep-set, eager, burning eyes. He had a way of bending to his audience when he spoke, with one long arm crooked behind him and the other extended to mark the sentences with a pointing finger, as if to remove the final trace of impersonality; to break down the last of the barriers of reserve which might be thrown up by the impenitent heart.

The hush remained unbroken till he announced his text in a voice that rang like an alarm-bell pealed in the dead of night. There are voices and voices, but only now and then one which is pitched in the key of the spheral harmonies. When the Reverend Silas hurled out the Baptist's words, *Repent ye: for the kingdom of heaven is at hand!* the responsive thrill from the packed benches was like the sympathetic vibration of harp-strings answering a trumpet blast.

The thin, large-jointed hand went up for silence, as if there could be a silence more profound than that which already hung on his word. Then he began slowly, and in phrase so simple that the youngest child could not fail to follow him, to draw the picture of that Judean morning scene on the banks of the Jordan, of the wild, unkempt, skin-clad forerunner, thundering forth his message to a sin — cursed world. On what deaf ears had it fallen among the multitude gathered on Jordan's bank! On what deaf ears would it fall in Zoar church this night!

He classed them rapidly, and with a prescient insight into the mazes of human frailty that made it seem as if the doors of all hearts were open to him: the Pharisee, who paid tithes — mint, anise and cummin — and prayed daily on the street corners, and saw no need for repentance; the youth and the maiden, with their lips to the brimming cup of worldly pleasures, saying to the faithful monitor, yet a little while longer and we will hear thee; the man and woman grown, fighting the battle for bread, living toilfully for time and the things that perish, and hearing the warning voice faintly and ever more faintly as the years pass; the aged, steeped and sodden in sin unrepented of, and with the spiritual senses all dulled and blunted by lifelong rebellion, willing now to hear and obey, it might be, but calling in vain on the merciful and long-suffering God they had so long rejected.

Then, suddenly, he passed from pleading to denunciation. The setting of The Great White Throne and the awful terrors of the Judgment Day were depicted in words that fell from the thin lips like the sentence of an inexorable judge.

"'Depart from me, ye cursed, into everlasting fire, prepared for the devil and his angels!'" he thundered, and a shudder ran through the crowded church as if an earthquake had shaken the valley. "There is your end, impenitent soul; and, alas! for you, it is only the beginning of a fearful eternity! Think of it, you who have time to think of everything but the salvation of your soul, your sins, and the awful doom which is awaiting you! Think of it, you who are throwing your lives away in the pleasures of this world; you who have broken God's commands; you who have stolen when you thought no eye was on you; you who have so often committed murder in your hating hearts! Think not that you will be suffered to escape! Every servant of the most high God who has ever declared His message to you will be there to denounce you: I, Silas Crafts, will meet you at the judgment-seat of Christ to bear my witness against you!"

A man, red-faced and with the devil of the cup of trembling peering from under his shaggy eyebrows, rose unsteadily from his seat on the bench nearest the door.

"'Sh! he's fotched Tike Bryerson!" flew the whisper from lip to ear; but the man with the trembling madness in his eyes was backing toward the door. Suddenly he stooped and rose again with a backwoodsman's rifle in his hands, and his voice sheared the breathless silence like the snarl of a wild beast at bay.

"No, by jacks, ye won't witness ag'inst me, Silas Crafts; ye'll be dead!"

The crack of the rifle went with the words, and at the flash of the piece the man sprang backward through the doorway and was gone. Happily, he had been too drunk or too tremulous to shoot straight. The preacher was unhurt, and he was quick to quell the rising tumult and to turn the incident to good account.

"There went the arrow of conviction quivering to the heart of a murderer!" he cried, dominating the commotion with his marvelous voice. "Come back here, Japheth Pettigrass; and you, William Layne: God Almighty will deal with that poor sinner in His own way. For him, for every impenitent soul here tonight, the hour has struck. 'Now is the accepted time; now is the day of salvation.' While we are singing, *Just as I am, without one plea*, let the doors of divine mercy stand opened wide, and let every hard heart be softened. Come, ye disconsolate; come forward to the mercy-seat as we sing."

The old, soul-moving, revival hymn was lifted in a triumphant burst of sound, and Thomas Jefferson's heart began to pound like a trip-hammer. Was this his call — his one last chance to enter the ark of safety? Just there was the pinch. A saying of Japheth Pettigrass's, overheard in Hargis's store on the first day of the meetings, flicked into his mind and stuck there: "Hit's scare, first, last, and all the time, with Brother Silas. He knows mighty well that a good bunch o' hickories, that'll bring the blood every cut, beats a sugar kittle out o' sight when it comes to fillin' the anxious seat." Was it really his call? Or was he only scared?

The twelve-year-old brain grappled hardily with the problem which has thrown many an older wrestler. This he knew: that while he had been listening with outward ears to the restless champing and stamping of the horses among the pines, but with his inmost soul to the burning words of his uncle, the preacher, a great fear had laid hold of him — a fear mightier than desire or shame, or love or hatred, or any spring of action known to him. It was lifting him to his feet; it was edging him past the others on the bench and out into the aisle with the mourners who were crowding the space in front of the pulpit platform. At the turn he heard his mother's low-murmured, "I thank Thee, O God!" and saw the grim, set smile on his father's face. Then he fell on his knees on the rough-hewn floor, with the tall mountaineer called William Layne on his right, and on his left a young girl from the choir who was sobbing softly in her handkerchief.

June being the queen of the months in the valleys of Tennessee, the revival converts of Little Zoar had the pick and choice of all the Sundays of the year for the day of their baptizing.

The font was of great nature's own providing, as was the mighty temple housing it, — a clear pool in the creek, with the green-walled aisles in the June forest leading down to it, and the blue arch of the flawless June sky for a dome resplendent.

All Paradise was there to see and hear and bear witness, as a matter of course; and there were not wanting farm-wagon loads from the great valley and from the Pine Knob highlands. Major Dabney was among the onlookers, sitting his clean-limbed Hambletonian, and twisting his huge white mustaches until they stood out like strange and fierce-looking horns. Also, in the outer ranks of skepticism, Major Dabney's foreman and horse-trader, Japheth Pettigrass, found a place. On the opposite bank of the stream were the few negroes owning Major Dabney now as "Majah Boss," as some of them, — most of them, in fact — had once owned him as "Mawstuh Majah"; and mingling freely with them were the laborers, white and black, from the Gordon iron-furnace.

Thomas Jefferson brought up memories from that solemn rite administered so simply and yet so impressively under the June sky, with the many-pointing forest spires to lift the soul to heights ecstatic. One was the singing of the choir, minimized and made celestially sweet by the lack of bounding walls and roof. Another was the sight of his father's face, with the grim smile gone, and the steadfast eyes gravely tolerant as he — Thomas Jefferson — was going down into the water. A third — and this might easily become the most lasting of all — was the memory of how his mother clasped him in her arms as he came up out of the water, all wet and dripping as he was, and sobbed over him as if her heart would break.

II

THE CEDARS OF LEBANON

Thomas Jefferson's twelfth summer fell in the year 1886; a year memorable in the annals of the Lebanon iron and coal region as the first of an epoch, and as the year of the great flood. But the herald of change had not yet blown his trumpet in Paradise Valley; and the world of russet and green and limestone white, spreading itself before the eyes of the boy sitting with his hands locked over his knees on the top step of the porch fronting the Gordon homestead, was the same world which, with due seasonal variations, had been his world from the beginning.

Centering in the broad, low, split-shingled house at his back, it widened in front to the old-fashioned flower garden, to the dooryard with its thick turf of uncut Bermuda grass, to the white pike splotched by the shadows of the two great poplars standing like sentinels on either side of the gate, to the wooded hills across the creek.

It was a hot July afternoon, a full month after the revival, and Thomas Jefferson was at that perilous pass where Satan is said to lurk for the purpose of providing employment for the idle. He was wondering if the shade of the hill oaks would be worth the trouble it would take to reach it, when his mother came to the open window of the living-room: a small, fair, well-preserved woman, this mother of the boy of twelve, with light brown hair graying a little at the temples, and eyes remindful of vigils, of fervent beseeching, of mighty wrestlings against principalities and powers and the rulers of the darkness of this world.

"You, Thomas Jefferson," she said gently, but speaking as one having authority, "you'd better be studying your Sunday lesson than sitting there doing nothing."

"Yes'm," said the boy, but he made no move other than to hug his knees a little closer. He wished his mother would stop calling him "Thomas Jefferson." To be sure, it was his name, or at least two-thirds of it; but he liked the "Buddy" of his father, or the "Tom-Jeff" of other people a vast deal better.

Further, the thought of studying Sunday lessons begot rebellion. At times, as during those soul-stirring revival weeks, now seemingly receding into a far-away past, he had moments of yearning to be wholly sanctified. But the miracle of transformation which he had confidently expected as the result of his "coming through" was still unwrought. When John Bates or Simeon Cantrell undertook to bully him, as aforetime, there was the same intoxicating experience of all the visible world going blood-red before his eyes — the same sinful desire to slay them, one or both. And as for Sunday lessons on a day when all outdoors was beckoning —

He stole a glance at the open window of the living-room. His mother had gone about her housework, and he could hear her singing softly, as befitted the still, warm day:

"O for a heart to praise my God!"

and it nettled him curiously. All hymns were beginning to have that effect, and this one in particular always renewed the conflict between the yearning for sanctity and a desire to do something desperately wicked; the only middle course lay in flight. Hence, the battle being fairly on, he stole another glance at the window, sprang afoot, and ran silently around the house and through the peach orchard to clamber over the low stone wall which was the only barrier on that side between the wilderness and the sown.

Once under the trees on the mountain side, the pious prompting knocked less clamorously at the door of his heart; and with its abatement the temptation to say or do the desperate thing became less insistent, also. It was always that way. When he was by himself in the forest, with no particularly gnawing hunger for righteousness, the devil let him alone. The thick wood was the true whisk to brush away all the naggings and perplexities that swarmed, like house-flies in the cleared lands. Nance Jane, the cow that did not know enough to come home at milking-time, knew that. In the hot weather, when the blood-sucking horse-flies and sweat-bees were worst, she would crash through the thickest underbrush and so be swept clean of her tormentors.

Emulating Nance Jane, Thomas Jefferson stormed through the nearest sassafras thicket and emerged regenerate. What next? High up on the mountain side, lifted far above Sunday lessons and soul conflicts and perplexing questions that hung answerless in a person's mind, was a place where the cedars smelled sweet and the west wind from the "other mountain" plashed cool in your face what time a sun-smitten Paradise Valley was like an oven. It would be three good hours before he would have to go after Nance Jane; and the Sunday lesson — but he had already forgotten about the Sunday lesson.

Three-quarters of the first hour were gone, and he was warm and thirsty when he topped the last of the densely-wooded lower slopes and came out on a high, rock-strewn terrace thinly set with mountain cedars. Here his feet were on familiar ground, and a little farther on, poised on the very edge of the terrace and overtopping the tallest trees of the lower slopes, was the great, square sandstone boulder which was his present Mecca.

On its outward face the big rock, gray, lichened and weather-worn, was a miniature cliff as high as the second story of a house; and at this cliff's foot was a dripping spring with a deep, crystalline pool for its basin. There was a time when Thomas Jefferson used to lie flat on his stomach and quench his thirst with his face thrust into the pool. But that was when he had got no farther than the Book of Joshua in his daily-chapter reading of the Bible. Now he was past Judges, so he knelt and drank from his hands, like the men of Gideon's chosen three hundred.

His thirst assuaged, he ascended the slope of the terrace to a height whence the flat top of the cubical boulder could be reached by the help of a low-branching tree. The summit of the great rock was one of the sacred places in the temple of the solitudes; and when the earth became too thickly peopled for comfort, he would come hither to lie on the very brink of the cliff overhanging the spring, heels in air, and hands for a chin-rest, looking down on a removed world mapping itself in softened outlines near and far.

Men spoke of Paradise as "the valley," though it was rather a sheltered cove with Mount Lebanon for its background and a semicircular range of oak-grown hills for its other rampart. Splitting it endwise ran the white streak of the pike, macadamized from the hill quarry which, a full quarter of a century before the Civil War, had furnished the stone for the Dabney manor-house; and paralleling the road unevenly lay a ribbon of silver, known to less poetic souls than Thomas Jefferson's as Turkey Creek, but loved best by him under its almost forgotten Indian name of Chiawassee.

Beyond the valley and its inclosing hills rose the "other mountain," blue in the sunlight and royal purple in the shadows — the Cumberland: source and birthplace of the cooling west wind that was whispering softly to the cedars on high Lebanon. Thomas Jefferson called the loftiest of the purple distances Pisgah, picturing it as the mountain from which Moses had looked over into the Promised Land. Sometime he would go and climb it and feast his eyes on the sight of the Canaan beyond; yea, he might even go down and possess the good land, if so the Lord should not hold him back as He had held Moses.

That was a high thought, quite in keeping with the sense of overlordship bred of the upper stillnesses. To company with it, the home valley straightway began to idealize itself from the uplifted point of view on the mount of vision. The Paradise fields were delicately-outlined squares of vivid green or golden yellow, or the warm red brown of the upturned earth in the fallow places. The old negro quarters on the Dabney grounds, many years gone to the ruin of disuse, were vine-grown and invisible save as a spot of summer verdure; and the manor-house itself, gray, grim and forbidding to a small boy scurrying past it in the deepening twilight, was now no more than a great square roof with the cheerful sunlight playing on it.

Farther down the valley, near the place where the white pike twisted itself between two of the rampart hills to escape into the great valley of the Tennessee, the split-shingled roof under which Thomas Jefferson had eaten and slept since the earliest beginning of memories became also a part of the high-mountain harmony; and the ragged, red iron-ore beds on the slope above the furnace were softened into a blur of joyous color.

The iron-furnace, with its alternating smoke puff and dull red flare, struck the one jarring note in a symphony blown otherwise on great nature's organ-pipes; but to Thomas Jefferson the furnace was as much a part of the immutable scheme as the hills or the forests or the creek which furnished the motive power for its air-blast. More, it stood for him as the summary of the world's industry, as the white pike was the world's great highway, and Major Dabney its chief citizen.

He was knocking his bare heels together and thinking idly of Major Dabney and certain disquieting rumors lately come to Paradise, when the tinkling drip of the spring into the pool at the foot of his perch was interrupted by a sudden splash.

By shifting a little to the right he could see the spring. A girl of about his own age, barefooted, and with only her tangled mat of dark hair for a head covering, was filling her bucket in the pool. He broke a dry twig from the nearest cedar and dropped it on her.

"You better quit that, Tom-Jeff Gordon. I taken sight o' you up there," said the girl, ignoring him otherwise.

"That's my spring, Nan Bryerson," he warned her dictatorially.

The girl looked up and scoffed. Hers was a face made for scoffing: oval and finely lined, with a laughing mouth and dark eyes that had both the fear and the fierceness of wild things in them.

"Shucks! it ain't your spring any more'n it's mine!" she retorted. "Hit's on Maje' Dabney's land."

"Well, don't you muddy it none," said Thomas Jefferson, with threatening emphasis.

For answer to this she put one brown foot deep into the pool and wriggled her toes in the sandy bottom. Things began to turn red for Thomas Jefferson, and a high, buzzing note, like the tocsin of the bees, sang in his ears.

"Take your foot out o' that spring! Don't you mad me, Nan Bryerson!" he cried.

She laughed up at him and flung him a taunt. "You don't darst to get mad, Tommy-Jeffy; *you've got religion.*"

It is a terrible thing to be angry in shackles. There are similes — pent volcanoes, overcharged boilers and the like — but they are all inadequate. Thomas Jefferson searched for missiles more deadly than dry twigs, found none, and fell headlong — not from the rock, but from grace. "*Damn!*" he screamed; and then, in an access of terrified remorse: "Oh, hell, hell, hell!"

The girl laughed mockingly and took her foot from the pool, not in deference to his outburst, but because the water was icy cold and gave her a cramp.

"Now you've done it," she remarked. "The devil'll shore get ye for sayin' that word, Tom-Jeff."

There was no reply, and she stepped back to see what had become of him. He was prone, writhing in agony. She knew the way to the top of the rock, and was presently crouching beside him.

"Don't take on like that!" she pleaded. "Times I cayn't he'p bein' mean: looks like I was made thataway. Get up and slap me, if you want to. I won't slap back."

But Thomas Jefferson only ground his face deeper into the thick mat of cedar needles and begged to be let alone.

"Go away; I don't want you to talk to me!" he groaned. "You're always making me sin!"

"That's because you're Adam and I'm Eve, ain't it? Wasn't you tellin' me in revival time that Eve made all the 'ruction 'twixt the man and God? I reckon she was right sorry; don't you?"

Thomas Jefferson sat up.

"You're awfully wicked, Nan," he said definitively.

"'Cause I don't believe all that about the woman and the snake and the apple and the man?"

"You'll go to hell when you die, and then I guess you'll believe," said Thomas Jefferson, still more definitively.

She took a red apple from the pocket of her ragged frock and gave it to him.

"What's that for?" he asked suspiciously.

"You eat it; it's the kind you like — off 'm the tree right back of Jim Stone's barn lot," she answered.

"You stole it, Nan Bryerson!"

"Well, what if I did? You didn't."

He bit into it, and she held him in talk till it was eaten to the core.

"Have you heard tell anything more about the new railroad?"

she asked.

Thomas Jefferson shook his head. "I heard Squire Bates and Major Dabney naming it one day last week."

"Well, it's shore comin' — right thoo' Paradise. I heard tell how it was goin' to cut the old Maje's grass patch plumb in two, and run right smack thoo' you-uns' peach orchard."

"Huh!" said Thomas Jefferson. "What do you reckon my father'd be doing all that time? He'd show 'em!"

A far-away cry, long-drawn and penetrating, rose on the still air of the lower slope and was blown on the breeze to the summit of the great rock.

"That's maw, hollerin' for me to get back home with that bucket o' water," said the girl; and, as she was descending the tree ladder: "You didn't s'picion why I give you that apple, did you, Tommy-Jeffy?"

"'Cause you didn't want it yourself, I reckon," said the second Adam.

"No; it was 'cause you said I was goin' to hell and I wanted comp'ny. That apple was stole and you knowed it!"

Thomas Jefferson flung the core far out over the tree-tops and shut his eyes till he could see without seeing red. Then he rose to the serenest height he had yet attained and said: "I forgive you, you wicked, wicked girl!"

Her laugh was a screaming taunt.

"But you've et the apple!" she cried; "and if you wasn't scared of goin' to hell, you'd cuss me again — you know you would! Lemme tell you, Tom-Jeff, if the preacher had dipped me in the creek like he did you, I'd be a mighty sight holier than what you are. I cert'nly would."

And now anger came to its own again.

"You don't know what you're talking about, Nan Bryerson! You're nothing but a — a miserable little heathen; my mother said you was!" he cried out after her.

But a back-flung grimace was all the answer he had.

III

OF THE FATHERS UPON THE CHILDREN

Thomas Jefferson's grandfather, Caleb the elder, was an old man before his son, Caleb the younger, went to the wars, and he figured in the recollections of those who remembered him as a grim, white-haired octogenarian who was one day carried home from the iron-furnace which he had built, and put to bed, dead in every part save his eyes. The eyes lived on for a year or more, following the movements of the sympathetic or curious visitor with a quiet, divining gaze; never sleeping, they said — though that could hardly be — until that last day of all when they fixed themselves on the wall and followed nothing more in this world.

Caleb, the son, was well past his first youth when the Civil War broke out; yet youthful ardor was not wanting, nor patriotism, as he defined it, to make him the first of the Paradise folk to write his name on the muster-roll of the South. And it was his good fortune, rather than any lack of battle hazards, that brought him through the four fighting years to the Appomattox end of that last running fight on the Petersburg and Lynchburg road in which, with his own hands, he had helped to destroy the guns of his battery.

Being alive and not dead on the memorable April Sunday when his commander-in-chief signed the articles of capitulation in Wilmer McLean's parlor in Appomattox town, this soldier Gordon was one among the haggard thousands who shared the enemy's rations to bridge over the hunger gap; and it was the sane, equable Gordon blood that enabled him to eat his portion of the bread of defeat manfully and without bitterness.

Later it was the steadfast Gordon courage that helped him to mount the crippled battery horse which had been his own contribution to the lost cause; to mount and ride painfully to the distant Southern valley, facing the weary journey, and the uncertain future in a land despoiled, as only a brave man might.

His homing was to the old furnace and the still older house at the foot of Lebanon. The tale of the years succeeding may be briefed in a bare sentence or two. It was said of him that he reached Paradise and the old homestead late one evening, and that the next day he was making ready for a run of iron in the antiquated blast-furnace. This may be only neighborhood tradition, but it depicts the man: sturdy, tenacious, dogged; a man to knot up the thread of life broken by untoward events, following it thereafter much as if nothing had happened.

Such men are your true conservatives. When his son was born, nine years after the great struggle had passed into history, Caleb, the soldier, was still using charcoal for fuel and blowing his cupola fire with the wooden air-pump whose staves had been hooped together by the hands of his father, and whose motive power was a huge overshot wheel swinging rhythmically below the stone dam in the creek.

The primitive air-blast being still in commission, it may itself say that the South, in spite of the war upheaval and the far more seismic convulsion of the reconstruction period, was still the Old South when Caleb married Martha Crafts.

It was as much a love match as middle-age marriages are wont to be, and following it there was Paradise gossip to assert that Caleb's wife brought gracious womanly reforms to the cheerless bachelor house at the furnace. Be this as it may, she certainly brought one innovation — an atmosphere of wholesome, if somewhat austere, piety hitherto unbreathed by the master or any of his dusky vassals.

Such moderate prosperity as the steadily pulsating iron-furnace could bring was Martha Gordon's portion from the beginning. Yet there was a fly in her pot of precious ointment; an obstacle to her complete happiness which Caleb Gordon never understood, nor could be made to understand. Like other zealous members of her communion, she took the Bible in its entirety for her creed, striving, as frail humanity may, to live up to it. But among the many admonitions which, for her, were no less than divine commands, was one which she had wilfully disregarded: *Be ye not unequally yoked together with unbelievers.*

Caleb respected her religion; stood a little in awe of it, if the truth were known, and was careful to put no straw of hindrance in the thorny upward way. But there are times when neutrality bites deeper than open antagonism. In the slippery middle ground of tolerance there is no foothold for one who would push or pull another into the kingdom of Heaven.

Under such conditions Thomas Jefferson was sure to be the child of many prayers on the mother's part; and perhaps of some naturally prideful hopes on Caleb's. When a man touches forty before his firstborn is put into his arms, he is likely to take the event seriously. Martha Gordon would have named her son after the great apostle of her faith, but Caleb asserted himself here and would have a manlier name-father for the boy. So Thomas Jefferson was named, not for an apostle, nor yet for the statesman — save by way of an intermediary. For Caleb's "Thomas Jefferson" was the stout old schoolmaster-warrior, Stonewall Jackson; the soldier iron-master's general while he lived, and his deified hero ever afterward.

When the mother was able to sit up in bed she wrote a letter to her brother Silas, the South Tredegar preacher. On the margin of the paper she tried the name, writing it "Reverend Thomas Jefferson Gordon." It was a rather appalling mouthful, not nearly so euphonious as the name of the apostle would have been. But she comforted herself with the thought that the boy would probably curtail it when he should come to a realizing sense of ownership; and "Reverend" would fit any of the curtailments.

So now we see to what high calling Thomas Jefferson's mother purposed devoting him while yet he was a helpless monad in pinning-blankets; to what end she had striven with many prayers and groanings that could not be uttered, from year to year of his childhood.

Does it account in some measure for the self-conscious young Pharisee kneeling on the top of the high rock under the cedars, and crying out on the girl scoffer that she was no better than she should be?

IV

THE NEWER EXODUS

One would always remember the first day of a new creation; the day when God said, *Let there be light.*

It has been said that nothing comes suddenly; that the unexpected is merely the overlooked. For weeks Thomas Jefferson had been scenting the unwonted in the air of sleepy Paradise. Once he had stumbled on the engineers at work in the "dark woods" across the creek, spying out a line for the new railroad. Another day he had come home late from a fishing excursion to the upper pools to find his father shut in the sitting-room with three strangers resplendent in town clothes, and the talk — what he could hear of it from his post of observation on the porch step — was of iron and coal, of a "New South," whatever that might be, and of wonderful changes portending, which his father was exhorted to help bring about.

But these were only the gentle heavings and crackings of the ground premonitory of the real earthquake. That came on a day of days when, as a reward of merit for having faultlessly recited the eighty-third Psalm from memory, he was permitted to go to town with his father. Behold him, then, dangling his feet — uncomfortable because they were stockinged and shod — from the high buggy seat while the laziest of horses ambled between the shafts up the white pike and around and over the hunched shoulder of Mount Lebanon. This in the cool of the morning of the day of revelations.

In spite of the premonitory tremblings, the true earthquake found Thomas Jefferson totally unprepared. He had been to town often enough to have a clear memory picture of South Tredegar — the prehistoric South Tredegar. There was a single street, hub-deep in mud in the rains, beginning vaguely at the steamboat landing, and ending rather more definitely in the open square surrounding the venerable court-house of pale brick and stucco-pillared porticoes. There were the shops — only Thomas Jefferson and all his kind called them "stores" — one-storied, these, the wooden ones with lying false fronts to hide the mean little gables; the brick ones honester in face, but sadly chipped and crumbling and dingy with age and the weather.

Also, there were houses, some of them built of the pale red brick, with pillared porticoes running to the second story; hip-roofed, with a square balustered observatory on top; rather grand looking and impressive till you came near enough to see that the bricks were shaling, and the portico floors rotting, and the plaster falling from the pillars to show the grinning lath-and-frame skeletons behind.

Also, on the banks of the river, there was the antiquated iron-furnace which, long before the war, had given the town its pretentious name. And lastly, there was the Calhoun House, dreariest and most inhospitable inn of its kind; and across the muddy street from it the great echoing train-shed, ridiculously out of proportion to every other building in the town, the tavern not excepted, and to the ramshackle, once-a-day train that wheezed and rattled and clanked into and out of it.

Thomas Jefferson had seen it all, time and again; and this he remembered, that each time the dead, weather-worn, miry or dusty dullness of it had crept into his soul, sending him back to the freshness of the Paradise fields and forests at eventide with grateful gladness in his heart.

But now all this was to be forgotten, or to be remembered only as a dream. On the day of revelations the earlier picture was effaced, blacked out, obliterated; and it came to the boy with a pang that he should never be able to recall it again in its entirety. For the genius of modern progress is contemptuous of old landmarks and impatient of delays. And swift as its race is elsewhere, it is only in that part of the South which has become "industrial" that it came as a thunderclap, with all the intermediate and accelerative steps taken at a bound. Men spoke of it as "the boom." It was not that. It was merely that the spirit of modernity had discovered a hitherto overlooked corner of the field, and made haste to occupy it.

So in South Tredegar, besprent now before the wondering eyes of a Thomas Jefferson. The muddy street had vanished to give place to a smooth black roadway, as springy under foot as a forest path, and as clean as the pike after a sweeping summer storm. The shops, with their false fronts and shabby lean-to awnings, were gone, or going, and in their room majestic vastnesses in brick and cut stone were rising, by their own might, as it would seem, out of disorderly mountains of building material.

Street-cars, propelled as yet by the patient mule, tinkled their bells incessantly. Smart vehicles of many kinds strange to Paradise eyes rattled recklessly in and out among the street obstructions. Bustling throngs were in possession of the sidewalks; of the awe-inspiring restaurant, where they gave you lemonade in a glass bowl and some people washed their fingers in it; of the rotunda of the Marlboro, the mammoth hotel which had grown up on the site of the old Calhoun House, — distressing crowds and multitudes of people everywhere.

Thomas Jefferson, awe-struck and gaping, found himself foot-loose for a time in the Marlboro rotunda while his father talked with a man who wanted to bargain for the entire output of the Paradise furnace by the year. The commercial transaction touched him lightly; but the moving groups, the imported bell-boys, the tesselated floors, frescoed ceiling and plush-covered furniture — these bit deeply. Could this be South Tredegar, the place that had hitherto figured chiefly to him as "court-day" town and the residence of his preacher uncle? It seemed hugely incredible.

After the conference with the iron buyer they crossed the street to the railway station; and again Thomas Jefferson was foot-loose while his father was closeted with some one in the manager's office.

An express train, with hissing air-brakes, Solomon-magnificent sleeping cars, and a locomotive large enough to swallow whole the small affair that used to bring the once-a-day train from Atlanta, had just backed in, and the boy took its royal measure with eager and curious eyes, walking slowly up one side of it and down the other.

At the rear of the string of Pullmans was a private car, with a deep observation platform, much polished brass railing, and sundry other luxurious appointments, apparent even to the eye of unsophistication. Thomas Jefferson spelled the name in the medallion, "Psyche," — spelled it without trying to pronounce it — and then turned his attention to the people who were descending the rubber-carpeted steps and grouping themselves under the direction of a tall man who reminded Thomas Jefferson of his Uncle Silas with an indescribable something left out of the face.

"As I was about to say, General, this station building is one of the relics. You mustn't judge South Tredegar — our new South Tredegar — by this. Eh? — I beg your pardon, Mrs. Vanadam? Oh, the hotel? It is just across the street, and a very good house; remarkably good, indeed, all things considered. In fact, we're quite proud of the Marlboro."

One of the younger women smiled.

"How enthusiastic you are, Mr. Parley. I thought we had outgrown all that — we moderns."

"But, my dear Miss Elleroy, if you could know what we have to be enthusiastic about down here! Why, these mountains we've been passing through for the last six hours are simply so many vast treasure-houses; coal at the top, iron at the bottom, and enough of both to keep the world's industries going for ages! There's millions in them!"

Thomas Jefferson overheard without understanding, but his

eyes served a better purpose. Away back in the line of the Scottish Gordons there must have been an ancestor with the seer's gift of insight, and some drop or two of his blood had come down to this sober-faced country boy searching the faces of the excursionists for his cue of fellowship or antipathy.

For the sweet-voiced young woman called Miss Elleroy there was love at first sight. For a severe, be-silked Mrs. Vanadam there was awe. For the portly General with mutton-chop whiskers, overlooking eyes and the air of a dictator, there was awe, also, not unmingled with envy. For the tall man in the frock-coat, whose face reminded him of his Uncle Silas, there had been shrinking antagonism at the first glance — which keen first impression was presently dulled and all but effaced by the enthusiasm, the suave tongue, and the benignant manner. Which proves that insight, like the film of a recording camera, should have the dark shutter snapped on it if the picture is to be preserved.

Thomas Jefferson made way when the party, marshaled by the enthusiast, prepared for its descent on the Marlboro. Afterward, the royalties having departed and a good-natured porter giving him leave, he was at liberty to examine the wheeled palace at near-hand, and even to climb into the vestibule for a peep inside.

Therewith, castles in the air began to rear themselves, tower on wall. Here was the very sky-reaching summit of all things desirable: to have one's own brass-bound hotel on wheels; to come and go at will; to give curt orders to a respectful and uniformed porter, as the awe-inspiring gentleman with the mutton-chop whiskers had done.

Time was when Thomas Jefferson's ideals ran quite otherwise: to a lodge in some vast wilderness, like the rock-strewn slopes of high Lebanon; to the company of the birds and trees, of the wide heavens and the shy wild creatures of the forest. But it is only the fool or the weakling who may not reconsider.

Notwithstanding, when the day of revelations was come to an end, and the ambling horse was inching the ancient buggy up the homeward road, the boy found himself turning his back on the wonderful new world with something of the same blessed sense of relief as that which he had experienced in former home-goings from South Tredegar, the commonplace.

At the highest point on the hunched shoulder of the mountain Thomas Jefferson twisted himself in the buggy seat for a final backward look into the valley of new marvels. The summer day was graying to its twilight, and a light haze was stealing out of the wooded ravines and across from the river. From the tall chimneys of a rolling-mill a dense column of smoke was ascending, and at the psychological moment the slag flare from an iron-furnace changed the overhanging cloud into a fiery ægis.

Having no symbolism save that of Holy Writ, Thomas Jefferson's mind seized instantly on the figure, building far better than it knew. It was a new Exodus, with its pillar of cloud by day and its pillar of fire by night. And its Moses — though this, we may suppose, was beyond a boy's imaging — was the frenzied, ruthless spirit of commercialism, named otherwise, by the multitude, Modern Progress.

V

THE DABNEYS OF DEER TRACE

If you have never had the pleasure of meeting a Southern gentleman of the patriarchal school, I despair of bringing you well acquainted with Major Caspar Dabney until you have summered and wintered him. But the Dabneys of Deer Trace — this was the old name of the estate, and it obtains to this day among the Paradise Valley folk — figure so largely in Thomas Jefferson's boyhood and youth as to be well-nigh elemental in these retrospective glimpses.

To know the Major even a little, you should not refer him to any of the accepted types, like Colonel Carter, of Cartersville, or that other colonel who has made Kentucky famous; this though I am compelled to write it down that Major Caspar wore the soft felt hat and the full-skirted Prince Albert coat, without which no reputable Southern gentleman ever appears in the pages of fiction. But if you will ignore these concessions to the conventional, and picture a man of heroic proportions, straight as an arrow in spite of his sixty-eight years, full-faced, well-preserved, with a massive jaw, keen eyes that have lost none of their lightnings, and huge white mustaches curling upward militantly at the ends you will have the Major's outward presentment.

Notwithstanding, this gives no adequate hint of the contradictory inner man. By turns the most lovingly kind and the most violent, the most generously magnanimous and the most vindictive of the unreconstructed minority, Caspar Dabney was rarely to be taken for granted, even by those who knew him best. Of course, Ardea adored him; but Ardea was his grandchild, and she was wont to protest that she never could see the contradictions, for the reason that she was herself a Dabney.

It was about the time when Thomas Jefferson was beginning to reconsider his ideals, with a leaning toward brass-bound palaces on wheels and dictatorial authority over uniformed lackeys and other of his fellow creatures, that fate dealt the Major its final stab and prepared to pour wine and oil into the wound — though of the balm-pouring, none could guess at the moment of wounding. It was not in Caspar Dabney to be patient under a blow, and for a time his ragings threatened to shake even Mammy Juliet's loyalty — than which nothing more convincing can be said.

"'Fo' Gawd, Mistuh Scipio," she would say, when the master had sworn volcanically at her for the fifth time in the course of one forenoon, "I'se jus' erbout wo'ed out! I done been knowin'

Mawstuh Caspah ebber sence I was Ol' Mistis's tiah-'ooman — dat's what she call me in de plantashum days — an' I ain't nev' seen him so fractious ez he been sence dat letter come tellin' him come get dat po' li'l gal-child o' Mawstuh Louis's. Seems lak he jus' gwine r'ar round twel he hu't somebody!"

Scipio, the Major's body-servant, had grown gray in the Dabney service, and he was well used to the master's storm periods.

"Doan' you trouble yo'se'f none erbout dat, Mis' Juliet. Mawstuh Majah tekkin' hit mighty hawd 'cause Mawstuh Louis done daid. But bimeby you gwine see him climm on his hawss an' ride up yondeh to whah de big steamboats comes in an' fotch dat li'l gal-child home; an' den: uck — uh-h! look out, niggahs! dar ain't gwine be nuttin' on de top side dishyer yearth good ernough for li'l Missy. You watch what I done tol' you erbout dat, now!"

Scipio's prophecy, or as much of it as related to the bringing of the orphaned Ardea to Deer Trace Manor, wrought itself out speedily, as a matter of course, though there was a vow to be broken by the necessary journey to the North. At the close of the war, Captain Louis, the Major's only son, had become, like many another hot-hearted young Confederate, a self-expatriated exile. On the eve of his departure for France he had married the Virginia maiden who had nursed him alive after Chancellorsville. Major Caspar had given the bride away, — the war had spared no kinsman of hers to stand in this breach, — and when the God-speeds were said, had himself turned back to the weed-grown fields of Deer Trace Manor, embittered and hostile, swearing never to set foot outside of his home acres again while the Union should stand.

For more than twenty years he kept this vow almost literally. A few of the older negroes, a mere handful of the six score slaves of the old patriarchal days, cast in their lot with their former master, and with these the Major made shift thriftily, farming a little, stockraising a little, and, unlike most of the war-broken plantation owners, clinging tenaciously to every rood of land covered by the original Dabney title-deeds.

In this cenobitic interval, if you wanted a Dabney colt or a Dabney cow, you went, or sent, to Deer Trace Manor on your own initiative, and you, or your deputy, never met the Major: your business was transacted with lean, lantern-jawed Japheth Pettigrass, the Major's stock-and-farm foreman. And although the Dabney stock was pedigreed, you kept your wits about you; else Pettigrass got much the better of you in the trade, like the shrewd, calculating Alabama Yankee that he was.

Ardea was born in Paris in the twelfth year of the exile; and the Virginian mother, pining always for the home land, died in the fifteenth year. Afterward, Captain Louis fought a long-drawn, losing battle, figuring bravely in his infrequent letters to his father as a rising miniature painter; figuring otherwise to the students of the Latin Quarter as "*ce pauvre Monsieur D'Aubigné;*" leading his little girl back and forth between his lodgings and the studio where he painted pictures that nobody would buy, and eking out a miserable existence by giving lessons in English when he was happy enough to find a pupil.

The brave letters imposed on the Major, as they were meant to do; and Ardea, the loyal, happening on one of them in her first Deer Trace summer, read it through with childish sobs and never thereafter opened her lips on the story of those distressful Paris days. Later she understood her father's motive better: how he would not be a charge on an old man rich in nothing but ruin; and the memory of the pinched childhood became a thing sacred.

How the Major, a second Rip Van Winkle, found his way to New York, and to the pier of the incoming French Line steamer, must always remain a mystery. But he was there, with the fierce old eyes quenched and swimming and the passionate Dabney lips trembling strangely under the great mustaches, when the black-frocked little waif from the Old World ran down the landing stage and into his arms. Small wonder that they clung to each other, these two at the further extremes of three generations; or that the child opened a door in the heart of the fierce old partizan which was locked and doubly barred against all others.

As may be imagined, the Major got away from Yankeeland with his charge as soon as a train could be made to serve; and he was grim and forbidding to all and sundry until the Cumberland Mountains had displaced the Alleghanies and the Blue Ridge on the western horizon. Indeed, the grimness, — to all save Ardea, — persisted quite to and through the transformed and transforming city at the eastern foot of Lebanon. Major Caspar was not in tune with the bravura of modern progress, and if he had been, his hatred of Northern importations of whatever nature would have made and kept him hostile.

But when the ancient carriage, with Scipio and Ardea's one small steamer trunk on the box, had topped the shrugged shoulder of Lebanon, and that view which we have seen from the summit of Thomas Jefferson's high rock among the cedars opened out before the eyes of the wondering child, the Major grew eloquent.

"Look youh fill, my deah child; thah it lies — God's country, and youh's and mine; the fines', the most inspiring, the most beautiful land the sun eveh shone on! And whilst you are givin' praise to youh Makeh for creatin' such a Gyarden of Eden, don't forget to thank him on youh bended knees for not putting anything oveh yondeh in ouh home lot to tempt these house-buildin', money-makin', schemin' Yankees that are swarming again oveh the land like anotheh plague of Egyptian locus'es."

"These — Yankees?" queried Ardea. In his later years the exiled Captain Louis had remembered only that he was an American, and his child knew no North nor South.

The Major did not explain. Not that there were any compunctions of conscience concerning the planting of the seed of sectionalism in this virgin soil, quite the contrary. He abstained because he made sure that time, and the Dabney blood, would do it better.

So he talked to the small one of safely prehistoric things, showing her the high mountain battle-field where John Sevier had broken the power of the savage Chickamaugas, and, as the carriage rolled down toward the head of Paradise, the tract of land where the first Dabney had sent his ax-men to blaze the trees for his lordly boundaries.

It was all new and very strange to a child whose only outlook on life had been urban and banal. She had never seen a mountain, and nothing more nearly approaching a forest than the parked groves of the Bois de Boulogne. Would it be permitted that she should sometimes walk in the woods of the first Dabney, she asked, with the quaint French twisting of the phrases that she was never able fully to overcome.

It would certainly be permitted; more, the Major would make her a deed to as many of the forest acres as she would care to include in her promenade. By which we see that the second part of Unc' Scipio's prophecy was finding its fulfilment in the beginning.

How the French-born child fitted into the haphazard household at Deer Trace Manor, with what struggles she came through the inevitable attack of homesickness, and how Mammy Juliet and every one else petted and indulged her, are matters which need not be dwelt on. But we shall gladly believe that she was too sensible, even at the early and tender age of ten, to be easily spoiled.

Many foolish things have been said and written about the wax-like quality of a child's mind; how each new impression effaces the old, and how character in permanence is not to be looked for until the bones have stopped growing. Yet who has not known criminals at twelve, and saints and angels, and wise men and women — in fine, the entire gamut of humanity — in short frocks or knee-breeches?

Ardea, child of adversity and the Paris ateliers, brought one lasting memory up out of those early Deer Trace Manor years: she was always immeasurably older than such infants as Mammy Juliet and Uncle Scipio. And this also she remembered: that when these and all the others, including her grandfather and Japheth Pettigrass, were busily leveling all the barriers of restraint for her, she had built some of her own and set herself the task of living within them.

I am sure she began to realize, almost at the first, that she must rise superior to the Dabney weakness, which, as exemplified by the Major, was ungoverned, and perhaps ungovernable, temper. At all events, she never forgot a summer day soon after her arrival when she first saw her grandfather transformed into a frenzied madman.

He was sitting on the wide portico, smoking his long-stemmed pipe and directing Japheth Pettigrass, who was training the great crimson-rambler rose that ran well up to the eaves. Ardea, herself, was on the lawn, playing with her grandfather's latest gift, a huge, solemn-eyed Great Dane, so she did not see the man who had dismounted at the gate and walked up the driveway until he was handing his card to her grandfather.

When she did see him, she looked twice at him; not because he was trigly clad in brown duck and tightly-buttoned service leg-gings, but because he wore his beard trimmed to a point, after the manner of the students in the Latin Quarter, and so was reminis-cent of things freshly forsaken.

She had succeeded in making the Great Dane carry her on his back quite all the way around the circular coleus bed when the explosion took place. There was a startling thunderclap of fierce words from the portico, and she slipped from the dog's back and stared wide-eyed. Her grandfather was on his feet, towering above the visitor as if he were about to fall on and crush him.

"Bring youh damned Yankee railroad through my fields and pastchuhs, suh? Foul the pure, God-given ai-ah of this peaceful Gyarden of Eden with youh dust-flingin', smoke-pot locomo-tives? Not a rod, suh! not a foot or an inch oveh the Dabney lands! Do I make it plain to you, suh?"

"But Major Dabney — one moment; this is purely a matter of business; there is nothing personal about it. Our company is able and willing to pay liberally for its right of way; and you must remember that the coming of the railroad will treble and qua-druple your land values. I am only asking you to consider the matter in a business way, and to name your own price."

Thus the smooth-spoken young locating engineer in brown duck, serving as plowman for his company. But there be tough old roots in some soils, roots stout enough to snap the colter of the commercializing plow, — as, for example, in Paradise Valley, owned, in broken areas, principally by an unreconciled Major Dabney.

"Not anotheh word, or by Heaven, suh, you'll make me lose my tempah! You add insult to injury, suh, when you offeh me youh contemptible Yankee gold. When I desiah to sell my birthright for youh beggahly mess of pottage, I'll send a black boy in town to infawm you, suh!"

It is conceivable that the locating engineer of the Great Southwestern Railway Company was younger than he looked; or, at all events, that his experience hitherto had not brought him in contact with fire-eating gentlemen of the old school. Else he would hardly have said what he did.

"Of course, it is optional with you, Major Dabney, whether you sell us our right of way peaceably or compel us to acquire it by condemnation proceedings in the courts. As for the rest — is it possible that you don't know the war is over?"

With a roar like that of a maddened lion the Major bowed himself, caught his man in a mighty wrestler's grip and flung him broadcast into the coleus bed. The words that went with the fierce attack made Ardea crouch and shiver and take refuge behind the great dog. Japheth Pettigrass jumped down from his step-ladder and went to help the engineer out of the flower bed. The Major had sworn himself to a stand, but the fine old face was a terrifying mask of passion.

"The old firebrand!" the engineer was muttering under his breath when Pettigrass reached him; but the foreman cut him short.

"You got mighty little sense, looks like, to me. Stove up any?"

"Nothing to hurt, I guess."

"Well, your hawss is waitin' for ye down yonder at the gate, and I don't b'lieve the Major is allowin' to ask ye to stay to supper."

The railroad man scowled and recovered his dignity, or some portion of it.

"You're a hospitable lot," he said, moving off toward the driveway. "You can tell the old maniac he'll hear from us later."

Pettigrass stooped with his back to the portico and patted the dog.

"Don't you look so shuck up, little one," he whispered reassuringly to Ardea. "There ain't nothin' goin' to happen, worse than has happened, I reckon." But Ardea was mute.

When the engineer had mounted and ridden away down the pike, the foreman straightened himself and faced about. The Major had dropped into his big armchair and was trying to relight his pipe. But his hands shook and the match went out.

Pettigrass moved nearer and spoke so that the child should not hear. "If you run me off the place the nex' minute, I'm goin' to tell you you ort to be tolerably 'shamed of yourse'f, Maje' Dabney. That po' little gal is scared out of a year's growin', right now."

"I know, Japheth; I know. I'm a damned old heathen! For, insultin' as he was, the man was for the time bein' my guest, suh — my guest!"

"I'm talkin' about the little one — not that railroader. So far as I know, he earned what he got. I allowed they'd make some sort of a swap with you, so I didn't say anything when they was layin' out their lines thoo' the hawss-lot and across the lower corn-field this mornin' — easy, now; no more r'arin' and t'arin' with that thar little gal not a-knowin' which side o' the earth's goin' to cave in next!"

The Major dropped his pipe, laid fast hold of the arms of his chair, and breathed hard.

"Laid out *theyuh* lines — across *my* prope'ty? Japheth, faveh me by riding down to the furnace and askin' Caleb Gordon if he will do me the honor to come up heah — this evenin', if he can. I — I — it's twenty yeahs and mo' since I've troubled the law cou'ts of ouh po', Yankee-ridden country with any affai-ah of mine; and now — well, I don't know — I don't know," with a despondent shake of the leonine head.

After Pettigrass had gone on his errand the Major rose and went unsteadily into the house. Then, and not till then, Ardea got up on her knees and put her arms around the neck of the Great Dane.

"O, Hector!" she whispered; "me, I am Dabney, too! Once the gamins killed a poor little cat of mine; and I forgot God — the good God — and said wicked things; and I could have torn them into little, little pieces! But we — we shall be very good and patient after this, won't we, Hector — you and me — no, you and *I*? What is it when you lick my face that way? Does it mean that you understand?"

VI

BLUE BLOOD AND RED

In a world full of puzzling questions for Thomas Jefferson, one of the chief clustering points of the persistent "whys" was Major Dabney's attitude, as a Man of Sin, and as the natural overlord of Paradise Valley.

That the Major was a Man of Sin there could be no manner of doubt. During the revival he had been frequently and pointedly prayed for by that name, and the groans from the Amen corner were conclusively damning. Just what the distinction was between a Man of Sin and a sinner — spelled with a small "s" — was something which Thomas Jefferson could never quite determine; but the desire to find out made him spy on Major Dabney at odd moments when the spying could be done safely and with a clear field for retreat in the event of the Major's catching him at it.

Thus far the spying had been barren of results — of that kind which do not have to be undone and made over to fit in with other things. Once, Thomas Jefferson had been picking blackberries behind the wall of his father's infield when the Major and Squire Bates had met on the pike. There was some talk of the new railroad; and when the Squire allowed that it was certain to come through Paradise, the Major had taken the name of God in vain in a way that suggested the fiery blast roaring from the furnace lip after the iron was out.

This was one of the results. But on reflection, Thomas Jefferson decided that this could not be The Sin. Profane swearing — that was what the Sunday-school lesson-leaf called it — was doubtless a mortal sin in a believer; was not he, Thomas Jefferson, finding the heavens as brass and the earth a place of fear and trembling because of that word to Nan Bryerson? But in other people — well, he had heard his father swear once, when one of the negroes at the furnace had opened the sand at the end of the sow and let the stream of molten iron run out into the creek.

The charge of profanity being tried and found wanting in the Major's case, there remained that of violence. One day, Tike Bryerson — Nan's father and the man who had tried to kill his Uncle Silas in the revival meeting — was beating his horses because they would not take the water at the lower ford. Tike had been stilling more pine-top whisky, and had been to town with some jugs hidden under the cornstalks in his wagon-bed. When he did that, he always came back with his eyes red like a squirrel's, and everybody gave him all the road.

But this time the Major had happened along, and when Tike would not stop beating the horses for a shouted cursing-out from the bank, the Major had spurred his Hambletonian into the creek and knocked Tike winding. More than that, he had made him lead his team out of the ford and go back to the bridge crossing.

Being himself committed to the theory of turning the other cheek, Thomas Jefferson could not question the acute sinfulness of all this; yet it did not sufficiently account for the Major as a Man of Sin. Had not Peter, stirred, no doubt, by some such generous rage as the Major's, snatched out his sword and smitten off a man's ear?

In the other field, that of overlordship, the subtleties were still more elusive. That the negroes, many of whom were the sons and daughters of the Major's former slaves, should pass the old-time "Mawstuh" on the pike with uncovered heads and respectful heel-scrapings, was a matter of course. Thomas Jefferson was white, free, and Southern born. But why his own father and mother should betray something of the same deference was not so readily apparent.

On rare occasions the Major, riding to or from the cross-roads post-office in Hargis's store, would rein in his horse at the Gordon gate and ask for a drink of water from the Gordon well. At such times Thomas Jefferson remarked that his mother always hastened to serve the Major with her own hands; this notwithstanding her own and Uncle Silas's oft-repeated asseveration touching the Major's unenviable preëminence as a Man of Sin. Also, he remarked that the Major's manner at such moments was a thing to dazzle the eye, like the reflection of the summer sun on the surface of burnished metal. But beneath the polished exterior, the groping perceptions of the boy would touch a thing repellent; a thing to stir a slow current of resentment in his blood.

It was Thomas Jefferson's first collision with the law of caste; a law Draconian in the Old South. Before the war, when Deer Trace Manor had been a seigniory with its six score black thralls, there had been no visiting between the great house on the inner knoll and the overgrown log homestead at the iron furnace. Quarrel there was none, nor any shadow of enmity; but the Dabneys were lords of the soil, and the Gordons were craftsmen.

Even in war the distinction was maintained. The Dabneys, father and son, were officers, having their commissions at the enrolment; while Caleb Gordon, whose name headed the list of the Paradise volunteers, began and ended a private in the ranks.

In the years of heart-hardenings which followed, a breach was opened, narrow at first, and never very deep, but wide enough to serve. Caleb Gordon had accepted defeat openly and honestly, and for this the unreconstructed Major had never fully forgiven him. It was an added proof that there was no redeeming drop of the *sang azure* in the Gordon veins — and Major Caspar was as scrupulously polite to Caleb Gordon's wife as he would have been, and was, to the helpmate of Tike Bryerson, mountaineer and distiller of illicit whisky.

Thomas Jefferson was vaguely indignant when Pettigrass came to ask his father to go forthwith to the manor-house. In the mouth of the foreman the invitation took on something of the flavor of a command. Besides, since the Major's return from New York, Thomas Jefferson had a grudge against him of a purely private and personal nature.

None the less, he was eager for news when his father came back, and though he got it only from overhearing the answer to his mother's question, it was satisfyingly thrilling.

"It's mighty near as we talked, Martha. The Major lumps the railroad in with all the other improvements, calls 'em Yankee, and h'ists his battle-flag. The engineer, that smart young fellow with the peaked whiskers and the eye-glasses, went to see him this evenin' about the right of way down the valley, and got himself slung off the porch of the great house into a posy bed."

"There is going to be trouble, Caleb; now you mark my words. You mustn't mix up in it."

"I don't allow to, if I can he'p it. The railroad's goin' to be a mighty good thing for us if I can get Mr. Downing to put in a side-track for the furnace."

Following this there were other conferences, the Major unbending sufficiently to come and sit on the Gordon porch in the cool of the evening. The iron-master, as one still in touch with the moving world, gave good advice. Failing to buy, the railroad company might possibly seek to bully a right of way through the valley. But in that case, there would certainly be redress in the courts for the property owners. In the meantime, nothing would be gained by making the contest a personal fight on individuals.

So counseled Caleb Gordon, sure, always, of his own standing-ground in any conflict. But from the last of the conferences the Major had ridden home through the fields; and Thomas Jefferson, with an alert eye for windstraws of conduct, had seen him dismount now and then to pull up and fling away the locating stakes driven by the railroad engineers.

In such a contention, in an age wholly given over to progress, there could be, one would say, no possible doubt of the outcome.

Giving the Major a second and a third chance to refuse to grant an easement, the railroad company pushed its grading and track-laying around the mountain and up to the stone wall marking the Dabney boundary, quietly accumulated the necessary material, and on a summer Sunday morning — Sunday by preference because no restraining writ could be served for at least twenty-four hours — a construction train, black with laborers, whisked around the nose of the mountain and dropped gently down the grade to the temporary end of track.

It was Thomas Jefferson who gave the alarm. Little Zoar, unable to support a settled pastor, was closed for the summer, but Martha Gordon kept the fire spiritual alight by teaching her son at home. One of the boy's Sunday privileges, earned by a faultless recitation of a prescribed number of Bible verses, was forest freedom for the remainder of the forenoon. It was while he was in the midst of the Beatitudes that he heard the low rumble of the coming train, and it was only by resolutely ignoring the sense of hearing that he was enabled to get through, letter-perfect.

"'Blessed are ye, when men shall revile you and persecute you,'" he chanted monotonously, with roving eyes bent on finding his cap with the loss of the fewest possible seconds — "'and shall say all manner of evil against you falsely, for my sake,' — and that's all." And he was off like a shot.

"Mind, now, Thomas Jefferson; you are not to go near that railroad!" his mother called to him as he raced down the path to the gate.

Oh, no; he would not go near the railroad! He would only run up the pike and cut across through the Dabney pasture to see if the train were really there.

It was there, as he could tell by the noise of hissing steam when the cross-cut was reached. But the parked wooding of the pasture still screened it. How near could he go without being "near" in the transgressing sense of the word? There was only one way of finding out — to keep on going until his conscience pricked sharply enough to stop him. It was a great convenience, Thomas Jefferson's conscience. As long as it kept quiet he could be reasonably sure there was no sin in sight. Yet he had to confess that it was not always above playing mean tricks; as that of sleeping like a log till after the fact, and then rising up to stab him till the blood ran.

He was halfway across the pasture when the crash of a falling tree stopped him in mid-rush. And in the vista opened by the felled tree he saw a sight to make him turn and race homeward faster than he had come. The invaders, hundreds strong, had torn down the boundary wall and the earth for the advancing embankment was flying from uncounted shovels.

Caleb Gordon was at work in the blacksmith shop, Sunday-repairing while the furnace was cool, when Thomas Jefferson came flying with his news. The iron-master dropped his hammer and cast aside the leather apron.

"You hear that, Buck?" he said, frowning across the anvil at his helper, a white man and the foreman of the pouring floor.

The helper nodded, being a man of as few words as the master.

"Well, I reckon we-all hain't got any call to stand by and see them highflyers ride it roughshod over Major Dabney thataway," said Gordon briefly. "Go down to the shanties and hustle out the day shift. Get Turk and Hardaway and every white man you can lay hands on, and all the guns you can find. And send one o' the black boys up the hill to tell the Major. Like as not, he ain't up yet."

Helgerson hastened away to obey his orders, and Caleb Gordon went out to the foundry scrap yard. In the heap of broken metal lay an old cast-iron field-piece, a relic of the battle which had one day raged hotly on the hillside across the creek. A hundred times the iron-master had been on the point of breaking it up for re-melting, and as often the old artilleryman in him had stayed his hand.

Now it was quickly hoisted in the crane shackle, — Thomas Jefferson sweating manfully at the crab crank, — clamped on the axle of a pair of wagon wheels, cleaned, swabbed, loaded with quarry blasting powder and pieces of broken iron to serve for grape, and trundled out on the pike at the heels of the ore team.

By this time Helgerson had come up with the furnace men, a motley crew in all stages of Sunday-morning dishevelment, and armed only as a mob may arm itself at a moment's notice. Caleb, the veteran, looked the squad over with a slow smile gathering the wrinkles at the corners of his eyes.

"You boys'll have to make up in f'erceness what-all you're lacking in soldier-looks," he observed mildly. Then he gave the word of command to Helgerson. "Take the gun and put out for the major's hawss-lot. I'll be along as soon as I can saddle the mare."

Thomas Jefferson went with his father to the stable and helped silently with the saddling. Afterward he held the mare, gentling her in suppressed excitement while his father went into the house for his rifle.

Martha Gordon met her husband at the door. She had seen the volunteer gun crew filing past on the pike.

"What is it, Caleb?" she asked anxiously.

He made no attempt to deceive her.

"The railroaders are allowin' to take what the Major wouldn't sell 'em — the right of way through his land down the valley. Buddy brought the word."

"Well?" she said, love and fear hardening her heart. "The railroad would be a good thing for us — for the furnace. You know you said it would."

He shook his head slowly.

"I reckon we mustn't look at it thataway, Martha. I'm going to stand by my neighbor, like I'd expect him to stand by me. Let me get my gun; the boys'll be there ahead o' me, and they won't know what to do."

"Caleb! There will be bloodshed; and you remember what the Word says: 'whoso sheddeth man's blood. . . .' And on the Lord's Day, too!"

"I know. But ain't it somewhere in the same Good Book that it says there's a time for peace and a time to make war? And then that there passage about lovin' your neighbor. Don't hender me, little woman. There ain't goin' to be no blood shed — onless them bushwhackers are a mighty sight f'ercer for it than what I think they are."

She let him go without further protest, not because he had convinced her, but because she had long since come to know this man, who, making her lightest wish his law in most things, could be as inflexible as the chilled iron of the pouring floor at the call of loyalty to his own standard of right and wrong. But when he passed down the path to the gate she knelt on the door-stone and covered her face with her hands.

Gordon gathered the slack of the reins on the neck of the mare and put a leg over the saddle.

"That'll do, Buddy," he said. "Run along in to your mammy, now."

But Thomas Jefferson caught again at the bridle and held on, choking.

"O pappy! — take me with you! I — I'll die if you don't take me with you!"

Who can tell what Caleb Gordon saw in his son's eyes when he bent to loosen the grip of the small brown hand on the rein? Was it some sympathetic reincarnation of his own militant soul striving to break its bonds? Without a word he bent lower and swung the boy up to a seat behind him. "Hold on tight, Buddy," he cautioned. "I'll have to run the mare some to catch up with the boys."

And the mother? She was still kneeling on the door-stone, but the burden of her prayer was not now for Caleb Gordon. "O Lord, have mercy on my boy! Thou knowest how, because of my disobedience, he has the fierce fighting blood and the stubborn unbelief of all the Gordons to contend with: save him alive and make him a man of peace and a man of faith, I beseech Thee, and let not the unbelief of the father or the unfaithfulness of the mother be visited on the son!"

When the one-piece battery dashed at a clumsy gallop through the open gate of the Dabney pasture and swung with a sharp turn into the vista of felled trees, Thomas Jefferson beheld a thing to set his heritage of soldier blood dancing through his veins. Standing fair in the midst of the ax-and-shovel havoc and clearing a wide circle to right and left with the sweep of his old service cavalry saber, was the Major, coatless, hatless, cursing the invaders with mighty and corrosive soldier oaths, and crying them to come on, the unnumbered host of them against one man.

Opposed to him the men of the construction force, generaled by the young engineer in brown duck and buttoned leggings, were deploying cautiously to surround him. Gordon spoke to his mare; and when he drew rein and wheeled to shout to the gun crew, Thomas Jefferson heard the engineer's low-toned order to the shovelers: "Be careful and don't hurt him, boys. He's the old maniac who threw me off the veranda of his house. Two of you take him behind, and —"

The break came on the uprush of the unanticipated reinforcements. With the battle readiness of a disciplined soldier, Caleb Gordon whipped from the saddle and ran to help the gun crew slue the makeshift field-piece into position.

"Fall back, Major!" he shouted; "fall back on your front line and give the artillery a chanst at 'em. I reckon a dose o' broken pot-iron'll carry fu'ther than that saber o' yourn. Buddy, hunt me a punk match, quick, will ye?"

[Illustration: "Fall back, Major!" he shouted; "give the artillery a chanst"]

Thomas Jefferson ran to the nearest rotting log, but one of the negroes was before him with a blazing pitch-pine splint. There was a respectful recoil in the opposing ranks which presently became a somewhat panicky surge to the rear. The shovelers, more than half of whom were negroes, had not come out to be blown from a cannon's mouth by a grim-faced veteran who was so palpably at home with the tools of his trade.

"That's right: keep right on goin'!" yelled the iron-master, waving his blazing slow-match dangerously near to the priming. "Keep it up, 'r by the Lord that made ye —"

There was no need to specify the alternative. For now the panic had spread by its own contagion, and the invaders were fighting among themselves for place on the flat-cars. And while yet the rear guard was swarming upon the engine, hanging by toe- and hand-holds where it could, the train was backed rapidly out of range.

Caleb Gordon kept his pine splint alight until the echoes of the engine's exhaust came faintly from the overhanging cliffs of the mountain.

"They've gone back to town, and I reckon the fire's plum' out for today, Major," he drawled. "Buck and a few o' the boys'll stay by the gun, against their rallyin' later on, and you might as well go home to your breakfast. Didn't bring your hawss, did ye? Take the mare, and welcome. Buddy and me'll walk."

But the Major would not mount, and so the two men walked together as far as the manor-house gates, with Thomas Jefferson a pace in the rear, leading the mare.

It was no matter of wonder to him that his father and the Major marched in solemn silence to the gate of parting. But the wonder came tumultuously when the Major wheeled abruptly at the moment of leave-taking and wrung his father's hand.

"By God, suh, you are a right true-hearted gentleman, and my very good friend, *Mistuh* Gordon!" he said, with the manner of one who has been carefully weighing the words beforehand. "If you had been given youh just dues, suh, you'd have come home from F'ginia wearin' youh shouldeh-straps." And then, with a little throat-clearing pause to come between: "Damn it, suh; an own brotheh couldn't have done'mo'! I — I've been misjudgin' you, Caleb, all these yeahs, and now I'm proud to shake you by the hand and call you my friend. Yes, suh, I am that!"

It was, in a manner not to be understood by the Northern alien, the accolade of knighthood, and Caleb Gordon's toil-rounded shoulders straightened visibly when he returned the hearty hand-grasp. And as for Thomas Jefferson: in his heart gratified pride flapped its wings and crowed lustily; and for the moment he was almost willing to bury that private grudge he was holding against Major Dabney — almost, but not quite.

VII

THE PRAYER OF THE RIGHTEOUS

Having come thus far with Thomas Jefferson on the road to whatever goal he will reach, it is high time we were looking a little more closely into this matter of his grudge against Major Dabney.

Primarily, it based itself upon the dominant quality in a masterful character; namely, a desire to possess the earth and its fullness without partnership encumbrances.

From a time back of which memory refused to run, the woods and the fields of Paradise Valley, the rampart hills and the backgrounding mountain side, had belonged to Thomas Jefferson by the right of discovery. The Bates boys and the Cantrells lived over in the great valley of the Tennessee, and when they planned a fishing excursion up Turkey Creek, they recognized Thomas Jefferson's suzerainty by announcing that they were coming over to *his* house. In like manner, the Pendrys and the Lumpkins and the Hardwicks were scattered at farm-width intervals down the pike, and the rampart hills marked the boundary of their domain on that side.

Now from possession which is recognized unquestioningly by one's compeers to fancied possession in fee simple is but a step; and from that to the putting up of "No Trespass" signs the interval can be read only on a micrometer scale. Wherefore, Thomas Jefferson had developed a huge disgust on hearing that Major Dabney was going to upset the natural order of things by bringing his granddaughter to Deer Trace Manor. If Ardea — the very name of her had a heathenish sound in his Scripturally-trained ear — had been a boy, the matter would have simplified itself. Thomas Jefferson had a sincere respect for his own prowess, and a boy might have been mauled into subjection. But a girl!

His lip curled stiffly at the thought of a girl, a town girl and therefore a thing without legs, or at best with legs only half useful and totally unfit for running or climbing trees, dividing the sovereignty of the fields and the forest, the swimming-hole and the perch pools in the creek, with him! She would do it, or try to do it. A girl would not have any more sense than to come prying around into all the quiet places to say, "This is my grandfather's land. What are *you* doing here?"

At such thoughts as these a queer prickling sensation like a hot shiver would run over him from neck to heel, and his eyes would gloom sullenly. There would be another word to put with that; a word of his own choosing. No matter if her grandfather, the terrifying Major, did own the fields and the wood and the stream: God was greater than Major Dabney, and had he not often heard his mother say on her knees that the fervent, effectual prayer of the righteous availeth much? If it should avail even a little, there would be no catastrophe, no disputed sovereignty of the woods, the fields and the creek.

It was in the middle of a sultry afternoon in the hotter half of August, two weeks or such a matter after the Great Southwestern Railway had given up the fight for Paradise Valley to run its line around the encompassing hills, that Thomas Jefferson was cast alive into the pit of burnings.

He made sure he should always remember his latest glimpse of the pleasant, homely earth. He was sitting idly on the porch step, letting his gaze go adrift over the nearer green-clad hills to the purple deeps of the western mountain, already steeped in shadow. The pike was deserted, and the shrill hum of the house-flies played an insistent tune in which the low-pitched boom of a bumblebee tumbling awkwardly among the clover heads served for an intermittent bass.

Suddenly into the hot silence came the quick *cloppity-clop* of galloping hoofs. Thomas Jefferson's heart was tender on that side of it which was turned toward the dumb creatures, and his thought was instantly pitiful and indignant. Who would be cruel enough to gallop a horse in such weltering weather?

The unspoken query had its answer when Major Dabney's fleet saddle stallion thundered up to the gate in a white nimbus of dust, and the Major flung himself from the saddle and called loudly for Mistress Gordon. Thomas Jefferson sprang up hastily to forward the cry, fear clutching at his heart; but the Major was before him in the wide passage opening upon the porch.

"My deah Mistress Gordon! We are in a world of trouble at the manor-house! Little Ardea, my grand-daughteh, was taken sick last night, and today she's out of huh head — think of it, *out of huh head!* I'm riding hotfoot for Doctah Williams, but Lord of Heaven! it'll be nigh sundown befo' I can hope to get back with him. Could you, my deah madam, faveh us —"

Thomas Jefferson heard no more; would stay to hear no more. The forest, always his refuge in time of trial, reached a long finger of scattering oaks down to the opposite side of the creek, and thither he fled, cold to the marrow of his bones, though the sun-heated stone coping of the dam on which he crossed the stream went near to blistering his bare feet as he ran.

From the crotch of one of the oaks — his watch-tower in other periods of stress — he saw the Major mount and continue his gallop eastward on the pike; and a little later the ancient Dabney family carriage came and went in a smother of white dust, wheeling in front of the home gate and pausing only long enough to take up his mother hastening to the rescue.

After that he was alone with the hideous tumult of his thoughts. The girl would die. He was as sure of it as if the heavens and the earth had instantly become articulate to shout the terrible sentence. God had taken him at his word! There would be no intruder to tell him that the woods and the creek belonged to her grandfather. She would be dead; slain by the breath of his mouth. And for all the years and years and ages to come, he would be roasting and grilling in that place prepared for the devil and his angels — and for murderers!

In the acutest misery of it a trembling fit seized him and the oak seemed to rock and sway as if to be rid of him. When the fit passed he slid to the ground and flung himself face downward under the spreading branches. The grass was cool to his face, but there was no moisture in it, and he thought of Dives praying that Lazarus might come and put a drop of water on his tongue.

Then the torment took a new and more terrible form. Though he had never been inside of the gray stone manor-house, his imagination transported him thither; to the house and to a darkened room on the upper floor with a bed in it, and in the bed a girl whose face he could not see.

The girl was dying: the doctor had told his mother and the Major, and they were all waiting. Thomas Jefferson had never seen any one die, only a dog that Tike Bryerson had shot on one of his drunken home-goings. But death was death, to a dog or to a girl; and vivid imagination supplied the appalling details. Over and over again in pitiless minuteness the heartbreaking scene was repeated: the little twitchings of the bed-clothing, the tossing of the girl's arms in the last desperate struggle for breath, his mother's low sobs, and the haggard face of the old Major.

Thomas Jefferson dug his fingers and toes into the grass and bit a mouthful of it to stifle the cry wrung from him by the torturing poignancy of it. Was there no way of escape?

He turned over and sat up to try to think it out. Yes, there was a way — the way which would be taken by the boy in the Sunday-school books. He would say he was sorry, and would have his sins washed away, and there would be rejoicing in Heaven over the one sinner who had repented. Of course, the girl would die, just the same, and all the misery his sin had caused would remain unchanged. But *he* would escape.

For one unworthy moment Thomas Jefferson was fiercely tempted. Then the dogged Gordon blood reasserted itself. He had done the dreadful thing: he had asked God to take this girl out of his way, and now he would accept what he had coveted and would not try to sneak out of paying. It comforted him a little to think that, after all, there must eventually be some sort of end to the torment, away on in the eternities to come. When he had suffered all he could suffer, not even God could make him suffer any more.

When he finally recrossed the creek on the dam head it was supper-time, and his mother had returned. The misery had now settled into dumb despair, both more and less agonizing than the acute remorse of the afternoon. What he needed to know was told in his mother's answer to his father's inquiry: "Yes; she is a very sick child. I'm going up again after supper to stay as long as I'm needed. It's a judgment on the Major; he has been setting the creature above the Creator."

Thomas Jefferson knew well enough that the judgment was his, and not the Major's; but he let his supper choke him in silence. Afterward, when his mother had gone back to the house of anxiety and he was alone with his father, there were some vague promptings toward confession and a cry for human sympathy. What sealed his lips was the conviction that his father would comfort him without understanding, just as his mother would understand and condemn him. Early in the evening his father went back to the furnace and his chance was lost.

For four heart-searching days Thomas Jefferson lived and endured, because living and enduring were the two unalterable conditions of the brimstone pit to which he had consigned himself. During these days his mother came and went, and prayed oftener than usual — not for the girl's life, as Thomas Jefferson noticed with deep stirrings of bitterness, but that the dispensation of Providence might inure to the lasting and eternal benefit of an impenitent and idolatrous Major Dabney.

Throughout these four days the sickening August heat remained unbroken; but on the fifth the thunderheads began to gather and a fresh breeze swept down from the slopes of the distant Cumberland; a wind smelling sweetly of rain and full of cooling promise.

On this fifth day, Thomas Jefferson, lying in wait at the gate of the manor-house grounds, waylaid Doctor Williams coming out, and asked the question which had hitherto had its doleful answer without the necessity of asking. If the doctor had struck him with the buggy whip the shock would not have been more real than that consequent on the snapping of mental tension strings and the surging, strangling uprush of the tidal wave of relief.

"Little Ardea?" said the doctor. "Oh, she'll do well enough now, I hope. The fever is broken and she's asleep."

Thomas Jefferson shut the gate mechanically when the doctor

had driven out; but when there was nothing more to hold him, he scrambled over the stone wall on the opposite side of the pike and ran for the hills like one demented.

The girl would live! Hell had yawned and cast him up once more on the pleasant, homely earth; and now the gentle rain of penitence, which could never water the dry places for a soul in torment, drenched him like the real rain which was falling to slake the thirst of the parched fields and the brittle-leaved, rustling forest.

For a long time he lay on his face on the first bit of tree-sheltered grass he had come to, caring nothing for the storm which was driving all the wild creatures of the wood to cover. God had not been so pitiless, after all. There was yet a balm in Gilead.

And for the future? O just Heavens! how straitly and circumspectly he would walk all the days of his life! Never again should Satan, going about like a roaring lion, take him unawares. He would even learn to love the girl, as one should love an enemy; and when she should come and tell him that all the sacred places were hers by her grandfather's right, he would smile reproachfully, like the boy being led forth to the stake in the *Book of Martyrs*, and say —

But the time was not yet fully come for self-pityings; and when Thomas Jefferson went home after the shower, not even the soggy chill of his wet clothes could depress the spirit which had made good its footing on the high mount of humility.

VIII

THE BACKSLIDER

It was late in September before the dreaded invasion of the sacred places, foreboded by Thomas Jefferson's prophetic soul, became one of the things to be looked back on; and the interval had sufficed for another change of heart, or, more correctly, for a descent to the valley of things as they are from the top of that high mountain of spiritual humility.

Thomas Jefferson did not analyze the reactionary process. But the milestones along the backward way were familiar.

In a little while he found that he was once more able to say his prayers at bedtime with the old glibness, and with the comfortable feeling that he had done his whole duty if he remained on his knees for sixty full ticks of the heirloom grandfather clock. It was an accomplishment on which he prided himself, this knack of saying his prayers and counting the clock ticks at the same time. Stub Helgerson, whose mother was a Lutheran and said her prayers out of a book, could not do it. Thomas Jefferson had asked him.

A little farther along he came to the still more familiar milestone of the doubtful questionings. Did God really trouble Himself about the millions of things people asked Him to do? It seemed highly incredible, not to say impossible, in the very nature of it. And if He did, would He make one person sick for the sake of making another person sorry? These questions were answerless, like so many of the others; but after the perplexity had been pushed aside, the doubt remained.

Coming down by such successive steps from the mount of penitent thanksgivings, it was but a short time before he found himself back on the old camping-ground of sullen resentment.

When the girl got well enough to go about, she would find him out and warn him off; or perhaps she might do even worse, and tag him. In either case he should hate her, and there was a sort of ferocious joy in the thought that she would doubtless be a long time getting well, and would probably not be able to find him if he kept far enough out of her way.

Acting on this wise conclusion, he carefully avoided the manor-house and its neighborhood, making a wide circuit when he went fishing in the upper pools. And once, when his father had sent him with a message to the Major, he did violence to his own sense of exact obedience by transferring the word at the house gate to Mammy Juliet's grandson, Pete.

But when one's evil star is in the ascendent, precautions are like the vain strugglings of the fly in the web. The day of reckoning may be postponed, but it will by no means be effaced from the calendar. One purple and russet afternoon, when all the silent forest world was steeped in the deep peace of early autumn, Thomas Jefferson was fishing luxuriously in the most distant of the upper pools. There were three fat perch gill-strung on a forked withe under the overhanging bank, and a fourth was rising to the bait, when the peaceful stillness was rudely rent by a crashing in the undergrowth, and a great dog, of a breed hitherto unknown to Paradise, bounded into the little glade to stand glaring at the fisherman, his teeth bared and his back hairs bristling.

Now Thomas Jefferson in his thirteenth year was as well able to defend himself as any clawed and toothed creature of the wood, and fear, the fear of anything he could face and grapple with, was a thing unknown. Propping his fishing pole so that no chance of a nibble might be lost in the impending struggle, he got on his knees and picked out the exact spot in the dog's neck where he would drive the bait knife home when hostilities actual should begin.

"Oh, please! Don't you hurt my dog!" said a rather weak little voice out of the rearward void.

But, gray eyes human, holding brown canine in an unwinking gaze: "You come round here and call him off o' me."

"He is not wishing to hurt you, or anybody," said the voice. "Down, Hector!"

The Great Dane passed from suspicious rigidity and threatening lip twitchings to mighty and frivolous gambolings, and Thomas Jefferson got up to give him room. A girl — *the* girl, as some inner sense instantly assured him — was trying to make the dog behave. So he had a chance to look her over before the battle for sovereignty should begin.

There was a little shock of disdainful surprise to go with the first glance. Somehow he had been expecting something very different; something on the order of the Queen of Sheba — done small, of course — as that personage was pictured in the family Bible; a girl, proud and scornful, and possibly wearing a silk dress and satin shoes.

Instead, she was only a pale, tired baby in a brier-torn frock; a girl whose bones showed brazenly at every angle, and whose only claim to a second glance lay in her thick mop of reddish-brown hair and in a pair of great, slate-blue eyes two sizes too large for the thin face. A double conclusion came and sat in Thomas Jefferson's mind: she was rather to be contemptuously pitied than feared; and as for looks — well, she was not to be thought of in the same day with black-eyed Nan Bryerson.

When the dog was reduced to quietude, the small one repaid Thomas Jefferson's stare with a level gaze out of the over-sized eyes.

"Was it that you were afraid of Hector?" she asked.

"Huh!" said Thomas Jefferson, and the scorn was partly for her queer way of speaking and partly for the foolishness of the question. "Huh! I reckon you don't know who I am. I'd have killed your dog if he'd jumped on me, maybe."

"Me? I do know who you are. You are Thomas Gordon. Your mother took care of me and prayed for me when I was sick. Hector is a — an extremely good dog. He would not jump at you."

"It's mighty lucky for him he didn't," bragged Thomas Jefferson, with a very creditable imitation of his father's grim frown. Then he sat down on the bank of the stream and busied himself with his fishing-tackle as if he considered the incident closed.

"What is it that you are trying to do?" asked Ardea, when the silence had extended to the third worm impaled on the hook and promptly abstracted therefrom by a wily sucker lying at the bottom of the pool.

"I was fishin' some before you and your dog came along and scared all the perch away," he said sourly. Then, turning suddenly on her: "Why don't you go ahead and say it? Is it 'cause you're afeard to?"

"I don't know what you mean."

"I know what you're going to say; you are going to tell me this is your grandfather's land and run me off. But I ain't aimin' to go till I'm good and ready."

She looked down on him without malice.

"You are such a funny boy," she remarked, and there was something in her way of saying it that made Thomas Jefferson feel little and infantile and inferior, though he was sure there must be an immense age difference in his favor.

"Why?" he demanded.

"Oh, I don't know; just because you are. If you knew French I could explain it better that way."

"I don't know anybody by that name, and I don't care," said Thomas Jefferson doggedly; and went back to his fishing.

Followed another interval of silence, in which two more worms were fed to the insatiable sucker at the bottom of the pool. Then came the volcanic outburst.

"I think you are mean, mean!" she sobbed, with an angry stamp of her foot. "I — I want to go ho-ome!"

"Well, I reckon there ain't anybody holdin' you," said Thomas Jefferson brutally. He was intent on fixing the sixth worm on the hook in such fashion as permanently to discourage the bait thief, and was coming to his own in the matter of self-possession with grateful facility. It was going to be notably easy to bully her — another point of difference between her and Nan Bryerson.

"I know there isn't anybody holding me, but — but I can't find the way."

That any one could be lost within an easy mile of the manor-house was ridiculously incredible to Thomas Jefferson. Yet there was no telling, in the case of a girl.

"You want me to show you the way?" he asked, putting all the ungraciousness he could muster into the query.

"You might tell me, I should think! I've walked and walked!"

"I reckon I'd better take you; you might get lost again," he said, with gloomy sarcasm. Then he consumed all the time he could for the methodical disposal of his fishing-tackle. It would be good for her to learn that she must wait on his motions.

She waited patiently, sitting on the ground with one arm around the neck of the Great Dane; and when Thomas Jefferson stole a glance at her to see how she was taking it, she looked so tired and thin and woebegone that he almost let the better part of him get the upper hand. That made him surlier than ever when he finally recovered his string of fish from the stream and said: "Well, come on, if you're comin'."

He told himself, hypocritically, that it was only to show her what hardships she would have to face if she should try to tag him, that he dragged her such a weary round over the hills and through the worst brier patches and across and across the creek, doubling and circling until the easy mile was spun out into three uncommonly difficult ones. But at bottom the motive was purely wicked. In all the range of sentient creatures there is none so innately and barbarously cruel as the human boy-child; and this was the first time Thomas Jefferson had ever had a helplessly pliable subject.

The better she kept up, the more determined he became to break her down; but at the very last, when she stumbled and fell in an old leaf bed and cried for sheer weariness, he relented enough to say: "I reckon you'll know better than to go projectin' round in the woods the next time. Come on — we're 'most there, now."

But Ardea's troubles were not yet at an end. She stopped crying and got up to follow him blindly over more hills and through other brier tangles; and when they finally emerged in the cleared lands, they were still on the wrong side of the creek.

"It's only about up to your chin; reckon you can wade it?" asked Thomas Jefferson, in a sudden access of heart-hardening. But it softened him a little to see her gather her torn frock and stumble down to the water's edge without a word, and he added: "Hold on; maybe we can find a log, somewhere."

There was a foot log just around the next bend above, as he very well knew, and thither he led the way. The dog made the crossing first, and stood wagging his tail encouragingly on the bank of safety. Then Thomas Jefferson passed his trembling victim out on the log.

"You go first," he directed; "so 't I can catch you if you slip."

For the first time she humbled herself to beg a boon.

"Oh, you please go first, so I won't have to look down at the water!"

"No; I'm coming behind — then I can catch you if you get dizzy and go to fall," he said stubbornly.

"Will you walk right up close, so I can know you are there?"

Thomas Jefferson's smile was cruelly misleading, as were his words. "All you'll have to do will be to reach your hand back and grab me," he assured her; and thereupon she began to inch her way out over the swirling pool.

When he saw that she could by no possibility turn to look back, Thomas Jefferson deliberately sat down on the bank to watch her. There had never been anything in his life so tigerishly delightful as this game of playing on the feelings and fears of the girl whose coming had spoiled the solitudes.

For the first few feet Ardea went steadily forward, keeping her eyes fixed on the Great Dane sitting motionless at the farther end of the bridge of peril. Then, suddenly the dog grew impatient and began to leap and bark like a foolish puppy. It was too much for Ardea to have her eye-anchor thus transformed into a dizzying whirlwind of gray monsters. She reached backward for the reassuring hand: it was not there, and the next instant the hungry pool rose up to engulf her.

In all his years Thomas Jefferson had never had such a stab as that which an instantly awakened conscience gave him when she slipped and fell. Now he was her murderer, beyond any hope of future mercies. For a moment the horror of it held him vise-like. Then the sight of the Great Dane plunging to the rescue freed him.

"Good dog!" he screamed, diving headlong from his own side of the pool; and between them Ardea was dragged ashore, a limp little heap of saturation, conscious, but with her teeth chattering and great, dark circles around the big blue eyes.

Thomas Jefferson's first word was masculinely selfish.

"I'm awful sorry!" he stammered. "If you can't make out to forgive me, I'm going to have a miser'ble time of it after I get home. God will whip me worse for this than He did for the other."

It was here, again, that she gave him the feeling that she was older than he.

"It will serve you quite right. Now you'd better get me home as quick as ever you can. I expect I'll be sick again, after this."

He held his peace and walked her as fast as he could across the fields and out on the pike. But at the Dabney gates he paused. It was not in human courage to face the Major under existing conditions.

"I reckon you'll go and tell your gran'paw on me," he said hopelessly.

She turned on him with anger ablaze.

"Why should I not tell him? And I never want to see you or hear of you again, you cruel, hateful boy!"

Thomas Jefferson hung about the gate while she went stumbling up the driveway, leaning heavily on the great dog. When she had safely reached the house he went slowly homeward, wading in trouble even as he waded in the white dust of the pike. For when one drinks too deeply of the cup of tyranny the lees are apt to be like the little book the Revelator ate — sweet as honey in the mouth and bitter in the belly.

That evening at the supper-table he had one nerve-racking fear dispelled and another confirmed by his mother's reply to a question put by his father.

"Yes; the Major sent for me again this afternoon. That child is back in bed again with a high fever. It seems she was out playing with that great dog of hers and fell into the creek. I wanted to tell the Major he is just tempting Providence, the way he makes over her and indulges her, but I didn't dare to."

And again Thomas Jefferson knew that he was the one who had tempted Providence.

IX

THE RACE TO THE SWIFT

From the grave and thoughtful vantage-ground of thirteen, Thomas Jefferson could look back on the second illness of Ardea Dabney as the closing incident of his childhood.

The industrial changes which were then beginning, not only for the city beyond the mountain, but for all the region round about, had rushed swiftly on Paradise; and the old listless life of the unhasting period soon receded quickly into a far-away past, rememberable only when one made an effort to recall it.

First had come the completion of the Great Southwestern. Diverted by the untiring opposition of Major Dabney from its chosen path through the valley, it skirted the westward hills, passing within a few hundred yards of the Gordon furnace. Since business knows no animosities, the part which Caleb Gordon and his gun crew had played in the right-of-way conflict was ignored. The way-station at the creek crossing was named Gordonia, and it was the railway traffic manager himself who suggested to the iron-master the taking of a partner with capital, the opening of the vein of coking coal on Mount Lebanon, the installation of coking-ovens, and the modernizing and enlarging of the furnace and foundry plant — hints all pointing to increased traffic for the road.

With the coming of Mr. Duxbury Farley to Paradise, Thomas Jefferson lost, not only the simple life, but the desire to live it. This Mr. Farley, whom we have seen and heard, momentarily, on the station platform in South Tredegar, the expanded, hailed from Cleveland, Ohio; was, as he was fond of saying pompously, a citizen of no mean city. His business in the reawakening South was that of an intermediary between cause and effect; the cause being the capital of confiding investors in the North, and the effect the dissipation of the same in various and sundry development schemes in the new iron field.

To Paradise, in the course of his goings to and fro, came this purger of other men's purses, and he saw the fortuitous grouping of the possibilities at a glance: abundant iron of good quality; an accessible vein of coal, second only to Pocahontas for coking; land cheap, water free, and a persuadable subject in straightforward, simple-hearted Caleb Gordon.

Farley had no capital, but he had that which counts for more in the promoter's field; namely, the ability to reap where others had sown. His plan, outlined to Caleb in a sweeping cavalry-dash of enthusiasm, was simplicity itself. Caleb should contribute the raw material — land, water and the ore quarry — and it should also be his part to secure a lease of the coal land from Major Dabney. In the meantime he, Farley, would undertake to float the enterprise in the North, forming a company and selling stock to provide the development capital.

The iron-master demurred a little at first. There were difficulties, and he pointed them out.

"I don't know, Colonel Farley. It appears like I'm givin' all I've got for a handout at the kitchen door of the big company. Then, again, there's the Major. He's pizon against all these improvements. You don't know the Major."

"On the contrary, my dear Mr. Gordon, it is because I do know him, or know of him, that I am turning him over to you. You are the one person in the world to obtain that coal lease. I confess I couldn't touch the Major with a ten-foot pole, any more than you could go North and get the cash. But you are his neighbor, and he likes you. What you recommend, he'll do." Thus the enthusiast.

"Well, I don't know," said Caleb doubtfully; "I reckon I can try. He can't any more 'n fire me, like he did the Southwestern right-o'-way man. But then, about t'other part of it: I've got a little charcoal furnace here that don't amount to much, maybe, but it's all mine, and I'm the boss. When this other thing goes through, the men who are putting up the money will own it and me. I'll be just about as much account as the tag on a shoe-string."

This part of the conference was held on the slab-floored porch of the oak-shingled house, with Thomas Jefferson as a negligible listener. Since he was listening with both eyes and ears, he saw something in Mr. Duxbury Farley's face that carried him swiftly back to the South Tredegar railway station and to that first antipathetic impression. But again the suave tongue quickly turned the page.

"Don't let that trouble you for a moment, Mr. Gordon," was the reassuring rejoinder. "I shall see that your apportionment of stock in the company is as large as the flotation scheme will stand; and as I, too, shall be a minority stock-holder, I shall share your risk. But there will be no risk. If the Lord prospers us, we shall both come out of this rich men, Mr. Gordon."

The slow smile that Thomas Jefferson knew so well came and went like a flitting shadow.

"I reckon the Lord don't make n'r meddle much with these here little child's playhouses of our'n," said Caleb; and then he gave his consent to the promoter's plan.

Singularly or not, as we choose to view it, the difficulties effaced themselves at the first onset. Though tact was no part of

Caleb Gordon's equipment, his presentation of the matter to Major Dabney became so nearly a personal asking — with Mr. Duxbury Farley and the Northern capitalists distantly backgrounding — that the Major granted the lease of the coal lands on purely personal grounds; would, indeed, have waived the matter of consideration entirely, if Caleb had not insisted. Had not the iron-master been raised to the high degree of fellowship by the hand that signed the lease?

On his part, Mr. Duxbury Farley was equally successful. A company was formed, the charter was obtained, and the golden stream began to flow into the treasury; into it and out again in the raceway channels of development. Thomas Jefferson stood aghast when an army of workmen swept down on Paradise and began to change the very face of nature. But that was only the beginning.

For a time Chiawassee Coal and Iron figured buoyantly in the market quotations, and delegations of stock-holders, both present and prospective, were personally conducted to the scene of activities by enthusiastic Vice-President Farley. But when these had served their purpose a thing happened. One fine morning it was whispered on 'Change that Chiawassee iron would not Bessemer, and that Chiawassee coke had been rejected by the Southern Association of Iron Smelters.

Followed a crash which was never very clearly understood by the simple-hearted soldier iron-master, though it was merely a repetition of a lesson well conned by the earlier investors in Southern coal and iron fields. Caleb's craft was the making of iron; not the financing of top-heavy corporations. So, when he was told that the company had failed, and that he and Farley had been appointed receivers, he took it as a financial matter, of course, somewhat beyond his ken, and went about his daily task of supervision with a mind as undisturbed as it would have been distraught had he known something of the subterranean mechanism by which the failure and the receivership had been brought to pass.

Why Mr. Duxbury Farley spared the iron-master in the freezing-out process was an unsolved riddle to many. But there were reasons. For one, there was the lease of the coal lands, renewable year by year — this was Caleb's own honest provision inserted in the contract for the Major's protection — and renewable only by the Major's friend. Further, a practical man at the practical end of an industry is a sheer necessity; and by contriving to have honest Caleb associated with himself in the receivership, a fine color of uprightness was imparted to the promoter's far-reaching plan of aggrandizement.

So, later, when the reorganization was effected; when the

troublesome, dividend-hungry stock-holders of the original company were eliminated by due process of law, Caleb's name appeared on the Farley slate with the title of general manager of the new company — for the same good and sufficient reasons.

It was during the fervid six months of Chiawassee Coal and Iron development that Thomas Jefferson had passed from the old life to the new — from childhood to boyhood.

Simultaneously, there were the coal-mines opening under the cliffs of Mount Lebanon, the long, double row of coking-ovens building on the flat below the furnace, and the furnace itself taking on undreamed-of magnitudes under the hands of the army of workmen. Thomas Jefferson did his best to keep the pace, being driven by a new and eager thirst for knowledge mechanical, and by a gripping desire to be present at all the assemblings of all the complicated parts of the threefold machine. And when he found it impossible to be in three places at one and the same moment, it distressed him to tears.

Of the home life during that strenuous interval there was little more than the eating and sleeping for one whose time for the absorbent process was all too limited. Also, the perplexing questions reaching down into the under-soul of things were silent. Also, again — mark of a change so radical that none but a Thomas Jefferson may read and understand — an awe-inspiring Major Dabney had ceased to be the first citizen of the world, that pinnacle being now occupied by a tall, sallow, smooth-faced gentleman, persuasive of speech and superhuman in accomplishment, who was the life and soul of the activities, and whom his father and mother always addressed respectfully as "Colonel" Farley.

One day, in the very heat of the battle, this commanding personage, at whose word the entire world of Paradise was in travail, had deigned to speak directly to him — Thomas Jefferson. It was at the mine on the mountain. The workmen were bolting into place the final trestle of the inclined railway which was to convey the coal in descending carloads to the bins at the coke-ovens, and Thomas Jefferson was absorbing the details as a dry sponge soaks water.

"Making sure that they do it just right, are you, my boy?" said the great man, patting him approvingly on the shoulder. "That's good. I like to see a boy anxious to get to the bottom of things. Going to be an iron-master, like your father, are you?"

"N-no," stammered the boy. "I wisht I was!"

"Well, what's to prevent? We are going to have the completest plant in the country right here, and it will be a fine chance for your father's son; the finest in the world."

"'Tain't goin' to do me any good," said Thomas Jefferson dejectedly. "I got to be a preacher."

Mr. Duxbury Farley looked down at him curiously. He was a religious person himself, coming to be known as a pillar in St. Michael's Church at South Tredegar, a liberal contributor, and a prime mover in a plan to tear down the old building and to erect a new one more in keeping with the times and South Tredegar's prosperity. Yet he was careful to draw the line between religion as a means of grace and business as a means of making money.

"That is your mother's wish, I suppose: and it's a worthy one; very worthy. Yet, unless you have a special vocation — but there; your mother doubtless knows best. I am only anxious to see your father's son succeed in whatever he undertakes."

After that, Thomas Jefferson secretly made Success his god, and was alertly ready to fetch and carry for the high priest in its temple, only the opportunities were infrequent.

For, wide as the Paradise field seemed to be growing from Thomas Jefferson's point of view, it was altogether too narrow for Duxbury Farley. The principal offices of Chiawassee Coal and Iron were in South Tredegar, and there the first vice-president was building a hewn-stone mansion, and had become a charter member of the city's first club; was domiciled in due form, and was already beginning to soften his final "r's," and to speak of himself as a Southerner — by adoption.

So sped the winter and the spring succeeding Thomas Jefferson's thirteenth birthday, and for the first time in his life he saw the opening buds of the ironwood and the tender, fresh greens of the herald poplars, and smelled the sweet, keen fragrance of awakening nature, without being moved thereby.

Ardea he saw only now and then, as old Scipio drove her back and forth between the manor-house and the railway station, morning and evening. He had heard that she was going to school in the city, and as yet there were no stirrings of adolescence in him to make him wish to know more.

As for Nan Bryerson, he saw her not at all. For one thing, he climbed no more to the spring-sheltering altar rock among the cedars; and for another, among all the wild creatures of the mountain, your moonshiner is the shyest, being an anachronism in a world of progress. One bit of news, however, floated in on the gossip at Little Zoar. It related that Nan's mother was dead, and that the body had lain two days unburied while Tike was drowning his sorrow in a sea of his own "pine-top."

In the new life, as in the old, summer followed quickly on the heels of spring, and when the hepaticas and the violets were gone, and the laurel and the rhododendron were decking the cliffs of

Lebanon in their summer robes of pink and white and magenta, another door was opened for Thomas Jefferson.

Vaguely it had been understood in the Gordon household that Mr. Duxbury Parley was a widower with two children: a boy, some two years older than Thomas Jefferson, at school in New England, and a girl younger, name and place of sojourn unknown. The boy was coming South for the long vacation, and the affairs of Chiawassee Coal and Iron — already reaching out subterraneously toward the future receivership — would call the first vice-president North for the better portion of July. Would Mrs. Martha take pity on a motherless lad, whose health was none of the best, and open her home to Vincent?

Mrs. Martha would and did; not ungrudgingly on the vice-president's account, but with many misgivings on Thomas Jefferson's. She was finding the surcharged industrial atmosphere of the new era inimical at every point to the development of the spiritual passion she had striven to arouse in her son; to paving the way for the realizing of that ideal which had first taken form when she had written "Reverend Thomas Jefferson Gordon" on the margin of the letter to her brother Silas.

As it fell out, the worst happened that could happen, considering the apparent harmlessness of the exciting cause. Vincent Farley proved to be an anemic stripling, cold, reserved, with no surface indications of moral depravity, and with at least a veneer of good breeding. But in Thomas Jefferson's heart he planted the seed of discontent with his surroundings, with the homely old house on the pike, unchanged as yet by the rising tide of prosperity, and more than all, with the prospect of becoming a chosen vessel.

It was of no use to hark back to the revival and the heart-quaking experiences of a year agone. Thomas Jefferson tried, but all that seemed to belong to another world and another life. What he craved now was to be like this envied and enviable son of good fortune, who wore his Sunday suit every day, carried a beautiful gold watch, and was coolly and complacently at ease, even with Major Dabney and a foreign-born and traveled Ardea.

Later in the summer the envy died down and Thomas Jefferson developed a pronounced case of hero-worship, something to the disgust of the colder-hearted, older boy. It did not last very long, nor did it leave any permanent scars; but before Thomas Jefferson was fully convalescent the subtle flattery of his adulation warmed the subject of it into something like companionship, and there were bragging stories of boarding-school life and of the world at large to add fresh fuel to the fire of discontent.

Though Thomas Jefferson did not know it, his deliverance on

that side was nigh. It had been decided in the family council of two — with a preacher-uncle for a casting-vote third — that he was to be sent away to school, Chiawassee Coal and Iron promising handsomely to warrant the expense; and the decision hung only on the choice of courses to be pursued.

Caleb had marked the growing hunger for technical knowledge in the boy, and had secretly gloried in it. Here, at least, was a strong stream of his own craftsman's blood flowing in the veins of his son.

"It'd be a thousand pities to spoil a good iron man and engineer to make a poor preacher, Martha," he objected; this for the twentieth time, and when the approach of autumn was forcing the conclusion.

"I know, Caleb; but you don't understand," was the invariable rejoinder. "You know that side of him, because it's your side. But he is my son, too; and — and Caleb, the Lord has called him!"

Gordon's smile was lenient, tolerant, as it always was in such discussions.

"Not out loud, I reckon, little woman; leastwise, Buddy don't act as if he'd heard it. As I've said, there's plenty of time. He's only a little shaver yet. Let him try the school in the city for a year 'r so, goin' and comin' on the railroads, nights and mornin's, like the Major's gran'daughter. After that, we might see."

But now Martha Gordon was fighting the last great battle in the war of spiritual repression which had been going on ever since the day when that text, *Be ye not unequally yoked together with unbelievers*, had been turned into a whip of scorpions to chasten her, and she fought as those who will not be denied the victory. Caleb yielded finally, but with some such hand-washing as Pilate did when he gave way to the pressure from without.

"I aim to do what's for the best, Martha, but I own I hain't got your courage. You've been shovin' that boy up the steps o' the pulpit ever since he let on like he could understand what you was sayin' to him, and maybe it's all right. I've never been over on your side o' that fence, and I don't know how things look over there. But if it was my doin's, I'd be prayin' mighty hard to whatever God I believed in not to let me make a hypocrite out'n o' Buddy. I would *so*."

Thomas Jefferson was told what was in store for him only a short time before his outsetting for the sectarian home school in a neighboring state, which was the joint selection of his mother and Uncle Silas. He took it with outward calm, as he would have taken anything from a prize to a whipping. But there was dumb rebellion within when his mother read him the letter he was to carry to the principal — a letter written by Brother Crafts to one of like precious faith, commending the lamb of the flock, and definitely committing that lamb as a chosen vessel. It was unfair, he cried inwardly, in a hot upflash of antagonism. He might choose to be a preacher; he had always meant to be one, for his mother's sake. But to be pushed and driven —

He took his last afternoon for a ramble in the fields and woods beyond the manor-house, in that part of the valley as yet unfurrowed by the industrial plow. It was not the old love of the solitudes that called him; it was rather a sore-hearted desire to go apart and give place to all the hard thoughts that were bubbling and boiling within.

A long circuit over the boundary hills brought him at length to the little glade with the pool in its center where he had been fishing for perch on that day when Ardea and the great dog had come to make him back-slide. He wondered if she had ever forgiven him. Most likely she had not. She never seemed to think him greatly worth while when they happened to meet.

He was sitting on the overhanging bank, just where he had sat that other day, when suddenly history repeated itself. There was a rustling in the bushes; the Great Dane bounded out, though not as before to stand menacing; and when he turned his head she was there near him.

"Oh, it's you, is it?" she said coolly; and then she called to the dog and made as if she would go away. But Thomas Jefferson's heart was full, and full hearts are soft.

"You needn't run," he hazarded. "I reckon I ain't going to bite you. I don't feel much like biting anybody today."

"You did bite me once, though," she said airily.

"And you've never forgiven me for it," he asserted, in deepest self-pity.

"Oh, yes, I have; the Dabneys always forgive — but they never forget. And me, I am a Dabney."

"That's just as bad. You wouldn't be so awful mean to me if you knew. I — I'm going away."

She came a little nearer at that and sat down beside him on the yellow grass with an arm around the dog's neck.

"Does it hurt?" she asked. "Because, if it does, I'm sorry; and I'll promise to forget."

"It does hurt some," he confessed. "Because, you see, I'm going to be a preacher."

"You?" she said, with the frank and unsympathetic surprise of childhood. Then politeness came to the rescue and she added: "I'm sorry for that, too, if you are wanting me to be. Only I should think it would be fine to wear a long black robe and a pretty white surplice, and to learn to sing the prayers beautifully, and all that."

Thomas Jefferson was honestly horrified, and he looked it.

"I'd like to know what in the world you're talking about," he said.

"About your being a minister, of course. Only in France, they call them priests of the church."

The boy's lips went together in a fine straight line. Not for nothing did the blood of many generations of Protestants flow in his veins. "Priest" was a Popish word.

"The Pope of Rome is antichrist!" he declared authoritatively.

She seemed only politely interested.

"Is he? I didn't know." Then, with a tactfulness worthy of graver years, she drew away from the dangerous topic. "When are you going?"

"Tomorrow."

"Is it far?"

"Yes; it's an awful long ways."

"Never mind; you'll be coming back after a while, and then we'll be friends — if you want to."

Surely Thomas Jefferson's heart was as wax before the fire that day.

"I'm mighty glad," he said. Then he got up. "Will you let me show you the way home again? — the short, easy way, this time?"

She hesitated a moment, and then stood up and gave him her hand.

"I'm not afraid of you now; *we* don't hate him any more, do we, Hector?"

And so they went together through the yellowing aisles of the September wood and across the fields to the manor-house gates.

X

THE SHADOW OF THE ROCK

Tom Gordon — Thomas Jefferson now only in his mother's letters — was fifteen past, and his voice was in the transition stage which made him blushingly self-conscious when he ran up the window-shade in the Pullman to watch for the earliest morning outlining of old Lebanon on the southern horizon.

There had been no home-going for him at the close of his first year in the sectarian school. The principal had reported him somewhat backward in his studies for his age, — which was true enough, — and had intimated that a summer spent with the preceptor who had the vacation charge of the school buildings would be invaluable to a boy of such excellent natural parts. So Tom had gone into semi-solitary confinement for three months with a man who thought in the dead languages and spoke in terms of ancient history, studying with sullen resentment in his heart, and charging his imprisonment to his preacher-uncle, who was, indeed, chiefly responsible.

He had mourned that loss of liberty all through his second year, and was conscious the while that it would prove the parent of a still greater loss. It is the exile's anchorage in a shifting world to think of the home haven as unchanged and unchanging; as a place where by and by the thread of life as it was may be knotted up with that of life as it shall be. But Tom remembered that he had left Paradise in the midst of convulsive upheavals, and was correspondingly fearful.

The sickening sense of unfamiliarity seized him when the train stopped for breakfast in the city which had once been the village of the single muddy street. The genius of progress had transformed it so completely that there was nothing but the huge, backgrounding mass of Lebanon, visible from the windows of the station breakfast-room, to identify the grave of the old and the birthplace of the new.

The boy laid desperate eye-holds on the comforting solidity of the background, and would not loose them when the train sped away southward again through mile-long yards with their boundaries picked out by black-vomiting factory chimneys. The mountain, at least, was unchanged, and there might be hope for the country beyond.

But the homesickness returned with renewed qualms when the train had doubled the nose of Lebanon and threaded its way among the hills to the Paradise portal. Gordonia, of the single side-track, had grown into a small iron town, with the Chiawassee plant flanking a good half mile of the railway; with a cindery street or two, and a scummy wave of operatives' cottages and laborers' shacks spreading up the hillsides which were stripped bare of their trees and undergrowth.

Tom's eyes filled, and he was wondering faintly if the desolating tide of progress had topped the hills to pour over into the home valley beyond, when his father accosted him. There was a little shock at the sight of the grizzled hair and beard turned so much grayer; but the welcoming was like a grateful draft of cool water in a parched wilderness.

"Well, now then! How are ye, Buddy, boy? Great land o' Canaan! but you've shot up and thickened out mightily in two years, son."

Tom was painfully conscious of his size. Also of the fact that he was clumsily in his own way, particularly as to hands and feet. The sectarian school dwelt lightly on athletics and such purely mundane trivialities as physical fitness and the harmonious education of the growing body and limbs.

"Yes; I'm so big it makes me right tired," he said gravely, and his voice cracked provokingly in the middle of it. Then he asked about his mother.

"She's tolerable — only tolerable, Buddy. She allows she don't have enough to keep her doin' in the new — " Caleb pulled himself up abruptly and changed the subject with a ponderous attempt at levity. "What-all have you done with your trunk check, son? Now I'll bet a hen worth fifty dollars ye've gone and lost it."

But Tom had not; and when the luggage was found there was another innovation to buffet him. The old buggy with its high seat had vanished, and in its room there was a modern surrey with a negro driver. Tom looked askance at the new equipage.

"Can't we make out to walk, pappy?" he asked, dropping unconsciously into the child-time phrase.

"Oh, yes; I reckon we could. You're not too young, and I'm not so terr'ble old. But — get in, Buddy, get in; there'll be trampin' enough for ye, all summer long."

The limestone pike was the same, and the creek was still rushing noisily over the stones in its bed, as Tom remarked gratefully. But the heaviest of the buffets came when the barrier hills were passed and the surrey horses made no motion to turn in at the gate of the old oak-shingled house beyond the iron-works.

"Hold on!" said Tom. "Doesn't the driver know where we live?"

The old-time, gentle smile wrinkled about the iron-master's eyes.

"That's the sup'rintendent's office and lab'ratory now, son. It was getting to be tolerable noisy down here for your mammy, so nigh to the plant. And we allowed to s'prise you. We've been buildin' us a new house up on the knoll just this side o' Major Dabney's."

It was the cruelest of the changes — the one hardest to bear; and it drove the boy back into the dumb reticence which was a part of his birthright. Had they left him nothing by which to remember the old days — days which were already beginning to take on the glamour of unutterable happiness past?

Nevertheless, he could not help looking curiously for the new home — the old being irretrievably sacked and ruined; but there were more shocks to come between. One of Mr. Duxbury Farley's side issues had been a real estate boom for Paradise Valley proper. South Tredegar being prosperous, the time had seemed propitious for the engrafting of the country-house idea. By some means, marvelous to those who knew Major Dabney's tenacious land-grip, the promoter had bought in the wooded hillsides facing the mountain, cut them into ten-acre residence plots, run a graveled drive on the western side of the creek to front them, and presto! the thing was done.

Tom saw well-kept lawns, park-like groves and pretentious country villas where he had once trailed Nance Jane through the "dark woods," and his father told him the names and circum-stance of the owners as they drove up the pike. There was Rockwood, the summer home of the Stanleys, and The Dell, owned, and inhabited at intervals, by Mr. Young-Dickson, of the South Tredegar potteries. Farther along there was Fairmount, whose owner was a wealthy cotton-seed buyer; Rook Hill, which Tom remembered as the ancient roosting ground of the migratory winter crows; and Farnsworth Park, ruralizing the name of its builder. On the most commanding of the hillsides was a pile of rough-cut Tennessee marble with turrets and many gables, rejoicing in the classic name of Warwick Lodge. This, Tom was told, was the country home of Mr. Farley himself, and the house alone had cost a fortune.

At the turn in the pike where you lost sight finally of the iron-works, there was a new church, a miniature in native stone of good old Stephen Hawker's church of Morwenstow. Tom gasped at the sight of it, and scowled when he saw the gilded cross on the tower.

"Catholic!" he said. "And right here in our valley!"

"No," said the father; "it's 'Piscopalian. Colonel Farley is one o' the vestries, or whatever you call 'em, of St. Michael's yonder in town. I reckon he wanted to get his own kind o' people round him out here, so he built this church, and they run it as a sort of side-show to the big church. Your mammy always looks the other way when we come by."

Tom looked the other way, too, watching anxiously for the first sight of the new home. They reached it in good time, by a graveled driveway leading up from the white pike between rows of forest trees; and there was a second negro waiting to take the team, when they alighted at the veranda steps.

The new house was a two-storied brick, ornate and palpably assertive, with no suggestion of the homely country comfort of the old. Yet, when his mother had wept over him in the wide hall, and there was time to go about, taking it all in like a cat exploring a strange garret, it was not so bad.

Or rather, let us say, there were compensations. The love of luxury is only dormant in the heart of the hardiest barbarian; and the polished floors and soft-piled rugs, the bath-room with its great china dish, and the carpeted stair with the old grandfather clock ticking bravely on the landing, presently began to thrum the tuneful chord of pride. Perhaps Ardea Dabney would not laugh and say, "What a funny, *funny* old place!" as she had once said when the Major had brought her to the log-walled homestead on the lower pike.

Still, there were incongruities — hopeless janglings of things married by increasing prosperity, but never meant to be bedfellows in the harmonious course of nature. One was the unblushing effrontery of the new brick pairing itself brazenly with the venerable gray stone manor-house on the adjoining knoll — impudence perceivable even to a hobbledehoy fresh from the school desk and the dormitory. Another was the total lack of sympathy between the housing and the housed.

This last was painfully evident in all the waking hours of the household. Tom observed that his father escaped early in the morning, and lived and moved and had his being in the industries at the lower end of the valley, as of old. But his mother's occupation was quite gone. And the summer evenings, sat out decorously on the ornate veranda, were full of constraint and awkward silences, having no part nor lot with those evenings of the older time on the slab-floored porch of the old homestead on the pike.

But there were compensations again, even for Martha Gordon, and Tom discovered one of them on the first Wednesday evening after his arrival. The new home was within easy walking distance of Little Zoar, and he went with his mother to the prayer-meeting.

The upper end of the pike was unchanged, and the little, weather-beaten church stood in its groving of pines, the same yesterday, today and for ever. Better still, the congregation, the small Wednesday-night gathering at least, held the familiar faces of the country folk. The minister was a young missionary, zealously earnest, and lacking as yet the quality of hardness and doctrinal precision which had been the boy's daily bread and meat at the sectarian school. What wonder, then, that when the call for testimony was made, the old pounding and heart-hammering set in, and duty, *duty*, duty, wrote itself in flaming letters on the dingy walls?

Tom set his teeth and swallowed hard, and let a dozen of the others rise and speak and sit again. He could feel the beating of his mother's heart, and he knew she was praying silently for him, praying that he would not deny his Master. For her sake, then . . . but not yet; there was still time enough — after the next hymn — after the next testimony — when the minister should give another invitation. He was chained to the bench and could not rise; his tongue clave to the roof of his mouth and his lips were like dry leaves. The silences grew longer; all, or nearly all, had spoken. He was stifling.

"*Whosoever therefore shall confess me before men, him will I confess also before my Father which is in heaven. But whosoever shall deny me before men, him will I also deny before my Father which is in heaven.*" It was the solemn voice of the young minister, and Tom staggered to his feet with the lamps whirling in giddy circles.

"I feel to say that the Lord is precious to my soul tonight. Pray for me, that I may ever be found faithful."

He struggled through the words of the familiar form gaspingly and sat down. A burst of triumphant song arose,

> "*O happy day, that fixed my choice*
> *On Thee, my Saviour and my God!*"

and the ecstatic aftermath came. Truly, it was better to be a doorkeeper in the house of God than to dwell in the tents of wickedness. What bliss was there to be compared with this heartmelting, soul-lifting blessing for duty done?

It went with him a good part of the way home, and Martha Gordon respected his silence, knowing well what heights and depths were engulfing the young spirit.

But afterward — alas and alas! that there should always be an "afterward"! When Tom had kissed his mother good night and was alone in his upper room, the reaction set in. What had he done? Were the words the outpouring of a full heart? Did they really mean anything to him, or to those who heard them? He grasped despairingly at the fast-fading glories of the vision, dropping on his knees at the bedside. "O God, let me see Thee and touch Thee, and be sure, *sure!*" he prayed, over and over again; and so finally sleep found him still on his knees with his face buried in the bed-clothes.

XI

THE TRUMPET-CALL

For the first few vacation days Tom rose with the sun and lived with the industries, marking all the later expansive strides and sorrowing keenly that he had not been present to see them taken in detail.

But this was a passing phase. When the mechanical hunger was sated; when he had started and stopped every engine in the big plant, had handled the levers of the great steam-hoist that shot the coal-cars from the mine to the coke-yard bins, and had prevailed on the engineer of the dinkey engine to let him haul out and dump a pot of slag, he had a sharp relapse into the primitive, and went roaming afield in search of his lost boyhood.

It was not to be found in any of the valley haunts, these having been transformed by the country-house colony. The old water-wheel below the dam hung motionless, being supplanted by the huge, modern, blowing-engines; and the black wash from the coal-mines had driven the perch from the pools and spoiled the swimming-holes in the creek. In the farther forests of the rampart hills the chopper's ax had been busy; and the blackberry patches in all the open spaces were sacked daily by chattering swarms of the work-people's children, white and black.

On the third morning Tom turned his steps despairingly toward the slopes of the mountain. He was at a pass when he would have given worlds to find one of the sacred places undesecrated. And there remained now only the high altar under the cedars of Lebanon to be visited.

It comforted him not a little to find that he had the old-time, burning thirst when he came within earshot of the dripping spring under the great rock. But when he would have knelt to drink from his palms like Gideon's men, there was no pool in the rocky basin. A barrel had been sunk in the sand-filled crevice, and a greedy pipe-line sucked up the water as fast as it trickled from the rock, to pass it on to one of the thirsty mechanisms in the iron plant a thousand feet below.

In its way this was the final straw, and Tom sat down beside the utilized spring with a lump in his throat. Afterward, he slaked his thirst as he could at the trickle from the rock's lip, and then set his face toward the higher steeps. Major Dabney, — not yet fully in tune with his new neighbors of the country-house colony, — and his granddaughter were spending the summer at Crestcliffe Inn, the new hotel on top of the mountain, and Tom felt that Ardea would understand if he could find and tell her. There are times when one must find a sympathetic ear, or be rent and torn by the pent-up things within.

In one sense the sympathy quest was a devitalizing failure. When he reached the summit of the mountain, hot and tired and dusty, the mere sight of the great hotel, with its thronged verandas and its overpowering air of grandeur and exclusiveness, quenched all desires save that which prompted a hasty retreat. The sectarian school paid as little attention to the social as to the athletic side of its youth; and Tom Gordon at fifteen past was as helpless conventionally as if he had never set foot outside of Paradise.

But at the retractive moment he ran plump into the Major, stalking grandly along the tile-paved walk and smoking a wartime cheroot of preposterous length. The despot of Paradise, despot now only by courtesy of the triumphant genius of modernity, put on his eye-glasses and stared Thomas into respectful rigidity.

"Why, bless my soul! — if it isn't Captain Gordon's boy! Well, well, you young limb! If you didn't faveh youh good fatheh in eve'y line and lineament of youh face, I should neveh have known you — you've grown so. Shake hands, suh!"

Tom did it awkwardly. It is a gift to be able to shake hands easily; a gift withheld from most girls and all boys up to the soulful age. But there was worse to follow. Ardea was somewhere on the peopled verandas, and the Major, more terrible in his hospitality than he had ever appeared in the old-time rage-fits, dragged his hapless victim up and down and around and about in search of her. "Not say 'Howdy' to Ardea? Why, you young cub, where are youh mannehs, suh?" Thus the Major, when the victim would have broken away.

It was a fiery trial for Tom — a way-picking among red-hot plowshares of embarrassment. How the well-bred folk smiled, and the grand ladies drew their immaculate skirts aside to make passing-room for his dusty feet! How one of them wondered, quite audibly, where in the world Major Dabney had unearthed that young native! Tom was conscious of every fleck of dust on his clothes and shoes; of the skilless knot in his necktie; of the school-desk droop in his shoulders; of the utter superfluousness of his big hands.

And when, at the long last, Ardea was discovered sitting beside a gorgeously-attired Queen of Sheba, who also smiled and examined him minutely through a pair of eye-glasses fastened on the end of a gold-mounted stick, the place of torment, wherever and whatever it might be, held no deeper pit for him. What he had climbed the mountain to find was a little girl in a school frock, who had sat on the yellowing grass with one arm around the neck of a great dog, looking fearlessly up at him and telling him she was sorry he was going away. What he had found was a very statuesque little lady, clad in fluffy summer white, with the other Ardea's slate-blue eyes and soft voice, to be sure, but with no other reminder of the lost avatar.

From first to last, from the moment she made room for him, dusty clothes and all, on the settee between herself and the Queen of Sheba, Tom was conscious of but one clearly-defined thought — an overmastering desire to get away — to be free at any cost. But the way of escape would not disclose itself, so he sat in stammering misery, answering Ardea's questions about the sectarian school in bluntest monosyllables, and hearing with his other ear a terrible Major tell the Queen of Sheba all about the railroad invasion, and how he — Tom Gordon — had run to find a punk match to fire a cannon in the Dabney cause.

All of which was bad enough, but the torture rack had still another turn left in its screw. After he had sat for awkward hours, as it seemed, though minutes would have measured it, there was a stir on the veranda and he became vaguely conscious of an impending catastrophe.

"Grandpa is telling you you must stay to luncheon with us," prompted Ardea. "Will you take me in?"

The Major had already given his arm to the Queen of Sheba, and there was no help for the helpless. Tom crooked his arm as stiffly as possible and said "May I?" — which was an inspiration — and they got to the great dining-room with no worse mishap than a collision at the door brought about by his stepping on the train of one of the grand ladies.

But at luncheon his troubles began afresh; or rather, a new and more agonizing set of them took the field. The fourth seat at the small table was occupied by the lady with the stick eye-glasses, and Tom was made aware that she was a Dabney cousin once removed. Thereupon, what little dexterity was left in him fled away, and the table-trial, under the smiling eyes of a Miss Euphrasia, became a chapter of horrors.

From absently picking and choosing among the forks, and trying to drink his bouillon out of the cup in which it was served, to upsetting his glass of iced tea, he stumbled on in a dream of awkwardness; and when, to cover the tea mishap, Ardea, emulating the lady hostess who broke one of her priceless tea-cups at a similar crisis, promptly overturned her own glass, he was unreasonable enough to be angry.

Taking it all in all, anger was coming to be the one constant quantity in the procession of varying emotions. By what right did this hollow, insincere, mocking world, of whose very existence he had been in utter ignorance, make him a butt for its well-bred sneers? Its fashions and fripperies and meaningless forms were not beyond learning; and, by Heaven! he would learn them, too, and put them all to shame. They should see!

And Ardea: was she laughing at him, too, in the depths of her big, beautiful eyes? No, that was too much; he would never believe that. But she was insincere, like the rest of them. It was acting a lie for her to make-believe clumsiness just to keep the others from laughing at him. She must stand with her kind.

From that station to the top of the high, bare crag of righteous condemnation was but a short stage in the wrathful journey; and while he was choking over the meal of strange dishes the zealous under-thought was reaching out into the future.

Some day, when his tongue should be loosed, he would stand before this mocking, smiling, heathenish world with the open Bible in his hand; then it should be taught what it needed to know — that while it was saying it was rich, and increased with goods, and had need of nothing, it was wretched and miserable and poor and blind and naked.

So it came about that it was the convert of Little Zoar, and not the self-pitying youth searching for his lost boyhood, who escaped finally from the entanglements of Major Dabney's hospitality.

On the way down the cliff path the fire burned and the revival zeal was kindled anew. There had been times, in the last year, especially, when he had thought coldly of the disciple's calling and was minded to break away and be a skilled craftsman, like his father. Now he was aghast to think that he had ever been so near the brink of apostasy. With the river of the Water of Life springing crystal clear at his feet, should he turn away and drink from the bitter pools in the wilderness of this world? With prophetic eye he saw himself as another Boanerges, lifting, with all the inspiring eloquence of the son of thunder, the Baptist's soul-shaking cry, *Repent ye: for the kingdom of heaven is at hand!*

The thought thrilled him, and the fierce glow of enthusiasm became an intoxicating ecstasy. The tinkling drip of falling water broke into the noonday silence of the forest like the low-voiced call of a sacred bell. For the first time since leaving the mountain top he took note of his surroundings. He was standing beside the great, cubical boulder under the cedars — the high altar in nature's mountain tabernacle.

Ah, Martha Gordon, mother of many prayers, look now, if you can, but not too closely or too long! Is it merely the boy you have molded and fashioned, or is it the convinced and consecrated evangelist of the future, who falls on his knees beside the great rock, with head bent and fingers tightly interlocked, groping desperately for words in which to rededicate himself to the God of your fathers?

Thomas Jefferson had the deep peace of the fully committed when he rose from his knees and went to drink at the spouting rock lip. It was decided now, this thing he had been holding half heartedly in abeyance. There would be no more dallying with temptation, no more rebellion, no more irreverent stumblings in the dark valley of doubtful questions. More especially, he would be vigilant to guard against those backslidings that came so swiftly on the heels of each spiritual quickening. His heart was fixed, so irrevocably, so surely, that he could almost wish that Satan would try him there and then. But the enemy of souls was nowhere to be seen in the leafy arches of the wood, and Tom bent again to take a second draft at the spouting rock lip.

XII

THE IRON IN THE FORGE FIRE

He was bending over the sunken barrel. A shadow, not his own, blurred the water mirror. He looked up quickly.

"Nan!" he cried.

She was standing on the opposite side of the barrel basin, looking down on him with good-natured mockery in the dark eyes.

"I 'lowed maybe you wouldn't have such a back load of religion after you'd been off to the school a spell," she said pointedly. And then: "Does it always make you right dry an' thirsty to say your prayers, Tommy-Jeffy?"

Tom sat back on his heels and regarded her thoughtfully. His first impulse was out of the natural heart, rageful, wounded vanity spurring it on. It was like her heathenish impertinence to look on at such a time, and then to taunt him about it afterward.

But slowly as he looked a curious change came over him. She was the same Nan Bryerson, bareheaded, barelegged, with the same tousled mat of dark hair, and the same childish indifference to a whole frock. And yet she was not the same. The subtle difference, whatever it was, made him get up and offer to shake hands with her, — and he thought it was the newly-made vows constraining him, and took credit therefor.

"You can revile me as much as you like now, Nan," he said, with prideful humility. "You can't make me mad any more, like you used to."

"Why can't I?" she demanded.

"Because I'm older now, and — and better, I hope. I shall never forget that you have a precious soul to save."

Her response to this was a scoffing laugh, shrill and challenging. Yet he could not help thinking that it made her look prettier than before.

"You can laugh as much as you want to; but I mean it," he insisted. "And, besides, Nan, — of all the things that I've been wanting to come back to, you're the only one that isn't changed." And again he thought it was righteous guile that was making him kind to her.

In a twinkling the mocking hardness went out of her eyes and she leaned across the barrel mouth and touched his hand.

"D'you reckon you shorely mean that, Tom Gordon?" she said; and the lips which lent themselves so easily to scorn were tremulous. She was just his age, and womanhood was only a step across the threshold for her.

"Of course, I do. Let me carry your bucket for you."

She had hung the little wooden piggin under the drip of the spring and it was full and running over. But when he had lifted it out for her, she rinsed and emptied it.

"I just set it there to cool some," she explained. "I'm goin' up to Sunday Rock afte' huckleberries. Come and go 'long with me, Tom."

He assented with a willingness as eager as it was unaccountable. If she had asked him to do a much less reasonable thing, he was not sure that he could have refused.

And as they went together through the wood, spicy with the June fragrances, questions like those of the boyhood time thronged on him, and he welcomed them as a return of at least one of the vanished thrills — and was grateful to her.

Why had he never before noticed that she was so much prettier than any other girl he had ever seen? What was there in the touch of her hand to make him feel like the iron in the forge fire — warm and glowing and putty-soft and yielding? Other girls were not that way. Only a half hour since, Ardea Dabney had put her hand in his when she had said good-by, and that feeling was the kind you have when you have climbed through breathless summer woods to a high mountain top and the cool breeze blows through your hair and makes you quietly glad and lifted-up and satisfied.

These were questions to be buried deep in the secret places, and yet he had a curious eagerness to talk to Nan about them; to find out if she could understand. But he could not get near to any serious or confidential side of her. Her mood was playful, hilarious, daring. Once she ran squirrel-like out on the bole of a great tree leaning to its fall over the cliff, hung her piggin on a broken limb, and told him he must go after it. Next it was a squeeze through some "fat-man's-misery" crevice in the water-worn sandstone, with a cry to him to come on if he were not a girl-boy. And when they were fairly under the overhanging cliff face of Sunday Rock, she darted away, laughing back at him over her shoulder, and daring him to follow her along a dizzy shelf halfway up the crag; a narrow ledge, perilous for a mountain goat.

This, as he remembered later, was the turning-point in her mood. In imagination he saw her try it and fail; saw her lithe, shapely beauty lying broken and mangled at the cliff's foot; and in three bounds he had her fast locked in his restraining arms. She strove with him at first, like a wrestling boy, laughing and taunting him with being afraid for himself. Then —

Tom Gordon, clean-hearted as yet, did not know precisely what happened. Suddenly she stopped struggling and lay panting in his arms, and quite as suddenly he released her.

"Nan!" he said, in a swiftly submerging wave of tenderness, "I didn't go to hurt you!"

She sank down on a stone at his feet and covered her face with her hands. But she was up again and turning from him with eyes downcast before he could comfort her.

"I ain't hurt none," she said gravely. And then: "I reckon we'd better be gettin' them berries. It looks like it might shower some; and paw'll kill me if I ain't home time to get his supper."

Here was an end of the playtime, and Tom helped industriously with the berry-picking, wondering the while why she kept her face turned from him, and why his brain was in such a turmoil, and why his hands shook so if they happened to touch hers in reaching for the piggin.

But this new mood of hers was more unapproachable than the other; and it was not until the piggin was filled and they had begun to retrace their steps together through the fragrant wood, that she let him see her eyes again, and told him soberly of her troubles: how she was fifteen and could neither read nor write; how the workmen's children in Gordonia hooted at her and called her a mountain cracker when she went down to buy meal or to fill the molasses jug; and, lastly, how, since her mother had died, her father had worked little and drunk much, till at times there was nothing to eat save the potatoes she raised in the little patch back of the cabin, and the berries she picked on the mountain side.

"I hain't never told anybody afore, and you mustn't tell, Tom. But times I'm scared paw'll up and kill me when — when he ain't feelin' just right. He's some good to me when he ain't red-eyed; but that ain't very often, nowadays."

Tom's heart swelled within him; and this time it was not the heart of the Pharisee. There is no lure known to the man part of the race that is half so potent as the tale of a woman in trouble.

"Does — does he beat you, Nan?" he asked; and there was wrathful horror in his voice.

For answer she bent her head and parted the thick black locks over a long scar.

"That's where he give me one with the skillet, a year come Christmas. And this," — opening her frock to show him a black-and-blue bruise on her breast, — "is what I got only day afore yesterday."

Tom was burning with indignant compassion, and bursting because he could think of no adequate way of expressing it. In all his fifteen years no one had ever leaned on him before, and the sense of protectorship over this abused one budded and bloomed like a juggler's rose.

"I wish I could take you home with me, Nan," he said simply.

There was age-old wisdom in the dark eyes when they were lifted to his.

"No, you don't," she said firmly. "Your mammy would call me a little heathen, same as she used to; and I reckon that's what I am — I hain't had no chanst to be anything else. And you're goin' to be a preacher, Tom."

Why did it rouse a dull anger in his heart to be thus reminded of his own scarce-cooled pledge made on his knees under the shadowing cedars? He could not tell; but the fact remained.

"You hear me, Nan; I'm going to take care of you when I'm able. No matter what happens, I'm going to take care of you," was what he said; and a low rumbling of thunder and a spattering of rain on the leaves punctuated the promise.

She looked away and was silent. Then, when the rain began to come faster: "Let's run, Tom. I don't mind gettin' wet; but you mustn't."

They reached the great rock sheltering the barrel-spring before the shower broke in earnest, and Tom led the way to the right. Half-way up its southern face the big boulder held a water-worn cavity, round, and deeply hollowed, and carpeted with cedar needles. Tom climbed in first and gave her a hand from the mouth of the little cavern. When she was up and in, there was room in the nest-like hollow, but none to spare. And on the instant the summer shower shut down upon the mountain side and closed the cave mouth as with a thick curtain.

There was no speech in that little interval of cloud-lowering and cloud-lifting. The boy tried for it, would have taken up the confidences where the storm-coming had broken them off; but it was blankly impossible. All the curious thrills foregone seemed to culminate now in a single burning desire: to have it rain for ever, that he might nestle there in the hollow of the great rock with Nan so close to him that he could feel the warmth of her body and the quick beating of her heart against his arm.

Yet the sleeping conscience did not stir. The moment of recognition was withheld even when the cloud curtain began to lift and he could see the long lashes drooped over the dark eyes, and the flush in the brown cheek matching his own.

"Nan!" he whispered, catching his breath; "you're — you're the —"

She slipped away from him before he could find the word, and a moment later she was calling to him from below that the rain was over and she must hurry.

He walked beside her to the door of the miserable log shack under the second cliff, still strangely shaken, but striving manfully to be himself again. The needed fillip came when the mountaineer staggered to the threshold to swear thickly at his daughter. In times past, Tom would quickly have put distance between himself and Tike Bryerson in the squirrel-eyed stage of intoxication. But now his promise to Nan was behind him, and the Gordon blood was to the fore.

"It was my fault that Nan stayed so long," he said bravely; and he was immensely relieved when Bryerson, making quite sure of his identity, became effusively hospitable.

"Cap'n Gordon's boy — 'f cou'se; didn't make out to know ye, 't firs'. Come awn in the house an' sit a spell; come in, I say!"

Again, for Nan's sake, Tom could do no less. It was the final plunge. The boy was come of abstinent stock, which was possibly the reason why the smell of the raw corn liquor with which the cabin reeked gripped him so fiercely. Be that as it may, he could make but a feeble resistance when the tipsy mountaineer pressed him to drink; and the slight barrier went down altogether when he saw the appealing look in Nan's eyes. Straightway he divined that there would be consequences for her when he was gone if the maudlin devil should be aroused in her father.

So he put the tin cup to his lips and coughed and strangled over a single swallow of the fiery, nauseating stuff; did this for the girl's sake, and then rose and fled away down the mountain with his heart ablaze and a fearful clamor as of the judgment trumpet sounding in his ears.

For now the sleeping conscience was broad awake and plying its merciless dagger; now, indeed, he knew very well what he had done — what he had been doing since that fatal moment at the barrel-spring when he had fallen under the spell of Nan Bryerson's beauty; nay, back of that — how the up-bubbling of zeal had been nothing more than wounded vanity; the smoke of a vengeful fire of anger lighted by a desire to strike back at those who had laughed at him.

The next morning he came hollow-eyed to his breakfast, and when the chance offered, besought his father to give him one of the many boy's jobs in the iron plant during the summer vacation — asked and obtained.

And neither the hotel on the mountain top nor the hovel cabin under the second cliff saw him more the long summer through.

XIII

A SISTER OF CHARITY

It was just before the Christmas holidays, in his fourth year of the sectarian school, that Tom Gordon was expelled.

Writing to the Reverend Silas at the moment of Tom's dismissal, the principal could voice only his regret and disappointment. It was a most singular case. During his first and second years Thomas had set a high mark and had attained to it. On the spiritual side he had been somewhat non-committal, to be sure, but to offset this, he had been deeply interested in the preparatory theological studies, or at least he had appeared to be.

But on his return from his first summer spent at home there was a marked change in him, due, so thought Doctor Tollivar, to his association with the rougher class of workmen in the iron mills. It was as if he had suddenly grown older and harder, and the discipline of the school, admirable as the Reverend Silas knew it to be, was not severe enough to reform him.

"It grieves me more than I can tell you, my dear brother, to be obliged to confess that we can do nothing more for him here," was the concluding paragraph of the principal's letter, "and to add that his continued presence with us is a menace to the morals of the school. When I say that the offense for which he is expelled is by no means the first, and that it is the double one of gambling and keeping intoxicating liquors in his room, you will understand that the good repute of Beersheba was at stake, and there was no other course open to us."

It was as well, perhaps, for what remained of Tom's peace of mind that he knew nothing of this letter at the time of its writing. The long day had been sufficiently soul-harrowing and humiliating. Since the morning exercises, when he had been publicly degraded by having his sentence read out to the entire school, he had spent the time in his room, watched, if not guarded, by some one of the assistants. And now he was to be shipped off on the night train like a criminal, with no chance for a word of leave-taking, however much he might desire it.

He was tramping up and down with his hands in his pockets, the Gordon scowl making him look like a young thunder-cloud, when one of the preceptors came to drive with him to the railroad station. It was the final indignity, and he resented it bitterly.

"I can make out to find my way down to the train without troubling you, Mr. Martin," he burst out in boyish anger.

"Doubtless," said the preceptor, quite unmoved. "But we are

still responsible for you. Doctor Tollivar wishes me to see you safely aboard your train, and I shall certainly do so. Take the side stairway down, if you please."

The principal's buggy was waiting at the gate, and the preceptor drove. Tom sat back under the hood with his overcoat across his knees. The evening was freezing cold, with an edged wind, and the drive to the station was a hilly mile. If it had been ten miles he would not have moved or opened his lips.

As it chanced, there were no other passengers for the train, which was a through south-bound express. Tom was meaning to sit up all night and think; and the most comfortless seat in the smoking-car would answer. There would be the meeting with his father and mother in the morning, and he thought he should not dare to let sleep come between. He had a firm grip of himself now, and it must not be relaxed until that meeting was over.

But the preceptor had already stepped to the ticket window. "That sleeping-car reservation for Thomas Gordon — have you secured it?" he asked of the agent; and Tom heard the reply: "Lower ten in car number two." That disposed of the seat in the smoker and the bit of penance, and he was unreasonable enough to be resentful for favors.

Hence, when the train came to a stand beside the platform, he went straight to the Pullman, ignoring his keeper. But the preceptor followed him to the car step, held out his hand coldly, and said: "I'm sorry for you, Gordon. Good-by."

Tom drew himself up stiffly, overlooking the extended hand.

"'Good-by' — that is 'God be with you,' isn't it, Mr. Martin? I reckon you don't mean that. Good night." And this is the way Thomas Jefferson turned his back on three and a half years of Beersheba, with hot tears in his eyes and an angry word on his lips.

The Pintsch lights were burning brightly in the Pullman, and these — and the tears — blinded him. Some of the sections in the middle of the car were made down for the night, and while he was stumbling in the wake of the porter over the shoes and the hand-bags left in the aisle, the train started.

"Lower ten, sah," said the black boy, and went about his business in the linen locker. But Tom stood balancing himself with the swaying of the car and staring helplessly at the occupant of lower twelve, a young girl in a gray traveling coat and hat, sitting with her face to the window.

"Why, you — somebody!" she exclaimed, turning to surprise him in the act of glowering down on her. "Do you know, I thought there might be just one chance in a thousand that you'd go home for Christmas, so I made the porter tell me when we were coming to Beersheba. Why don't you sit down?"

Tom edged into the opposite seat and shook hands with her, all in miserable, comfortless silence. Then he blurted out:

"If I'd had any idea you were on this train, I'd have walked."

Ardea laughed, and for all his misery he could not help remarking how much sweeter the low voice was growing, and how much clearer the blue of her eyes was under the forced light of the gas-globes. He had seen her only two or three times since that blush-kindling noon at Crestcliffe Inn. Their Paradise goings and comings had not coincided very evenly.

"You are just the same rude boy, aren't you?" she said leniently. "Are there no girls in Beersheba to teach you how to be nice?"

"I didn't mean it that way," he hastened to say. "I'm always saying the wrong thing to you. But if you only knew, you wouldn't speak to me; much less let me sit here and talk to you."

"If I only knew what? Perhaps you would better tell me and let me judge for myself," she suggested; and out of the past came a flick of the memory whip to make him feel again that she was immeasurably his senior.

"I'm expelled," he said bluntly.

"Oh!" For a full minute, as it seemed to him, she looked stead-fastly out of the window at the wall of blackness flitting past, and the steady drumming of the wheels grated on his nerves and got into his blood. When it was about to become unbearable she turned and gave him her hand again. "I'm just as sorry as I can be!" she declared, and the slate-blue eyes confirmed it.

Tom hung his head, just as he had in the trying interview with Doctor Tollivar. But he told her a great deal more than he had told the principal.

"It was this way: three of the boys came to my room to play cards — because their rooms were watched. I didn't want to play — oh, I'm none too good;" — this in answer to something in her eyes that made him eager to tell her the exact truth — "I've done it lots of times. But that night I'd been thinking — well, I just didn't want to, that's all. Then they said I was afraid, and of course, that settled it."

"Of course," she agreed loyally.

"Wait; I want you to know it all," he went on doggedly. "When Martin — he's the Greek and Latin, you know — slipped up on us, there was a bottle of whisky on the table. He took down our names, and then he pointed at the bottle, and said, 'Which one of you does that belong to?' Nobody said anything, and after it began to get sort of — well, kind of monotonous, I picked up the bottle and offered him a drink, and put it in my pocket. That settled *me*."

"But it wasn't yours," she averred.

His smile was a rather ferocious grin. "Wasn't it? Well, I took it, anyway; and I've got it yet. Now see here: that's my berth over there and I'm going over to it. You needn't let on like you know me any more."

"Fiddle!" she said, making a face at him. "You say that like a little boy trying, oh, so hard, to be a man. I'll believe you are just as bad as bad can be, if you want me to; but you mustn't be rude to me. We don't play cards or drink things at Carroll College, but some of us have brothers, and — well, we can't help knowing."

Tom was soberly silent for the space of half a hundred rail-lengths. Then he said: "I wish I'd had a sister; maybe it would have been different."

She shook her head.

"No, indeed, it wouldn't. You're going to be just what you are going to be, and a dozen sisters wouldn't make any difference."

"One like you would make a lot of difference." It made him blush and have a slight return of the largeness of hands; but he said it.

She laughed. "That's nice. You couldn't begin to say anything like that the day you came up to Crestcliffe Inn. But I mean what I say. Sisters wouldn't help you to be good, unless you really wanted to be good yourself. They're just comfortable persons to have around when you are taking your whipping for being naughty."

"Well, that's a good deal, isn't it?"

Again she made the adorable little face at him. "Do you want me to be your sister for a little while — till you get out of this scrape? Is that what you are trying to say?"

He took heart of grace, for the first time in three bad days. "Say, Ardea; I'm hunting for sympathy; just as I used to a long time ago. But you mustn't mix up with me. I'm not worth it."

"Oh, I suppose not; no boy is. But tell me; what are you going to do when you get back to Paradise?"

"Why — I don't know; I haven't thought that far ahead; go to work in the iron plant and be a mucker all the rest of my life, I reckon."

"How silly! You are nearly eighteen, now, aren't you? — and about six feet tall?"

"Both," he said briefly.

"And all the way along you've been meaning to be a minister?"

He gritted his teeth. "That's all over, now; I reckon it's been over for a long time."

"That is more serious. Does your mother know?"

He shook his head.

"She mustn't, Tom; it will just break her heart."

"As if I didn't know!" he said bitterly. "But, Ardea, I haven't been quite square with you. The way I told it about the cards and the whisky you might think —"

"I know what you are going to say. But it needn't make any all-the-time difference, need it? You've been backsliding — isn't that what you call it? — but now you are sorry, and —"

"No; that's the worst of it. I'm not sorry, the way I ought to be. Besides, after what I've been these last two years — but you can't understand; it would just be mockery — mocking God. I told you I wasn't worth your while."

She smiled gravely. "You are such a boy, Tom. Don't you know that all through life you'll have two kinds of friends: those who will stand by you because they won't believe anything bad about you, and those who will take you for just what you are and still stand by you?"

He scowled thoughtfully at her. "Say, Ardea; I'd just like to know how old you are, anyhow! You say things every once in a while that make me feel as if I were a little kid in knee-breeches."

She laughed in his face. "That is the rudest thing you've said yet! But I don't mind telling you — since I'm to be your sister. I'll be seventeen a little while after you're eighteen."

"Haven't you ever been foolish, like other girls?" he asked.

She laughed again, more heartily than ever. "They say I'm the silliest tomboy in our house, at Carroll. But I have my lucid intervals, I suppose, like other people, and this is one of them. I am going to stand by you tomorrow morning, when you have to tell your father and mother — that is, if you want me to."

His gratitude was too large for speech, but he tried to look it. Then the porter came to make her section down, and he had to say good night and vanish.

XIV

ON JORDAN'S BANK

Ardea saw cause for increasing satisfaction in Thomas Jefferson the next morning, when they sat together in section nine to give the porter a chance to rehabilitate ten and twelve.

He had grown so much surer of himself in the two years, and his manners were gratefully improved. Also, she was constrained to admit — frank glances of the slate-blue eyes appraising him — that he was developing hopefully in the matter of good looks. The dust-colored hair of boyhood had become a sort of viking yellow, and the gray eyes, so they should not be overcast by trouble shadows, were honest and fearless.

Then, too, the Gordon jaw was beginning to assert itself — square in the angle and broad at the point of the chin, with a deep cleft to mark its center. Ardea thought it would not be well, later on, for those who should find that jaw and chin opposing them. There would certainly be stubborn and aggressive resistance — and none too much mercy when the fight should end.

The improved manners were pleasantly apparent when the train reached South Tredegar. There were twenty minutes for breakfast, and Tom bestirred himself manfully, and as if the awkward day at Crestcliffe Inn had never been; helping Ardea with her coat, steering her masterfully through the crowd, choosing the fortunate seats at the most convenient table, and commanding the readiest service in spite of the hurry and bustle.

Ardea marked it all with a little thrill of vicarious triumph, which was straightway followed by a little pang personal. What had wrought the change in him? Was it merely the natural chivalry of the coming man breaking through the crust of boyish indifference to the social conventions? Or was it one of the effects of the late plunge into rebellious wickedness?

She hoped it was the chivalry, but she had a vague fear that it was the wickedness. There was a young woman among the seniors in Carroll College who was old in a certain brilliant hardness of mind — a young woman with a cynical outlook on life, and who was not always regardful of her seed-sowing in fresher hearts. Ardea remembered a saying of hers, flung out one evening in the college parlors when the talk of her group had turned on the goodness of good boys: "Why can't you be sincere with yourselves? Not one of you has any use for the truly good boy until after he has learned how to respect you by being a bad boy. You haven't been saying it in so many words, perhaps, but that is the crude fact." Was this the secret of Tom's new acceptability? Ardea hoped it was not — and feared lest it might be.

When they were once more in the train, and the mile-long labyrinth of the factory chimneys had been threaded and left behind, Thomas Jefferson gave proof of another and still more gratifying change.

"Say, Ardea," he began, "you said last night that you'd stand by me in what I've got to face this morning. That's all right; and I reckon I'll never live long enough to even it up with you. But, of course, you know I'm not going to let you do it."

"Why not?" she asked.

"Because I'm not mean enough, or coward enough. After a while, if you get a chance to sort of make it easier for mother —"

"I'll do that, if I can," she promised quickly. "But I hope you are not going to break her heart, Tom."

"You can be mighty sure I'm not; if anything I can do now will help it. But — but, say, Ardea, I can't go back and begin all over again. I should be the meanest, low-down thing in all this world — and that's a hypocrite."

"Oh!" said Ardea, catching her breath. Her religion was very much a matter of fact to her, and the thought of Tom — Martha Gordon's son — stumbling in the plain path of belief was dismaying. "Why would you have to be a hypocrite? Do you mean that you are not sure you ought to be a minister?"

"I mean that I don't know any more what I believe and what I don't believe. I feel as if I'd just like to let myself alone on that side for a while, and make everybody else let me alone. It seems — but you don't know; a girl can't know."

She smiled up at him, and the smile effaced some of the trouble furrows between his eyes.

"Last night you were telling me that I seemed ages older than you; what is it that I can't know?"

"Stumpings like mine, — a man's stumpings," he said, with a touch of the old self-assurance. "You've swallowed your religion whole; it's the best thing for a girl to do, I reckon. But I've got to have whys and wherefores; I've always had to have them. And there are no wherefores in religion; just none whatever."

She was plainly shocked. "O Tom!" she urged; "think of your mother!"

"Thinking of her isn't going to change the value of pi any," he rejoined soberly. "I suppose I've thought of her, and of what she wants me to be, ever since the first day I went to Beersheba. The first two years I tried, honestly tried. But it's no use. It appears like we've got so far away from taw that we can't even see what-all we're aiming at. I've been grinding theology till I'm fairly sick of the word, and I've learned just one thing, Ardea, and that is that you can't prove a single theorem in it."

"But there are some things that don't appear to need any proof; one seems to have been born knowing them. Don't you feel that way?"

He shook his head slowly.

"I used to think I did; but now I'm afraid I don't. I can't remember the time when I wasn't asking why. Don't they teach you to ask why at Carroll?"

"Not in matters of — of conscience."

"Well, they don't at Beersheba, when you come right down to it. And when you do ask, they put you off with a text out of the Bible that, just as like as not, doesn't come within a row of apple-trees of hitting the mark. I remember one time I said something about the 'why' to Doctor Tollivar. He sniffled — he *does* sniffle, Ardea — and said: 'Mr. Gordon, I recommend that you read what Paul says to the Romans, fourteen and twenty-three: "He that doubteth is damned." And you will note the verb in the original — *is damned*, present tense.' Do you happen to remember the verse?"

Ardea confessed ignorance, and he went on, with a lip-curl of contempt.

"Well, the whole chapter is about being careful for the weak brother. The Romans used to eat the flesh of the animals offered in the sacrifices to the gods, and some of the Christian Romans didn't seem to be strong enough or sensible enough to eat it as just plain, every-day meat. They tangled it up with the idol worship. So Paul, or whoever it was that wrote the chapter, said: 'He that doubteth is damned if he eat, because he eateth not of faith,' that is, the Christian faith, I suppose, which would teach him that the meat wasn't any the worse for having been offered to a block of wood or stone called a god. Now, honestly, Ardea, what would you think of a teacher who would deliberately cut a verse in two in the middle and make his half of it mean something else, just to put a fellow down?"

"It doesn't seem quite honest," she could not help admitting.

"Honest! It's low-down trickery. And they all do it. Last year when I was going up to Beersheba I happened to sit in the same seat with a Catholic priest. We got to talking, I don't remember just how, and I said something about doubting the Pope's infalli-bility. Out pops the same old text: 'My son, hear the words of the holy Apostle, Saint Paul — " He that doubteth is damned!"' He was old enough to be my father, but I couldn't help slapping the other half of the verse at him, and saying that we'd most luckily escape because there wasn't any dinner-stop for our train."

The flippant tone of all this disheartened Thomas Jefferson's listener, and a silence succeeded which lasted until the train had stormed around the nose of Lebanon and the whistle was blowing for Gordonia. Then Tom said: "I didn't mean to hurt you; but now you see why I can't go back and begin all over again." And she nodded assent.

There was no one at the station to meet the disgraced one, news of the disaster at Beersheba being as yet only on the way. Thomas Jefferson was rather glad of it; especially glad that there was no one from Woodlawn — this was the name of the new home — to recognize him and ask discomforting questions. But Ardea was expected, and the Dabney carriage, with old Scipio on the box, was drawn up beside the platform.

Tom put Ardea into the carriage and was giving her hand luggage to Scipio when she called to him.

"Isn't there any one here to meet you, Tom?"

"They don't know I'm coming," he explained. Whereupon she quickly made room for him, holding the door open. But he hung back.

"I reckon I'd better ride on the box with Unc' Scipio," he suggested.

"I am sure I don't know why you should," she objected.

He told her straight; or at least gave her his own view of it.

"By tomorrow morning everybody in Gordonia and Paradise Valley will know that I'm home in disgrace. It won't hurt Unc' Scipio any if I'm seen riding with him."

It was the first time that he had been given to see the Dabney imperiousness shining star-like in Miss Ardea's slate-blue eyes.

"I wish you to get your hand-bag and ride in here with me," she said, with the air of one whose wish was law. But when he was sitting opposite and the carriage door was shut, she smiled companionably across at him and added: "You foolish boy!"

"It wasn't foolish," he maintained doggedly. "I know what I ought to do — and I'm not doing it. Everybody around here knows both of us, and —"

"Hush!" she commanded. "I refuse to hear another word. I said you were a foolish boy, and it will be inexcusably impolite in you to prove that you are not."

Tom was glad enough to be silent; and it came to him, after a little, that she was giving him a chance to pull himself together to meet the ordeal that was before him. In all the misery of the moment — the misery which belongs to those who ride to the block, the gallows or other mortal finalities — he marveled that she could be a girl and still be so thoughtful and far-seeing; and once again it made him feel young and inadequate and awkwardly her inferior.

At the Woodlawn gates she pulled the old-fashioned, check-strap signal, and Scipio reined in his horses.

"Are you quite sure you don't want me to go in with you?" she asked, while Tom was fumbling the door-latch.

He nodded and said: "There'll be trouble enough to go around among as many as can crowd in, all right. But I can't let you."

"Still, you won't say you don't want me?"

"No; lying isn't one of the things I was expelled for. When I stand up to my mother to tell her what I've got to tell her, I'd be glad if there was a little fise-dog sniffling around to back me up. But I'm not going to call in the neighbors — you, least of all."

"You are disappointing me right along — and I'm rather glad," she said. And then, almost wistfully: "You are going to be good, aren't you, Tom?"

His look was so sober that it was well-nigh sullen. "I'm going to say what I've got to say, and then hold my tongue if I have to bite it," he answered. "Good-by; and — and a Merry Christmas, and — thank you."

He shut the carriage door and gave Scipio the word to go on; and afterward stood at the gate looking after the great lumbering ark on wheels until it turned in at the Deer Trace driveway and was lost in the winding avenue of thick-set evergreens. Then he let himself in at the home gate, walking leaden-footed toward the ornate house at the top of the knoll and wishing the distance were ten times as great.

When he reached the house there was an ominous air of quiet about it, and a horse and buggy, with a black boy holding the reins, stood before the door. Tom's heart came into his mouth. The turnout was Doctor Williams's.

"Who's sick?" he asked of the boy who was holding the doctor's horse, and his tongue was thick with a nameless fear.

The black boy did not know; and Tom crept up the steps and let himself in as one enters a house of mourning, breaking down completely when he saw his father sitting bowed on the hall seat.

"You, Buddy? — I'm mighty glad," said the man; and when he held out his arms the boy flung himself on his knees beside the seat and buried his face in the cushions.

"Is she — is she going to die?" he asked; when the dreadful words could be found and spoken.

"We're hoping for the best, Buddy, son. It's some sort of a stroke, the doctor says; it took her yesterday morning, and she hasn't been herself since. Did somebody telegraph to you?"

Tom rocked his head on the cushion. How could he add to the blackness of darkness by telling his miserable story of disgrace?

Yet it had to be done, and surely no hapless penitent in the confessional ever emptied his soul with more heartfelt contrition or more bitter remorse.

Caleb Gordon listened, with what inward condemnings one could only guess from his silence. It was terrible! If his father would strike him, curse him, drive him out of the house, it would be easier to bear than the stifling silence. But when the words came finally they were as balm poured into an angry wound.

"There, there, Buddy; don't take on so. You're might' nigh a man, now, and the sun's still risin' and settin' just the same as it did before you tripped up and fell down. And it'll go on risin' and settin', too, long after you and me and all of us have quit goin' to bed and gettin' up by it. If it wasn't for your poor mammy —"

"That's it — that's just it," groaned Tom. "It would kill her, even if she was well."

"Nev' mind; you're here now, and I reckon that's the main thing. If she gets up again, of course she'll have to know; but we won't cross that bridge till we come to it. And Buddy, son, whatever happens, your old pappy ain't goin' to believe that you'll be the first Gordon to die in the gutter. You've got better blood in you than what that calls for."

Tom felt the lightening of his burden to some extent; but beyond was the alternative of suffering, or causing suffering. He had never realized until now how much he loved his mother; how large a place she had filled in his life, and what a vast void there would be when she was gone. He was yet too young and too self-centered to know that this is the mother-cross: to live for love and to be crowned and enthroned oftenest in memory.

For days, — days which brought back the boyhood agony of the time when he had believed himself to be Ardea's murderer, — he went softly about the house, sharing, with his father and his uncle, the watch in the sick-room; doing what little there was to be done in dumb hopelessness, and beating at times on the brazen gates of Heaven in sheer despair. There was no answer to his prayers; in his inmost soul he knew there would not be; but even in this the eternal query assailed him. Was it for lack of faith that no whisper of reply came from the unseen world beyond the veil? Or was it only because there was no ear to hear, no voice to answer? He could not tell. He made sure he was doomed to live and die, buffeting with these submerging waves of doubt — doubt of himself on one hand, and of God on the other.

In that time of sore trial, his Uncle Silas's forbearance wiped out many a score of boyish resentment. There was no word of reproach, still less the harsh arraignment and condemnation to which he began to look forward on the day when Doctor Tollivar had announced his purpose of writing the facts to his brother in the faith. But Tom remarked that in the daily morning and evening prayers his uncle spoke of him as a soul in peril, and he wondered that this pointed reference, which once would have stirred the pool of bitterness to its bottom, now left him unmoved and immovable. Later, he knew it was because there was now no pool of bitterness to be stirred; the spiritual well-springs had failed and there was no water in them — either for healing or for penitential cleansing.

The fifth day after his homecoming was Christmas Eve. Late in the afternoon, when the doctor had made his second visit and had gone away, leaving no word of encouragement for the watchers, Tom left the house and took the path that led up through the young orchard to the foot of Lebanon.

He was deep within the winter-stripped forest on the mountain side, plunging upward through the beds of dry leaves in the little hollows, when he met Ardea. She was coming down with her arms full of holly, and for the moment he forgot his troubles in the keen pleasure of looking at her. It had not occurred to him sooner to think of her as other than the girl of his boyhood days, grown somewhat, as he himself had grown. But now he saw that she was very beautiful.

None the less, his greeting was a brotherly reproof.

"I'd like to know what you're thinking of, tramping around on the mountain alone," he said, frowning at her.

"I have been thinking of you, most of the time, and wishing you could be with me," she answered, so artlessly as to mollify him instantly.

[Illustration: "I have been wishing you could be with me."]

"I ought to row you like smoke, but when you say things like that, I can't. Don't you know you oughtn't to go projecting around in the woods all alone?"

"I have always done it, haven't I? And Hector was with me till a few minutes ago, when he took it into his foolish old head to run after a rabbit. Is your mother any better this afternoon?"

"Sit down," he commanded abruptly. "I want to talk to you."

She hung the bunch of holly on the twigged limb of a small oak and sat down on a moss-covered rock. Tom sprawled at her feet in the dry leaves, and for a little while he was silent.

"You haven't told me yet how your mother is," she reminded him.

"She is just the same; lying there so still that you have to look close to see whether she is breathing. The doctor says that if there isn't a change pretty soon, she'll die."

"O Tom!"

He looked up at her with the old boyish frown pulling his eyebrows together.

"She's been good to God all her life; what do you reckon He's letting her die this way for?"

It was a terrible question, made more terrible by the savage hardihood that lay behind it. Ardea could not reason with him; and she felt intuitively that at this crisis only reason would appeal to him. Yet she could not turn him away empty-handed in his hour of need.

"How can we tell?" she said, and there were tears in her voice. "We only know that He does everything for the best."

"Yes; that is what they tell us. But how are we going to *know*?" he demanded.

The girl's faith was as simple and confiding as it was defenseless under any fire of argument.

"I suppose we can't know, in your sense of the word. But we can believe."

"*I* can't," said Tom fiercely. "I can pretend to; I reckon I've been pretending to all my life; but now I've got to a place where I can't feel anything that I can't touch, nor hear anything that doesn't make a noise, nor see anything that everybody else can't see. From what you've said at different times, you seem to be able to do all these things. Do you really believe?"

"I hope I do," she answered, and her voice was low and very earnest. But she would be altogether honest. "Perhaps you wouldn't call it 'belief unto righteousness,' as your Uncle Silas would say. I've never thought much about such things — in the way he says we ought to think about them. They seem to me to be true, like the — well, like the stars and the universe. You don't think about the universe all the time; but you know it is there, and that you are a little, tiny fraction of it, yourself."

But these were abstractions, and Tom's need was terribly concrete.

"I suppose you mean you haven't been converted, and all that; never mind about that. What I want to know is, did you ever ask God for anything and get it?"

"Why, yes; I ask Him for things every day, and get them. Don't you?"

"No, not now. But are you sure the things you ask for are not things that you'd get anyway?" he persisted.

She was growing a little restive under the fire of relentless questions. There are modesties in religion as in morals, — inner shrines to be defended at any and all costs. In the Crafts part of Thomas Jefferson's veins ran the blood of those who had fought with the sword in one hand and the Bible in the other, stabling their horses overnight in the enemy's churches. Ardea rose and began to untangle the great bunch of holly.

"I think we had better be going," she said, ignoring his clenching question. "Cousin Euphrasia gets nervous about me, sometimes, as you made believe you were."

He did not look around, or make any move toward getting up. But there was a new note of hardness in his voice when he said: "I thought you'd have to dodge, just like all the others, if I could only make out to throw straight enough. 'Way down deep inside of you, you don't believe God worries Himself much about what happens to us little dry leaves in His big woods."

"Oh, but I do! — that is, I believe He cares. The things you spoke of are things I might easily be deprived of; and I choose to believe that He gives and continues them."

He was quiet for a full minute, sitting with his knees drawn up to his chin and his hands tightly clasped over them. When he looked up at her his face was the face of one tormented.

"I wish you'd ask Him to let my mother live!" he said brokenly. "I've tried and tried, and the words just die in my mouth."

There is a Mother of Sorrows in every womanly heart, to whom the appeal of the stricken is never made in vain. Ardea saw only a boy-brother crying out in his pain, and she dropped on her knees and put her arms around his neck and wept over him in a pure transport of sisterly sympathy.

"Indeed and indeed I will help, Tom! And you mustn't let it drive you out into the dark. You poor boy! I know just how it hurts, and I'm so sorry for you!"

He freed himself gently from the comforting arms, got up rather unsteadily, and lifted her to her feet. Then the manly bigness of him sent the hot blood to her cheeks and she was ashamed.

"O Tom!" she faltered; "what must you think of me!"

He turned to gather up the scattered holly.

"I think God made you — and that was one time when His hand didn't tremble," he said gravely.

They had picked their way down the leaf-slippery mountain side and he was giving her the bunch of holly at the Dabney orchard gate before he spoke again. But at the moment of leave-taking he said:

"How did you know what I needed more than anything else in all the world, Ardea?"

She blushed painfully and the blue eyes were downcast.

"You must never speak of that again. I didn't stop to think. It's a Dabney failing, I'm afraid — to do things first and consider them afterward. It was as if we were little again, and you had fallen down and hurt yourself."

"I know," he acquiesced, with the same manly gentleness that had made her ashamed. "I won't speak of it any more — and I'll never forget it the longest day I live. Good-by."

And he went the back way to his own orchard gate, plunging through the leaf beds with his head down and his hands in his pockets, struggling as he could to stem the swift current which was whirling him out beyond all the old landmarks. For now he was made to know that boyhood was gone, and youth was going, and for one intoxicating moment he had looked over the mountain top into the Promised Land of manhood.

XV

NOËL

The night was far spent and the Christmas dawn was graying in the remotest east when Tom, sleeping in his clothes on a lounge before the fire in the lower hall, roused himself and went noiselessly up stairs to beg his father to go and lie down for a little while.

There was a trained nurse from South Tredegar in charge of the sick-room; but from the beginning the three — husband, brother and son — had kept watch at the bedside of the stricken one. There was little to be done; nothing, in fact; and the nurse would have spared them the nights. Yet no one of the three would surrender his privilege.

His father relieved, Tom mended the fire in the grate; and when he found the nurse dozing in her chair, he woke her and persuaded her to go and rest in the adjoining room, promising to call her instantly if she were needed.

Left alone with his mother, he tiptoed to the bedside and stood for many minutes looking with sorrow-blurred eyes at the still, rigid face on the pillow. It was terribly like death; so like, that more than once he laid his hand softly on the bed-covering to make sure that she still breathed. When he could bear it no longer, he crossed the room to the western window, drawing the draperies and standing between them to stare miserably out into the calm, starlit void. While he looked, a meteor burned its way across the inverted bowl of the heavens, and its passing kindled the embers of the inextinguishable fire.

And, lo, the star . . . came and stood over where the young child was. The curtains of the void were parted by invisible hands, and down the long vista of the centuries he saw the familiar scene of the Nativity, dwelt on so often and so faithfully in his childhood training that it seemed almost like a part of the material scheme of the universe: the Babe in the manger; the shepherds watching their flocks; the heavenly host singing the triumphant anthem of the ages, *Glory to God in the highest, and on earth, peace*; the star of Bethlehem shining serenely above a world lying in darkness and in the shadow of death.

Was it all true? or was it only a beautiful myth? If it were true, where was the proof? Not in history, for this, the most wonderful and miraculous thing in all the story of mankind, stands unrecorded save by the pens of those who were themselves under the spell of it. In subsequent marvels and wonder-workings? — he shook his head mournfully. If any such there had been, those impartial witnesses who must have known and should have spoken were silent, and now all the earth was silent: storms rose in their fury and were calmed for no man's *Peace, be still*; earthquakes engulfed pagan and Christian believer alike; all nature was cruel, relentless, mechanical.

Was there nothing then to reach down the ages from that Christmas morning so long ago to make the beautiful first-century myth a latter-day reality? Tom cast about him hopelessly. There was the Church — one and indivisible, if the myth were true. The slow Gordon smile gathered at the corners of his eyes. He remembered a thing his mother had said to him long ago, when, in a moment of boyish confidence, he had told her of the climb to Crestcliffe Inn and its purpose. "Ardea's a dear girl, as the children of this world go, Thomas; she's been right loving and kind to me since we've come to be such close neighbors. But" — with a note of solemn warning in her voice — "you must never forget that she's an Episcopalian, a lost soul, dead in forms and ceremonies and trespasses and sins." So his mother scoffed at Ardea's faith; and Ardea — no, she did not scoff, her contempt was too generous for that; but it was there, just the same. And the Methodists fellowshiped neither, and the Baptists excluded the Methodists, and the Catholics retorted to the Protestant charge of apostasy with the centuries-old cry of "heretics all"! Which of the scores of divisions and subdivisions was the one true indivisible body of Christ? Tom shook his head again. There was no hope of proof in the churches.

And the world? He was only now verging on manhood, and he had seen little of the world. But that little was frankly indifferent to the things which, if they were worthy of belief, should shake an unsaved world to its very foundations. Its people bought and sold, built houses and laid up stores of the things that perish, grasped, overreached, did what they listed. But for that matter, even those who professed to be followers of the Christ, who asserted most loudly their belief in the unproved things, fought and struggled and sinned in common with the worldlings, as far as Tom could see.

He turned from the window and from the vision, and went to stand with his back to the flickering blaze in the grate. It was going to leave a huge rift in his life when this thing, with all its rootings and anchorings in childhood and boyhood, was torn out and cast aside. The mere thought of it was appalling. What would there be to fill the void?

As if the question had evoked them, alluring shapes began to rise out of the depths. Ambition, though he knew it not by name, was the first that beckoned. The craftsman's blood stirred to its reawakening: to know how, and to do things; to compel the iron and steel and the stubborn forces of nature. This would be worthwhile; but better still, he would learn to be a leader of men. The magic vista opened again, but this time it stretched away into the future, and he saw himself keeping step with the ever-advancing march of progress — nay, even setting the pace in his own corner of the vast field. His father was content to follow; he would learn the trick of it and lead. The Farleys were said to be rich and steadily growing richer — not out of Chiawassee Iron, to be sure, but in others of their multifarious out-reachings; very good, — he would be rich, too. What a Duxbury Farley could do, he would do; on a larger scale and with a stubborner patience. He —

It was a mere turning of the head that sent the air-castles tumbling and left him choking in the dust of their dissolution. Something, he fancied it was a noise or some slight movement, made him look quickly toward the bed; and at sight of the still, white face among the pillows, boyish love — God Himself has made no stronger passion — swept doubt, distrust, rebellion, worldly ambition, all, into the abyss of renunciation. He went softly, groping because the quick tears blinded him, to kneel at the bedside. She was his mother; for one thing she had lived and striven and prayed; living or dying she must not, she should not, be disappointed. And if his service must be of the lip and not of the heart, she should never suspect, never, never!

And so it came about that he knelt in the graying dawn of the Christmas morning, with his soul in thick darkness, lifting the prayer that in some form has shaped itself in all the ages on lips of trembling: "O God, if there be a God, have mercy on my soul, if I have a soul!"

XVI

THE BUBBLE, REPUTATION

It was not until late in the afternoon of Christmas Day that Ardea was able to slip away from her guests long enough to run over to apprise herself of the condition of things at the Gordon house.

Tom opened the door for her, and he made her come to the fire before he would answer her questions. Even then he sat glowering at the cheerful blaze as if he had forgotten her presence; and she was womanly enough, or amiable enough, to let him take his own time. When he began, it was seemingly at a great distance from matters present and pressing.

"Say, Ardea; do you believe in miracles?" he asked abruptly.

It was a large question to be answered offhand, but she broke the back of it with a simple, "Yes."

"How do you account for them? Did God make His laws so they could be taken apart and put together again when some little human ant loses its way on a grass stalk or drops its grain of sugar?"

"I don't know," she confessed frankly. "I am not sure that I ever tried to account for them; I suppose I have swallowed them whole, as you say I have swallowed my religion."

"Well, you believe in them, anyway," he said, "and that makes it easier to hit what I'm aiming at. Do you reckon they stopped short in the Apostles' time?"

"I don't know that, either," she admitted.

"You ought to know it, if you're consistent," he said, bluntly dogmatic. "Any answer to any prayer would be a miracle."

"Would it? I never happened to think of it that way."

"It certainly would. You chop a tree in two and it falls; that's cause and effect. If you ask God to make it stand up after it's cut in two, and it does stand, that's a miracle."

"You are the queerest boy," she commented. "I ran over here just for a minute to ask how your mother is, and you won't tell me."

"I'm coming to that," he rejoined gravely. "But I wanted to get this other thing straightened out first. Now tell me this: did you pray for my mother last night, like you said you would?"

Once again he was offending the guardian of the inner shrines, and her heightened color was not all the reflection of the ruddy firelight.

"You can be so barbarously personal when you try, Tom," she protested. And then she added: "But I did."

"Well, the miracle was wrought. Early this morning mother came to herself and asked for something to eat. Doctor Williams has been here, and now he tells us all the things he wouldn't tell us before. It was some little clot in one of the veins or arteries of the brain, and nine times out of ten there is no hope."

"O Tom! — and she will get well again?"

"She has more chances today of getting well than she had last night of dying — so the doctor says. But it's a miracle, just the same."

"I'm so glad! And now I really must go home." And she got up.

"No, sit down; I'm not through with you yet. I want to know what you think about promises."

She smiled and pushed her chair back from the soft-coal blaze in the fireplace.

"Don't you know you are a perfect 'old man of the sea,' Tom?"

"That's all right; but tell me: is a bad promise better broken or kept?"

"I am sure I couldn't say without knowing the circumstances. Tell me all about it," and she resigned herself to listen.

"It was at daybreak this morning. I was alone with mother, looking at her lying there so still and helpless — dead, all but the little flicker of breath that seemed just about ready to go out. It came over me all of a sudden that I couldn't disappoint her, living or dead; that I'd have to go on and be what she has always wanted me to be. And I promised her."

"But she couldn't hear you?"

"No; it was before she came to herself. Nobody heard me but God; and I reckon He wasn't paying much attention to anything I said."

"Why do you say that?"

"Because — well, because it wasn't the kind of a promise that makes the angels glad. I said I'd go on and do it, if I had to be a hypocrite all the rest of my life."

"O Tom! would you have to be?"

"That's the way it looks to me now. I told you the other day that I didn't know what I believed and what I didn't believe. But I do know some of the *don'ts*. For instance: if there is a hell — and I'm not anyways convinced that there is — I don't believe — but what's the use of cataloguing it? They'd ask me a string of questions when I was ordained, and I'd have to lie like Ananias."

She rose and met his gloomy eyes fairly.

"Tom Gordon, if you should do that, you would be the wickedest thing alive — the basest thing that ever breathed!"

"That's about the way it strikes me," he said coolly. "So you see it comes down to a case of big wicked or little wicked; it's been that way all along. Did you know that one time I asked God to kill you?"

She looked horrified, as was her undoubted right.

"Why, of all things!" she gasped.

"It's so. I took a notion that I'd be mad because your grandfather brought you here to Paradise. And when you took sick — well, I reckon there isn't any hell deeper or hotter than the one I frizzled in for about four days that summer."

It was too deep in the past to be tragic, and she laughed.

"I used to think then that you were the worst, as well as the queerest, boy I had ever seen."

"And now you know it," he said. Then: "What's your rush? I'm not trying to get rid of you now."

"I positively must go back. We have company, and I ran away without saying a word."

"Anybody I know?" inquired Tom.

"Three somebodies whom you know, or ought to know, very well: Mr. Duxbury Farley, Mr. Vincent Farley, Miss Eva Farley."

His eyes darkened suddenly.

"I'd like to know how under the sun they managed to get on your grandfather's good side!" he grumbled.

Ardea Dabney's expressive face mirrored dawning displeasure.

"Why do you say that?" she retorted. "Eva was my classmate for years at Miss De Valle's."

He made a boyish face of disapproval, saying bluntly: "I don't care if she was. You shouldn't make friends of them. They are not fit for you to wipe your shoes on."

For the second time since his homecoming, Tom saw the Dabney imperiousness flash out; saw and felt it.

"You ought to be ashamed of yourself, Tom Gordon! Less than an hour ago, we were speaking of you, and of what happened at Beersheba. Mr. Farley and his son both stood up for you."

"And you took the other side, I reckon," he broke out, quite unreasonably. It had not as yet come to blows between him and his father's business associates, but it made him immeasurably dissatisfied to find them on social terms at Deer Trace Manor.

"Perhaps I did, and perhaps I did not," she answered, matching his tartness.

"Well, you can tell them both that I'm much obliged to them for nothing," he said, rising and going to the door with her. "They would be mighty glad to see it patched up again and me back in the Beersheba school."

"Of course they would; so would all of your friends."

"But they are not my friends. They have fooled my father, and they'll fool your grandfather, if he doesn't watch out. But they can't fool me."

He had opened the outer door for her, and she drew herself up till she could face him squarely, slate-blue eyes flashing scornfully into sullen gray.

"That is the first downright cowardly thing I have ever known you to say!" she declared. "And I wish you to know, Mr. Thomas Jefferson Gordon, that Mr. Duxbury Farley and Mr. Vincent Farley and Miss Eva Farley are my guests and my friends!" And with that for her leave-taking, she turned her back on him and went swiftly across the two lawns to the great gray house on the opposite knoll.

For the first fortnight of his mother's convalescence Tom slept badly, and his days were as the days of the accused whose sentence has been suspended; jail days, these, with chains to clank when he thought of the promise made in the gray Christmas dawn; with whips to flog him when the respite grew shorter and the time drew near when his continued stay at home must be explained to his mother.

Ardea had gone back to Carroll the Saturday before New Year's, and there was no one to talk to. But for that matter, he had cut himself out of her confidence by his assault on the Farleys. Every morning for a week after the Christmas-day clash, Scipio came over with the compliments of "Mawsteh Majah," Miss Euphrasia, and Miss Dabney, and kindly inquiries touching the progress of the invalid. But after New Year's, Tom remarked that there were only the Major and Miss Euphrasia to send compliments, and despair set in. For out of his boyhood he had brought up undiminished the longing for sympathy, or rather for a burden-bearer on whom he might unload his troubles, and Ardea had begun to promise well.

It was on a crisp morning in the second week of January when the prolonged agony of suspense drove him to the mountain. His mother was sitting up, and was rapidly recovering her strength. His father had gone back to his work in the iron plant, and his uncle was preparing to return to his charge in South Tredegar. With Uncle Silas and the nurse both gone, Tom knew that the evil hour must come speedily; and it was with some half cowardly hope that his uncle would break the ice for him that he ran away on the crisp morning of happenings.

With no particular destination in view, it was only natural that his feet should find the familiar path leading up to the great boulder under the cedars. He had not visited the rock of the spring since the summer day when he and Nan Bryerson had taken refuge from the shower in the hollow heart of it, nor had he seen Nan since their parting at the door of her father's cabin under the cliff. Rumor in Gordonia had it that Tike Bryerson had been hunted out by the revenue officers; and, for reasons which he would have found it difficult to declare in words, Tom had been shy about making inquiries.

For this cause an apparition could scarcely have startled him more than did the sight of Nan filling her bucket at the trickling barrel-spring under the cliff face of the great rock. He came on her suddenly at the end of the long climb up the wooded slopes, at a moment when — semi-tropical growth having had two full seasons in which to change the natural aspect of things — he was half bewildered with the unwonted look of the place. But there was no doubt about it; it was Nan in the flesh, a little fuller in the figure, something less childish in the face, but with all the fascinating, wild-creature beauty of the child-time promise to dazzle the eye and breed riot in the brain of the boy-man.

When she stood up with a little cry of pleased surprise, the dark eyes lighting quick joy-fires, and the welcoming blush mounting swiftly to neck and cheek, Tom thought she was the most alluring thing he had ever looked on. Yet the bottom stone in the wall of recrudescent admiration was the certainty that he had found a sympathetic ear.

"Did you know I was coming? Were you waiting for me, Nan?" he bubbled, gazing into the great black eyes as eagerly as a freed dog plunges into the first pool that offers.

"How could I be knowin' to it?" she asked, taking him seriously, or appearing to. "I nev' knowed school let out this time o' year."

"It's let out for me, Nan," he said meaningly. "I came home — for good — nearly three weeks ago. My mother has been sick. Didn't you hear of it?"

She shook her head gravely.

"I hain't been as far as Paradise sence paw and me moved back from Pine Knob, two months ago. I don't hear nothin' any more."

In times long past, Tom, valley-born and of superior clay, used to be scornful of the mountain dialect. Now, on Nan's lips, it charmed him. It was blessedly reminiscent of the care-free days of yore.

"Say, Nan; I hope you haven't got to hurry home," he interposed, when she stooped to lift the overflowing bucket. "I want to talk to you — to tell you something."

She looked up quickly, and there were scrolls unreadable in the black eyes.

"Air you a man now, Tom-Jeff, or on'y a boy like you used to be?" she asked.

Tom squared his broad shoulders and laughed.

"I'm big enough to be in my own way a good deal of the time. I believe I could muddy Sim Cantrell's back for him now, at arm-holts."

But there was still a question in the black eyes.

"Where's your preacher's coat, Tom-Jeff? I was allowin' you'd be wearin' it nex' time we met up."

"I reckon there isn't going to be any preacher's coat for me, Nan; that's one of the things I want to talk to you about. Let's go over yonder and sit down in the sun."

The place he chose for her was a flat stone half embedded in the up-climbing slope beyond the great boulder. She sat facing the path and the spring, listening, while Tom, stretched luxuriously on a bed of dry leaves at her feet, told her what had befallen; how he had been turned out of Beersheba, and what for; how, all the former things having passed away, he was torn and distracted in the struggle to find a footing in the new order.

In the midst of it he had a feeling that she was only dimly apprehending; that some of his keenest pains — most of them, perhaps — did not appeal to her. But there was comfort in her bodily presence, in the listening ear. It was a shifting of the burden in some sort, and there be times when the humblest pack animal may lighten a king's load.

His fears touching her understanding, or her lack of it, were confirmed when he had reached a stopping-place.

"They-all up yonder in that school where you was at hain't got much sense, it looks like to me," was her comment. "You're a man growed now, Tom-Jeff, and if you want to play cards or drink whisky, what-all business is it o' their'n?"

He smiled at her elemental point of view; laughed outright when the significance of it struck him fairly. But it betokened allegiance of a kind to gladden the heart of the masculine tyrant, and he rolled the declaration of fealty as a sweet morsel under his tongue.

"You stand by your friends, right or wrong, don't you, girl?" he said, in sheerest self-gratulation. "That's what I like in you. You asked me a little while back if I was a man or a boy; I believe you could make a man of me, Nan, if you'd try."

He was looking up into her face as he said it and the change that came over her lighted a strange fire in his blood. The black eyes kindled it, and the red lips, half parted, blew it into a blaze. His face flushed and he broke the eye-hold and looked down. In their primal state, when Nature mothered the race, the man was less daring than the woman.

"If you'd said that two year ago," she began, in a half whisper that melted the marrow in his bones. "But you was on'y a boy then; and now I reckon it's too late."

"You mean that you don't care for me any more, Nan? I know better than that. You'd back me if I had come up here to tell you that I'd killed somebody. Wouldn't you, now?"

He waited overlong for his answer. There were sounds in the air: a metallic tapping like the intermittent drumming of a woodpecker mingled with a rustling as of some small animal scurrying back and forth over the dead leaves. The girl leaned forward, listening intently. Then three men appeared in the farther crooking of the spring path, and at the first glimpse of them she slipped from the flat stone to cower behind Tom, trembling, shaking with terror.

"Hide me, Tom-Jeff! Oh, for God's sake, hide me, quick!" she panted. "Lookee there!"

He looked and saw the three men walking slowly up the pipe-line which drained the barrel-spring. They were too far away to be recognizable to him, and since they were stopping momently to examine the pipe, there was good hope of an escape unseen.

Tom waited breathless for the propitious instant when the tapping of the pipe-men's hammers should drown the noise of a dash for effacement. When it came, he flung himself backward, whipped Nan over his head and out of the line of sight as if she had been feather-light, and rolled swiftly after her.

Before she could rise he had picked her up and was dragging her to the climbing point under the lip of the boulder cave.

"Up with you!" he commanded, making a step of his hand. "Give me your foot and then climb to my shoulder — quick!" But she drew back.

"Oh, I can't!" she gasped. "I — I'm too skeered!"

Tom's brows went together in the Gordon frown. Bone-meltings and blood-firings apart, he was neither a fool nor a dastard, and he was older now than on that day when the storm had driven them to take refuge in the heart of the great rock. And since he had decided that the cavern was only big enough for one, he had meant to put Nan up, going himself to meet the intruders to make sure that they should not discover her. But her trembling fit — a new and curious thing in the girl who used to make his flesh creep with her reckless daring — spoiled the plan.

"Can't you climb up?" he demanded.

She shook her head despairingly, and he lost no time in trying to persuade her. Jumping to catch the lip of the cavern's mouth, he ascended cat-like, and a moment later he had drawn her up after him.

"I'd like to know what got the matter with you all at once," he said severely, when they were crowded together in the narrow rock cell; and then, without waiting for her answer: "You stay here while I drop down and keep those fellows away from this side of things."

But it was too late. The men were already at the barrel-spring, as an indistinct murmur of voices testified. The girl had another trembling fit when she heard them, and Tom's wonder was fast lapsing into contempt or something like it.

"Oh-h-h!" she shuddered. "Do you reckon they saw us, Tom-Jeff?"

"I shouldn't wonder," he whispered back unfeelingly. "We could see them plain enough."

"He'll kill me, for shore, Tom-Jeff! O God!"

Tom's lip curled. The wolf does not mate with the jackal. Not all her beauty could atone for such spiritless cringing. Love would have pitied her, but passion is not moved by qualities opposite to those which have evoked it.

"Then you know them — or one of them, at least," he said. "Who is he?"

She would not tell; and since the murmur of voices was still plainly audible, she begged in dumb-show for silence. Whereupon Tom shut his mouth and did not open it again until the sound of the voices had died away and the fainter tappings of the hammers on the pipe-line advertised the retreat of the inspection party.

"They're gone now," he said shortly. "Let's get out of here before we stifle."

But a second time ill chance intervened. Tom had a leg over the brink and was looking for a soft leaf bed to drop into, when the baying of a hound broke on the restored quiet of the mountain side. "Oh, dang it all!" said Tom heartily, and drew back into hiding.

The girl's ague fit of fear had passed, and she seemed less concerned about the equivocal situation than a girl should be; at least, this is the way Tom's thought was shaping itself. He tried to imagine Ardea in Nan's place, but the thing was baldly unimaginable. A daughter of the Dabneys would never run and cower and beg to be hidden at the possible cost of her good name. And Nan's word did not help matters.

"What makes you so cross to me, Tom-Jeff?" she asked, when he drew back with the impatient exclamation. "I hain't done nothin' to make you let on like you hate me, have I?"

"I don't hate you," said Tom, frowning. "If I did, I shouldn't care." Just then the hound burst out of the laurel thicket on the brow of the lower slope, running with its nose to the ground, and he added: "That's Japhe Pettigrass's dog; I hope to goodness he isn't anywhere behind it."

But the horse-trader was behind the dog; so close behind that he came out on the continuation of the pipe-line path while the hound was still nosing among the leaves where Tom had lain sunning himself and telling his tale of woe.

"Good dog — seek him! What is it, old boy?" Pettigrass came up, patted the hound, and sat down on the flat stone to look on curiously while the dog coursed back and forth among the dead leaves. "Find him, Cæsar; find him, boy!" encouraged Japheth; and finally the hound pointed a sensitive nose toward the rift in the side of the great boulder and yelped conclusively.

"D'ye reckon he climm up thar', Cæsar?" Pettigrass unfolded his long legs and stood up on the flat stone to attain an eye-level with the interior of the little cavern. Tom crushed Nan into the farthest cranny, and flattened himself lizard-like against the nearer side wall. The horse-trader looked long and hard, and they could hear him still talking to the dog.

"You're an old fool, Cæsar — that's about what you are — and Solomon allowed thar' wasn't no fool like an old one. But you needn't to swaller that whole, old boy; I've knowed some young ones in my time — sometimes gals, sometimes boys, sometimes *both*. But thar' ain't no 'possum up yonder, Cæsar; you've flew the track this time, for certain. Come on, old dog; let's be gettin' down the mountain."

The baying dog and the whistling man were still within hearing when Tom swung Nan lightly to the ground and dropped beside her. No word was spoken until she had emptied and refilled her bucket at the spring, then Tom said, with the bickering tang still on his tongue:

"Say, Nan, I want to know who it is that's going to kill you if he happens to find you talking to me."

She shook her head despondently. "I cayn't nev' tell you that, Tom-Jeff."

"I'd like to know why you can't."

"Because he'd shore kill me then."

"Then I'll find out some other way."

"What differ' does it make to you?" she asked; and again the dark eyes searched him till he was fain to look away from her.

"I reckon it doesn't make any difference, if you don't want it to. But one time you were willing enough to tell me your troubles, and —"

"And I'll nev' do it nare 'nother time; never, *never*. And let me tell you somethin' else, Tom-Jeff Gordon: if you know what's good for you, don't you nev' come anigh me again. One time we usen to be a boy and a girl together; you're nothin' but a boy yet, but I — oh, God, Tom-Jeff — I'm a woman!"

And with that saying she snatched her bucket and was gone before he could find a word wherewith to match it.

XVII

ABSALOM, MY SON!

Three days after the episode at the barrel-spring, Tom went afield again, this time to gather plunging courage for the confession to his mother — a thing which, after so many postponements, could be put off no longer.

It was more instinct than purpose that led him to avoid the mountain. Thinking only of the crying need for solitude, he crossed the pike and the creek and rambled aimlessly for an hour or more over that farther hill ground beyond the country-house colony where he had once tried to break the Dabney spirit in a weary, bedraggled little girl with colorless lips and saucer-like eyes.

When he recrossed the stream, at a point some distance above the boy-time perch pools, the serving foot-log chanced to be that used by the Little Zoar folk coming from beyond the boundary hills. Following the windings of the path he presently came out in the rear of the weather-beaten, wooden-shuttered church standing, blind-eyed and silent, in week-day desertion in the midst of its groving of pines.

The spot was rife with memories, and Tom passed around the building to the front, treading softly as on hallowed ground. Whatever the future might hold for him, there would always be heart-stirring recollections to cluster about this frail old building sheltered by the whispering pines.

How many times he had sat on the steps in the door-opening days of boyhood, looking out across the dusty pike and up to the opposing steeps of Lebanon lifting the eastward horizon halfway to the zenith! Leg-weariness, and a sudden desire to live over again thus much of the past turning him aside, he went to sit on the highest of the three steps, with the brooding silence for company and the uplifted landscape to revamp the boyhood memories.

The sun had set for Paradise Valley, but his parting rays were still volleying in level lines against the great gray cliffs at the top of Lebanon, silvering the bare sandstone, blackening the cedars and pines by contrast, and making a fine-lined tracery, blue on gray, of the twigs and leafless branches of the deciduous trees. Off to the left a touch of sepia on the sky-line marked the chimneys of Crestcliffe Inn, and farther around, and happily almost hidden by the shouldering of the hills, a grayer cloud hung over the industries at Gordonia.

Nearer at hand were the wooded slopes of the Dabney lands — lordly forests culled and cared for through three generations of land-lovers until now their groves of oaks and hickories, tulip-trees and sweet-and black-gums were like those the pioneers looked on when the land was young.

Thomas Jefferson had the appreciative eye and heart of one born with a deep and abiding love of the beautiful in nature, and for a time the sunset ravishment possessed him utterly. But the blurring of the fine-lined traceries and the fading of the silver and the gray into twilight purple broke the spell. The postponed resolve was the thing present and pressing. His mother was as nearly recovered as she was ever likely to be, and his uncle would be returning to South Tredegar in the morning. The evil tale must be told while there was yet one to whom his mother could turn for help and sympathy in her hour of bitter disappointment.

He was rising from his seat on the church step when he heard sounds like muffled groans. Recovering quickly from the first boyish startle of fear oozing like a cool breeze blowing up the back of his neck, he saw that the church door was ajar. By cautiously adding another inch to the aperture he could see the interior of the building, its outlines taking shape when his eyes had become accustomed to darkness relieved only by the small fan-light over the door. Some one was in the church: a man, kneeling, with clasped hands uplifted, in the open space fronting the rude pulpit. Tom recognized the voice and withdrew quickly. It was his Uncle Silas, praying fervently for a lost sheep of the house of Israel.

In former times, with grim rebellion gripping him as it gripped him now, Tom would have run away. But there was a prompting stronger than rebellion: a sudden melting of the heart that made him remember the loving-kindnesses, and not any of the austerities, of the man who was praying for him, and he sat down on the lowest step to wait.

The twilight was glooming to dusk when Silas Crafts came out of the church and locked the door behind him. If he were surprised to find Tom waiting for him, he made no sign. Neither was there any word of greeting passed between them when he gathered his coat tails and sat down on the higher step, self-restraint being a heritage which had come down undiminished from the Covenanter ancestors of both. A little grayer, a little thinner, but with the deep-set eyes still glowing with the fires of utter convincement and the marvelous voice still unimpaired, Silas Crafts would have refused to believe that the passing years had changed him; yet now there was kinsman love to temper solemn austerity when he spoke to the lost sheep — as there might not have been in the sterner years.

"The way of the transgressor is hard, grievously hard, Thomas. I think you are already finding it so, are you not?"

Tom shook his head slowly.

"That doesn't mean what it used to, to me, Uncle Silas; nothing means the same any more. It's just as if somebody had hit that part of me with a club; it's all numb and dead. I'm sure of only one thing now: that is, that I'm not going to be a hypocrite after this, if I can help it."

The man put his hand on the boy's knee.

"Have you been that all along, Thomas?"

"I reckon so," — monotonously. "At first it was partly scare, and partly because I knew what mother wanted. But ever since I've been big enough to think, I've been asking why, and, as you would say, doubting."

Silas Crafts was silent for a moment. Then he said:

"You have come to the years of discretion, Thomas, and you have chosen death rather than life. If you go on as you have begun, you will bring the gray hairs of your father and mother in sorrow to the grave. Leaving your own soul's salvation out of the question, can you go on and drag an upright, honorable name in the dust and mire of degradation?"

"No," said Tom definitely. "And what's more, I don't mean to. I don't know what Doctor Tollivar wrote you about me, and it doesn't make any difference now. That's over and done with. You haven't been seeing me every day for these three weeks without knowing that I'm ashamed of it."

"Ashamed of the consequences, you mean, Thomas. You are not repentant."

"Yes, I am, Uncle Silas; though maybe not in your way. I don't allow to make a fool of myself again."

The preacher's comment was a groan.

"Tom, my boy, if any one had told me a year ago that a short twelvemonth would make you, not only an apostate to the faith, but a shameless liar as well —"

Tom started as if he had been struck with a whip.

"Hold on, Uncle Silas," he broke in hardily. "That's mighty near a fighting word, even between blood kin. When have you ever caught me in a lie?"

"Now!" thundered the accusing voice; "this moment! You have been giving me to understand that your sinful rebellion at Beersheba was the worst that could be charged against you. Answer me: isn't that what you want me to believe?"

"I don't care whether you believe it or not. It's so."

"It is not so. Here, at your own home, when your mother had just been spared to you by the mercies of the God whose commandments you set at naught, you have been wallowing in sin — in crime!"

Tom locked his clasped fingers fast around his knees and would not open the flood-gates of passion.

"If I can sit here and take that from you, it's because it isn't so," he replied soberly.

Silas Crafts rose, stern and pitiless.

"Wretched boy! Out of your own mouth you shall be convicted. Where were you on Wednesday morning?"

Tom had to think back before he could place the Wednesday morning, and his momentary hesitation was immediately set down to the score of conscious guilt.

"I was at home most of the time; between ten o'clock and noon I was on the mountain."

"Alone?"

"No; not all of the time."

"You say well. There were three of you: a hardened, degraded boy, a woman no less wicked and abandoned, and the devil who tempted you."

The flood-gates of passion would hold no longer.

"It's a lie!" he denied hotly. "I just happened to meet Nan Bryerson at the spring under the big rock, and —"

"Well, go on," said the inexorable voice.

Tom choked in a sudden fit of rage and helplessness. He saw how incredible the simple truth would sound; how like a clumsy equivocation it must appear to one who already believed the worst of him. So he took refuge in the last resort alike of badgered innocence and hardened guilt.

"I don't have to defend myself!" he burst out. "If you can believe I'm that low-down, you're welcome to!" Then, abruptly: "I reckon we'd better be going on home; they'll be waiting dinner for us at the house."

He got on his feet with that, but the accuser was still confronting him, with the dark eyes glowing and a monitory finger pointed to detain him.

"Not yet, Thomas Gordon; there is a duty laid on me. I had hoped and prayed that I might find you repentant; you are not repentant."

"No," said Tom, and he confirmed it with an oath in sheer bravado.

"Peace, miserable boy! God is not mocked. Your father has a letter from Doctor Tollivar; the doors of Beersheba are open to you again. I had hoped — " The pause was not for effect. It was merely that the man and the kinsman in Silas Crafts had throttled the righteous judge. "It breaks my heart, Thomas, but I must say it. You have put it out of your power to say with the Psalmist, 'I will wash mine hands in innocency: so will I compass thine altar, O Lord.' You must give up all thoughts of going back to Beersheba."

"Don't trouble yourself," said Tom, with more bravado. "I wouldn't go back there if it was the only place on earth." Then suddenly: "Who was it that told on me, Uncle Silas?"

"Never mind about that. It was one who could have no object in misstating the fact — which you have not denied. Let us go home."

The mile walk down the pike, lying white and ghostly under the starlight, was paced in silence, man and boy striding side by side and each busy with his own thoughts. As they were passing the Deer Trace gates a loose-jointed figure loomed black against the palings, and the voice of Japheth Pettigrass said:

"Why, howdy, Brother Silas! Thought ye'd gone back to South Tredegar. When are ye comin' out to Little Zoar ag'in to give us another o' them old-fashioned, spiritual times o' refreshin' from the presence of the Lord?"

Silas Crafts turned short on the scoffer.

"Why do you ask that, Japheth Pettigrass? The Lord will deal with you, one day."

"Yes, I reckon so; that's what makes me say what I does. There's a heap o' sinners left round here, yit, Brother Silas. There's the Major, for one, and I know you're always countin' me in for another. I dunno but you might snatch me as a brand from the burnin', if you could make out to try it one more lap around the you'se. I been thinkin' right p'intedly about —"

But the preacher had cut in with a curt "Good night," and was gone, with his broad-shouldered nephew at his heels; and the horse-trader went on, with the stars for his audience.

"Look at that, now, will ye? Old Brother Silas is gettin' right smart tetchy with the passin' of the years; he is, so. But he's a powerful preacher. If anybody ever gits me for a star in their crown, it's Brother Silas ag'inst the field, even money up."

Pettigrass turned and was groping for the gate latch when a hand fell on his shoulder, and a clutch that was more than half a blow twirled him about to face the roadway. He was doubling his fists for defense when he saw who his assailant was.

"Why, Tom-Jeff! what's ailin' ye?" he began; but Tom broke in with gaspings of rage.

"Japhe Pettigrass, what did you think you saw last Wednesday forenoon up yonder at Big Rock Spring on the mountain? Tell it straight, this time, or by the God you don't believe in, I'll dig the truth out of you with my bare hands!"

"Sho, now, Tom-Jeff; don't you git so servigrous over nothin'.

I didn't see nothin' but a couple o' young fly-aways playin' 'possum in a hole in the big rock. And I'll leave it to you if I didn't call Cæsar off and go my ways, jes' like I'd like to be done by."

"Yes," snarled Tom, dog-mad and furious in this second submergence of the wave of wrath. "Yes; and then you came straight down here and told my uncle!" The hand he had been holding behind him came to the front, clutching a stone snatched up from the metaling of the pike as he ran. "If I should break your face in with this, Japhe Pettigrass, it wouldn't be any more than you've earned!"

"By gravy! *I* tell Brother Silas on you, Tom-Jeff? You show me the man 'at says I done any such low-down thing as that, and I'll frazzle a fifty-dollar hawsswhip out on his ornery hide — I will, so. Say, boy; you don't certain'y believe that o' me, do ye?"

"I don't want to believe it of you, Japhe," quavered Tom, as near to tears as the pride of his eighteen years would sanction. "But somebody saw and told, and made it a heap worse than it was." He leaned over the top of the wall and put his face in the crook of his elbow, being nothing better than a hurt child, for all his bigness.

"Well, now; I wouldn't let a little thing like that gravel me, if I was you, Tom-Jeff," said Pettigrass, turned comforter. "Nan's a mighty pretty gal, and you ort to be willin' to stand a little devilin' on her account — more especially as you've —"

Tom put up his arm as if to ward a blow.

"Don't you say it, Japhe, or I'll go mad again," he broke out.

"I ain't sayin' nothin'. But who do you reckon it was told on you? Was there anybody else in the big woods that mornin'?"

"Yes; there were three men testing the pipe-line. We both saw them, and Nan was scared stiff at sight of one of them; that's why I put her up in that hole."

"Who was the man?"

"I don't know. I didn't recognize any of them — they were too far off when I saw them. And afterward, Nan wouldn't tell me."

"Did any of 'em see you and Nan?"

"I thought not. Nan was sitting on the flat rock where you stood and looked into the cave, and when she began to whimper, I flung her over into the leaves and ran with her to the hole."

"H'm," said Japheth. "When you find out who that feller is that Nan's skeered of, you can lay your hand on the man that told Brother Silas on you. But I wouldn't trouble about it none, if I was you. You've got a long ways the best of him, whoever he is, and —"

But Tom had turned to go home, feeling his way by the wall because the angry tears were still blinding him, and the horse-trader fell back into his star-gazing.

"Law, law," he mused; "'the horrible pit an' the miry clay.' What a sufferin' pity it is we pore sinners cayn't dance a little now and ag'in 'thout havin' to walk right up and pay the fiddler! Tom-Jeff, there, now, he's a-thinkin' the price is toler'ble high; and I don't know but it is — I don't know but what it is."

The dinner at Woodlawn that night was a stiff and comfortless meal, as it had come to be with the taking on of four-tined forks and the other conventions for which an oak-paneled dining-room in an ornate brick mansion sets the pace. Caleb Gordon was fathoms deep in the mechanical problems of the day's work, as was his wont. Silas Crafts was abstracted and silent. Tom's food choked him, as it had need under the sharp stress of things; and the convalescent housemother remained at table only long enough to pour the coffee.

Tom excused himself a few minutes later, and followed his mother to her room, climbing the stair to her door, leaden-footed and with his heart ready to burst.

"Is that you, Thomas?" said the gentle voice within, answering his tap on the panel. "Come in, son; come in and sit by my fire. It's right chilly tonight."

Thomas Jefferson entered and placed his chair so that she could not see him without turning, and for many minutes the silence was unbroken. Then he began, as begin he must, sometime and in some way.

"Mammy," he said, feeling unconsciously for the childish phrase, "Mammy, has Uncle Silas been telling you anything about me?"

She gave a little nod of assent.

"Something, Thomas, but not a great deal. You have had some trouble with Doctor Tollivar?"

"Yes."

"I have known that for some little time. Your uncle might have told me more, but I wouldn't let him. There has never been anything between us to break confidence, Tom. I knew you would tell me yourself, when the time came."

"I have come to tell you tonight, mammy. You must hear it all, from beginning to end. It goes back a long way — back to the time when you used to let me kneel with my head in your lap to say my prayers; when you used to think I was good. . . ."

The fire had died down to a few glowing masses of coke on the grate bars when he had finished the story of his wanderings in the valley of dry bones. Through it all, Martha Gordon had sat silent and rigid, her thin hands lying clasped in her lap, and her low willow rocking-chair barely moving at the touch of her foot on the fender.

But when it was over; when Tom, his voice breaking in spite of his efforts to control it, told her that he could walk in the way she had chosen for him only at the price a conscious hypocrite must pay, she reached up quickly and took him in her arms and wept over him as those who sorrow without hope, crying again and again, *"O my son Absalom, my son, my son Absalom! would God I had died for thee, O Absalom, my son, my son!"*

XVIII

THE AWAKENING

Once in a lifetime for every youngling climbing the facile or difficult slope of the years there comes a day of realization, of a sudden extension of vision, of Rubicon-crossing from the hither shore of joyous and irresponsible adolescence to that further one of conscious grapplings with the adult fact.

For Thomas Jefferson, grinding tenaciously in the Boston technical school, whither he had gone late in the winter of Beersheban discontent, the stream-crossing fell in the spring of the panic year 1893, what time he was twenty-one, a quarter-back on his college eleven, fit, hardy, studious and athletic; a pacesetter for his fellows and the pride of the faculty, but still little more than an overgrown, care-free boy in his outlook on life. Glimpses there had been over into the Promised Land of manhood, but the brimming cup of college work and play quaffed in health-giving heartiness is the elixir of youth. The speculative habit of the boy slept in the college undergraduate. The days were full, each of the things of itself, and if Tom looked forward to the workaday future, — as he did by times, — the boyish impatience to be at it was gone. Chiawassee Consolidated was moderately prosperous; the home letters were mere chronicles of sleepy Paradise. The skies were clear, and the present was acutely present. Tom studied hard and played hard; ate like an ogre and slept like a log. And when he finally awoke to find himself stumbling bewildered on the bank of the epoch-marking Rubicon, he was over and across before he could realize how so narrow a stream should fill so vast a chasm.

The call of the ferryman — to keep the figure whole — was a letter from his father, a letter longer than the commonplace chronicles, and painfully written with the mechanic hand on both sides of a company letter-head. Caleb Gordon wrote chiefly of business. Mutterings of the storm of financial depression were already in the air. Iron, more sensitive than the stock-market, was the barometer, and its readings in the Southern field were growing portentous. Within the month several of the smaller furnaces had gone out of blast, and Chiawassee Consolidated, though still presenting a fair exterior, was, Caleb feared, rotten at heart. What would Tom advise?

Tom found this letter in his mail-box one evening after a strenuous day in the laboratory; and that night he sat up with the corpse of his later boyhood, though he was far enough from putting it that way. His father was in trouble, and the letter was a call for help. It seemed vastly incredible. Thomas Jefferson's ideal of steady courage, of invincible human puissance, was formed on the model of the stout-hearted old soldier who had fought under Stonewall Jackson. What a trumpet blast of alarm must have sounded to make such a man turn to a raw recruit for help!

Suddenly Tom began to realize that he was no longer a raw recruit, a boy to ride care-free while men were afoot and fighting. It astounded him that the realization had been so slow in arriving. It was as if he had been led blindfolded to the firing line, there to have the bandage plucked from his eyes by an unseen hand. Tumultuously it rushed on him that he was weaponed as the men of his father's generation could not be; that his hand could be steady and his heart fearless under threatenings that might well shake the courage of the old man who had borne only the burden and the heat of the day of smaller things.

He sat long with his elbows on the study table and his chin resting on his hands. The room was small but the walls gave before the steady gaze of the gray eyes, and Tom saw afar; down a vistaed highway wherein a strong man walked, leading a boy by the hand. Swiftly, with a click like that of the mechanism in a kinetoscope, the scene changed. The highway was the same, but now the man's steps had grown cautious and uncertain and he was groping for the shoulder of the boy, as for a leaning-staff.

Tom broke the eye-hold on the vision and sprang up to pace the narrow limits of the study.

"It's up to me," he mused, "and I'd like to know what I've been thinking of all this time. Why, pappy's old! he was forty before I was born. And I've been up here taking it easy and having all sorts of a good time, while he's been playing Sindbad to Duxbury Farley's Old Man of the Sea. Coming, pappy!" he shouted; and forthwith flung himself down at the table to write a letter that was to put new life into a weary old man who was fighting against odds in the far-away Southland.

The lone soldier was to take heart of grace, remembering that he had a son; remembering also that the son was now a man grown, stout of arm, steady of head, and otherwise fighting-fit. If the storm should come, the watchword must be to hold on all, keeping steerage-way on the Chiawassee Consolidated craft at all hazards. The June examinations were not far off, and these disposed of, the man-son would be ready to lay hold. Meanwhile, let Caleb Gordon, in his capacity of principal minor stock-holder, insist on a full and exact statement of the company's affairs, and — here the new manhood asserted itself boldly — let that statement, or a copy of it, come to Boston by the first mail.

To this letter there was a grateful reply in which Tom read with a smile his father's half bewildered attempt to get over to the new point of view. It began, "Dear Buddy," and ended, "Your affectionate pappy," but there was man-to-man matter between the salutation and the signature. The inquiry into the affairs of Chiawassee Consolidated had revealed little or nothing more than the general manager already knew. The president had turned the inquiring stock-holder over to Dyckman, the bookkeeper, with instructions to give Mr. Gordon the fullest possible information, and:

"Dyckman slid out of it, smooth and easy-like," Caleb's letter went on. "He allowed he was *mighty* busy, right about then. Wouldn't I just make myself at home and examine the books for myself? I reckon that was about what Farley wanted him to do. I'm no book expert, and I couldn't make head or tail out of Dyckman's spider tracks. Looks to me like all the books are good for is to keep people from finding where the company is at. What little I found out, young Norman told me. He says we're in a hole, and the first wagon-load of dirt that comes along will bury us out of sight."

Tom, driven now with the closing work of the college year, yet took time to write another heartening letter to the hard-pressed old soldier. It had been his good fortune to win the Clarkson prize for crucible tests, and to have gained thereby a speaking acquaintance with the multimillionaire iron king who had founded it. Mr. Clarkson did not believe that the financial storm would grow to panic size. As for himself, Tom thought the hazard was less in the times than in the Farleys. Father Caleb was to keep his finger on the pulse of the main office, wiring Boston at the first sign of its weakening.

The junior metallurgical was in the thick of the June examinations when the catastrophe befell. The brief story of it came to Tom in the first dictated letter he had ever received from his father, and the tremulous shakiness of the signature pointed eloquently to the reason. Chiawassee Consolidated was out of blast — "temporarily suspended," in the pleasant euphemism of the elder Farley; the force, clerical and manual, was discharged, with only Dyckman left in the deserted South Tredegar offices to answer questions; and the three Farleys, with Major Dabney, Ardea and Miss Euphrasia, were to spend the summer in Europe.

Caleb wrote in some bitterness of spirit. Though the Gordon holdings in the company, increased from time to time as the ironmaster had prospered, amounted to a little more than a third of the capital stock, everything had been done secretly. The general manager's own notice of the shut-down had come in the posted

"Notice to Employees." When the Farleys should leave, he would be utterly helpless; on their return they could repudiate everything he might do in their absence. Meantime, ruin was imminent. The affairs of the company were in the utmost confusion; the treasury was empty, and there were no apparent assets apart from the idle plant. Creditors were pressing; the discharged workmen, led by the white coal-miners, were on the verge of riot; and Major Dabney's royalties on the coal lands were many months in arrears.

Tom rose promptly to the occasion, and in all the stress of things found space to wonder how it chanced that he knew instinctively what to do and how to go about it. Before his information was an hour old a rush telegram had gone to his father, asking from what port and by what steamer the Farleys would sail; asking also that certain documents be sent to a given New York address by first mail.

This done, he laid the exigencies frankly before the examiners in the technical school, praying for such lenity as might be extended under the circumstances. Since all things are possible for an honor-man, beloved of those whose mission it is to grind the human weapon to its edge, the difficulties in this field vanished. Mr. Gordon could go on with the examinations until his presence was needed elsewhere; and after the stressful moment was passed he could return and finish.

Tom, the boy, could not have gone on. It would have been blankly impossible. But Tom, the man, was a new creature. While waiting for the reply to his telegram, he plunged doggedly back into the scholastic whirlpool, kicked, struggled, strangled, got his head above water, and found, vastly to his own amazement, that the thing was actually compassable in spite of the mighty distractions.

The return telegram from Gordonia was a day late. Knowing diplomacy only by name, Caleb Gordon had gone directly to Dyckman for information regarding the Farleys' movements. Dyckman was polite to the general manager, but unhappily he knew nothing of Mr. Farley's plans. Caleb tried elsewhere, and the little mystery thickened. At his club, Mr. Farley had spoken of taking a Cunarder from Boston; to a friend in the South Tredegar Manufacturers' Association he had confided his intention of sailing from Philadelphia. But at the railway ticket office he had engaged Pullman reservations for six persons to New York.

This last was conclusive, as far as it went; and Japheth Pettigrass supplied the missing item. The Dabneys and the Farleys made one party, and Japheth knew the steamer and the sailing date.

"Party will sail by White Star Line Baltic, New York, to-morrow. New York address, Fifth Avenue Hotel. Papers to you care 271 Broadway by mail yesterday," was the message which was signed for by the doorkeeper at the mines and metallurgy examination room in Boston, late in the forenoon of the second day; and Tom looked at the clock. Nothing would be gained by taking a train which would land him in New York late in the evening; so he plunged again into the examination pool and thought no more of Chiawassee Consolidated until his paper on qualitative analysis had been neatly folded, docketed and handed to the examiner.

The hands of his watch were pointing to eight o'clock the following morning when Tom made his way through the throng in the Grand Central station and found a cab. The sailing hour of the *Baltic* was ten, and he picked his cabman accordingly.

"I shall want you for a couple of hours, and it's double fare if you don't miss. 271 Broadway, first," was his fillip for the driver; and he was speedily rattling away to the down-town address.

The taking of the cab was his first mistake, and he discovered it before he had gone very far. Time was precious, and the horse, pushed to the police limit, was too slow. Tom signaled his Irishman.

"Get me over to the Elevated, and then go to Madison Square and wait for me," he ordered; and by this change of conveyance he obtained his mail and won back to the Fifth Avenue Hotel by late breakfast time.

From that on, luck was with him. The Farleys, father and son, were in the lobby of the hotel, waiting for the others to come down to the café breakfast. Tom saw them, confronted them, and went at things very concisely.

"I have come all the way from Boston to ask for a few minutes of your time, Mr. Farley," he said to the president. "Will you give it to me now?"

"Surely!" was the genial reply, and the promoter signed to his son and drew apart with the importunate one. "Well, go on, my boy; what can I do for you at this last American moment? — some message from your good father?"

"No," said Tom shortly; "it's from me, individually. You know in what shape you have left things at home; they've got to be stood on their feet before you go aboard the *Baltic*."

"What's this — what's this? Why, my dear young man! what can you possibly mean?" — this in buttered tones of the gentlest expostulation.

"I mean just about what I say. You have smashed Chiawassee Consolidated, and now you are going off to leave my father to hold the bag. Or rather I should say, you are taking the bag with you."

The president was visibly moved.

"Why, Thomas — you must be losing your mind! You've — you've been studying too hard; that's it — the term work up there in Boston has been too much for you."

"Cut it out, Mr. Farley," said Tom savagely, all the Gordon fighting blood singing in his veins. "You've got a thing to do, and it is going to be done before you leave America. Will you talk straight business, or not?"

The president adjusted his eye-glasses, and gave this brand-new Gordon a calm over-look.

"And if I decline to discuss business matters with a rude school-boy?" he intimated mildly.

"Then it will be rather the worse for you," was the defiant rejoinder. "Acting for my father and the minority stock-holders, I shall try to have you and your son held in America, pending an expert examination of the company's affairs."

It was a long shot, with a thousand chances of missing. If there was anything criminal in the Farley administration, the evidences were doubtless well buried. But Tom was looking deep into the shifty blue eyes of his antagonist when he fired, and he saw that he had not wholly missed. None the less, the president attempted to carry it off lightly.

"What do you think of this, Vincent?" he said, turning to his son. "Here is Tom Gordon — our Tom — talking wildly about investigations and arrests, and I don't know what all. Shall we give him his breakfast and send him back to school?"

Tom cut in quickly before Vincent could make a reply.

"If you're sparring to gain time, it's no use, Mr. Farley. I mean what I say, and I'm dead in earnest." Then he tried another long shot: "I tell you right now we've had this thing cocked and primed ever since we found out what you and Vincent meant to do. You must turn over the control of Chiawassee Consolidated, legally and formally, to my father before you go aboard the *Baltic*, or — *you don't go aboard*!"

"Let me understand," said the treasurer, cutting in. "Are you accusing us of crime?"

"You will find out what the accusation is, later on," said Tom, taking yet another cartridge from the long-range box. "What I want now is a plain, straightforward yes or no, if either of you is capable of saying it."

The president took his son aside.

"Do you suppose Dyckman has been talking too much?" he asked hurriedly.

Vincent shook his head.

"You can't tell . . . it looks a little rocky. Of course, we had a right to do as we pleased with our own, but we don't want to have an unfriendly construction put on things."

"But they can't do anything!" protested the president. "Why, I'd be perfectly willing to turn over my private papers, if they were asked for!"

"Yes, of course. But there would be misconstruction. There is that contract with the combination, for example; we had a right to manipulate things so we'd have to close down, and it might not transpire that we made money by doing it. But, on the other hand, it might leak out, and there'd be no end of a row. Then there is another thing: there is somebody behind this who is bigger than the old soldier or this young foot-ball tough. It's too nicely timed."

"But, heavens and earth! you wouldn't turn the property over to Gordon, would you?"

The younger man's smile was a mere contortion of the lips. "It's a sucked orange," he said. "Let the old man have it. He may work a miracle of some sort and pull out alive. I should call it a snap, and take him up too quick. If he wins out, so much the better for all concerned. If he doesn't, why, we left the property entirely in his hands, and he smashed it. Don't you see the beauty of it?"

The president wheeled short on Tom.

"What you may think you are extorting, my dear boy, you are going to get through sheer good-will and a desire to give your father every chance in the world," he said blandly. "We discussed the plan of electing him vice-president, with power to act, before we left home, but there seemed to be some objections. We are willing to give him full control — and this altogether apart from any foolish threats you have seen fit to make. Bring your legal counsel to Room 327 after breakfast and we will go through the formalities. Are you satisfied?"

"I shall be a lot better satisfied after the fact," said Tom bluntly; and he turned away to avoid meeting Major Dabney and the ladies, who were coming from the elevator to join the two early risers. He had seen next to nothing of Ardea during the three Boston years, and would willingly have seen more. But the new manhood was warning him that time was short, and that he must not mix business with sentiment. So Ardea saw nothing but his back, which, curiously enough, she failed to recognize.

Picking up his cab at the curb, Tom had himself driven quickly to the office of the corporation lawyer whose name he had obtained from Mr. Clarkson the day before, and with whom he had made a wire appointment before leaving Boston. The attorney was waiting for him, and Tom stated the case succinctly, adding a brief of the interview which had just taken place at the hotel.

"You say they agreed to your proposal?" observed the lawyer. "Did Mr. Farley indicate the method?"

"No."

"Have you a copy of the by-laws of your company?"

Tom produced the packet of papers received that morning from his father, and handed the required pamphlet to Mr. Croswell.

"H'm — ha! the usual form. A stock-holders' meeting, with a resolution, would be the simplest way out of it; but that can't be held without the published call. You say your father is a stock-holder?"

"He has four hundred and three of the original one thousand shares. I hold his proxy."

The attorney smiled shrewdly.

"You are a very remarkable young man. You seem to have come prepared at all points. I assume that you are acting under your father's instructions?"

"Why, with his approval, of course," Tom amended. "But it is my own initiative, under the advice of a good friend of mine in Boston, thus far. Oh, I know what I'm about," he added, in answer to the latent question in the lawyer's eyes.

"You seem to," was the laconic reply. "Now let us see exactly what it is that you want Mr. Farley to concede."

"I want him to turn over the entire control of the company's business, operative and financial, to my father."

The lawyer smiled again.

"That is a pretty big asking. Have you any reason to suppose that Mr. Farley will accede to any such demand?"

"Yes; I have very good reasons, but I reckon we needn't go into them here and now. The time is too short; their liner sails at ten."

The attorney tilted his chair and became reflective.

"The simple way out of it is to have Mr. Farley constitute your father, or yourself, his proxy to vote his stock at a certain specified meeting of the stock-holders, which can be called later. Of course, with a majority vote of the stock, you can rearrange matters to suit yourselves, subject only to Mr. Farley's disarrangement when he resumes control of his holdings. How would that serve?"

"You're the doctor," said Tom bruskly. "Any way to get him out and get my father in."

"It's the simplest way, as I say. But if the property is worth anything at all, I should think Mr. Farley would fight you to a finish before he would consent."

"You fix up the papers, Mr. Croswell, and I'll see to it that he consents. Make the proxy run in my father's name."

The attorney went into another room and dictated to his stenographer. While he was absent, Tom sat, watch in hand, counting the minutes. It was his first pitched battle with the Farleys, and victory promised. But with industrial panic in the air the victory threatened to be of the Cadmean sort, and a scowl of anxiety gathered between his eyes.

"Never mind," he gritted, with an out-thrust of the square jaw; "it's the Gordon fighting chance; and pappy says that's all we've ever asked — it's all I'm going to ask, anyway. But I wish Ardea wasn't going over with that crowd!"

The conference in Room 327, Fifth Avenue Hotel, held while the carriages were waiting to take the steamer party to the pier, was brief and businesslike. Something to Tom's surprise, Major Dabney was present; and a little later he learned, with a shock of resentment, that the Major was also a minority stock-holder in the moribund Chiawassee Consolidated. The master of Deer Trace was as gracious to Caleb Gordon's son as only a Dabney knew how to be.

"Nothing could give me greateh pleasure, my deah boy, than this plan of having youh fatheh in command at Gordonia," he beamed, shaking Tom's hand effusively. "I hope you'll have us all made millionaihs when we get back home again; I do, for a fact, suh."

Tom smiled and shook his head.

"It looks pretty black, just now, Major. I'm afraid we're in for rough weather."

"Oh, no; not that, son; a meah passing cloud." And then, with the big Dabney laugh: "You youngstehs oughtn't to leave it for us old fellows to keep up the stock of optimism, suh. A word in youh ear, young man: if these heah damned Yankee rascals would quit thei-uh monkeying right heah in Wall Street, the country would take on a new lease of life, suh; it would for a fact," and he said it loudly enough to be heard in the corridor.

During this bit of side play the attorney was laboring with the two Farleys, and Tom, watching narrowly, saw that there was a hitch of some kind.

"What is it?" he demanded, turning shortly on the trio at the table.

The lawyer explained. Mr. Farley thought the plan proposed was entirely too far-reaching in its effects, or possible effects. He was willing to delegate his authority as president of the company to Caleb Gordon in writing. Would not that answer all the requirements?

Tom asked his attorney with his eyes if it would answer, and read the negative reply very clearly. So he shook his head.

"No," he said, turning his back on the Major and lowering his voice. "We must have your proxy, Mr. Farley."

"And if I don't choose to accede to your demands?"

"I don't think we need to go over that ground again," said Tom coolly. "If you don't sign that paper, you'll miss your steamer."

The president glanced toward the open door, as if he half expected to see an officer waiting for him. Then he said, "Oh, well; it's as broad as it is long," and signed.

The leave-takings were brief, and somewhat constrained, save those of the genial Major. Tom pleaded business, further business, with his attorney, when the Major would have had him wait to tell the ladies good-by; hence he saw no more of the tourists after the conference broke up.

Not to lose time, Tom took a noon train back to Boston, first wiring his father to try and keep things in *statu quo* at Gordonia for another week at all hazards. Winning back to the technical school, he plunged once more into the examination whirlpool, doing his best to forget Chiawassee Consolidated and its mortal sickness for the time being, and succeeding so well that he passed with colors flying.

But the school task done, he turned down the old leaf, pasting it firmly in place. Telegraphing his father to meet him, on the morning of the third day following, at the station in South Trede-gar, he allowed himself a few hours for a run up the North Shore and a conference with the Michigan iron king; after which he turned his face southward and was soon speeding to the battle-field through a land by this time shaking to its industrial founda-tions in the throes of the panic earthquake.

XIX

ISSACHAR

In accordance with Tom's telegram, Caleb Gordon met his son at the station in South Tredegar, and they went together to breakfast in one of the dining-rooms of the Marlboro. Tom's heart burned within him when he saw how the late stress of things had aged his father, and for the first time in his life he opened a vengeance account: if the Farleys ever came back there should be reckoning for more than the looting of Chiawassee Consolidated. But this was only the primitive under-thought. Uppermost at the moment was the joy of the young soldier arrived, fit and vigorous, on his maiden battle-field.

"You don't know how good it seems to get back home again, pappy," he said, over the bacon and eggs. "I've been grinding pretty hard this year, and now it's over, I feel as if I could whip my weight in wildcats, as Japheth used to say. By the way, how is Japheth?"

Caleb Gordon smiled in spite of the corroding industrial anxieties.

"Japheth's going to surprise you some, I reckon, son; he's gone and got religion."

Tom put down his knife and fork.

"Why, the old sinner!" he laughed. "How did that happen?"

"Oh, just about the way it always does," said Caleb slowly. "The spirit moved your Uncle Silas to come out to Little Zoar and hold a protracted meetin', and Japhe joined the mourners and was gathered into the fold."

"Pshaw!" said Tom, in good-natured incredulity. "Why, the very meat and marrow of his existence is his horse-trading; and who could swap horses and tell the truth at the same time?"

"I don't know," was the doubtful reply. "But Brother Japheth allows that's about what he aims to do. It's sort o' curious the way it works out, too. About a week after the baptizin', Jim Bledsoe came down from Pine Knob with a horse to swap. 'Long about sundown he met up with Japhe, and struck him for a trade on a piebald that the Major wouldn't let run in the same lot with the Deer Trace stock. They had it up one side and down the other; Brother Japhe tryin' to tell Bledsoe that his piebald was about the no-accountest horse in the valley, and Jim takin' it all by contraries and gettin' more and more p'intedly anxious to trade."

"Well?" said Tom, enjoying his return to nature like any creature freed of the urban cage.

"They came to the trade, after a tolerable spell of it," Caleb went on, "and the last thing I heard Japhe say was, 'now you recollect, Brother Bledsoe, I done told you that there piebald's no account on the face of the earth — a-lovin' of my neighbor like I promise' Brother Silas I would.'"

Tom laughed again. There was the smell of the good red soil in the little story, a whiff of the home earth reminiscent and heartening. But the under-thought laid hold on Japheth and his change of heart.

"Japhe was about the last man in Paradise, always excepting Major Dabney," he said half musingly. "Haven't you often wondered what sort of a maggot it is that gets into the human brain to give it the superstitious twist?"

Caleb's gentle frown was the upcast of paternal bewilderment, partly prideful, partly disconcerting. He was not yet fully acquainted with this young giant with the frank face, the sober gray eyes, and the conscious grasp of himself. More than once since their meeting at the steps of the Pullman car he had felt obliged to reassure himself by saying, "This is Tom; this is my son." There were so many and such marked changes: the quick, curt speech, caught in the Northland; the nervous, sure-footed stride, and the athletic swing of the shoulders; the easy manner and confident air, not of college-boy conceit, but of the assurance of young manhood; and, lastly, this blunt right-about-face in matters of religion. Caleb was not quite sure that this latter change was entirely welcome.

"Whereabouts did ye learn to call it superstition, son? Not at your mammy's knee, leastwise," he said, in sober deprecation.

Tom shook his head. "No; and not altogether at yours. But I guess I've worked around to your point of view, after so long a time."

"It's your mammy's faith, all the same, Buddy," said the father gravely. "Let's not belittle it any more'n we can help."

"I don't belittle it," was the quick response. "In some of its phases it is grand — magnificent. We can't always be prying into the cause; the effect is what counts. And there is no denying that the fairy tale which we call Christianity has built some of the most godlike heroes the world has ever seen."

"You're right sure now that it is a fairy story, son?" said the old man, a little wistfully.

"There is no doubt about that," was the decisive rejoinder. "There is room for credulity only in ignorance. Any thinking person who is brought face to face with the materialistic facts —"

Caleb held up a toil-hardened hand.

"Hold on, Buddy; you'll have to pick a place where the water deepens sort o' gradually for the old man or you'll have him flounderin'. I reckon I been sittin' up on the bank all my life, waitin' for somebody to come along and pole the bottom for me in that pool."

"No," said Tom definitively. "There isn't any bank to that pool. You're in it, or you are out of it; one or the other. That was the notion I took with me to Boston. I thought I'd get well up above the eternal wrangle and look down on it — wouldn't believe, wouldn't disbelieve. It can't be done. Jesus, Himself, said, if they've reported Him straight, 'He that is not with me is against me.'"

"Well," said the father, still deprecating, "that's some farther along than I've ever been able to get — not sayin' that I wouldn't be willin' to go." And then: "You don't allow to argue with your mammy about these things, do you, Tom?"

Tom's rejoinder was gravely considerate.

"It is a sealed book between us, now, pappy. She knows — and knows it can't be helped. If I wasn't her son, I hope I should still be the last person in the world to try to shake her faith — or any one's, for that matter. I have merely turned my own back — because I had to."

The old man put down his coffee-cup and the look in his eyes was half appealing.

"What was it turned you, son? — nothing I've ever said or done, I hope?"

Tom shook his big blond head slowly.

"No, not directly; though I suppose a man does go back to his father for a measuring-stick. But indirectly you, and the other Gordons, are responsible for the best there is in me — and that's the questioning part. Given the doubt, I hunted till I found the man who could resolve or confirm it."

"Who was he?" inquired Caleb, willing to hear more particularly.

"His name is Bauer — the man I've been rooming with. He is a German biologist who was to have been educated for the Lutheran ministry. His people made the capital mistake of sending him to Freiburg for a couple of years as a preliminary, and, when they found out what the German university had done for him, they sent him to Boston, under the impression that the Puritan American city might correct some of his materialism."

Caleb smiled. "That ain't just the way we think of Boston over here," he remarked.

"No; and, of course, Bauer didn't change his point of view. We used to have it up hill and down. I had Scripture — mother and the Beershebans had taught me that — and Bauer had immense reading, flinty Dutch common sense, and a huge lack of the reverence for the so-called sacred subjects which seems to be ingrained in every race but the Teutonic. I fought hard, both for mother's sake and because it was the first time I had ever met a man with his sword out on the other side."

"Well?" said Caleb.

"He downed me, horse, foot and artillery; made me realize as I never had before what an absolute begging of the premises the entire Christian argument is."

"But how?" persisted the iron-master.

"Held me up at the muzzle of the cold facts. For example: do you happen to know that the oldest Bible manuscripts in existence go back only to the fourth century, and are doubtless copies of copies of copies?"

The father had pushed back his chair and was trying to fold his napkin in the original creases.

"No; there's a heap o' things I don't know, son, but I'm willin' to learn. One o' these days, if we ever get out o' this business tangle alive, we'll sit down quiet together and you'll do for me what this Dutchman has done for you. For, in spite of what you say, I've been sittin' on the fence all these years, and I reckon you're the one to help me down."

Tom smiled first at the thought of it and then grew suddenly sober. It is one thing to be serenely critical for oneself, and quite another to set the pace for a disciple. And when that disciple chances to be one's father?

"I don't know about that, pappy," he said, rather dubiously. "I'd like to have you meet some of the people on my side of the road first. Maybe you wouldn't like the company."

But Caleb would not have it so. "If they're good enough for you, son, they're good enough for me," he said. "Not but what there's some mighty good folks trampin' along on the other side, too."

"Yes, and some mighty bad ones," said Tom, thinking of the promoter vestryman of St. Michael's and his Bible-class-teaching son. "We are going right now to investigate the financiering methods of a pair of them. Is Dyckman still on duty? Or are the offices closed?"

"Dyckman's there," was the answer; and they left the breakfast-room together to go around the block and have themselves lifted to the fifth floor of the Coosa Building, where half a dozen gilt-lettered glass doors advertised the administrative headquarters of Chiawassee Consolidated.

If Caleb Gordon had been mildly bewildered by the outward and instantly visible changes in his college-bred son, he was quite lost in wondering admiration when the young man had climbed fairly into the business saddle and gathered his grip on the reins. Notwithstanding the fact of his stock-holding, Caleb the iron-master had always stood a little in awe of the general office grandeurs; of chief priest Dyckman in particular. But Tom seemed to recognize no distinctions of class, age, or previous condition of overlordship. Dyckman was found busily lounging in the absent president's easy-chair, smoking a good cigar and reading the morning papers. At the outset he was inclined to be genially supercilious, thus:

"Ah, good morning, Mr. Gordon! Hello, Tom! Back from college, are you? The books and papers? They are over in the vaults of the Iron City National — by Mr. Farley's orders. I suppose he thought they'd be safer there in case of fire. Won't you sit down and have a fresh cigar?"

What Tom said, or the precise wording of it, Caleb could never remember. But the staccato sentence or two had the effect of instantly electrifying Mr. Dyckman. Certainly; whatever Mr. Thomas desired should be done. He — Dyckman — had had no notice of the change in the plans of the company, and Mr. Farley's instructions —

Tom cut the oath of fealty short and stated his desires succinctly. The bookkeeper was to reassemble his office force immediately, taking particular care to reinstate Norman, the correspondence man. That done, he was to prepare full and complete exhibits of the company's condition: assets, liabilities, contracts, in short, the results in statement form of a thorough and searching house-cleaning in the accounting and administrative departments.

"I am going to put you on your good behavior, Dyckman," said the new tyrant in conclusion, driving the words home with a shrewd sword-thrust of the gray eyes. "At first I thought I'd bring an expert accountant down here from New York and put him on your books; but I'm going to spare you that — on one condition. Those exhibits must be made absolutely without fear or favor; they must contain the exact truth and all of it. If you tinker them, you'll not be able to run fast enough nor far enough to get away from me. Do I make it plain?"

"Very plain, indeed, Mr. Tom; the office boy would catch your meaning, I think."

"All right, then; gather up your force and pitch in. I haven't time to watch you, and I don't mean to take it. But I shall know it when you begin to flicker."

When the two early morning disturbers of Mr. Dyckman's peace were once more in the street and on the way to the station to take the train for Gordonia and the seat of war, Caleb found speech.

"Son," he said gravely, "do you know that you've made a mighty bitter enemy in the last fifteen minutes? Dyckman is Farley's confidential man, and when he gets his knife ground good and sharp he's goin' to cut you with it, once for himself and once for his boss."

Tom's laugh was an easing of strains.

"It does me a heap of good to know that I can crack the whip where you'd be putting on the brakes, pappy; it does, for a fact. But you needn't worry about Dyckman. He won't quarrel with his bread and butter. I don't care anything about his personal loyalty so long as he does his work."

Again Caleb had to withdraw a little and look his stalwart young captain over and say: "It is Tom; it's just Buddy, grown up and come to be a man." But it was hard to realize.

"I reckon you've got it all figured out — what-all we're goin' to do, Tom," he said, when they were seated in the car of the accommodation train.

"Yes, I think I have; at least, I have the beginning struck out. We are going to call a stock-holders' meeting, vote you into the presidency, take the bull squarely by the horns and blow in the Chiawassee furnace again — dig coal, roast coke and make iron."

"But, son! at the present price of iron, we can't make any money; couldn't clear a dollar a car if the buyers would push their cars right into our yard. And there ain't any buyers."

Tom was looking out of the window at the procession of smokeless factory chimneys. The blight had already fallen on the South Tredegar industries.

"It's going to be a battle to the strong, to the fellow who can wait, and work while he waits," he said, half to himself. Then, more particularly to his father's protest: "I know, we are in pretty bad shape. When we get those exhibits we shall find that the Farleys have picked the bones, leaving them for us to bury decently out of sight. Then, when the funeral is over, they'll come back and charge it all to the Gordon mismanagement. It's a cinch, isn't it?"

The old iron-master was silent for the train-speed's measuring of a long mile. Then he said slowly:

"I don't aim to go back on you, Buddy; not a foot 'r an inch. But it does seem to me like you put your finger in the fire when you hilt up Duxbury Farley for that proxy paper in New York. If we go under — and the good Lord only knows how we can he'p it — they'll come out of it with clean clothes, and we'll have to take all the mud-slingin', just as you say."

Tom's smile would have stamped him as the son of the grim old ex-artilleryman in any court of inquiry.

"Did your old general ever go into battle with the idea that he was bound to be licked, pappy?" he asked.

"Who? Stonewall Jackson? Well, I reckon not, son."

"Neither shall we," said Tom laconically. "We are going in to win. We are in bad shape, I admit, but we are better off than a lot of these furnaces that are shutting down. We have our own ore beds, and our own coking plant. Our coal costs us seventy-five cents less than Pocahontas, our water is free, and we can hold the property as long as we can stand the sheriff off. My notion is to make iron and hold it; stack it in the yards, mortgage it for what we can get, and make more iron. Some day the country will get iron hungry; then we'll have it to sell when the other fellows will have to make it first and sell it afterward. Have I got it straight?"

Caleb nodded.

"Yes; I don't know but what you have. What's puzzlin' me right now, son, is *where* you got it."

Tom's laugh was a tonic for sore nerves.

"I'd like to know what you've been spending your good money on me for if it wasn't to give me a chance to get it. Do you think I've been playing foot-ball all the time?"

"No; but — well, Tom, the last I knew of you, you was just a little shaver, spattin' around barefooted in the dust o' the Paradise pike, and I can't seem to climb up to where you're at now."

Tom laughed again.

"You'll come to it, after while. I reckon I haven't much more sense, in some ways, than the little shaver had; but I've been trying my level best to learn my trade. There is only one thing about this tangle that is worrying me: that's the labor end of it."

"We can get all the labor we want," said Caleb.

"Yes; but didn't you write me that the men were on strike?"

"I said the white miners were likely to make trouble if they got hungry enough."

"Was there any pay in arrears when you shut down?"

"No. Farley wanted to scale the men, but I fought him out o' that."

"Good! Then what are they kicking about?"

"Oh, because they're out of a job. There are always a lot of keen noses in a crowd the size of ours, and they've smelled out some o' the Farley doin's. Of course, they don't believe in the cry of hard times; laborin' men are always the last to believe that."

The train was tracking thunderously around the nose of Lebanon, and Tom was looking out of the window again, this time for the first glimpse of the Gordonia chimney-stacks and the bounding hills of the home valley.

"That is where you will have to put your shoulder into the collar with me, pappy," he said. "Most of the older men know me as a boy who has grown up among them. When I spring my proposition, they'll howl, if only for that reason."

But now Caleb was shaking his gray head more dubiously than ever.

"You won't get any help from the men, Buddy, more 'n what you pay for. You know the whites — Welshmen, Cornishmen, and a good sprinklin' o' 'huckleberries.' And the blacks don't count, one way or the other."

The engineer of the accommodation had whistled for Gordonia, and Tom was gathering his dunnage.

"Our scramble is going to depend very largely on the outcome of the meeting which I'm going to ask you to call for say, two o'clock this afternoon on the floor of the foundry building," he said. "Will you stay in town and get the men together, while I go home and see mother and shape up my talk?"

Caleb Gordon acquiesced, glad of a chance to have somewhat to do. And so, in the very beginning of things, it was the son and not the father who took the helm of the tempest-driven ship.

XX

DRY WELLS

As early as one o'clock in the afternoon, the elder Helgerson, acting as day watchman at the iron-works, had opened the great yard gates, and the men began to gather by twos and threes and in little caucusing knots on the sand floor of the huge, iron-roofed foundry building. Some of the more heedful set to work making seats of the wooden flask frames and bottom boards; and in the pouring space fronting one of the cupolas they built a rough-and-ready platform out of the same materials.

As the numbers increased the men fell into groups, dividing first on the color-line, and then by trades, with the white miners in the majority and doing most of the talking.

"What's all this buzzin' round about young Tom?" queried one of the men in the miners' caucus. "Might' nigh every other word with old Caleb was, 'Tom; my son, Tom.' Why, I riccollect him when he wasn't no more'n knee-high to a hop-toad!"

"Well, you bet your life he's a heap higher'n that now," said another, who had chanced to be at the station when the Gordons, father and son, left the train together. "He's a half a head taller than the old man, an' built like one o' Maje' Dabney's thoroughbreds. But I reckon he ain't nothin' but a school-boy, for all o' that."

"Gar-r-r!" spat a third. "We've had one kid too many in this outfit, all along. I'll bet, if the truth was knowed, th't that young Farley'd skin a louse for the hide and tallow."

"Yes," chimed in a fourth, a "huckleberry" miner from the Bald Mountain district, "and I reckon whar thar's sich a hell of a smoke, thar's a right smart heap o' fire, ef it could on'y be on-kivered."

But all of this was in a manner beside the mark, and there were many to inquire what the Gordons were going to do. Ludlow, check weigher in Number Two entry, and the head of the local union, took it on himself to reply.

"B'gosh! I don't b'lieve the old man knows, himself. He fit around and fit around, talkin' to me, and never said nothin' more'n that there was goin' to be a meetin' here at two o'clock, and Tom — his son Tom — was goin' to speak to it."

"All right; we're a-waitin' on son Tom right now," said a grizzled old coal-digger on the outer edge of the group. "And ef he's got anything to say, he cayn't say hit none too sudden. My ol' woman told me this mornin' she was a-hittin' the bottom o' the meal bar'l, kerchuck! ever' time she was dippin' into hit. Hit's erbout time there was somepin doin', ez I allow."

"Saw it off!" warned Ludlow. "Here they come, both of 'em."

Tom and his father had entered the building from the cupola side, and Tom mounted the flask-built platform while the men were scattering to find seats. He made a goodly figure of young manhood, standing at ease on the pile of frames until quiet should prevail, and the glances flung up from the throng of workmen were friendly rather than critical. When the time came, he began to speak quietly, but with a certain masterful quality in his voice that unmistakably constrained attention.

"I suppose you have all been told why the works are shut down — why you are out of a job in the middle of summer; and I understand you are not fully satisfied with the reason that was given — hard times. You have been saying among yourselves that if the president and the treasurer could go off on a holiday trip to Europe, the situation couldn't be so very desperate. Isn't that so?"

"That's so; you've hit it in the head first crack out o' the box," was the swift reply from a score of the men.

"Good; then we'll settle that point before we go any further. I want to tell you men that the hard times are here, sure enough. We are all hoping that they won't last very long; but the fact remains that the wheels have stopped. Let me tell you: I've just come down from the North, and the streets of the cities up there are full of idle men. All the way down here I didn't see a single iron-furnace in blast, and those of you who have been over to South Tredegar know what the conditions are there. Mr. Farley has gone to Europe because he believes there is nothing to be done here, and the facts are on his side. For anybody with money enough to live on, this is a mighty good time to take a vacation."

There was a murmur of protest, voicing itself generally in a denial of the possibility for men who wrought with their hands and ate in the sweat of their brows.

"I know that," was Tom's rejoinder. "Some of us can't afford to take a lay-off; I can't, for one. And that's why we are here this afternoon. Chiawassee can blow in again and stay in blast if we've all got nerve enough to hang on. If we start up and go on making pig, it'll be on a dead market and we'll have to sell it at a loss or stack it in the yards. We can't do the first, and I needn't tell you that it is going to take a mighty long purse to do the stacking. It will be all outgo and no income. If —"

"Spit it out," called Ludlow, from the forefront of the miners' division. "I reckon we all know what's comin'."

Gordon thrust out his square jaw and gave them the fact bluntly.

"It's a case of half a loaf or no bread. If Chiawassee blows in again, it will be on borrowed money. If you men will take half pay in cash and half in promises, the promised half to be paid when we can sell the stacked pig, we go on. If not, we don't. Talk it over among yourselves and let us have your decision."

There was hot caucusing and a fair imitation of pandemonium on the foundry floor following this bomb-hurling, and Tom sat down on the edge of the platform to give the men time. Caleb Gordon sat within arm's reach, nursing his knee, diligently saying nothing. It was Tom, undoubtedly, but a Tom who had become a citizen of another world, a newer world than the one the ex-artilleryman knew and lived in. He — Caleb — had freely predicted a riot as the result of the half pay proposal; yet Tom had applied the match and there was no explosion. The buzzing, arguing groups were not riotous — only fiercely questioning.

It was Ludlow, hammering clamorously for silence on the shell of the big crane ladle, who acted as spokesman when the uproar was quelled.

"You're all right, Tom Gordon — you and your daddy. But you've hit us plum' 'twixt dinner and supper. If you two was the company —"

Tom stood up and interrupted.

"We are the company. While Mr. Farley is away we're the bosses; what we say, goes."

"All right," Ludlow went on. "That's a little better. But we've got a kick or two comin'. Is this half pay goin' to be in orders on the company's store?"

"I said cash," said Tom briefly.

"Good enough. But I s'pose we'd have to spend it at the company's store, jest the same, 'r get fired."

"No!" — emphatically. "I'm not even sure that we should reopen the store. We shall not reopen it unless you men want it. If you do want it, we'll make it strictly coöperative, dividing the profits with every employee according to his purchases."

"Well, by gol, that's white, anyway," commented one of the coke burners. "Be a mighty col' day in July when old man Farley'd talk as straight as that."

"Ag'in," said Ludlow, "what's this half pay to be figured on — the reg'lar scale?"

"Of course."

"And what security do we have that t'other half'll be paid, some time?"

"My father's word, and mine."

"And if old man Farley says no?"

"Mr. Farley is out of it for the present, and he has nothing to say about it. You are making this deal with Gordon and Gordon."

"Well, now, that's a heap more like it." Ludlow turned to the miners. "What d'ye say, boys? Fish or cut bait? Hands up!"

There was a good showing of hands among the white miners and the coke burners, but the negro foundry men did not vote. Patty, the mulatto foreman who was Helgerson's second, explained the reason.

"You ain't said nuttin' 'bout de foundry, Boss Tom. W-w-w-we-all boys been wukkin' short ti-ti-time, and m-m-m-makin' pig ain't gwine give we-all n-n-nuttin' ter do." Patty had a painful impediment in his speech, and the strain of the public occasion doubled it.

"We are going to run the foundry, too, Patty, and on full time. There will be work for all of you on the terms I have named."

Caleb Gordon closed his eyes and put his face in his hands. For weeks before the shut-down the foundry had been run on short time, because there was no market for its miscellaneous output. Surely Tom must be losing his mind!

But the negro foundry men were taking his word for it, as the miners had. "Pup-pup-put up yo' hands, boys!" said Patty, and again the ayes had it.

Tom looked vastly relieved.

"Well, that was a short horse soon curried," he said bruskly. "The power goes on tomorrow morning, and we'll blow in as soon as the furnaces are relined. Ludlow, you come to the office at five o'clock and I'll list the shifts with you. Patty, you report to Mr. Helgerson, and you and the pattern-maker show up at half past five. I want to talk over some new work with you. Anybody else got anything to say? If not, we'll adjourn."

Caleb followed his son out and across the yard to the old log homestead which still served as the superintendent's office and laboratory. When the door was shut, he dropped heavily into a chair.

"Son," he said brokenly, "you're — you're crazy — plum' crazy. Don't you know you can't do the first one o' these things you've been promisin'?"

Tom was already busy at the desk, emptying the pigeonholes one after another and rapidly scanning their contents.

"If I believed that, I'd be taking to the high grass and the tall timber. But don't you worry, pappy; we're going to do them — all of them."

"But, Buddy, you can't sell a pound of foundry product! We may be able to make pig cheaper than some others, but when it comes to the foundry floor, South Tredegar can choke us off in less'n a week."

"Wait," said Tom, still rummaging. "There is one thing we can make — and sell."

"I'd like tolerable well to know what it is," was the hopeless rejoinder.

"You ought to know, better than any one else. It's cast-iron pipe — water-pipe. Where are the plans of that invention of yours that Farley wouldn't let you install?"

Caleb found the blue-prints, and his hands were trembling. The invention, a pit machine process for molding and casting water-and gas-pipe at a cost that would put all other makers of the commodity out of the field, had been wrought out and perfected in Tom's second Boston year. It was Caleb's one ewe lamb, and he had nursed it by hand through a long preparatory period.

Tom took the blue-prints and spread them on the desk, absorbing the details as his father leaned over him and pointed them out. He saw clearly that the invention would revolutionize pipe-making. The accepted method was to cast each piece separately in a floor flask made in two parts, rammed by hand, once for the drag and again for the cope, with reversings, crane-handlings and all the manipulations necessary for the molding of any heavy casting. But the new process substituted machinery. A cistern-like pit; a circular table pivoted over it, with a hundred or more iron flasks suspended upright from its edges; a huge crane carrying a mechanical ram, these were the main points of the machine which, with a single small gang of men, would do the work of an entire foundry floor.

"It's great!" said Tom enthusiastically. "I got your idea pretty well from your letters, but you've improved on it since then. I wonder Farley didn't snap at it."

"He was willin' to," said Caleb grimly. "Only he wanted me to transfer the patents to the company; in other words, to make him a present of the controlling interest. I bucked at that, and we come near havin' a fall-out. If there was any market for pipe now —"

"There is a market," said Tom hopefully. "I got a pointer on that before I left Boston. Did I tell you I had a little talk with Mr. Clarkson the day I came away?"

"No."

"Well, I did. I told him the conditions and asked his advice. Among other things, I spoke of this pipe pit of yours, and he said at once, 'There is your chance. Cast-iron water-pipe is like bread, or sugar, or butcher's meat — it's a necessity, in good times or bad. If that machine is practicable, you can make pipe for less than half the present labor cost.' Then we talked ways and means. Money is tighter than a shut fist — up East as well as everywhere else. But men with money to invest will still bet on a sure thing. Mr.

Clarkson advised me to try our own banks first. Failing with them, he authorized me to call on him. Now you know where I'm digging my sand."

The old iron-master sat back in his chair with his hands locked over one knee, once more taking the measure of this new creation calling itself Tom Gordon and purporting to be his son.

"Say, Buddy," he said at length, "are there many more like you out yonder in the big road? — young fellows that can walk right out o' school and tell their daddies how to run things?"

Tom's laugh was boyishly hearty.

"Plenty of 'em, pappy; lots of 'em! The old world is moving right along; it would be a pity if it didn't, don't you think? But about this pipe business: I want you to make over these patents to me."

"They're yours now, Tom; everything I've got will be yours in a little while," said the father; but his voice betrayed the depth of that thrust. Was the new Tom beginning so soon to grasp and reach out avariciously for the fruit of the old tree?

"You ought to know I don't mean it that way," said Tom, frowning a little. "But here is the way it sizes up. There is money in this pipe-making; some money now, and big money later on. Farley has refused to go into it unless you make it a company proposition; as president and a controlling stock-holder you can't very well go into it now without making it in some sort a company proposition. But you can transfer the patents to me, and I can contract with Chiawassee Consolidated to make pipe for me."

Caleb Gordon's frown matched that of his son.

"That would certainly be givin' Colonel Duxbury a dose of his own medicine; but I don't like it, Tom. It looks as if we were taking advantage of him."

"No. I'd make the proposition to him, personally, if he were here, and the boss; and he'd be a fool if he didn't jump at it," said Tom earnestly. "But there is more to it than that. If we make a go of this, and don't protect ourselves, the two Farleys will come back and put the whole thing in their pockets. I won't go into it on any such terms. When they do come back, I'm going to have money to fight them with, and this is our one little ghost of a chance. Ring up Judge Bates and get him to come over here and make a legal transfer of these patents to me."

The thing was done, though not without some misgivings on Caleb's part. Honesty and fair dealing, even with a known enemy, had been the rule of his life; and while he could not put his finger on the equivocal thing in Tom's plan, he was vaguely troubled. Analyzed after the fact, the trouble was vicarious, and for Tom. It defined itself more clearly when they went together to South

Tredegar to have an attorney draw up the agreement under which Tom's pipe venture was to be conducted. Tom, as the owner of the patents, was fair with the Chiawassee Consolidated, but he was not liberal; indeed, he would have been quite illiberal if the attorney had not warned him that an agreement, to be defensible, must be equitable as well as legal.

At this stage in the journey Tom could not have accounted for himself in the ethical field. Something, a thing intangible, had gone out of him. He could not tell what it was; but he missed it. The kindly Gordon nature was intact, or he hoped it was, but the neighbor-love, which was his father's rule of life, seemed not to have come down to him in its largeness. Ruth for the Farleys was not to be expected of him, he argued; but behind this was a vaster ruthlessness, arming him to win the industrial battle, making him a hard man as he had suddenly become a strong one.

And the experiences of the summer were all hardening. He plunged headlong into the world of business, into a panic-time competition which was in grim reality a fight for life, and there seemed to be little to choose between trampling or being trampled. By early autumn the iron industries of the country were gasping, and the stacks of pig in the Chiawassee yards, kept down a little during the summer by a few meager orders, grew and spread until they covered acres. As long as money could be had, the iron was bonded as fast as it was made, and the proceeds were turned into wages to make more. But when money was no longer obtainable from this source, the pipe venture was the only hope.

With the entire foundry force at the Chiawassee making pipe, Tom had gone early into the market with his low-priced product. But the commercial side of the struggle was fire-new to him, and he found himself matched against men who knew buying and selling as he knew smelting and casting. They routed him, easily at first, with increasing difficulty as he learned the new trade, but always with certainty. It was Norman, the correspondence man, transformed now into a sales agent, who gave him his first hint of the inwardnesses.

"We're too straight, Mr. Gordon; that's at the bottom of it," he said to Tom, over a grill-room luncheon at the Marlboro one day. "It takes money to make money."

Tom's eyebrows went up and his ears were open. The battle had grown desperate.

"Our prices are right," he said. "Isn't that enough?"

"No," said Norman, looking down. Like all the others, he stood a little in awe of the young boss.

"Why?"

"Four times out of five we have to sell to a municipal committee, and the other time we have to monkey with the purchasing agent of a corporation. In either case it takes money — other money besides the difference in price."

Tom wagged his head in a slow affirmative. "It's rotten!" he said.

Norman smiled.

"It's our privilege to cuss it out; but it's a condition."

Tom was in town that day for the purpose of taking a train to Louisville, where he was to meet the officials of an Indiana city forced, despite the hard times, to relay many miles of worn-out water-mains. He made a pencil computation on the back of an envelope. The contract was a large one, and his bid, which he was confident was lower than any competitor could make, would still stand a cut and leave a margin of profit. Before he took the train he went to the bank, and, when he reached the Kentucky metropolis, his first care was to assure the "wheel-horse" member of the municipal purchasing board that he was ready to talk business on a modern business basis.

Notwithstanding, he lost the contract. Other people were growing desperate, too, it appeared, and his bribe was not great enough. One member of the committee stood by him and gave him the facts. A check had been passed, and it was a bigger check than Tom could draw without trenching on the balance left in the Iron City National to meet the month's pay-roll at Gordonia.

"You sent a boy to mill," said the loyal one. "And now it's all over, I don't mind telling you that you sent him to the wrong mill, at that. Bullinger's a hog."

"I'd like to do him up," said Tom vindictively.

"Well, that might be done, too. But it would cost you something."

Tom did not take the hint; he was not buying vengeance. But on the way home he grew bitterer with every subtracted mile. He could meet one more pay-day, and possibly another; and then the end would come. This one contract would have saved the day, and it was lost.

The homing train, rushing around the boundary hills of Paradise, set him down at Gordonia late in the afternoon. There was no one at the station to meet him, but there was bad news in the air which needed no herald to proclaim it. Though it still wanted half an hour of quitting time, the big plant was silent and deserted.

Tom walked out the pike and found his father smoking gloomily on the Woodlawn porch.

"You needn't say it, son," was his low greeting, when Tom had flung himself into a chair. "It was in the South Tredegar papers this morning."

"What was in the papers?"

"About our losin' the Indiany contract. I reckon it was what did the business for us, though there were a-plenty of black looks and a storm brewin' when we missed the pay-day yesterday."

Tom started as if he had been stung.

"Missed the pay-day? Why, I left money in bank for it when I went to Louisville!"

"Yes, I know you did. When Dyckman didn't come out with the pay-rolls yesterday evening I telephoned him. He said Vint Farley, as treasurer of the company, had made a draft on him and taken it all."

Tom sprang out of his chair and the bitter oaths upbubbled and choked him. But he stifled them long enough to say: "And the men?"

"The miners went out at ten o'clock this morning. The blacks would have stood by us, but Ludlow's men drove 'em out — made 'em quit. We're done, Buddy."

Tom dashed his hat on the floor, and the Gordon rage, slow to fire and fierce to scorch and burn when once it was aflame, made for the moment a yelling, cursing maniac of him. In the midst of it he turned, and the tempest of imprecation spent itself in a gasp of dismay. His mother was standing in the doorway, thin, frail, with the sorrow in her eyes that had been there since the long night of chastenings three years agone.

As he looked he saw the growing pallor in her face, the growing speechless horror in her gaze. Then she put out her hands as one groping in darkness and fell before he could reach her.

It was her stalwart son who carried Martha Gordon to her room and laid her gently on the bed, with the husband to follow helplessly behind. Also, it was Tom, tender and loving now as a woman, who sat upon the edge of the bed, chafing the bloodless hands and striving as he could to revive her.

"I'm afeard you've killed her for sure, this time, son!" groaned the man.

But Tom saw the pale lips move and bent low to catch their whisperings. What he heard was only the echo of the despairing cry of the broken heart: "*Would God I had died for thee, O Absalom, my son!*"

XXI

GILGAL

In these days of slowing wheels and silenced anvils South Trede-gar had its own troubles, and when some one telephoned the editor of the *Morning Tribune* that Chiawassee Consolidated had succumbed at last, he did not deem it worth while to inquire whether the strike at Gordonia was the cause or the consequence of the sudden shut-down.

But a day or two later, when rumors of threatened violence began to trickle in over the telephone wires, a *Tribune* man called, in passing, at the general offices in the Coosa Building, and was promptly put to sleep by the astute Dyckman, who, for reasons of his own, was quite willing to conceal the true state of affairs. Yes, there was a suspension of active operations at Gordonia, and he believed there had been some hot-headed talk among the miners. But there would be no trouble. Mr. Farley was at present in London negotiating for English capital. When he should return, the capital stock of the company would be increased, and the plant would probably be removed to South Tredegar and en-larged.

All of which was duly jotted down to be passed into the *Tri-bune*'s archives; and the following morning Tom, doing guard duty with his father, the two Helgersons and a squad of the yard men at the threatened plant, read a pointless editorial in which misstatement of fact and sympathy for the absent and struggling Farleys were equally and impartially blended.

"Look at that!" he growled wrathfully, handing the paper across the office desk to Caleb. "One of these fine days I'm going to land that fellow Dyckman in the penitentiary."

The iron-master put on his spectacles and plodded slowly and conscientiously through the editorial, turning the paper, at length, to glance over the headings on the telegraphic page. In the middle of it he looked up suddenly to say:

"Son, what was the name o' that Indiany town with the big water-pipe contract?"

Tom gave it in a word, and Caleb passed the paper back, with his thumb on one of the press despatches.

"Read that," he said.

Tom read, and the wrathful scowl evoked by the foolish edito-rial gave place to a flitting smile of triumph. There was trouble in the Indiana city over the awarding of the pipe contract. In some way unknown to the press reporter, it had leaked out that a much lower bid than the one accepted had been ignored by the purchasing committee. A municipal election was pending, and the people were up in arms. Rumors of a wholesale indictment of the suspected officials were rife, and the city offices were in a state of siege.

Tom put the paper down and smote on the desk.

"Damn them!" he said; "I thought perhaps I could give them a run for their money."

"You?" said Caleb, removing his glasses. "How's that?"

The new recruit in the army of business chicane nodded his head.

"It was a shot in the dark, and I didn't want to brag beforehand," he explained. "I wrestled it out Saturday night when I was tramping the hills after Doc Williams had brought mother around. One member of the purchasing committee was ready to dodge; he gave me a pointer before I left Louisville. I didn't see anything in it then but revenge; but afterward I saw how we might spend some money to a possible advantage."

Caleb's eyes had grown narrow.

"I reckon I'm sort o' dull, Buddy; what-all did you do?"

"Wired the disgruntled one that there was a letter and a check in the mail for him, to be followed by another and a bigger if his pole proved long enough to reach the persimmons."

The old iron-master left his chair and began to walk the floor, six steps and a turn. After a little he said:

"Tom, is that business?"

"It is the modern definition of it."

"What's goin' to happen up yonder in Indiany?"

"If I knew, I'd be a good bit easier in my mind. What I'm hoping is that the rumpus will be big enough to make 'em turn the contract our way."

Caleb stopped short.

"My God!" he ejaculated. "Where's your heart, Buddy? Would you take the chance of sendin' these fellows to jail for the sake of gettin' that contract?"

"Cheerfully," said Tom. "They're rascals; I could have bought them if I'd had money enough; and the other fellow did buy them."

The old man resumed his monotonous tramp up and down the room. The hardness in Tom's voice unnerved him. After another interval of silence he spoke again.

"I wish you hadn't done it, son. It's a dirty job, any way you look at it."

Tom shrugged.

"Norman says it's a condition, not a theory; and he is right.

We are living under a new order of things, and if we want to stay alive, we've got to conform to it. It gagged me at first: I reckon there are some traces of the Christian tradition left. But, pappy, I'm going to win. That is what I'm here for."

Caleb Gordon shook his head as one who deprecates help-lessly, but he sat down again and asked Tom what the programme was to be.

"There is nothing for us to do but to sit tight and wait. If we get a telegram from Indiana before these idiots of ours lose their heads and go to rioting and burning, we shall still have a fighting chance. If not, we're smashed."

"You mustn't be too hard on the men, Buddy. They've been mighty patient."

The scowl deepened between the level gray eyes.

"If I could do what I'd like to, I'd fire the last man of them. It makes me savage to have them turn up and knock us on the head after we've been sweating blood to pull through. Have you seen Ludlow?"

"Yes; I saw him last night. He's right ugly; swore he wouldn't raise a hand even if the boys took kerosene and dynamite to us."

"Well, if they do, he'll be the first man to pay for it," said Tom; and he left the office and the house to make the round of the guarded gates.

Ludlow was as good as his word. On the night following the day of suspense an attempt was made to wreck the inclined rail-way running from the mines on Lebanon to the coke yard. It was happily frustrated; but when Tom and his handful of guards got back to the foot of the hill they found a fire started in a pile of wooden flasks heaped against the end of the foundry building.

The fire was easily extinguishable by a willing hand or two, but Tom tried an experiment. Steam had been kept up in a single battery of boilers against emergencies, and he directed Helgerson to throw open the great gates while he ran to the boiler room and sent the fire call of the huge siren whistle shrieking out on the night.

The experiment was only meagerly successful. Less than a score of the strikers answered the call, but these worked with a will, and the fire was quickly put out.

Tom was under the arc-light at the gates when the volunteers straggled out. He had a word for each man, — a word of appreciation and a plea for suspended judgment. Most of the men shook their heads despondently, but a few of them promised to stand on the side of law and order. Tom took the names of the few, and went back to his guard duty with the burden a little lightened. But the succeeding night there were more attempts at violence, three of them so determined as to leave no doubt that the crisis was at hand. This was Tom's discouraged admission when his father came to relieve him in the morning.

"We're about at the end of the rope," he said wearily, when Caleb had closed the door of the log-house yard office behind him. "The two Helgersons are played out, and neither of us can stand this strain for another twenty-four hours. I'm just about dead on my feet for sleep, and I know you are."

The old ex-artilleryman stifled a yawn, and admitted the fact.

"I'm gettin' right old and no-account, son; there's no denyin' that. And you can't make out to shoulder it all, stout as you are. But what-all can we do different?"

"I know what I'm going to do. I had a 'phone wire from Bradley, the sheriff, last night after you went home. He funked like a boy; said he couldn't raise a posse in South Tredegar that would serve against striking workmen. Then I wired the governor, and his answer came an hour ago. We can have the soldiers if we make a formal demand for them."

"But, Tom, son; you wouldn't do that!" protested Caleb tremulously. Then, getting up to walk the floor as was his wont under sharp stress: "Let's try to hold out a little spell longer, Buddy. It'll be like fire to tow; there'll be men killed — men that I've known ever since they were boys: men killed, and women made widders. Tom, I've seen enough of war to last me."

"I know," said Tom. None the less, he found a telegraph blank and began to write the message. There had been shots fired in the night, in a sally on the inclined railway, and one of them had scored his arm. If the rioters needed the strong hand to curb them, they should have it.

"Think of what it'll mean for this town that we've built up, son. We'll have to stay here — 'er leastwise, I will, and there'll be blood on the streets for me to see as long as I walk 'em."

"I know," Tom reiterated, in the same monotonous tone. But his pen did not pause.

"Then there's your mammy," Caleb pleaded, and now the pen stopped.

"Mother must not know."

"How can we he'p her knowin', Buddy? I tell you, son, the very stones o' Paradise'll rise up to testify against us, now, and at the last great day, maybe."

The frown deepened between the young man's eyes.

"The old, old phantom!" he said, half to himself. "Will it never be laid, even for those who know it to be a myth?" And then to his father: "It's no use, pappy. I tell you we've got to take this thing by the neck. See here; that's how near they came to settling me last night," and he showed the perforated coat-sleeve.

Caleb Gordon was silenced. He resumed his restless pacing while Tom signed the call for help, read it over methodically, and placed it between dampened sheets in the letter-press. He had pushed the electric button which summoned Stub Helgerson, when the door opened silently and Jeff Ludlow's boy thrust face and hand through the aperture.

"Well; what is it?" demanded Tom, more sharply than he meant to. The strain was beginning to tell on his nerves.

"Hit's a letter for you-all from Mr. Stamford at the dee-po," said the boy. "He allowed maybe you-all'd gimme a nickel for bringin' hit."

The coin was found and passed, and the small boy was whooping and yelling for Helgerson to come and let him through the gates when Tom tore the envelope across and read the telegram. It was from the Indiana city, and it was signed by the chairman of the Board of Public Works.

"Proposals for water-pipe have been reopened, and your bid is accepted. Wire how soon you can begin to ship eighteen-inch mains," was what it said. Tom handed it to his father and stepped quickly to the telephone. There was a little delay in getting the ear of the president of the Iron City National at South Tredegar, and the bounding, pulsing blood of impatience made it seem interminable.

"Is that you, Mr. Henniker? This is Gordon at the Chiawassee plant, Gordonia. We have secured that Indiana contract I was telling you about, and I'll be in to see you on the ten o'clock train. Will you save five minutes for me? Thank you. Good-by."

Tom hung the ear-piece on its hook and turned to face his father.

"Have you surrounded it?" he laughed, with a little quaver of excitement in his voice, which he had been careful to master in the announcement to the bank president. "We live, pappy; we live and win! Get word to the men to come up here at three o'clock for their pay. Tell them we blow in again tomorrow, and they can all come back to work and no questions asked. Can you stay on your feet long enough to do all that?"

Caleb was nodding gravely; yet bewilderment was still in the saddle.

"But the money for the pay-rolls, son — this is only an order to go to work," he said, fingering the telegram doubtfully.

Tom laughed joyously.

"If I can't make Mr. Henniker believe that he can afford to carry us a while longer on the strength of that bit of yellow paper, I'll rob his bank. You get the men together by three o'clock, and

I'll be here with the money. If I'm not, it will be because somebody has sandbagged me between the bank and the train."

Caleb was still wrestling with the incredible thing, but light was breaking in on him slowly.

"Hold on, son," he said, and the old-time smile was wrinkling at the corners of his eyes; "how much did you allow to make out o' this job? I disremember what you said when you talked about it before."

Tom checked off the items on his fingers.

"Enough to put us through the winter; enough to stand us on our feet independent of Duxbury Farley and his son; enough to let us pay Major Dabney the back royalties on the coal. More than this, it's going to use up iron — hundreds of tons of it. We'll buy out of our own yards, and the men shall have the back-pay dividends."

The general manager had taken his burned-out corn-cob pipe from his pocket and was looking at it speculatively.

"Well, now, if that's the case, I reckon I can go down to Hargis's and buy me a new pipe, Buddy; and I — I'll be switched if I don't do it right now."

And in such gladsome easing of the strain were the wheels of Chiawassee Consolidated oiled to their new whirlings on the road to fortune. If Caleb Gordon remembered how the miracle had been wrought, he said no word to clench his disapproval; and as for Tom — ah, well; it was not the first time in the history of the race that the end has served to justify the means — to make them clean and white and spotless, if need were.

XXII

LOVE

If Tom Gordon could have known how slightly the Dabney's European plans coincided with those of the Farleys, he might have had fewer heartburnings in those intervals when the harassing struggle for industrial existence gave him time to think of Ardea.

As a strict matter of fact, the voyage across, and some little guide-book touring of England, were the sum total of coincidence. On leaving London the Farleys set out on the grand tour which was to land them in Naples for the winter, while the Dabneys went directly to Paris and to a modest pension in the Rue Cambon to spend the European holiday in a manner better befitting the purse of a country gentleman.

So it befell that by the time Miss Eva Farley was rhapsodizing over the Rhine castles in twenty-page letters, boring Ardea a little, if the truth must be told, the Dabneys had settled down to their quiet life in the French capital. Ardea was anxious to do something with her music under a Parisian master — and was doing it. The Major found melancholy pleasure in reviewing at large the city of his son's long exile; and Miss Euphrasia came and went with one or the other of her cousins, as the exigencies of chaperonage or companionship constrained her.

In such moderate pleasuring the French summer began for the Major and his charges; so it continued, and so it ended; and late in September they began to talk about going home.

"We really mean it this time," wrote Ardea in a letter to Martha Gordon. "I confess we are all a little homesick for America, and Paradise, and dear old Deer Trace Manor. The Farleys are settled for the remainder of the year or longer in a fine old palazzo on the Bay of Naples, and we have a very pressing invitation to go and help them inhabit it. But thus far we have not been tempted beyond our strength. Major Grandpa is talking more and more pointedly about the Morgan mares, and is growing a habit of comparison-drawing in which America profits at the expense of Europe; so I suppose by the time you are reading this we shall have made our sailing arrangements. Nevertheless, the Naples invitation is dying hard. Eva seems to have set her heart on having us for the winter."

Ardea's figure of speech was no figure. The palazzo-sharing invitation did die hard; and when Miss Farley's letters failed, Mr. Vincent Farley made a journey to Paris for the express purpose of persuading the Dabneys to reconsider. Miss Euphrasia was neutral. The Major was homesick for a sight of his native Southland, but for Ardea's sake he generously concealed the symptoms — or thought he did. So the decision was finally left to Ardea.

She said no, and adhered to it, partly because she knew her grandfather was pining for Paradise, and partly on her own account. Ardea at twenty was a young woman who might have made King Solomon pause with suspended pen when he was writing that saying about his inability to find one woman among a thousand. She was not beautiful beyond compare, as the Southern young woman is so likely to be under the pencil of her loyal limners. She had the Dabney nose, which was not quite classical, and the Courtenay mouth, well-lined and expressive, rather than too suggestive, of feminine softness. But her eyes were beautiful, and her luxuriant masses of copper-gold hair fitted her shapely head like a glorious aureole; also, she had that indefinable adorableness called charm, and the sweet, direct, childlike frankness of speech which is its characteristic.

This was the external Ardea, known of men, and of those women who were large-minded enough not to envy her. But the inner Ardea was a being apart — high-seated, alone, self-sufficient in the sense that it saw too clearly to be hoodwinked, infinitely reasonable, with vision unclouded either by passion or the conventions. This inner Ardea knew Vincent Farley better than he knew himself: the small mind, the mask of outward correctness, the coldness of heart, the utter lack of the heroic soul-strength which, even in a brutal man, may sometimes draw and conquer and merge within itself the woman-soul that, yielding, still yields open-eyed and undeceived.

He was the most moderate of lovers, as such a man must needs be, but his anxiety to second the wishes of his father and sister was not to be misunderstood by the clear-eyed inner Ardea, whose intuition served her as a sixth sense. She knew that sometime he would ask her to marry him; and in that region where her answer should lie she found only a vast indecision. He was not her ideal, but the all-seeing inner self told her that she would never find the ideal. There comes to every woman, sooner or later, the conviction that if she would marry she must take men as they are, weighing the good against the evil, choosing as she may the man whose vices may be condoned or whose virtues are great enough to overshadow them. Ardea knew that Vincent Farley was not great in either field; but the little virtues were not to be despised. If he were not, in the best sense of the word, well-bred, he had at least been well nurtured, well schooled in the conventions. Ardea sighed. It was in her to be something more than the conventional wife, yet she saw no reason to believe that she would ever be called on to be anything else. By which it will be apparent that the sacred flame of love had not yet been kindled in her maiden heart.

As for Vincent Farley, the real man, Ardea's appraisal of him was not greatly at fault. He was tall, like his father, but there the resemblance paused. The promoter's shifty blue eyes were always at the point of lighting up with enthusiasm; the son's, of precisely the same hue, were cold and calmly calculating. The human polyhedron has as many facets as a curiously-cut gem, and Vincent Farley's gift lay in the ability always to present the same side to the same person. His attitude toward Ardea had always been a pose; but it was a pose maintained so faithfully that it had become one of the facets of the polyhedron. Such men do not love, as a woman defines love; they merely have the mating instinct. And even lust finds a cold hearth in such hearts, though on occasion it will rake the embers together and make shift to blow them into some brief, fierce flame. At times, Farley's thought of Ardea was libertine; but oftener she figured as the woman who would grace the home of affluence, giving it charm and tone. Also, he had an affection for the Dabney manorial acres, and especially for that portion of them overlying the coal measures.

The pose-facet was at the precisely effective angle when he came to Paris as his sister's messenger and pictured, with what warmth there was in him, the delights in the prospect of a Neapolitan winter. But Ardea, shrinking from a six months' guesting with any one, said no, and told her grandfather she was ready to go home.

The start was from Havre, and Vincent, with time on his hands, was her companion on the railway journey, her *courrier du place* in the embarkation, and her faithful shadow up to the instant when the warning cry for the shore-goers rang through the ship. It was scarcely a moment for sentimental passages, and under the most favoring conditions, Vincent Farley was something less than sentimental. Yet he found time to declare himself in conventional fashion, modestly asking only for the right to hope.

Ardea was not ready to give an answer, even to the tentative question; yet she did it — was, in a manner, surprised into doing it. For the young woman who has not loved, it is easy to doubt the existence of the seventh Heaven, or at least to reckon without its possibilities. At the very crucial moment the clear-sighted inner self was assuring her that this cold-eyed young man, who walked in the paths of righteousness because he found them easier and pleasanter than the way of the transgressor, was at best only a mildly exciting apotheosis of the negative virtues. But the negative virtues, failing to score brilliantly, nevertheless have the advantage of continuous innings. Ardea was turned twenty in the year of the European holiday, and she had — or believed she had — her heritage of the Dabney impetuosity well in hand. Vincent's self-restraint was admirable, and his gentle deference, conventional as it was, rose almost to the height of sentiment. So she gave him his answer; gave him her hand at parting, and stood dutifully fluttering her handkerchief for him while the liner drew out of its slip and pointed its prow toward the headlands.

With rough weather on the homeward passage, she had space and opportunity to consider the consequences. Being the only good sailor in the trio, she had her own self-communings for company during the greater part of the six days, and the incident sentimental took on an aspect of finality which was rather dismaying. It was quite in vain that she sought comfort in the reflection that she was committed to nothing conclusive. Vincent Farley had not taken that view of it. True, he had asked for nothing more than a favorable attitude on her part; but she thought he would be less than a man if he had not seen his final answer foreshadowed in her acquiescence.

The finality admitted, a query arose. Was Vincent Farley the man who, giving her his best, could call out the best there was in her? It annoyed her to admit the query, or rather the doubt which fathered it; it distressed her when the doubt appeared to grow with the lengthening leagues of distance.

Now vacillation was not a Dabney failing; and the aftermath of these storm-tossed musings made for Vincent Farley's cause. Romance also, in the eternal feminine, is a constant quantity, and if it be denied the Romeo-and-Juliet form of expression, will find another. Vincent Farley, as man or as lover, presented obstacles to any idealizing process, but Ardea set herself resolutely to overcome them. Distance and time have other potentialities besides the obliterative: they may breed halos. When the French liner reached its New York slip, Ardea was remembering only the studied kindnesses, the conventional refinements, the correctnesses which, if they did seem artificial at times, were so many guarantees of self-respect: when the Great Southwestern train had roared around the cliffs of Lebanon with the returning exiles, and the locomotive whistle was sounding for Gordonia, some other of the negative virtues had become definitely positive, and the halo was beginning to be distinctly visible.

How Tom Gordon had informed himself of the precise day and train of their homecoming, Ardea did not think to inquire. But he was on the platform when the train drew in, and was the first to welcome them.

She was quick to see and appreciate the changes wrought in him, by time, by the Boston sojourn, by the summer's struggle with adverse men and things — though of this last she knew nothing as yet. It seemed scarcely credible that the big, handsome young fellow who was shaking hands with her grandfather, helping Miss Euphrasia with her multifarious belongings, and making himself generally useful and hospitable, could be a later reincarnation of the abashed school-boy who had sweated through the trying luncheon at Crestcliffe Inn.

"Not a word for me, Tom?" she said, when the last of Cousin Euphrasia's treasures had been rescued from the impatient train porter and added to the heap on the platform.

"All the words are for you — or they shall be presently," he laughed. "Just let me get your luggage out of pawn and started Deer-Traceward, and I'll talk you to a finish."

She stood by and looked on while he did it. Surely, he had grown and matured in the three broadening years! There was conscious manhood, effectiveness, in every movement; in the very bigness of him. She had a little attack of patriotism, saying to herself that they did not fashion such young men in the Old World — could not, perhaps.

Mammy Juliet's grandson, Pete, was down with the family carriage, and he took his orders from Tom touching the bestowal of the luggage as he would have taken them from Major Dabney. Ardea marked this, too, and being Southern bred, wrote the Gordon name still a little higher on the scroll of esteem. Pete's respectful obedience was, in its way, a patent of nobility. The negro house-servant, to the manner born, draws the line sharply between gentle and simple and is swift to resent interlopings.

When Pete had done his office with the European gatherings of the party the ancient carriage looked like a van, and there was scant room inside for three passengers.

"That means us for old Longfellow and the buggy," said Tom to Ardea. "Do you mind? Longfellow is fearfully and wonderfully slow, same as ever, but he's reasonably sure."

"Any way," said Ardea; so he put her into the buggy and they drew in behind the carriage. Before they were halfway to the iron-works they had the pike to themselves, and Tom was not urging the leisurely horse.

"My land! but it's good for tired eyes to have another sight of you!" he declared, applying the remedy till she laughed and blushed a little. Then: "It has been a full month of Sundays. Do you realize that?"

"Since we saw each other? It has been much longer than that, hasn't it?"

"Not so very much. I saw you in New York the day you sailed."

"You did! Where was I?"

"You had just come down in the elevator at the hotel with your grandfather and Miss Euphrasia."

"And you wouldn't stop to speak to us? I think that was simply barbarous!"

"Wasn't it?" he laughed. "But the time was horribly unpropitious."

"Why?"

He looked at her quizzically.

"I'm wondering whether I'd better lie out of it; say I knew you were on your way to breakfast, and that I hoped to have a later opportunity, and all that. Shall I do it?"

She did not reply at once. The undeceived inner self was telling her that here lay the parting of the ways; that on her answer would be built the structure, formal or confidential, of their future intercourse. Loyalty to the halo demanded self-restraint; but every other fiber of her was reaching out for a reëstablishment of the old boy-and-girl openness of heart and mind. Her hesitation was only momentary.

"You are just as rude and Gothic as you used to be, aren't you, Tom? Don't you know, I'm childishly glad of it; I was afraid you might be changed in that way, too, — and I don't want to find anything changed. You needn't be polite at the expense of truth — not with me."

He looked at her with love in his eyes.

"This time, you mean — or all the time."

"All the time, if you like."

"I do like; there has got to be some one person in this world to whom I can talk straight, Ardea."

She laughed a little laugh of half constraint.

"You speak as if there had been a vacancy."

"There has been — for just about three years. I remember you told me once that I'd find two kinds of friends: those who would refuse to believe anything bad of me, and those who would size me up and still stick to me. You are the only one of that second lot I have discovered thus far."

"We are getting miles away from the Fifth Avenue Hotel," she reminded him.

"No; we are just now approaching it from the proper direction. I had my war paint on that morning, and I wasn't fit to talk to you."

"Business?" she queried.

"Yes. Didn't the Major tell you about it?"

"Not a word. I hope you didn't quarrel with him, too?"

He marked the adverb of addition and wondered if Vincent Farley had been less reticent than Major Dabney.

"No; I didn't quarrel with your grandfather."

"But you did quarrel with Mr. Farley? — or was it with Vincent?"

He smiled and shook his head.

"We can't do it, Ardea — go back to the old way, you know. You see there's a stump in the road, the very first thing."

"I shan't admit it," she said half defiantly. "I am going to make you like the Farleys."

He shook his head again. "You'll have to make a Christian of me first, and teach me how to love my enemies."

"Don't you do that now?"

"No; not unless you are my enemy; I love you."

She looked up at him appealingly.

"Don't make fun of such things, Tom. Love is sacred."

"I was never further from making fun of things in my life. I mean it with every drop of blood in me. You said you didn't want to find me changed; I'm not changed in that, at least."

"You ridiculous boy!" she said; but that was only a stop-gap, and Longfellow added another by coming to a stand opposite a vast obstruction of building material half damming the white road. "What are you doing here — building more additions?" she asked.

"No," said Tom. "It is a new plant — a pipe foundry."

"Don't tell me we are going to have more neighbors in Paradise," she said in mock concern.

"I'll tell you something that may shock you worse than that: the owner of this new plant has camped down right next door to Deer Trace."

"How dreadful! You don't mean that!"

"Oh, but I do. He's a young man, of poor but honest parentage, with a large eye for the main chance. I shouldn't be surprised if he took every opportunity to make love to you."

"How absurd you can be, Tom! Who is he?"

"He is Mr. Caleb Gordon's son. I think you think you know him, but you don't; nobody does."

"Really, Tom? Have you gone into business for yourself? I thought you had another year at Boston."

"I have another year coming to me, but I don't know when I shall get it. And I am in business for myself; though perhaps I should be modest and call it a firm — Gordon and Gordon."

"What does the firm do?"

"A number of things; among others, it buys the entire iron output of the Chiawassee Consolidated, just at present."

"Dear me!" she said; "how fine and large that sounds! If I should say anything like that you would tell me that Brag was a good dog, but —"

He grinned ecstatically. It was so like old times — the good old times — to be bandying good-tempered abuse with her.

"I do brag a lot, don't I? But have you ever noticed that I 'most always have something to brag about? This time, for instance. I built this new firm, and it is all that has kept Chiawassee from going into the sheriff's hands any time during the past six months."

Longfellow had picked his way judiciously around the obstructions and through the gap in the boundary hills, and was jogging in a vertical trot up the valley pike made clean and hard and stony-white by the sweeping and hammering of the autumn rains. The mingled clamor of the industries was left behind, but the throbbing pulsations of the big blowing-engines hung in the air like the sighings of an imprisoned giant. They were passing the miniature copy of Morwenstow Church when Ardea spoke again.

"You have been home all summer?" she asked.

"At home and on the road, trying to hypnotize somebody into buying something — anything — made out of cast-iron. Ah, girl! it's been a bitter fight!"

She was instantly sympathetic; more, there was a little thrill of vicarious triumph to go with the sympathy. She was sure he had won, or was winning, the battle.

"We read something about the hard times in the American papers," she said. "You don't know how far away anything like that seems when there is an ocean between. And I was hoping all the time that our homeland down here was escaping."

"Escaping? You came through South Tredegar a little while ago; it is dead — too dead to bury. You hear the sob of those blowing-engines? — you will travel two hundred miles in the iron belt before you will hear it again. When I came home in June we were smashed, like all the other furnaces in the South — only worse."

"How worse, Tom?"

He forgot the tacit truce for the moment.

"Duxbury Farley and his son had deliberately wrecked the company."

She laid a restraining hand on his arm.

"Let us understand each other," she said gently. "You must not say such things of Mr. Farley and — and his son to me. If you do, I can't listen."

"You don't believe what I say?"

"I believe you have convinced yourself. But you are vindictive;

you know you are. And I mean to be fair and just."

He let the plodding horse measure a full half mile before he turned and looked at her with anger and despair glooming in his eyes.

"Tell me one thing, Ardea, and maybe it will shut my mouth. What is Vincent Parley to you — anything more than Eva's brother?"

Another young woman might have claimed her undoubted right to evade such a pointed question. But Ardea saw safety only in instant frankness.

"He has asked me to be his wife, Tom."

"And you have consented?"

"I wonder if I have," she said half musingly.

"Don't you *know*?" he demanded. And then, "Ardea, I'd rather see you dead and in your coffin!"

"Just why — apart from your prejudice?"

"It's Beauty and the Beast over again. You don't know Vint Farley."

"Don't I? My opportunities have been very much better than yours," she retorted.

"That may be, but I say you don't know him. He is a whited sepulcher."

"But you can not particularize," she insisted. "And the evidence is all the other way."

Tom was silent. During the summer of strugglings he had gone pretty deeply into the history of Chiawassee Consolidated, and there was commercial sharp practice in plenty, with some nice balancings on the edge of criminality. Once, indeed, the balance had been quite lost, but it was Dyckman who had been thrust into the breach, or who had been induced to enter it by falsifying his books. Yet these were mere business matters, without standing in the present court.

"The evidence isn't all one-sided," he asserted. "If you were a man, I could convince you in two minutes that both of the Farleys are rascals and hypocrites."

"Yet they are your father's business associates," she reminded him.

He saw the hopelessness of any argument on that side, and was silent again, this time until they had passed the Deer Trace gates and he had cut the buggy before the great Greek-pillared portico of the manor-house. When he had helped her out, she thanked him and gave him her hand quite in the old way; and he held it while he asked a single blunt question.

"Tell me one thing more, Ardea: do you love Vincent Farley?"

Her swift blush answered him, and he did not wait for her

word.

"That settles it; you needn't say it in so many words. Isn't it a hell of a world, Ardea? I love you — love you as this man never will, never could. And with half his chance, I could have made you love me. I —"

"Don't, Tom! please don't," she begged, trying to free her hand.

"I must, for this once; then we'll quit and go back to the former things. You said a while ago that I was vindictive; I'll show you that I am not. When the time comes for me to put my foot on Vint Farley's neck, I'm going to spare him for your sake. Then you'll know what it means to have a man's love. Good-by; I'm coming over for a few minutes this evening if you'll let me."

XXIII

TARRED ROPES

"Now jest you listen at me, Tom-Jeff; you ain't goin' to make out to find no better hawss 'n that this side o' the Blue Grass. Sound as a dollar in lung *and* leg, highstepper — my Land! jest look at the way he holds his head — rides like a baby's cradle; why, that hawss is a perfect gentleman, Tom-Jeff."

Since her return from Europe Miss Ardea Dabney had taken to horseback riding, a five-mile canter before breakfast in the fine brisk air of the autumn mornings; and Tom had discovered that he needed a saddle animal. Wherefore Brother Japheth was parading a handsome bay up and down before the door of the small office building of the new foundry, descanting glowingly on its merits, while Tom lounged on the step and pretended to make difficulties.

"You think he's a pretty good horse, do you, Japhe — worth the money?" he queried, with the air of one who is about to surrender, not to the fact, but to the presentation of it.

"If you cayn't stable him this winter and then get your money back on him in ary hawss market this side o' the Ohio River, I'll eat hawss for the rest o' my bawn days. Now that's fair, ain't it?"

"It's more than fair; it's generous. But let me ask you: is this protracted-meeting talk you're giving me, or just plain, every-day horse lies?"

Brother Japheth halted the parade and there was aggrieved reproachfulness in every line of his long, lantern-jawed face.

"Now lookee here; I didn't 'low to find *you* a-sittin' in the seat of the scornful, Tom-Jeff; I shore didn't. Ain't the good cause precious to your soul no mo' sence you to'd loose f'om your mammy's apron-string?"

Tom's shrewd overlooking of the horse-trader spoke eloquently of the spiritual landmarks past and left behind.

"I don't know about you, Japhe. A fair half of the time you have me cornered; and the other half I'm wondering if you are just ordinary, canting hypocrite, like the majority of 'the brethren.'"

"Now see here, Tom-Jeff, you know a heap better'n that! First and fo'most, the majority ain't the majority, not by three sights and a horn-blow. Hit don't take more'n one good, perseverin' hypocrite in the chu'ch to spile the name o' chu'ch-member as fur as ye can holler it. You been on a railroad train and seen the conduc-tor havin' a furss with the feller 'at pays for one seat and tries to hog four, and you've set back and said, 'My gosh! what a lot o' swine the human race is when hit gits away f'om home!' And right at that ve'y minute, mebbe, ther' was forty-five 'r fifty other people in that cyar goin' erlong, mindin' their own business, and not hoggin' any more 'n they paid for."

Tom smiled. "And you think that's the way it is in the church, do you?"

"I don't think nare' thing about hit; I know sufferin' well that's the how of it. Lord forgive me! didn't I let one scribe-an'-Pharisee keep me out o' the Isra'l o' God for nigh on to twenty year?"

"Who was it?" asked Tom, tranquilly curious.

"That ther' Jim Bledsoe, Brother Bill Layne's brother-in-law. He kep' Brother Bill out, too, for a right smart spell."

Tom was turning the memory pages half absently.

"Let me see," he said. "Didn't I hear something about your whaling the everlasting daylights out of Bledsoe sometime last winter?"

Japheth hung his head after the manner of one who has spoiled a good argument by overstating it.

"That ther's jest like me," he said disgustedly. "I nev' do know enough to quit when I git thoo. Ain't it somewhere's in the Bible 'at it says some folks is bawn troublesome, and some goes round huntin' for trouble, and some has trouble jammed up ag'inst 'em?"

"You can't prove it by me," Tom laughed. "I believe Shakespeare said something like that about greatness."

"Well, nev' mind; whoa, Saladin, boy, we'll git round to you ag'in, bime-by. As I was sayin', this here furss with Jim Bledsoe jest natchelly couldn't be holped, nohow. Hit was thisaway: 'long late in the fall I swapped Jim a piebald that was jest erbout the no-accountest hawss 'at ever had a bit in his mouth. I done told Jim all his meanness; but Jim, he 'lowed I was lyin' and made the trade anyhow. Inside of a week he was back here, callin' me names. I turned him first one cheek and then t'other, like the Good Book says, till they was jest plum' wo' out; and then I says, says I: 'Lookee here, Jim, you've done smack' me on both sides o' the jaw, and that ther's your priv'lege — me bein' a chu'ch-member in good and reg'lar standin', and no low-down, in-fergotten, turkey-trodden hypocrite like you. But right here the torections erbout what I'm bounden to do sort o' peter out. I got as many cheeks to turn as any of 'em, but that ain't sayin' that the stock's immortil' With that he ups and allows a heap mo' things about my morils; and me havin' turned both cheeks till my neck ached, and not havin' any mo' *toe* turn, what-all could I do — what-all would you 'a' done, Tom-Jeff?"

"Don't ask me. I'm one of the hair-hung and breeze-shaken majority. I should most probably have punched his head."

"Well, that's jest what I did. I says, says I, 'Jim, whom the Lord loveth He chasteneth, and jest at this time present, I'm the instru*ment*.' And when the dust got settled down, Jim he druv' home with that ther' piebald, allowin' he wasn't such an all-fired bad hawss after all. But lookee here, Tom-Jeff, this ain't sellin' you the finest saddle-hawss in the valley. What do ye say about Saladin?"

"Oh, I don't know," said Tom. "I don't love horses very much. You know what the Bible says: *A horse is a vain thing for safety*. Is this bay going to make me lose my temper and knock his pinhead brains out the first time I put a leg over him?"

"No-o-o, suh! Why, he's as kind and gentle and lovin as a woman. You jest natchelly *couldn't* whup this here bay, Tom-Jeff!"

"All right, Japhe; I was only deviling you a little. Take him up to the Woodlawn stables and tell William Henry Harrison to give him the box stall. I'll try him tomorrow morning, if the weather is good."

Brother Japheth's business was concluded, and the architect who was building the latest extension to the pipe-pit floor was heading across the yard to consult the young boss. Pettigrass paused with his foot in the stirrup to say, "Old Tike Bryerson's on the rampage ag'in; folks up at the valley head say he's a-lookin' for you, Tom-Jeff."

"For me?" said Tom; then he laughed easily. "I don't owe him anything, and I'm not very hard to find. What's the matter?"

He thought it a little singular at the time that Japheth gave him a curious look and mounted and rode away without answering his question. But the building activities were clamoring for time and attention, and his father was waiting to consult him about a run of iron that was not quite up to the pipe-making test requirements. So he forgot Japheth's half accusing glance at parting, and the implied warning that had preceded it, until an incident at the day's end reminded him of both.

The incident turned on the fact of his walking home. Ordinarily he struck work when the furnace whistle blew, riding home with his father behind old Longfellow; but on this particular evening Kinderling, the architect, missed his South Tredegar train, and Tom spent an extra hour with him, discussing further and future possibilities of expansion. Kinderling got away on a later train, and Tom closed his office and took the long mile up the pike afoot in the dusk of the autumn evening, thinking pointedly of many things mechanical and industrial, and never by any chance forereaching to the epoch-marking event that was awaiting him at the Woodlawn gate.

His hand was upon the latch of the ornamental side wicket opening on the home foot-path when a woman, crouching in the shadow of the great-gate pillar, rose suddenly and stood before him. He did not recognize her at first; it was nearly dark, and her head was snooded in a shawl. Then she spoke, and he saw that it was Nancy Bryerson — a Nan sadly and terribly changed, but with much of the wild-creature beauty of face and form still remaining.

"You done forgot me, Tom-Jeff?" she asked; and then, at his start of recognition: "I allow I have changed some."

"Surely I haven't forgotten you, Nan. But you took me by surprise; and I can't see in the dark any better than most people. What are you doing down here in the valley so late in the evening?" He tried to say it superiorly, paternally, as an older man might have said it — and was not altogether successful. The mere sight of her set his blood aswing in the old throbbing ebb and flow, though, if he had known it, it was pity now rather than passion that gave the impetus.

"You allow it ain't fittin' for me to be out alone after night?" she said, with a hard little laugh. "I reckon it ain't goin' to hurt me none; anyways, I had to come. Paw's been red-eyed for a week, and he's huntin' for you, Tom-Jeff."

Then Tom recalled Japheth's word of the morning.

"Hunting for me? Well, I'm not very hard to find," he said, unconsciously repeating the answer he had made to the horse-trader's warning.

"Couldn't you make out to go off somewheres for a little spell?" she asked half pleadingly.

"Run away, you mean? Hardly; I'm too busy just at present. Besides, I haven't any quarrel with your father. What's he making trouble about now?"

She put her face in her hands, and though she was silent, he could see that sobs were shaking her. Being neither more nor less than a man, her tears made him foolish. He put his arm around her and was trying to find the comforting word, when the heavens fell.

How Ardea and Miss Euphrasia, going the round-about way from one house to the other to avoid the dew-wet grass of the lawns, came fairly within arm's-reach before he saw or heard them, remained a thing inexplicable. But when he looked up they were there, Miss Euphrasia straightening herself aloof in virtuous disapproval, and Ardea looking as if some one had suddenly shown her the head of Medusa.

Tom separated himself from Nan in hot-hearted confusion and stood as a culprit taken in the act. Nan hid her face again and turned away. It was Miss Dabney the younger who found words to break the smarting silence.

"Don't mind us, Mr. Gordon," she said icily. "We were going to Woodlawn to see if your father and mother could come over after dinner."

Tom smote himself alive and made haste to open the foot-path gate for them. There was nothing more said, or to be said; but when they were gone and he was once more alone with Nan, he was fighting desperately with a very manlike desire to smash something; to relieve the wrathful pressure by hurting somebody. Let it be written down to his credit that he did not wreak his vengeance on the defenseless. Thomas Jefferson, the boy, would not have hesitated.

[Illustration: Tom made haste to open the foot-path gate for them.]

"You were going to tell me about your father," he said, striving to hold the interruption as if it had not been, and yet tingling in every nerve to be free. "Did you come all the way down the mountain to warn me?"

She nodded, adding: "But that didn't make no differ'; I had to come anyway. He run me out, paw did."

"Heavens!" ejaculated Tom, prickling now with a new sensation. "And you haven't any place to stay?"

She shook her head.

"No. I was allowin' maybe your paw'd let me sleep where you-uns keep the hawsses — jest for a little spell till I could make out what-all I'm goin' to do."

He was too rageful to be quite clear-sighted. Yet he conceived that he had a duty laid on him. Once in the foolish, infatuated long-ago he had told her he would take care of her; he remembered it; doubtless she was remembering it, too. But her suggestion was not to be considered for a moment.

"I can't let you go to the stables," he objected. "The horse-boys sleep there. But I'll put a roof over you, some way. Wait here a minute till I come back."

His thought was to go to his mother and ask her help; but halfway to the house his courage failed him. Since the breach in spiritual confidence he had been better able to see the lovable side of his mother's faith; but he could not be blind to that quality of hardness in it which, even in such chastened souls as Martha Gordon's, finds expression in woman's inhumanity to woman. Besides, Ardea and her cousin were still in the way.

He swung on his heel undecided. On the hillside back of the new foundry there was a one-roomed cabin built on the Gordon land years before by a hermit watchman of the Chiawassee plant.

It was vacant, and Tom remembered that the few bits of furniture had not been removed when the old watchman died. Would the miserable shack do for a temporary refuge for the outcast? He concluded it would have to do; and, making a wide circuit of the house, he went around to the stables to harness Longfellow to the buggy. Luckily, the negroes were all in the detached kitchen, eating their supper, so he was able to go and come undetected.

When he drove down to the gate he found Nan waiting where he had left her; but now she had a bundle in her arms. As he got out to swing the driveway grille, the house door opened; a flood of light from the hall lamp banded the lawn, and there were voices and footsteps on the veranda. He flung a nervous glance over his shoulder; Ardea and her cousin were returning down the foot-path. Wherefore he made haste, meaning not to be caught again, if he could help it. But the fates were against him. Longfellow, snatched ruthlessly from his half emptied oat box, made equine protest, yawing and veering and earning himself a savage cut of the whip before he consented to place the buggy at the stone mounting-step.

"Quick!" said Tom, flinging the reins on the dashboard. "Chuck your bundle under the seat and climb in!"

But Nan was provokingly slow, and when she tried to get in with the bundle still in her arms, the buggy hood was in the way. Tom had to help her, was in the act of lifting her to the step, when the wicket latch, clicked and Ardea and Miss Euphrasia came out. They passed on without comment, but Tom could feel the electric shock of righteous scorn through the back of his head. That was why he drove halfway to the lower end of the pike before he turned on Nan to say:

"What's in that bundle you're so careful of? Why don't you put it under the seat?"

She looked around at him, and dark as it was, he saw that the great black eyes were shining with a strange light — strange to him.

"I reckon you wouldn't want me to do that, Tom-Jeff," she answered simply. "Hit's my baby — my little Tom."

He was struck dumb. It often happens that in the fiercest storm of gossip the one most nearly concerned goes his way without so much as suspecting that the sun is hidden. But Tom had not been exposed to the violence of the storm. Nan's shame was old, and the gossip tongues had wagged themselves weary two years before, when the child was born. So Tom was quite free to think only of his companion. A great anger rose and swelled in his heart. What scoundrel had taken advantage of an ignorance so profound as to be the blood sister of innocence? He would have given much to know; and yet the true delicacy of a manly soul made him hold his peace.

Thus it befell that they drove in silence to the deserted cabin on the hillside; and Tom went down to the foundry office and brought a lamp for light. The cabin was a mere shelter; but when he would have made excuses, Nan stopped him.

"Hit's as good as I been usen to, as you know mighty well, Tom-Jeff. I on'y wisht —"

He was on his knees at the hearth, kindling a fire, and he looked up to see why she did not finish. She was sitting on the edge of the old watchman's rude bed, bowed low over the sleeping child, and again sobs were shaking her like an ague fit. There was something heartrending in this silent, wordless anguish; but there was nothing to be said, and Tom went on making the fire. After a little she sat up and continued monotonously:

"*He* was liken to me thataway, too; the Man 'at I heard your Uncle Silas tellin' about one night when I sot on the doorstep at Little Zoar — He hadn't no place to lay His'n head; not so much as the red foxes 'r the birds . . . and I hain't."

The blaze was racing up the chimney now with a cheerful roar, and Tom rose to his feet, every good emotion in him stirring to its awakening.

"Such as it is, Nan, this place is yours, for as long as you want to stay," he said soberly. And then: "You straighten things around here to suit you, and I'll be back in a little while."

He was gone less than half an hour, but in that short interval he lighted another fire: a blaze of curiosity and comment to tingle the ears and loosen the tongues of the circle of loungers in Hargis's store in Gordonia. He ignored the stove-hugging contingent pointedly while he was giving his curt orders to the storekeeper; and the contingent avenged itself when he was out of hearing.

"Te-he!" chuckled Simeon Cantrell the elder, pursing his lips around the stem of his corn-cob pipe; "looks like Tom-Jeff was goin' to house-keepin' right late in the evenin'."

"By gol, I wonder what's doin'?" said another. "Reckon he's done tuk up with Nan Bryerson, afte' all's been said an' done?"

Bastrop Clegg, whose distinction was that of being the oldest loafer in the circle, spat accurately into the drafthole of the stove, sat back and tilted his hat over his eyes.

"Well, boys, I reckon hit's erbout time, ain't hit?" he moralized. "Leetle Tom must be a-goin' awn two year old; and I don't recommember ez Tom 'r his pappy has ever done a livin' thing for Nan."

Whereupon one member of the group got up and addressed himself to the door. It was Japheth Pettigrass; and what he said was said to the starlit night outside.

"My Lord! that ther' boy *was* lyin' to me, after all! I didn't believe hit that night when he r'ared and took on so to me and 'lowed to chunk me with a rock, and I don't want to believe hit now. But Lordy gracious! hit do look mighty bad, with him a-buyin' all that outfit and loadin' hit in his pappy's buggy; hit do, for shore!"

A half hour later, Brother Japheth, trudging back to Deer Trace on the pike, saw the light in the long-deserted cabin back of the new foundry plant; saw this and was overtaken at the Wood-lawn gates by Thomas Jefferson with Longfellow and the buggy. And he could not well help observing that the buggy had been lightened of its burden of household supplies.

Tom turned the horse over to William Henry Harrison and went in to his belated dinner somberly reflective. He was not sorry to find that his mother and father had gone over to the manor-house. Solitude was grateful at the moment; he was glad of the chance to try to think himself uninterruptedly out of the snarl of misunderstanding in which his impulsiveness had entangled him.

The pointing of the thought was to see Ardea and have it out with her at once. Reconsidered, it appeared the part of prudence to wait a little. The muddiest pool will settle if time and freedom from ill-judged disturbance be given it. But we, who have known Thomas Jefferson from his beginnings, may be sure that it was the action-thought that triumphed. *They also serve who only stand and wait,* was meaningless comfort to him; and when he had fin-ished his solitary dinner and had changed his clothes, he strode across the double lawns and rang the manor-house bell.

XXIV

THE UNDER-DEPTHS

The Deer Trace family and the two guests from Woodlawn were in the music-room when Tom was admitted, with Ardea at the piano playing war songs for the pleasuring of her grandfather and the ex-artilleryman. Under cover of the music, Tom slipped into the circle of listeners and went to sit beside his mother. There was a courteous hand-wave of welcome from Major Dabney, but Miss Euphrasia seemed not to see him. He saw and understood, and was obstinately impervious to the chilling east wind in that quarter. It was with Ardea that he must make his peace, and he settled himself to wait for his opportunity.

It bade fair to be a long time coming. Ardea's repertoire was apparently inexhaustible, and at the end of an added hour he began to suspect that she knew what was in store for her and was willing to postpone the afflictive moment. From the battle hymns of the Confederacy to the militant revival melodies best loved by Martha Gordon the transition was easy; and from these she drifted through a Beethoven sonata to Mozart, and from Mozart to Chopin.

Thomas Jefferson knew music as the barbarian knows it, which is to say that it lighted strange fires in him; stirred and thrilled him in certain heart or soul labyrinths locked against all other influences. As Ardea's fingers sought the changing chords he felt vaguely that she was speaking to him, now scorning, now rebuking, now pleading, but always in a tongue that he only half comprehended. He stole a glance at his watch, impatient to come to hand-grips with her and have it over. The suspense could not last much longer. It was past ten; the Major was dozing peacefully in his great armchair, and Miss Euphrasia yawned decorously behind her hand.

Ardea lingered lovingly on the closing harmonies of the nocturne, and when the final chord was struck her hands lingered on the keys until the sweet voices of the strings had sung themselves afar into the higher sound heaven. Then she turned quickly and surprised her anesthetized audience.

"You poor things!" she laughed. "In another five minutes the last one of you would have succumbed. Why didn't somebody stop me?"

The iron-master said something about the heavy work of the day, and helped his wife to her feet. The Major came awake with a start and bestirred himself hospitably, and Miss Euphrasia rose to speed the parting guests — or rather the two of them who had been invited. In the drift down the wide hall Ardea fell behind with Tom, whom Cousin Euphrasia continued to ignore.

"I came to tell you," he said in a low tone, snatching his opportunity. "I can't sleep until I have fought it out with you."

"You don't deserve a hearing, even from your best friend," was her discouraging reply; but when they were at the door she gave him a formal reprieve. "I shall walk for a few minutes on the portico to rest my nerves," she said. "If you want to come back —"

He thanked her gravely, and went obediently when his mother called to him from the steps. But on the Woodlawn veranda he excused himself to smoke a cigar in the open; and when the door closed behind the two in-going, he swiftly recrossed the lawns to pay the penalty.

The front door of the manor-house was shut and the broad, pillared portico was untenanted. He sat down in one of the rustic chairs and searched absently in his pockets for a cigar. Before he could find it the door opened and closed and Ardea stood before him. She had thrown a wrap over her shoulders, and the light from the music-room windows illuminated her. There was cool scorn in the slate-blue eyes, but in Tom's thought she had never appeared more unutterably beautiful and desirable — and unattainable.

"I have come," she said, in a tone that cut him to the heart for its very indifference. "What have you to say for yourself?"

He rose quickly and offered her the chair; and when she would not take it, he put his back to the wall and stood with her.

"I'm afraid I haven't left myself much to say," he began penitently. "I was born foolish, and it seems that I haven't outgrown it. But, really, if you could know —"

"Unhappily, I do know," she interrupted. "If I did not, I might listen to you with better patience."

"It did look pretty bad," he confessed. "And that's what I wanted to say; it looked a great deal worse than it was, you know."

"I *don't* know," she retorted.

"You are tangling me," he said, gaining something in self-possession under the flick of the whip. "First you say you know, and then you say you don't know. Which is which?"

"If you are flippant I shall go in," she threatened. "There are things that not even the most loyal friendship can condone."

"That's the difference between friendship and love," he asserted. "I believe I'd enjoy a little more real confidence and a little less of the dutiful kind of loyalty."

"You ask too much," she said, quite coolly. "Forgiveness implies penitence and continued good behavior."

"No, it doesn't, anything of the kind," he denied, matching her tone. "That is the purely pagan point of view, and you are barred from taking it. You are bound to consider the motive."

"I am bound to believe what I see with my own eyes," she rejoined. "Perhaps you can make it appear that seeing is not believing."

"Of course I can't, if you take that attitude," he complained. And then he said irritably: "You talk about friendship! You don't know the meaning of the word!"

"If I didn't, I should hardly be here at this moment," she suggested. "You don't seem to apprehend to what degrading depths you have sunk."

His sins in the business field rose before him accusingly and prompted his reply.

"Yes, I do; but that is another matter. We were speaking of what you saw this evening. Will you let me try to explain?"

"Yes, if you will tell the plain truth."

"Lacking imagination, I can't do anything else. Nan has had a falling-out with the old scamp of a moonshiner who calls himself her father. She came to me for help, and broke down in the midst of telling me about it. I can't stand a woman's crying any better than other men."

The slate-blue eyes were transfixing him.

"And that was all — absolutely all, Tom?"

"I don't lie — to you," he said briefly.

She gave him her hand with an impulsive return to the old comradeship. "I believe you, Tom, in the face of all the — the unlikelinesses. But please don't try me again. After what has happened — " she stopped in deference to something in his eyes, half anger, half bewilderment, or a most skilful simulation of both.

"Go on," he said; "tell me what has happened. I seem to have missed something."

"No," she said, with sudden gravity. "I don't want to be your accuser or your confessor; and if you should try to prevaricate, I should hate you!"

"There is nothing for me to confess to you, Ardea," he said soberly, still holding the hand she had given him. "You have known the worst of me, always and all along, I think."

"Yes, I *have* known," she replied, freeing the imprisoned hand and turning from him. "And I have been sorry, sorry; not less for you than for poor Nancy Bryerson. You know now what I thought — what I *had* to think — when I saw you with her this evening."

It was slowly beating its way into his brain. Little things, atoms of suggestion, were separating themselves from the mass of

things disregarded to cluster thickly on this nucleus of reveal-
ment: the old story of his companying with Nan on the mountain;
his uncle's and Japheth's accusation at the time; and now the old
moonshiner's enmity, Japheth's meaning look and distrustful
silence, Nan's appearance with a child bearing his own name, the
glances askance in Hargis's store when he was buying the little
stock of necessaries for the poor outcast. It was all plain enough.
For reasons best known to herself, Nan had not revealed the name
of her betrayer, and all Gordonia, and all Paradise, believed him to
be the man. Even Ardea . . .

She had moved aside out of the square of window light, and
he followed her.

"Tell me," he said thickly; "you heard this: you have believed
it. Have I been misjudging you?"

"Not more than I misjudged you, perhaps. But that is all over,
now: I am trusting you again, Tom. Only, as I said before, you
mustn't try me too hard."

"Let me understand," he went on, still in the same strained
tone. "Knowing this, or believing it, you could still find a place in
your heart for me — you could still forgive me, Ardea?"

"I could still be your friend; yes," she replied. "I believed —
others believed — that your punishment would be great enough;
there are all the coming years for you to be sorry in, Tom. But in
the fullness of time I meant to remind you of your duty. The time
has come; you must play the man's part now. What have you done
with her?"

"Wait a moment. I must know one other thing," he insisted.
"You heard this before you went to Europe?"

"Long before."

"And it didn't make any difference in the way you felt toward
me?"

"It did; it made the vastest difference." They were pacing
slowly up and down the portico, and she waited until they had
made the turn at the Woodlawn end before she went on. "I
thought I knew you when we were boy and girl together, and, girl-
like, I suppose I had idealized you in some ways. I thought I knew
your wickednesses, and that they were not weaknesses; so — so it
was a miserable shock. But it was not for me to judge you — only
as you might rise or sink from that desperate starting point. When
I came home I was sure that you had risen; I have been sure of it
ever since until — until these few wretched hours tonight. They
are past, and now I'm going to be sure of it some more, Tom."

It was his turn to be silent, and they had measured twice the
length of the pillared floor when at last he said:

"What if I should tell you that you are mistaken — that all of them are mistaken?"

"Don't," she said softly. "That would only be smashing what is left of the ideal. I think I couldn't bear that."

"God in Heaven!" he said, under his breath. "And you've been calling this friendship! Ardea, girl, it's *love*!"

She shook her head slowly.

"No," she rejoined gravely. "At one time I thought — I was afraid — that it might be. But now I know it isn't."

"How do you know it?"

"Because love, as I think of it, is stronger than the traditions, stronger than anything else in the world. And the traditions are still with me. I admit the existence of the social pale, and as long as I live within it I have a right to demand certain things of the man who marries me."

"And love doesn't demand anything," he said, putting the remainder of the thought into words for her. "You are right. If I could clear myself with a word, I should not say it."

"Why?"

"Because your — loyalty, let us call it, is too precious to be exchanged for anything else you could give me in place of it — esteem, respect, and all the other well-behaved and virtuous bestowals."

"But the loyalty is based on the belief that you are trying to earn the well-behaved approvals," she continued.

"No, it isn't. It exists 'in spite of' everything, and not 'because of' anything. The traditions may try to make you stand it on the other leg, it's a way they have; but the fact remains."

She shook her head in deprecation.

"The 'traditions,' are about to send me into the house, and the principal problem is yet untouched. What have you done with Nancy?"

He told her briefly and exactly, adding nothing and omitting nothing; and her word for it was "impossible."

"Don't you understand?" she objected. "I may choose to believe that this home making for poor Nan and her waif is merely a bit of tardy justice on your part and honor you for it. But nobody else will take that view of it. If you keep her in that little cabin of yours, Mountain View Avenue will have a fit — and very properly."

"I don't see why it should," he protested densely.

"Don't you? That's because you are still so hopelessly primeval. People won't give you credit for the good motive; they will quote that Scripture about the dog and the sow. You must think of some other way."

"Supposing I say I don't care a hang?"

"Oh, but you do. You have your father and mother and — and me to consider, however reckless you may be for yourself and Nancy. You mustn't leave her where she is for a single day."

"I can leave her there if I like. I've told her she may stay as long as she wants to."

They had paused in front of the great door, and Ardea's hand was on the knob.

"No," she said decisively, "you will have a perfect hornets' nest about your ears. Every move you make will be watched and commented on. Don't you see that you are playing the part of the headstrong, obstinate boy again?"

"Yet you think I ought to provide for Nan, in some way; how am I going to do it unless I ignore the hornets?"

"Now you are more reasonable," she said approvingly. "I shall ride tomorrow morning, and if you should happen to overtake me, we might think up something."

The door was opening gently under the pressure of her hand, but he was loath to go.

"I wouldn't take five added years of life for what I've learned tonight, Ardea;" he said passionately. And then: "Have you fully made up your mind to marry Vincent Farley?"

In the twinkling of an eye she was another woman — cold, unapproachable, with pride kindling as if she had received a mortal affront.

"Sometimes — and they are bad times for you, Mr. Gordon — I am tempted to forget the boy-and-girl anchorings in the past. Have you no sense of the fitness of things — no shame?"

"Not very much of either, I guess," he said quite calmly. "Love hasn't any shame; and it doesn't concern itself much about the fitness of anything but its object."

And then he bade her good night and went his way with a lilting song of triumph in his heart which not even the chilling rebuff of the leave-taking was sufficient to silence.

"She loves me! She would still love me if she were ten times Vincent Farley's wife!" he said, over and over to himself; the words were on his lips when he fell asleep, and they were still ringing in his ears the next morning at dawn-break when he rose and made ready to go to ride with her.

XXV

THE PLOW IN THE FURROW

One of Miss Ardea Dabney's illuminating graces was the ability to return easily and amicably to the *status quo ante bellum*; to "kiss and be friends," in the unfettered phrase of Margaret Catherwood, her chum and room-mate at Carroll College.

Wherefore, when Tom, mounted on Saladin, overtook her on the morning next after the night of offenses, she greeted him quite as if nothing had happened, challenging him gaily to a gallop with the valley head for its goal, and refusing to be drawn into anything more serious than joyous persiflage until they were returning at a walk down a boulder-strewn wood road at the back of the Dabney horse pasture. Then, and not till then, was the question of Nancy Bryerson's future suffered to present itself.

For Miss Dabney the question was settled before it came up for discussion. In the Major's young manhood Deer Trace had maintained a pack of foxhounds, and it was the Major's bride, a city-bred Charleston belle, who first objected to the dooryard kennels and the clamor of the dogs. Back of the horse pasture, and a hundred yards vertical above the road Ardea and Tom were traversing, a pocket-like glen indented the mountain side, and in this glen the kennels had been established, with a substantial log cabin for the convenience of the dog-keeper.

Dogs and dog-keeper had long since gone the way of most of the old-time Southern manorial largenesses; but the cabin still stood solidly planted in the midst of its overgrown garden patch, with a dense thicket of mountain laurel backgrounding it, and a giant tulip-tree standing sentinel over a gate hanging by one rusted hinge.

This was what Tom saw when he had followed Ardea's lead up the steep bit of path climbing from the road and the pasture wall, and it evoked memories. Often in the boyhood days, when the Nazarite fit was on, he had climbed to the deserted solitude of the glen to sit on the broad door-stone of the dog-keeper's cabin as a hermit at large, — monarch for the monastic moment of a kingdom as remote as that of John the Baptist in the Wilderness of Sin.

"I thought of it last night," said Ardea, nodding toward the cabin. "It is just the place for Nancy, if she can not, or will not, go back to her father. After breakfast, I shall send Dinah and a man up to set things in order, and she can come as soon as she likes. She won't mind the loneliness?"

Tom shook his head. "I should think not; she has never been used to anything else. I'll bring her and the youngster over in the buggy any time you telephone." He had quite forgotten his lesson of the previous evening.

"Indeed, you will do nothing of the kind," was the quick reply. "Japheth will go after her when we are ready; and if you are prudently wise you will have business in South Tredegar for the next few days."

The blue-grass, seeded once in the dog-keeper's dooryard, had spread to the farthest limits of the glen, and the autumn rains had given it a spring-like start. Tom let Saladin crop a dozen mouthfuls unchecked before he said:

"That looks like dodging; and I don't like to dodge."

"You will have to do many things you don't like before you say your *ave atque vale*," she remarked. "But you shall be permitted to carry your full share of the burden. I mean to let you give me some money, if you can afford it, and I'll spend it for you."

"Charity itself couldn't be kinder," he asseverated. "And, luckily, I can afford it. But —"

He was looking at her wistfully, and the old longing for sympathy, for the sympathy which has been quite to the bottom of the well where truth lies, was about to cry out against this riveting of the fetters of misunderstanding and false accusation.

"But you would rather spend it yourself?" she broke in, fancying she had divined his thought. "That cannot be. The one condition on which I shall consent to help is the completest isolation for Nan. You must promise me you will not try to see her. I am hoping against hope that none of the Mountain View Avenue people will find out what you did last night."

"Oh, confound their gossiping tongues!" he railed; adding hastily: "Not that I care so very much what they say, either."

Ardea let her horse pick his way down to the wood road, and when they were approaching the Deer Trace gate: "You haven't promised yet, Tom; and you must, you know."

"Not to see Nan? That's easy. I'll keep out of her way, if you can keep her out of mine. All I care is to know that she is comfortably provided for."

This he said, thinking only of the boy-time obligation voluntarily assumed; but it was quite inevitable that Ardea should mistake the motive.

"It is right and proper that you should care about that," she said judicially. And a little farther along she added: "But I don't like your attitude."

"I don't like it myself," he rejoined heartily. "I never wanted so badly to say things in all my life! But you've nailed the lid on and I can't."

"They are better unsaid," she returned quickly. "Will you take that for your cue in the future?"

"Certainly; it is for you to command," he said lightly, swinging from his saddle to open the pasture gate for her; and so the morning ride came to its end.

Since provincialism is by no means the exclusive distinction of the landward bred, there was an immediate restirring of the gossip pool when the story of Tom's befriending of Nancy Bryerson and her child got abroad in Gordonia and among the country colonists.

In the comment of the simpler-minded Gordonia folk, the iron-master's son had finally "made it up" with Nancy, and here the note of approval was not wholly lacking. There were good-hearted souls to say that boys will be boys, and to express the hope that Tom would go on from this beginning and make an honest woman of Nancy by marrying her.

Quite naturally, the point of view of the country-house people was different; more critical, if not less charitable. Though the social acceptance of the Gordons, as an ancient family, as friends of the Dabneys, and as land-holding neighbors was fairly complete, it still lacked somewhat of the class kinship which breeds leniency and the closed eye to the sins of its own household. But for Tom, personally, as a distinct social improvement on honest Caleb, the welcome into the charmed circle of Mountain View Avenue had been warm enough to make his sudden apparent relapse into the primitive figure as an affront to the colony. Hence, there were rods laid in pickle for the sinner, as when Mrs. Vancourt Henniker gave the footman at Rook Hill a hint that for the present the Misses Henniker were not at home to Mr. Thomas Gordon; and if Tom had known it, there were other and similar chastenings lying in wait for him behind more of the colonial doors.

But Tom did not know it. He was in the crucial month of the panic year, striving desperately to maintain the foothold given to him by the pipe-casting invention, and he had little time for the amenities. So it came about that he escaped for the moment; or, which was quite the same, he did not know he was pursued. Another Northern city, with its full complement of grafting officials, was in the market for some train-loads of water-mains, and again Thomas Jefferson was fighting the old battle of conscience against expediency, this time in the evil-smelling ditches where the dead and wounded lie.

"You are sure you went into it thoroughly, Norman?" he demanded of his lieutenant, when the latter returned from a personal reconnaissance of the field. "The break they are making at us seems almost too rank to be taken at its face value."

"Oh, yes; I dug it up from the bottom," said the henchman. "It's rotten and riotous. The political machine runs the town, and the bosses own the machine. So much to this one, so much to that, so much to half a dozen others, and we get the contract. Otherwise, most emphatically *nit*."

"That comes straight, does it?"

"As straight as a shot out of a gun. They got together on it, eight of the big bosses, called me in and told me flat-footed what we had to do," said the salesman. "Oh, I tell you, those fellows are on to their job."

"No chance to go behind the returns and stir up popular indignation, as we did in Indiana?" suggested Tom.

"No show on top of earth. The ring owns or controls two of the dailies, and has the other two scared. Besides, they've just had their municipal election."

The Gordon-and-Gordon manager was absently jabbing holes in the desk blotter with the paper-knife.

"Well, we can do what we have to, I suppose," he said, after a hesitant pause. "Say nothing to my father, but make your arrangements to take the train for the North again tonight. I'll meet you in town at the Marlboro at four o'clock."

To prepare for the new exigency, Tom took the afternoon local for South Tredegar. The lump sum required for the bribery was considerably in excess of his balance in bank. Notwithstanding the stringency of the times, he made sure he could borrow; but it was in some vague hope that the moral chasm might be widened to impassibility, or decently bridged for him, that he was moved to state the case in detail to President Henniker of the Iron City National. Mr. Vancourt Henniker could dig ditches, on occasion, making them too vast for the boldest borrower to cross; but Tom's credit was gilt-edged, and in the present instance the president chose rather to build bridges.

"We have to shut our eyes to a good many disagreeable things in business, Mr. Gordon," he said, genially didactic. "Our problem in this day and generation is so to draw the line of distinction that these necessary concessions to human frailty will not debauch us; may be made without prejudice to that high sense of personal honor and integrity which must be the corner-stone of any successful business career. This state of affairs which you describe is deplorable — most deplorable; but — well, we may think of such obstacles as we do of toll-gates on the highway. The road is a public utility, and it should be free; but we pay the toll, under protest, and pass on."

Mr. Henniker was a large man, benign and full-favored, not to say unctuous; and his manner in delivering an opinion was blandly impressive, and convincing to many. Yet Tom was not convinced.

"Of course, I came to ask for the loan, and not specially to justify it," he said, in mild irony which was quite lost on the philosopher in the president's chair. "I wasn't sure just how you would regard it if you should know the object for which we are borrowing, and this high sense of personal honor you speak of impelled me to be altogether frank with you."

"Quite right; you were quite right, Mr. Gordon," said the banker urbanely. "You are young in business, but you have learned the first lesson in the book of success — to be perfectly open and outspoken with your banker. As I have said, the venality of these men with whom you are dealing is most deplorable, but. . . ."

There was some further glozing over of the putrid fact, a good bit of it, and Tom sat back in his chair and listened, outwardly respectful, inwardly hot-hearted and contemptuous. Was this smooth-spoken, oracular prince of the market-place a predetermined hypocrite, shaping his words to fit the money-gathering end without regard to their demoralizing effect? Or was he only a subconscious Pharisee, self-deceived and complacent? Tom's thought ran lightning-like over the long list of the Vancourt Hennikers: men of the business world successful to the Croesus mark, large and liberal benefactors, founders of colleges, libraries and hospitals, gift-givers to their fellow men, irreproachable in private life, and yet apparently stone blind on the side of the larger equities. Could it be possible that such men deliberately admitted and accepted the double standard in morals? It seemed fairly incredible, and yet their lives appeared to proclaim it.

When the president had finished his apology for those who bow the head in the house of Rimmon, Tom rose to take his bit of approved paper around to the cashier's window. The bridge was built, and he meant to cross it; but he was honest enough, or blunt enough, to give his own point of view in a crisp sentence or two.

"I wish I could look at it in some such way as you do, Mr. Henniker, but I can't," he objected. "To me it is just plain bribery; the corrupting of officials who have sworn, among other things, to administer their offices honestly. I'm immoral, or unmoral, enough to yield to the apparent necessity, but it is quite without prejudice to a firm conviction that I am no better than the men I am going to purchase."

Having obtained the sinews of war, he kept the appointment with Norman, and their joint discussion of the business situation made him too late for the early dinner at Woodlawn. To complete the delay, the evening train lost half an hour with a hot box at a point a mile short of Gordonia. Two things came of these combined time-killings: a man in a slouched hat and the brown jeans of the mountaineers, who had been watching the Woodlawn gates since dusk from his hiding-place behind the field wall across the pike, got up stiffly and went away; and Tom reached home just in time to intercept Ardea on the steps of the picturesque veranda.

"Been visiting the little mother?" he asked, when she paused on the step above him.

"Yes — no; I ran over to tell you that we moved Nancy today."

"Oh! Well, that's comfortable. She was willing?"

"Y-es: almost, at first; and altogether willing when I told her that I — that she — " There was an embarrassed moment and then the truth came out. "Perhaps I should have asked you first: but she was quite satisfied when I told her that she owed her changed condition to the person whose duty it was to provide for her. You don't mind, do you?"

The question was almost a beseechment; but Tom was thinking of something else.

"No, I don't mind," he said absently, and the under-thought dealt savagely with Nan — with a woman who, for the sake of the loaves and the fishes, and the shielding of the real offender, would suffer an innocent man to go to the social gallows for lack of the word which would have cleared him. He laughed rather bitterly and added, out of the heart of the under-thought: "I'm glad I'm not naturally inclined to be pessimistic."

"What makes you say that?"

"Because, after hearing" — he changed his mind suddenly, and transferred the hard word from Nan to Mr. Vancourt Henniker — "after what I've been hearing this afternoon I find myself more in the notion of weeping with the angels than of laughing with the devils."

"What has happened?" she asked, sympathetically alive to his need in one breath, and keenly apprehensive for her own peace of mind in the next.

"An exceedingly small thing, as the world's measurements go. I was in town, and made a business call on Mr. Henniker. He's a member of your church, isn't he?"

"Of St. Michael's in the city," she corrected. "You know I claim membership here at home in St. John's."

"Well, it's all the same. He is what you would call a Christian man, I take it?"

"Why not?" she demanded. "What has he done to make you doubt it?"

"Oh, nothing worth mentioning, perhaps. I needed some money to bribe a lot of political grafters in a Pennsylvania city where I'm trying to sell a bill of water-pipe. I went to Mr. Henniker to borrow it."

"And, of course, he wouldn't let you have it for any such wretched purpose!" she flamed out.

"No, you are mistaken; it's just the other way around. I told him what it was for, hoping rather vaguely, I think, that he'd sit on me and make the crime impossible. But he didn't."

"You don't mean that he lent you the money after you had told him what you purposed doing with it?" It was too dark for him to see her face, but there was something like a breath-catching of horror in her voice.

"I'm sorry it shocks you, but he did. More than that, he took the trouble to try to explain away my scruples; made it seem quite a virtuous thing before he got through. You wouldn't believe it now, would you?"

"But, Tom! you didn't take the money?"

"How could I refuse so good a man? Norman is on his way to Pennsylvania at this present moment, with a letter of credit in his pocket big enough to make the mouth of even a professional grafter water. At least, I hope it is big enough."

She was hurt, shocked, horrified, and he knew it and found pleasure of a certain sort in the knowledge. When a man has done violence to his own best impulses, the thing that comes nearest to the holy joy of penitence is the unholy joy of making somebody else sorry for him. There were unmistakable tears in her voice when she said:

"Tom, why have you told me this — this unspeakable thing?"

"Why — I guess it was because I wanted to ask you how you supposed the Mr. Henniker kind of men square such things with their conscience; or don't they have any conscience?"

"That is *not* the reason," she faltered.

"You are right," he rejoined quickly. "It was diabolism pure and unstrained. I had hurt myself, and I wanted to pass it along — to hurt some one else. But it is too cold to keep you standing here. Won't you come in again?"

"No; I must go home." And she went down the broad steps.

He drew her arm through his and walked with her, down one grassy slope and up the other. At the manor-house steps he found at last sufficient grace to say: "It was a currish thing to do; will you forgive me, Ardea?"

"I don't know," she said, in a tone that thrilled him curiously. "Such things are hard to forgive. I don't mean your slapping me in the face with it, that is nothing. But to know that you have gone so far aside . . . that you have sunk your manhood and all the promise of it. . . ."

He nodded perfect intelligence. "I know; it's hell, Ardea. I've been frizzling in it for the past six months, more or less; ever since I came home with the one sole, single determination to climb out of the panic ditch if I had to make steps of dead bodies or lost souls. I'm doing it, and I'm paying the price. Sometimes I can find it in my heart to curse the mistaken mother-love that gave me to eat of the fruit of the tree of the knowledge of good and evil. I'm pagan in all else, but I can't sin like a pagan. Why is it? Why can't I be a smug, peaceful, sound-sleeping scoundrel like other men?"

She was standing on the step above him, as she had stood on the other side of the two dew-wet lawns.

"I have a theory," she rejoined, "but you wouldn't accept it. You'll never be able to do wrong without paying for it. Is it worth while to try?"

"Nothing is worth while — nothing at all. I don't mean that I'm going to quit; I shall doubtless go on trampling and grinding the face of the poor, and the rich, if they come in my way. But at the end of the ends I shall curse God and die, as Job's wife wanted him to."

She put her hands on his shoulders impulsively, and again the tears were in her voice.

"What can I say to help you, Tom? God knows I would do anything that a true friend may do!"

He freed himself of the touch of her hands, but very gently.

"There might have been a thing; but you have made it impossible. No, don't freeze me again — it's the last time. If I could have won your love . . . but what is the use of trying to put it in words; you know — you have always known. And now it is too late."

For a single instant Vincent Farley's chance of marrying the Deer Trace coal lands trembled in the balance. Ardea forgot him, forgot Nan, thought of nothing but the passionate yearning that was drawing her like gripping hands toward the man who had bared his inmost heart to her. Again she leaned on him with a touch so light that he scarcely felt it, and her lips brushed his forehead.

"It is not too late for you to be a man, noble, upright, honorable. Let the world find that for which it is looking, my friend — my brother: the strong man armed who can stand where others faint and fall. Oh, I wish I knew how to say the word that would make you the man you were meant to be!"

When it was said, she was gone and the sound of the closing door was in his ears when he turned and went slowly down the driveway and out on the white pike, lying like a snowy ribbon under the December stars. On the highway he hung undecided for a moment; but an hour later, William Layne, driving homeward from South Tredegar, overtook him plodding slowly southward far beyond the head of Paradise; and it was nearing midnight when he won back, pacing steadily past the Deer Trace and Woodlawn gates and holding his way down the pike to Gordonia.

The railway station was his goal; and when he had aroused the sleepy night operator and gained admittance, he sat at the telegraph table to write a message. It was to Norman, addressed to intercept the salesman at the breakfast stop.

"Cancel Pennsylvania date and come in at once to take managership of plant," was the wording of it; and at the breakfast-table the following morning Tom announced his intention of leaving the industrial plow in the furrow while he should go to Boston to complete his course in the technical school.

XXVI

AS WITH A MANTLE

The month of March in the great, southward-reaching bight of the Tennessee River is the pattern and form of fickleness climatic. Normally it is the time of starting sap and swelling buds and steaming leaf beds odorous of spring; the month when the migratory crows wing their flight northward, and Nature, lightest of winter sleepers in the azurine latitudes, stirs to her vernal awakening. None the less, in the Tennessee March the orchardist, watching the high-blown clouds in skies of the softest blue, is glad if the peach buds are slow in responding to the touch of the wooing airs, or, chewing a black birch twig as he makes the leisurely round of his line fence, warns his gardening neighbor that it is too early to plant beans. True, the poplars may be showing a tinge of green, and the buds of the hickory may have lighted their tiny candle flames on the winter-bared boughs; but the "blackberry winter" is yet to come, and there are rigorous possibilities still lingering in the high-flying clouds and the sudden-shifting winds.

It was on the fourth Sunday in the month that Ardea rose early and went fasting to the communion service at St. John's-in-Paradise. Primarily, St. John's was merely the religious factor in Mr. Duxbury Farley's scheme of country-colony promotion, and for the greater part of the year its silver-toned bell was silent and its appeal was mainly to the artistic eye. But latterly St. Michael's, the mother church in South Tredegar, had attained a new assistant rector whose zeal was not yet dulled by apathetic unresponsiveness on the part of the to-be-helped. Hence St. Michael's various missions flourished for the time, and once a month, if not oftener, the bell of St. John's sent its note abroad on the still morning air of Paradise.

On this particular Sunday morning Ardea was early at the church, and she was glad she had decided to wear her cloth gown. It had turned cooler in the night and the azure March sky was hidden behind a gray cloud mass which hung low on the slopes of the mountain. There was no fire in the church heater; and the few worshipers — the Vancourt Henniker girls, the two Misses Harrison, John Young-Dickson, of The Dell, dragged out at the chilly hour by his new wife, and Mrs. Schuyler Farnsworth and her daughter, all of the country-house colony beyond the creek — sat or knelt, and shivered through the service in decorous discomfort.

Miss Dabney was not looking quite as well as usual, as Miss

Betsy Harrison remarked to her sister, Miss Willie, in a church whisper. She had grown thinner during the winter, and though the slate-blue eyes were as clear and steadfast as before, there was a strained look in them like that in the eyes of the spent runner. Mountain View Avenue, rurally alert for something to talk about, decided it was trouble rather than ill health. Miss Eva Farley corresponded with Jessica Farnsworth, and there had been European hints of an understanding between Vincent and Ardea. Coupling this with young Gordon's ostentatious devotion, Nan's appearance, and Tom's sudden determination to go back to college, there was the groundwork for a very pretty story which sufficiently accounted for Miss Dabney's changed looks and for her growing reluctance to be included in the country colony's social divagations. She was engaged to one man and in love with another, who was clearly ineligible — this was the Mountain View Avenue summing-up of the matter; and some condemned and some pitied, and all were careful not to step within the barrier of aloofness with which Miss Dabney had of late surrounded herself.

On this Sunday morning of weather portents it chanced to be Ardea's turn to entertain the young minister, or rather to give him his breakfast after the service; and she waited for him in the vestibule after the others had gone. The outer doors were open, and she could see the gray cloud mass feathering on its under side and creeping lower on the slopes of Lebanon in every stormy gust of the chill wind.

"It was prudent to bring your overcoat this morning, Mr. Morelock," she said, when her guest emerged from the vesting-room with his cassock in a neat bundle under his arm. "If I'd had any idea it would turn cold so fast, I should have had the carriage come for us."

"Indeed, my dear Miss Dabney, if you could walk to church, I'm sure I can walk home with you," was the ready response; nevertheless, the rather fragile-looking young man shuddered a little in sympathy with the rawness of the wind. He was from well-sheltered New England, and he had not yet acquired the native Southron's indifference to weather discomforts; would never acquire them this side of a consumptive's grave, it was to be feared.

"The attendance was pretty good for such a disagreeable morning, don't you think?" Ardea ventured, trying to make talk as they breasted the gusts together on the Deer Trace side of the pike.

The young missioner shook his head rather despondently. "There are English churchmen among the English and Welsh miners at Gordonia, — quite a number of them," he rejoined. "Not one of them was present."

It was the clear-sighted inner Ardea that smiled. There was little in the stately service and luxurious appointments of the country colony's church to attract the working-men, and much to repel them. She wondered that Mr. Morelock, young as he was, did not understand this.

"The mission of St. John's is hardly to the working people of Gordonia, is it?" she said, more in exculpation than in criticism.

"Oh, my dear young lady! the church knows no class distinctions!" protested the zealous one warmly. "Her call is to rich and poor, gentle and simple, young and old alike; and it is imperative. I must make a round of visitation among these miners at the very first opportunity."

Ardea bent low to the buffet of a stronger blast and fought for a moment with her clinging skirts. When she had breath to say it, she said: "Will you really do that? Then let me tell you how. Come out here some week-day in your roughest clothes, and make your round among the men while they are at work in the mine. They will listen to you then."

"Bless me! what an idea!" he gasped.

"It is not original with me," was the gentle reply. "You will remember that the example was set a good many hundred years ago among the fishermen of Galilee. And, after all, Mr. Morelock, it is the only way. You can not reach down to a living soul on this earth — that is worth saving."

It had begun to rain in spiteful little dashes and squalls, and the clergyman was turning up the collar of his overcoat and buttoning it about his throat. Moreover, the wind had risen to half a gale, and talking was difficult when it was not wholly impossible. But when they reached the Deer Trace gates and the shelter of the driveway evergreens, he had a defensive word ready.

"I can't fully agree with you, you know, Miss Ardea," he said. "Of course, we must not reach down in the Pharisaical sense. But neither must we lower the dignity of the sacred calling."

Her smile was neither disloyal nor cynical; it was merely pitying. She was thinking in her heart of hearts how much this zealous young apostle had yet to learn.

"Do you call it undignified to be a man among men?" she asked; adding quickly: "But I know you don't. And what other way is open to the true brother-helper?"

"There is the church and its ministrations," he began, but she broke in.

"To get the drowning man ashore you have first to go down into the water and lay hold of him, Mr. Morelock. That means personal contact, personal association."

The young man was clearly bewildered. His experience thus

far had not been enriched by many intimacies with clear-eyed young women who calmly defined the larger humanities for him.

"I'm afraid I don't quite understand your point of view," he demurred.

"Don't you? I'm not sure that I can explain just what I mean. But it seems to me that really to help any one, you must know that one; not superficially, as people meet in ordinary ways, but intimately. And you can't hope to do that if you hold aloof; if you — if you — pose as a minister all the time." The word was not flattering, but she could lay hold of no other.

"Oh, I hope I don't do that!" he laughed. "But to creep around underground in a sooty coal-mine, a laughing-stock to those who know how to do it — er — professionally —"

"The men have to do it as breadwinners, Mr. Morelock, and the most ribald one of them wouldn't laugh at you. I wouldn't be afraid to promise that you could fill St. John's, forbidding as its atmosphere is to the average working-man, the very next Sunday after such a visitation."

Now this young zealot was a man of imagination, hidebound only in his traditions. Also, he was not above taking ideas where he found them.

"Really, Miss Dabney, I'm not sure but you have hold of the matter at the practical end," he conceded. "I — I'd like to talk with you further about it, when we have time. Do you suppose I could get permission to go into the mines during working-hours?"

"Certainly you could — for the mere asking. We can speak to Mr. Caleb Gordon about it after breakfast, if you wish. My! doesn't that rain sting! I'm glad we are at home."

"Yes; and it is freezing as it falls. At home in New England we should say it was too cold to rain."

"It is never too cold or too anything to rain here," she said; and she let him take her arm to help her up the slippery stone steps to the stately portico.

A moment later the hospitable door of the manor house yawned for them, and the warmth of the Major's welcome, the light and glow of the crackling wood fires, and the solid comfort of surrounding stone walls soon banished the memory of the small struggle with the elements.

"Oh, my deah suh! you are not going back to town this mo'ning!" protested the warm-hearted Major Caspar, as the quartet was rising from the breakfast-table an hour later. "Why, bless youh soul! I wouldn't think of letting you go from undeh my roof in such weatheh as this! Tell him it's his duty to stay, Ardea, my deah; persuade him that he'll neveh have a betteh oppo'tunity to wrestle with the wickedest old sinner in Paradise Valley."

Young Mr. Morelock objected, zealously at first, but less strenuously when Ardea drew the sash curtain and showed him the ice crust already an inch thick, coating tree trunk and twig, grass blade and graveled driveway.

"I doubt very much if the horses could keep their footing; and it is quite out of the question for you to walk to Gordonia," she decided. "We have the long-distance, and you can explain matters to Doctor Channing."

The young man called up St. Michael's rectory and explained first, and smoked companionably with the Major in the library afterward. Further along, there was a one-sided discussion polemical, it being meat and drink to Major Caspar to ensnare a young theologian to his discomfiture in the unaxiomatic field of religion. Ardea was in and out of the library frequently while the discussion was in progress, but she had little to say; indeed, there was scant room for a third when the Major was once well warmed to his favorite relaxation. But Morelock remarked as he might, in the few breathing-spaces allowed him by his host, that Miss Dabney seemed restless and anxious about something, and that she spent much of the time at the windows watching the steady growth of the ice sheet.

After luncheon they all gathered in the deep-recessed window of the music-room which commanded a view of the groved pasture with its background of mountain slope and precipice. The rain was still falling, and the temperature remained at the freezing-point, but the wind had gone down and the slow, measured swaying of the trees under the weight of the thickening armor of ice was portentous of disaster, if the weather conditions should continue unchanged.

But as yet the storm was only in the magnificent stage. Far and near, the outdoor world was a world of cold, white crystal, gleaming pure and unsullied under the gray skies. Even the blackened tree trunks had their shining panoply of silver; and from the eaves of the projecting window a fringe of huge icicles was lengthening drop by drop.

Miss Euphrasia thought of her roses, already in leaf, and refused to be enthusiastic over the supernal beauty of the crystalline stage settings. Major Caspar was anxious about the pasturing stock, and was relieved when Japheth Pettigrass came in sight, leading a slipping, sliding cavalcade of terrified horses to shelter in the great stables. The young clergyman's thoughts were with the ill-housed poor of the South Tredegar parish; and Ardea's — ?

Young Mr. Morelock put his private anxieties aside in deference to the growing terror in the eyes of his young hostess. He had known her but a short time, meeting her only as his St. John's-in-

Paradise duties gave him opportunity; but from the first she had stood to him as a type of womanly serenity and fortitude. Yet now she was visibly terrified and distressed, and the clergyman wondered. She had never before given him the impression that she belonged to the storm-fearing group of women.

"Can't we have a little music, Miss Ardea?" he asked, after a while, hoping to suggest a comforting diversion.

"You will have to excuse me," she said, in a low voice. "I — I think I am not quite well."

Cousin Euphrasia overheard the admission and recommended the quiet of up stairs, drawn curtains and possets. But Ardea let the suggestion fall to the ground, and a little while afterward Morelock surprised her at her forenoon occupation of going from window to window, with the look of distress rising to sharp agony when the overladen trees began to groan and crack under the crushing ice burden.

"What is it, Miss Dabney?" he said, out of the heart of sympathy, when he came on her alone in the library. "Is there anything I can do?"

"Yes," she rejoined quickly. "The moment the storm subsides even a little, I must go out. My excuse will be a desire to see, a thirst for fresh air — anything; and you must abet me if there is any opposition."

"But I thought you were afraid of the storm," he interposed.

"I? I should be out in it this minute if I thought grandfather wouldn't be tempted to lock me in my room for proposing such a thing. And I *must* go before dark, whatever happens."

The young man from New England was a gentleman born. He neither asked questions nor raised objections.

"Of course, you may command me utterly," he said warmly. "I'll help; and I'll go with you, if you will let me."

"That is what I want," she said frankly. "Will you propose it? I — I can't explain, even to my cousin."

"Certainly," he agreed; and a little later, when the temperature dropped the necessary three degrees and the rain stopped, he calmly announced his intention of taking Miss Ardea out to see the devastation which, by this time, was beginning to be apparent on all sides.

There was a protest, as a matter of course, quite shrill on the part of Miss Euphrasia, but not absolutely prohibitory on the Major's. Morelock saw to it that his charge was well wrapped; in her haste and agitation Ardea would have overlooked the common precautions. They used the side door for a sally-port, and were soon slipping and sliding almost helplessly across the lawn. Walking was next to impossible, and the crashes of falling branches and trees came like the detonations of quick-firing guns. The minister locked arms with the determined young woman at his side and picked the way for her as he could.

"This is something awful for you," he said, when they had covered half the distance to the nearest pasture wall. "Does the necessity warrant it?"

"It does," she rejoined; and they pressed on in awe-inspired silence to the gate which opened on the pasture grove.

The quarter of a mile intervening between the gate and that side of the inclosure bounded by the lower slope of the mountain was truly a passage perilous. A dozen times in the crossing Ardea fell, and so far from being able to save her, Morelock could do no more than fall with her. Once a great limb of a spreading oak split off with a clashing of ice and came sweeping down to give them the narrowest of escapes; and after that they kept the open where they might.

At a rude rock stile over the limestone boundary wall at the mountain's foot they paused to take breath.

"Is there much more of it?" asked the escort, regretting for the first time in his life, perhaps, that he had so studiously ignored the athletic side of his seminary training.

"The distance is nothing," she panted. "But we must take the path for a little way up the mountain. No, don't tell me it can't be done; it *must* be done," — this in answer to his dubious scanning of the glassy ascent.

Again his good breeding asserted itself.

"Certainly it can be done, if you so desire." And he picked up a stone and patiently hammered the ice from the steps of the stile so she could cross in safety.

It was no more than a three-hundred-yard dash up the slope to the dog-keeper's cabin in the little glen, but it was a fight for inches. Every stone, every hand-hold of bush or shrub or tuft of dried grass was an icy treachery. Ardea knew the mountain and the path, and was less helpless than she would otherwise have been; yet she was willing to confess that she could never have done it alone. With all their care and caution they were exhausted and breathless when they topped the acclivity and Morelock saw the cabin in the pocket cove, with the great tulip-tree in the dooryard bending and distorted and groaning like a living thing in agony.

"Isn't it terrible!" he said; but Ardea's glance had gone beyond the tortured tree to the shuttered windows and smokeless chimney of the cabin.

"Oh, let us hurry!" she gasped; but at the gate of the tiny dooryard she stopped in sudden embarrassment. "I can't take you into the house, Mr. Morelock. Will you wait for me here — just a moment?"

He said "Certainly," as he had been saying it from the first. But it was quite without prejudice to a healthy and growing curiosity. The small adventure was taking on an air of mystery which thickened momently, demanding insistently a complete rearrangement of his preconceived notions of Miss Ardea Dabney.

She left him at once and made her way cautiously to the ice-encrusted door-stone. What she saw, when she lifted the wooden latch and entered, was what she had been praying she might not see.

On the small hearth was a heap of white ashes, dead and cold, and the tomb-like chill of the tightly-closed room was benumbing. Asleep in the fireplace corner, his little knees drawn up to his chin and his face streaked with the dried tears, was the three-year-old baby who bore Tom Gordon's name. And on the bed in the recess at the back of the room, her hands clenched and her passionate face a mask of long-continued agony, lay the mother.

Ardea was white to the lips and trembling when she retreated to the door-stone and beckoned to her companion.

"Can you find the way back to Deer Trace alone?" she faltered. "There is trouble here, as I feared there might be — terrible trouble and suffering. Say to my cousin that I must have Aunt Eliza, if she has to crawl here on her hands and knees. Then telephone for Doctor Williams, at Gordonia. He'll come if you tell him the message is from me. Oh, please go, quickly!"

[Illustration: "Oh, please go quickly!"]

He was waiting only for her to finish.

"Is it quite safe for you here?" he asked.

"Quite; but I shall die of impatience if you don't hurry!" Then her good blood made its protest heard. "Oh, please forgive me! I don't forget that you are my guest, but —"

"Not a word, Miss Dabney. Shall I come back here with the woman or the doctor?"

"No; I'll send for you if — if there is no hope. Otherwise you could do nothing."

He lifted his hat and was gone, and she turned and reëntered the house of trouble, bravely facing that which had to be faced.

An hour later, when Doctor Williams, with Mammy Juliet's Pete chopping the way for him up the hazardous path, reached the end of his journey of mercy, there was a bright fire crackling on the hearth, and Miss Dabney was sitting before it, holding little Tom, who was still sleeping. Aunt Eliza, a deft middle-aged negress who had succeeded Mammy Juliet as housekeeper at Deer Trace, was bending over the bed, and the physician went quickly to stand beside her, shaking his head dubiously. A moment afterward he turned short on Ardea.

"You must go home, my dear — at once — and take the child with you. Pete is outside to help you, and my buggy is just at the foot of the path. I can't have you here."

"Can't I be of some use if I stay?" she pleaded.

"No; you'd only hinder. You are much too sympathetic. Don't delay; the minutes may count for lives," and the physician began to unbuckle the straps of the canvas-covered case he had brought with him.

Ardea wrapped the child hastily and gave him to Pete to carry, following as quickly as she could down the path made possible by the coachman's choppings. Happily, the doctor's horse was freshly shod, and the quarter-mile to the manor-house was measured in safety. Ardea left little Tom with Mammy Juliet at her cabin in the old quarters, and went up to the great house to wait anxiously for news. It was drawing on to the early dusk of the cloudy evening when she saw from the window of the music-room the muffled figure of Pete opening the pasture gate for the doctor to drive through. Instantly she flew to the door and out on the steps.

"Go in, child; go in," was the fatherly command. "I've got to stop to take Morelock in. I promised to carry him to the station."

"But Nancy?" she questioned anxiously.

"She will live," said the doctor briefly. And then he added with a frown: "But the child may not — which would doubtless be the best thing possible for all concerned. I'm afraid the woman is incorrigible." Then the professional part of him came to its own again: "You'll have to send somebody up there to relieve Eliza. Care is all that is needed now, but it mustn't be stinted."

There were tears standing in the slate-blue eyes of the listener, but Doctor Williams did not see them. If he had, he would not have understood; neither would he have plumbed the depths of misery in that whispered saying of Ardea's as she turned and fled to her room: "O Tom! how could you! how could you!"

XXVII

SWEPT AND GARNISHED

Thomas Jefferson Gordon, Bachelor of Science, and one of the six prize-men in his class, was expected home on the first day of July; and it was remarked as a coincidence by the curious that Deer Trace manor-house was closed for the summer no more than a week before the return of the Gordon black sheep.

That Tom was a black sheep, a hopeless and incorrigible social iconoclast, was no longer a matter of doubt in the minds of any. Something may be forgiven a promising young man who has been unhappy enough, or imprudent enough, to begin to make history for himself in the irresponsible 'teens; but also the act of oblivion may be repealed. When it became noised about that there were two children instead of one in the old dog-keeper's cabin in the glen, Mountain View Avenue was justly indignant, and even the lenient Gordonians scowled and shook their heads at the mention of the young boss's name. All the world loves a lover, as in just measure it despises a libertine; and there were fathers of daughters among the miner and foundry folk of the town.

On the lips of the transplanted urbanites of the hill houses comment was less elemental, but no less condemnatory. It was no wonder the Dabneys had closed their house and had gone to Crestcliffe Inn to save Ardea the humiliation of having to meet Tom before she was safely married to Vincent Farley. It was what any self-respecting young woman would wish under like trying conditions. The country colony approved; likewise, it commended Miss Dabney's foresight and prudence in causing the Bryerson woman and her two children to disappear from the cabin in the glen; though Mrs. Vancourt Henniker, in secret session over the tea-cups with the elder Miss Harrison, voiced her surprise that Ardea could continue to be charitable in that quarter.

"It is quite beyond me," was the matron's thin-lipped phrasing of it. "When one remembers that this wretched mountain girl has been Ardea's understudy from the very beginning — faugh! it is simply disgusting! I should think Ardea would never want to see or hear of her again."

To such an atmosphere of potential social ostracism Tom returned after the final scholastic triumph in Boston; and for the first few days he escaped asphyxiation chiefly because the affairs of Gordon and Gordon and the Chiawassee Consolidated gave him no time to test its quality.

But after the first week he began to breathe it unmistakably. One evening he called on the Farnsworths; the ladies were not at home to him. The next night he saddled Saladin and rode over to Fairmont; the Misses Harrison were also unable to see him, and the butler conveyed a deftly-worded intimation pointing to future invisibilities on the part of his mistresses. The evening being still young, Tom tried Rockwood and the Dell, suspicion settling into conviction when the trim maidservant at the Stanley villa went near to shutting the door in his face. At the Dell he fared a little better. The Young-Dicksons were going out for an after-dinner call on one of the neighbors, and Tom met them at the gate as he was dismounting. There were regrets apparently hearty; but in recasting the incident later, Tom remembered that it was the husband who did the talking, and that Mrs. Young-Dickson stood in the shadow of the gate tree, frigidly silent and with her face averted.

"Once more, old boy, and then we'll quit," he said to Saladin at the remounting, and the final rein-drawing was at the stone-pillared gates of Rook Hill. Again the ladies were not at home, but Mr. Vancourt Henniker came out and smoked a cigar with his customer on the piazza. The talk was pointedly of business, and the banker was urbanely gracious — and mildly inquisitive. Would there be a consolidation of the allied iron industries of Gordonia when the Farleys should return? Mr. Henniker thought it would be undeniably profitable to all concerned, and offered his services as financiering promoter and intermediary. Would Mr. Gordon come and talk it over with him — at the bank?

Tom found his father smoking a bedtime pipe on the picturesque veranda at Woodlawn when he reached home. Whistling for William Henry Harrison to come and take his horse, he drew up one of the porch chairs and filled and lighted his own pipe. For a time there was such silence as stands for communion between men of one blood, and it was the father who first broke it.

"Been out callin', son?" he asked, marking the Tuxedo and the white expanse of shirt front.

"No, I reckon not," was the reply, punctuated by a short laugh. "The Avenue seems to be depopulated."

"So? I hadn't heard of anybody goin' away," said Caleb the literal.

"Nor I," said Tom curtly; and the conversation paused until the iron-master had deliberately refilled and lighted his corn-cob.

"It's a-plenty onprofitable, Buddy, don't you reckon?" he ventured, referring to the social diversion.

There was a picric quality in Tom's tone when he replied: "The calling act? — I have certainly found it so tonight." Then, more humanely: "But as a means of relaxation it beats sitting here in the dark and stewing over tomorrow's furnace run — which is what you've been doing."

Caleb chuckled. "That's one time you missed the whole side o' the barn, Buddy. I was settin' here wonderin' if a man ever did get over bein' surprised at the way his children turn out."

"Meaning me?" said Tom, knocking the ash from his pipe and feeling in his pockets for a cigar.

"Yes, meanin' you, son. You've somehow got away from me again in these last six months 'r so."

"I'm older, pappy; and I hope I'm bigger and broader. I was a good bit of a kid a year ago; tough in some spots and fearfully and wonderfully raw in others. Do you recollect how I climbed up on the fence the first dash out of the box and read off the law to you about religion and such things?"

"I reckon so," said the iron-master. "And that's one o' the things — I ain't heard you cuss out the hypocrites once since you got back. Have you gone back on the Dutchman and his argy-ment?"

"Bauer, you mean? — no; only on the nullifying part of it. Bauer's no-religion doctrine is a doctrine of denial, and it's pure theory. What we have to deal with in this world is the practical human fact, and a good half of that is tangled up with some sort of religious belief or sentiment. At least, that's the way I'm finding it."

"It's the way it *is*," said Caleb sententiously. And after a pause: "I allow it helps some, too; greases the wheels some if it don't do anything more."

"It does much more," was the quick reply. "When you find it in a woman like Ardea Dabney, it raises her to the seventh power angelic. It is only when you find it, or some ghastly imitation of it, in such people as the Farleys. . . ." He changed the subject abruptly. "You said the Dabneys had gone up on the mountain for the summer, didn't you?"

"Yes. I believe they're allowin' to come back in August, in time for the weddin'."

The younger man's wince was purely involuntary. He had been trying latterly to train up to the degree of mental fitness which would enable him to think calmly of Ardea as another man's wife. The effort commended itself as a part of the new broadening process, but it was not entirely successful.

"You wrote me the Farleys would be back this month, didn't you?" he asked.

"The fifteenth," said Caleb; smoking reflectively through another long pause before he added. "And then come the business fireworks. Have you made up your mind what-all you're goin' to do, Buddy?"

"Oh, yes," said Tom, as if this were merely a matter in passing. "We'll consolidate the two plants and the coal-mine, if it's agreeable all around."

The iron-master took a fresh hitch in his chair. Truly, this was a retransformed Tom; a creature totally and radically different from the college junior who had sweltered through the industrial battle of the previous summer, breathing out curses and threatenings.

"Was you allowin' to let Colonel Duxbury climb into all three o' the saddles?" he inquired, keeping his emotions out of his voice as he could.

"That will be for you and Major Dabney to decide," was the even-toned response. "I would suggest a three-cornered alliance: a third to you, another to Farley, and the remaining third to the Major. The pipe foundry can't run without the furnace and, under present conditions, the furnace is pretty largely dependent on the pipe foundry for its market; and neither could run without the Major's coal."

"Yes, that scheme might carry far enough to hit three of us. But whereabouts do you figure out the fourth third for yourself, son?"

"Oh, I'm not in it; or I'm not going to be after the Farleys come back. I made up my mind to that six months ago," said Tom coolly.

"Great Peter!" ejaculated Caleb, stirred for once out of his slow-speaking, reticent habit. But he made amends by remaining silent for five full minutes before he hazarded the query: "Got something else on the string, Buddy?"

"Yes, two or three things," was Tom's immediate and frank rejoinder. "I can have a place as chemist with the steel people at Bethlehem; and Mr. Clarkson is anxious to have me to go to the New Arizona iron country for him."

It was the brightest of midsummer nights, and a late moon was swinging clear of the Lebanon sky-line, but the prospect of close-clipped lawn and stately trees suddenly went dim before the eyes of the old ex-artillery-man.

"You're all I got in this world, son, and I reckon it makes me sort o' narrow. I know in reason it must seem mighty little and pindlin' down here to you, after what you've seen out in the big road, and I ain't goin' to say a word. But if you can sort it round somehow in the mix-up so I can get a few thousand dollars quittin' money out of it — jest enough to keep your mammy and me from gettin' hongry what few years we've got to eat, I'd be mighty proud."

"Oh," said Tom, still unmoved, as it seemed, "we can do better than that, if you want to pull out. But I made sure you'd rather stay in and hold your job. I've a notion you'd find 'retiring' pretty hard work after so many years spent in the furnace yard."

"You're right about that, son; I sure would," agreed Caleb. Then he went back to the main proposition. "What-all makes you restless, Buddy? Is it because Chiawassee and the pipe-makin' ain't big enough for you?"

Tom answered promptly and without apparent reserve.

"The job's big enough, but I don't want to stay here and yoke up with the Farleys; they'd ruin me in a year."

"Get the better of you in the business — is that what you're aimin' to say?"

"Not exactly. I'm still brash enough to believe I could hold my own on that score. But — oh, well; you know what we found out last summer about their business methods. I can do business that way, too; as a matter of fact, I did do a good bit more of it last year than you knew anything about. But I'm out of it now, and I mean to stay out."

A longer interval of silence followed, and at the end of it another query.

"Is that all that's the matter, Buddy?"

"No — it isn't," hesitantly. "I'm seventeen other kinds of a fool, too, pappy."

"Reckon ye couldn't make out to onload the whole of it on to a pair o' right old shoulders, could ye, son Tom?" was the gentle invitation.

"I don't know why I shouldn't tell you. I'm foolish about Ardea; been that way ever since she used to wear frocks and I used to run barefoot. I don't believe I could stand it to stay here and be her husband's business partner."

Caleb was shrouding himself in tobacco smoke and nodding complete intelligence.

"How did you ever come to let her get away from you, son?" he asked.

"That's a large question — too big for me to answer, I'm afraid. I always knew we were meant for each other, and I guess I took too much for granted. Then Vint Farley came along, and I helped his case by pitching into him every time she gave me a chance. Naturally, she leaned the other way; and the European business settled it."

Caleb drew a long breath. "Reckon it's everlastin'ly too late now, do ye, Tom?"

The young man's smile was wintry.

"You said the wedding-day was set, didn't you?"

"Why, yes; *toe* be sure. Leastwise, your mammy talked like it was. But, lawzee, son! the Gordon stock don't lie down in the harness. Ardee thinks a heap o' you, and if you could jest've made out to keep from gettin' so everlastin'ly tangled with that gal o' Tike — " he stopped abruptly, but not quite soon enough, and the word was as the flick of a whip on a wound already made raw by the abrasion of the closed doors.

"So that miserable story has got around to you at last, has it?" said Tom, in fine scorn. "I did hope they'd spare you and mother."

"She's spared yet, so far as I know," said the father, with a backward nod to indicate the antecedent of the pronoun. Following which, he said what lay uppermost in his mind. "I been allowin' maybe you'd come back this time with your head sot on lettin' that gal alone, son."

Thomas Jefferson was on his feet and a hot anger wave was sweeping him back over the years to other times when things used to turn red under the rage blast. But he got some sort of grip on himself before the words came.

"You've believed all you've heard, have you? — condemned me before I could say a word in my own defense? That's what they've all done."

"I don't say that, son." Then, with a note of fatherly yearning in his voice: "I'm waitin' to hear that word right now, Buddy — or as much of it as ye can say honestly."

"You'll never hear it from me — never in this world or another. Now tell me who told you!"

"Why, it's in mighty near ever'body's mouth, son!" said Caleb, in mild surprise. "You certain'y didn't take any pains to cover it up."

"Didn't take any pains? Why, in the name of God, should I?" Tom burst out. After which he tramped heavily to the farther end of the veranda, refilled and lighted his pipe, and smoked furiously for a time, glooming over at the darkened windows of Deer Trace and letting bitter anger and disappointment work their will on him. And when he finally turned and tramped back it was only to say an abrupt "Good night," and to pass into the house and up to his room.

He thought he was alone in the moon-lighted dusk of the upper chamber when he closed the door and began to pace a rageful sentry-beat back and forth between the windows. But all unknown to him one of the three fell sisters, she of the implacable front and deep-set, burning eyes, had entered with him to pace evenly as he paced, and to lay a maddening finger on his soul.

Without vowing a vow and confirming it with an oath, he had

partly turned a new life-leaf on the night of heavenly comfort when Ardea had sent him forth to tramp the pike with her kiss of sisterly love still caressing him. Beyond the needs of the moment, the recall of Norman and the determination to turn his back on the world struggle for the time being, he had not gone in that first fervor of the uplifting impulse. But later on there had been other steps: a growing hunger for success with self-respect kept whole; a dulling of the sharp edge of his hatred for the Farleys; a meliorating of his fierce contempt for all the hypocrites, conscious and subconscious.

With the changing point of view had come a corresponding change in the life. The men of his class had marked it, and there were helping hands held out, as there always are when one struggles toward the forward margin of any Slough of Despond. He had even gone to church at long intervals, having there the good hap to fall under the influence of a man whose faults were neither of ignorance nor of insincerity.

In these surface-scratchings of the heart soil there had sprung up a mixed growth in which the tares of self-righteousness began presently to overtop the good grain of humility. One must not be too exacting. If the world were not all good, neither was it all bad; at all events, it was the part of wisdom to make the magnanimous best of it, and to be thankful that the day-star of reason had at last arisen for one's self. At the close of his college course he would go home prepared to deal firmly but justly with the Farleys, prepared to show Ardea and the small world of Paradise a pattern of business rectitude, of filial devotion, of upright, honorable manhood. As Ardea had said, the example was needed; it should be forthcoming. And perhaps, in the dim and distant future, Ardea herself would look back to the night when her word and her kiss had fashioned a man after her own heart, and be — not sorry (true love was still stronger than prideful Phariseeism here), but a little regretful, it might be, that her love could not have gone where it was sent.

And now. . . . With Alecto's maddening finger pressed on the soul-hurt, no man is responsible. After the furious storm of upbubbling curses had spent itself there was a little calm, not of surcease but of vacuity, since even the cursing vocabulary has its limitations. Then a grouping of words long forgotten arrayed itself before him, like the handwriting on the wall of Belshazzer's banqueting hall.

When the unclean spirit is gone out of a man, he walketh through dry places, seeking rest, and findeth none. Then he saith, I will return into my house from whence I came out; and when he is come, he findeth it empty, swept, and garnished. Then goeth he, and taketh with himself seven other spirits more wicked than himself, and they enter in and dwell there: and the last state of that man is worse than the first.

He put his hands before his face to shut out the sight of the words. Farther on, he felt his way across the room to stand at the window where he could look across to the gray, shadowy bulk of the manor-house, to the house and to the window of the upper room which was Ardea's.

"They've got me down," he whispered, as if the words might reach her ear. "The devils have come back, Ardea, my love; but you can cast them out again, if you will. Ah, girl, girl! Vincent Farley will never need you as I need you this night!"

XXVIII

THE BURDEN OF HABAKKUK

During the first half of the year 1894, with Norman too busy at the pipe foundry to worry him, and the iron-master president too deeply engrossed in matters mechanical, Mr. Henry Dyckman, still bookkeeper and cashier for Chiawassee Consolidated, had fewer nightmares; and by the time he had been a month in undisputed command at the general office he had given over searching for a certain packet of papers which had mysteriously disappeared from a secret compartment in his desk.

Later, when the time for the return of the younger Gordon drew near, there was encouraging news from Europe. Dyckman had not failed to keep the mails warm with reports of the Gordon and Gordon success; with urgings for the return of the exiled dynasty; and late in May he had news of the homecoming intention. From that on there were alternating chills and fever. If Colonel Duxbury should arrive and resume the reins of management before Tom Gordon should reappear, all might yet be well. If not, — the alternative impaired the bookkeeper's appetite, and there were hot nights in June when he slept badly.

When Tom's advent preceded the earliest date named by Mr. Farley by a broad fortnight or more, the bookkeeper missed other of his meals, and one night fear and a sharp premonition of close-pressing disaster laid cold hands on him; and nine o'clock found him skulking in the great train shed at the railway station, a ticket to Canada in his pocket, a goodly sum of the company's money tightly buckled in a safety-belt next to his skin — all things ready for flight save one, the courage requisite to the final step-taking.

The following morning the premonition became a certainty. In the Gordonia mail there was a note from the younger Gordon, directing him to come to the office of the pipe foundry, bringing the cash-book and ledger for a year whose number was written out in letters of fire in the bookkeeper's brain. He went, again lacking the courage either to refuse or to disappear, and found Gordon waiting for him. There were no preliminaries.

"Good morning, Dyckman," said the tyrant, pushing aside the papers on his desk. "You have brought the books? Sit down at that table and open the ledger at the company's expense account for the year. I wish to make a few comparisons," and he took a thick packet of papers from a pigeonhole of the small iron safe behind his chair.

Dyckman was unbuckling the shawl-strap in which he had

carried the two heavy books, but at the significant command he desisted, went swiftly to the door opening into the stenographer's room, satisfied himself that there were no listeners, and resumed his chair.

"You have cut out some of the preface, Mr. Gordon; I'll cut out the remainder," he said, moistening his dry lips. "You have the true record of the expense account in that package. I'm down and out; what is it you want?"

The inexorable one at the desk did not keep him in suspense.

"I want a written confession of just what you did, and what you did it for," was the direct reply. "You'll find Miss Ackerman's type-writer in the other room; I'll wait while you put it in type."

The bookkeeper's lips were dryer than before, and his tongue was like a stick in his mouth when he said:

"You're not giving me a show, Mr. Gordon; the poor show a common murderer would have in any court of law. You are asking me to convict myself."

Gordon held up the packet of papers.

"Here is your conviction, Mr. Dyckman — the original leaves taken from those books when you had them re-bound. I need your statement of the facts for quite another purpose."

"And if I refuse to make it? A cornered rat will fight for his life, Mr. Gordon."

"If you refuse I shall be reluctantly compelled to hand these papers over to our attorneys — reluctantly, I say, because you can serve me better just now out of jail than in it."

Dyckman made a final attempt to gain fighting space.

"It's an unfair advantage you're taking; at the worst, I am only an accessory. My principals will be here in a few days, and —"

"Precisely," was the cold rejoinder. "It is because your principals are coming home, and because they are not yet here, that I want your statement. Oblige me, if you please; my time is limited this morning."

There was no help for it, or none apparent to the fear-stricken; and for the twenty succeeding minutes the type-writer clicked monotonously in the small ante-room. Dyckman could hear his persecutor pacing the floor of the private office, and once he found himself looking about him for a weapon. But at the end of the writing interval he was handing the freshly-typed sheet to a man who was yet alive and unhurt.

Gordon sat down at his desk to read it, and again the roving eyes of the bookkeeper swept the interior of the larger room for the means to an end; sought and found not.

The eye-search was not fully concluded when Gordon pressed the electric button which summoned the young man who kept the local books of the Chiawassee plant across the way. While he waited he saw the conclusion of the eye-search and smiled rather grimly.

"You'll not find it, Dyckman," he said, divining the desperate purpose of the other; adding, as an afterthought: "and if you should, you wouldn't have the courage to use it. That is the fatal lack in your makeup. It is what kept you from taking the train last night with the money belt which you emptied this morning. You'll never make a successful criminal; it takes a good deal more nerve than it does to be an honest man."

The bookkeeper was sliding lower in his chair.

"I — I believe you are the devil in human shape," he muttered; and then he made an addendum which was an unconscious slipping of the under-thought into words: "It's no crime to kill a devil."

Gordon smiled again. "None in the least, — only you want to make sure you have a silver bullet in the gun when you try it."

Hereupon the young man from the office across the pike came in, and Gordon handed a pen to Dyckman.

"I want you to witness Mr. Dyckman's signature to this paper, Dillard," he said, folding the confession so that it could not be read by the witness; and when the thing was done, the young man appended his notarial attestation and went back to his duties.

"Well?" said Dyckman, when they were once more alone together.

"That's all," said Gordon curtly. "As long as you are discreet, you needn't lose any sleep over this. If you don't mind hurrying a little, you can make the ten-forty back to town."

Dyckman restrapped his books and made a show of hastening. But before he closed the office door behind him he had seen Gordon place the type-written sheet, neatly folded, on top of the thick packet, snapping an elastic band over the whole and returning it to its pigeonhole in the small safe.

Later in the day, Tom crossed the pike to the oak-shingled office of the Chiawassee Consolidated. His father was deep in the new wage scale submitted by the miners' union, but he sat up and pushed the papers away when his son entered.

"Have you seen this morning's *Tribune*?" asked Tom, taking the paper from his pocket.

"No; I don't make out to find much time for it before I get home o' nights," said Caleb. "Anything doin'?"

"Yes; they are having a hot time in Chicago and Pullman. The strike is spreading all over the country on sympathy lines."

"Reckon it'll get down to us in any way?" queried the ironmaster.

"You can't tell. I'd be a little easy with Ludlow and his outfit on that wage scale, if I were you."

"I don't like to be scared into doin' a thing."

"No; but we don't want a row on our hands just now. Farley might make capital out of it."

Caleb nodded. Then he said: "Didn't I see Dyckman comin' out of your shanty 'long about eleven o'clock?"

"Yes; he came out to do me a little favor, and it went mighty near to making him sweat blood. Shall you need me any more today?"

"No, I reckon not. Goin' away?"

"I'm going to town on the five-ten, and I may not be back till late."

Tom's business in South Tredegar was unimportant. There was a word or two to be said personally in the ear of Hanchett, the senior member of the firm of attorneys intrusted with the legal concernments of Gordon and Gordon, and afterward a solitary dinner at the Marlboro. But the real object of the town trip disclosed itself when he took an electric car for the foot of Lebanon on the line connecting with the inclined railway running up the mountain to Crestcliffe Inn. He had not seen Ardea since the midwinter night of soul-awakenings; and Alecto's finger was still pressing on the wound inflicted by the closed doors of Mountain View Avenue and his father's misdirected sympathy.

He found Major Dabney smoking on the hotel veranda, and his welcome was not scanted here, at least. There was a vacant chair beside the Major's and the Major's pocket case of long cheroots was instantly forthcoming. Would not the returned Bachelor of Science sit and smoke and tell an old man what was going on in the young and lusty world beyond the mountain-girt horizons?

Tom did all three. His boyish awe for the old autocrat of Paradise had mellowed into an affection that was almost filial, and there was plenty to talk about: the final dash in the technical school; the outlook in the broader world; the great strike which was filling all mouths; the business prospects for Chiawassee Consolidated.

The moment being auspicious, Tom sounded the master of the Deer Trace coal lands on the reorganization scheme, and found nothing but complaisance. Whatever rearrangement commended itself to Tom and his father, and to Colonel Duxbury Farley, would be acceptable to the Major.

"I reckon I can trust you, Tom, and my ve'y good friend, youh fatheh, to watch out for Ardea's little fo'tune," was the way he put it. "I haven't so ve'y much longeh to stay in Paradise," he went on, with a silent little chuckle for the grim pun, "and what I've got goes to her, as a matteh of cou'se." Then he added a word that set Tom to thinking hard. "I had planned to give her a little suhprise on her wedding-day: suppose you have the lawyehs make out that block of new stock to Mistress Vincent Farley instead of to me?"

Tom's hard thinking crystallized into a guarded query.

"Of course, Major Dabney, if you say so. But wouldn't it be more prudent to make it over in trust for her and her children before she becomes Mrs. Farley?"

The piercing Dabney eyes were on him, and the fierce white mustaches took the militant angle.

"Tell me, Tom, have you had *youh* suspicions in that qua'teh, too? I'm speaking in confidence to a family friend, suh."

"It is just as well to be on the safe side," said Tom evasively. There was enough of the uplift left to make him reluctant to strike his enemy in the dark.

"No, suh, that isn't what I mean. You've had youh suspicions aroused. Tell me, suh, what they are."

"Suppose you tell me yours, Major," smiled the younger man.

Major Dabney became reflectively reminiscent. "I don't know, Tom, and that's the plain fact. Looking back oveh ouh acquaintance, thah's nothing in that young man for me to put a fingeh on; but, Tom, I tell you in confidence, suh, I'd give five yeahs of my old life, if the good Lord has that many mo' in His book for me, if the blood of the Dabneys didn't have to be — uh — mingled with that of these heah damned Yankees. I would, for a fact, suh!"

Tom rose and flung away the stub of his third cheroot.

"Then you'll let me place your third of the new stock in trust for her and her children?" he said. "That will be best, on all accounts. By the way, where shall I find Miss Ardea?"

"She's about the place, somewhahs," was the reply; and Tom passed on to the electric-lighted lobby to send his card in search of her.

Chance saved him the trouble. Some one was playing in the music-room and he recognized her touch and turned aside to stand under the looped portières. She was alone, and again, as many times before, it came on him with the sense of discovery that she was radiantly beautiful — that for him she had no peer among women.

It was the score of a Bach fugue that stood on the music-rack, and she was oblivious to everything else until her fingers had found and struck the final chords. Then she looked up and saw him.

There was no greeting, no welcoming light in the slate-blue

eyes; and she did not seem to see when he came nearer and offered to shake hands.

"I've been talking to your grandfather for an hour or more," he began, "and I was just going to send my card after you. Haven't you a word of welcome for me, Ardea?"

Her eyes were holding him at arm's length.

"Do you think you deserve a welcome from any self-respecting woman?" she asked in low tones.

His smile became a scowl — the anger scowl of the Gordons.

"Why shouldn't I?" he demanded. "What have I done to make every woman I meet look at me as if I were a leper?"

She rose from the piano-stool and confronted him bravely. It was now or never, if their future attitude each to the other was to be succinctly defined.

"You know very well what you have done," she said evenly. "If you had a spark of manhood left in you, you would know what a dastardly thing you are doing now in coming here to see me."

"Well, I don't," he returned doggedly. "And another thing: I'm not to be put off with hard words. I ask you again what has happened? Who has been lying about me this time?"

Three other guests of the hotel were entering the music-room and the quarrel had to pause. Ardea had a nerve-shaking conviction that it would never do to leave it in the air. He must be made to understand, once for all, that he had sinned beyond forgiveness. She caught up the light wrap she had been wearing earlier in the evening and turned to one of the windows opening on the rear veranda. "Come with me," she whispered; and he followed obediently.

But there was no privacy to be had out of doors. There was a goodly scattering of people in the veranda chairs enjoying the perfect night and the white moonlight. Ardea stopped suddenly.

"You were intending to walk down to the valley?" she asked. He nodded.

"I will walk with you to the cliff edge."

It was a short hundred yards, and there were many abroad in the graveled walks: lovers in pairs, and groups of young people pensive or chattering. So it was not until they stood on the very battlements of the western cliff that they were measurably alone.

"Has no one told you what happened last March — on the day of the ice storm?" she asked coldly.

"No."

"Don't you know it without being told?"

"Of course, I don't; why should I?"

His angry impassiveness shook her resolution. It seemed incredible that the most accomplished dissembler could rise to such supreme heights of seeming.

"I used to think I knew you," she said, faltering, "but I don't. Why don't you despise hypocrisy and double-dealing as you used to?"

"I do; more heartily than ever."

"Yet, in spite of that, you have — oh, it is perfectly unspeakable!"

"I am taking your word for it," he rejoined gloomily. "You are denying me what the most wretched criminal is taught to believe is his right — to know what he is accused of."

"Have you forgotten that night last winter when you — when I saw you at the gate with Nancy Bryerson?"

"I'm not likely to forget it."

She seized her courage and held it fast, putting maidenly shame to the wall.

"Tom, it is a terrible thing to say — and your punishment will be terrible. *But you must marry Nancy!*"

"And father another man's child? — not much!" he answered brutally.

"And father your own children — two of them," she said, with bitter emphasis.

"Oh, that's it, is it?" he said, with a deeper scowl. "So there are two of them, are there? That's why no woman in Mr. Farley's country colony is at home to me any more, I suppose." And then, still more bitterly: "Of course, you are all sure of this? — Nan has at last confessed that I am the guilty man?"

"You know she has not, Tom. Her loyalty is still as strong and true at it is mistaken. But your duty remains."

He was standing on the brink of the cliff, looking down on Paradise Valley, spread like a silver-etched map far below in the moonlight. The flare and sough of the furnace at the iron-works came and went with regular intermittency; and just beyond the group of Chiawassee stacks a tiny orange spot appeared and disappeared like a will-o'-the-wisp. He was staring down at the curious spot when he said:

"If I say that I have no duty toward Nan, you will believe it is a lie — as you did once before. Have you ever reflected that it is possible to trample on love until it dies — even such love as I bear you?"

"It is a shame for you to speak of such things to me, Tom. Consider what I have endured — what you have made me endure. People said I was standing by you, condoning a sin that no right-minded young woman should condone. I bore it because I thought, I believed, you were sorry. And at that very time you were deceiving me — deceiving every one. You have dragged me in the very dust of shame!"

"There is no shame save what we make for ourselves," he retorted. "One day, according to your creed, we shall stand naked before your God, and before each other. In that day you will know what you have done to me tonight. No, don't speak, please; let me finish. The last time we were together you gave me a strong word, and — and you kissed me. For the sake of that word and that kiss I went out into the world a different man. For the little fragment of your love that you gave me then, I have lived a different man from that day to this. Now you shall see what I shall be without it."

Before he had finished she had turned from him gasping, choking, strangling in the grip of a mighty passion, new-born and yet not new. With the suddenness of a revealing flash of lightning she understood; knew that she loved him, that she had been loving him from childhood, not because, but in spite of everything, as he had once defined love. It was terrible, heartbreaking, soul-destroying. She called on shame for help, but shame had fled. She was cold with a horrible fear lest he should find out and she should be for ever lost in the bottomless pit of humiliation.

It was the sight of the little orange-colored spot glowing and growing beyond the Chiawassee chimneys that saved her.

"Look!" she cried. "Isn't that a fire down in the valley just across the pike from the furnace? It *is* a fire!"

He made a field-glass of his hands and looked long and steadily.

"You are quite right," he said coolly. "It's my foundry. Can you get back to the hotel alone? If you can, I'll take the short cut down through the woods. Good night, and — good-by." And before she could reply, he had lowered himself over the cliff's edge and was crashing through the underbrush on the slopes below.

XXIX

AS BRUTES THAT PERISH

It was the office building of the pipe foundry that burned on the night of July fifteenth, and the fire was incendiary. Suspicion, put on the scent by the night-watchman's story, pointed to Tike Bryerson as the criminal. The old moonshiner, in the bickering stage of intoxication, had been seen hanging about the new plant during the day, and had made vague threats in the hearing of various ears in Gordonia.

Wherefore the small world of Paradise and its environs looked to see a warrant sworn out for the mountaineer's arrest; and when nothing was done, gossip reawakened to say that Tom Gordon did not dare to prosecute; that Bryerson's crime was a bit of wild justice, so recognized by the man whose duty it was to invoke the law.

It was remarked, also, that neither of the Gordons had anything to say, and that an air of mystery enveloped the little that they did. The small wooden office building was a total loss, but the night shift at the Chiawassee had saved most of the contents; everything of value except the small iron safe which had stood behind the manager's desk in the private office. The safe, as the onlookers observed, was taken from the debris and conveyed, unopened, across the road to the Chiawassee laboratory and yard office. Whether or not its keepings were destroyed by the fire, was known only to the younger Gordon, who, as the foreman of the Chiawassee night shift informed a *Tribune* reporter, had broken it open himself, deep in the small hours of the night following the fire, and behind the locked door of the furnace laboratory.

At another moment South Tredegar newspaperdom might have made something of the little mystery. But there were more exciting topics to the fore. The great strike, with Chicago and Pullman as its storm-centers, was gripping the land in its frenzied fist, and the press despatches were greedy of space. Hence, young Gordon was suffered to open his safe in mysterious secrecy; to rebuild his burned office; and to let the incendiary, sufficiently identified by the watchman, it was believed, go scot-free.

With the greater land-wide interest to divert it, even Paradise failed to note the curious change that had come over the younger of the Gordons, dating from the night of burnings. But the few who came in contact with him in the business day saw and felt it. Miss Ackerman, the pipe-works stenographer, quit when her week was up. It was nothing that the young manager had said or done; but, as she confided to her sister, more fortunately situated in town, it was like being caged with a living threat. Even Norman, the trusted lieutenant, was cut out of his employer's confidence; and for hours on end in the business day the card "Not in" would be displayed on the glass-paneled door of the private room in the rebuilt office.

Not to make a mystery of it for ourselves, Tom had passed another milestone in the descent to the valley of lost souls. Or rather, let us say, he had taken a longer step backward toward the primitive. Daggered *amour-propre* is rarely a benign wound. Oftener than not it gangrenes, and there is loss of sound tissue and the setting-up of strange and malevolent growth. With the passing of the first healthful shock of honest resentment, Tom became a man of one idea. Somewhere in the land of the living dwelt a man who had robbed him, intentionally or otherwise, indirectly, but none the less effectually, of the ennobling love of the one woman; to find that man and to deal with him as Joab dealt with Amasa became the one thing worth living for.

The first step was taken in secrecy. One day a stranger, purporting to be a walking delegate for the United Miners, but repudiated as such by check-weigher Ludlow, took up his residence in Gordonia and began to interest himself, quite unminer-like, in the various mechanical appliances of the Chiawassee plant, and particularly in the different sources of its water supply.

Divested of his cloakings, this sham walking delegate was a Pinkerton man, detailed grudgingly from the Chicago storm-center on Tom's requisition. His task was to scrutinize Nancy Bryerson's past, and to identify, if possible, one or more of the three men who, in January of the year 1890, had inspected and repaired the pipe-line running from the coke-yard tank up to the barrel-spring on high Lebanon.

To the detective the exclusion card on Tom's door did not apply, and the conferences between the hired and the hirer were frequent and prolonged. If we shall overhear one of them — the final one, held on the day of the Farleys' return to Paradise and Warwick Lodge — it will suffice.

"It looks easy enough, as you say, Mr. Gordon," the human ferret is explaining; "but in point of fact there's nothing to work on — less than nothing. Three years ago you had no regular repair gang, and when a job of that kind was to be done, any Tom, Dick or Harry picked up a helper or two and did it. But I think you can bet on one thing: none of the three men who made that inspection is at present in your employ."

"In other words, you'd like to get back to your job at Pullman," snaps Tom.

"Oh, I ain't in any hurry! That job looks as if it would keep for a while longer. But I don't like to take a man's good money for nothing; and that's about what I'm doing here."

Tom swings around to his desk and writes a check.

"I suppose you have no further report to make on the woman?"

"Nothing of any importance. I told you where she is living — in a little cabin up on the mountain in a settlement called Pine Knob."

"Yes; but I found that out for myself."

"So you did. Well, she's living straight, as far as anybody knows; and if you can believe what you hear, the only follower she ever had was a young mountaineer named Kincaid. I looked him up; he's been gone from these parts for something over three years. He is ranching in Indian Territory, and only came back last week. You can check him off your list."

"He was never on, and I have no list," says the manhunter grittingly. "But I'll tell you one thing, Mr. Beckham," passing the signed check to the other, "I shall begin where you leave off, and end by finding my man."

"I hope you do, I'm sure," says the Pinkerton, moved by the liberal figure of the check. "And if there's anything more the Agency can do —"

In the afternoon of the same day, when the self-dismissed detective was speeding northward toward Chicago and the car-burners, Tom saddled the bay and rode long and hard over a bad mountain cart track to the hamlet of Pine Knob. It was a measure of his abandonment that he was breaking his promise to Ardea; and another of his reckless singleness of purpose that he rode brazenly through the little settlement to Nan's door, dismounted and entered as if he had right.

The cabin was untenanted, but he found Nan sitting on the slab step of a rude porch at the back, nursing her child. She greeted him without rising, and her eyes were downcast.

"I've come for justice, Nan," he said, without preface, seating himself on the end of the step and flicking the dust from his leggings with his riding-crop. "You know what they're saying about us — about you and me. I want to know who to thank for it: what is the man's name?"

She did not reply at once, and when she lifted the dark eyes to his they were full of suffering, like those of an animal under the lash.

"I nev' said hit was you," she averred, after a time.

"No; but you might as well. Everybody believes it, and you haven't denied it. Who is the man?"

"I cayn't tell," she said simply.

"You mean you won't tell."

"No, I cayn't; I'm livin' on his money, Tom-Jeff."

"No, you are not. What makes you say that?"

"She told me I was."

"Who? Miss Dabney?"

Her nod was affirmative, and he went on: "Tell me just what she said; word for word, if you can remember."

The answer came brokenly.

"I was ashamed — you don't believe hit, but hit's so. I allowed it was *her* money. When I made out like I'd run off, she said, 'No; it's his money 'at's bein' spent for you, and you have a right to it.'"

Tom was silent for a time; then he said the other necessary word.

"She believes I am the man who wronged you, Nan. It was my money."

The woman half rose and then sat down again, rocking the child in her arms.

"You're lyin' to me, Tom-Jeff Gordon. Hit's on'y a lie to make me tell!" she panted.

"No, it's the truth. I was sorry for you and helped you because — well, because of the old times. But everybody has misunderstood, even Miss Dabney."

Silence again; the silence of the high mountain plateau and the whispering pines. Then she asked softly:

"Was you aimin' to marry her, Tom-Jeff?"

His voice was somber. "I've never had the beginning of a chance; and besides, she is promised to another man."

The woman was breathing hard again. "I heerd about that, too — jest the other day. I don't believe hit!"

"It is true, just the same. But I didn't come out here to talk about Miss Dabney. I want to know a name — the name of a man."

She shook her head again and relapsed into unresponsiveness.

"I cayn't tell; he'd shore kill me. He's always allowed he'd do hit if I let on."

"Tell me his name, and I'll kill him before he ever gets a chance at you," was the savage rejoinder.

"D'ye reckon you'd do that, Tom-Jeff — for me?"

The light of the old allurement was glowing in the dark eyes when she said it, but there was no answering thrill of passion in his blood. For one moment, indeed, the bestial demon whispered that here was vengeance of a sort, freely proffered; but the fiercer devil thrust this one aside, and Tom found himself looking consciously and deliberately into the abyss of crime. Once he might have said such a thing in the mere exuberance of anger, meaning nothing more deadly than the retaliatory buffet of passion. But now —

It was as if the curtain of the civilizing, the humanizing, ages had been withdrawn a hand's-breadth to give him a clear outlook on primordial chaos. Once across the mystic threshold, untrammeled by the hamperings of tradition, unterrified by the threat of the mythical future, the human atom becomes its own law, the arbiter of its own momentary destiny. What it wills to do, it may do — if iron-shod chance, blind and stumbling blindly, does not happen to trample on and efface it. Who first took it on him to say, *Thou shalt not kill*? What were any or all of the prohibitions but the frantic shrillings of some of the atoms to the others?

In the clear outlook Thomas Gordon saw himself as one whose foot was already across the threshold. True, he had thus far broken with the world of time-honored traditions only in part. But why should he scruple to be wholly free? If the man whose deed of brutality or passion was disturbing the chanceful equilibrium for two other human dust-grains should be identified, why should he not be effaced?

The child at Nan's breast stirred in its sleep and threw up its tiny hands in the convulsive movement which is the human embryo's first unconscious protest against the helplessness of which it is born inheritor. Tom stood up, beating the air softly with the hunting-crop.

"The man has spoiled your life, Nan; and, incidentally, he has muddied the spring for me — robbed me of the love and respect of the one woman in the world," he said, quite without heat. "If I find him, I think I shall blot him out — like that." A bumblebee was bobbing and swaying on a head of red clover, and the sudden swish of the hunting-crop left it a little disorganized mass of black and yellow down and broken wing-filaments.

The glow in the dark eyes of the woman had died down again, and her voice was hard and lifeless when she said:

"But not for me, Tom-Jeff; you ain't wantin' to kill him like my brother would, if I had one."

"No; not at all for you, Nan," he said half absently. And then he tramped away to the gate, and put a leg over Saladin, and rode down the straggling street of the little settlement, again in the face and eyes of all who cared to see.

The bay had measured less than a mile of the homeward way when there came a clatter of hoof-beats in the rear. Tom awoke out of the absent fit, spoke to Saladin and rode the faster. Nevertheless, the pursuing horseman overtook him, and a drawling voice said:

"Hit's right smart wicked to shove the bay thataway downhill, son."

Tom pulled his horse down to a walk. He was in no mood for companionship, but he knew Pettigrass would refuse to be shaken off.

"Where have you been?" he asked sourly.

"Me? I been over to McLemore's Valley, lookin' at some brood-mares that old man Mac is tryin' to sell the Major."

"Did you come through Pine Knob?"

"Shore, I did. I was a-settin' on Brother Bill Layne's porch whilst you was talkin' to Nan Bryerson. Seems sort o' pitiful you cayn't let that pore gal alone, Tom-Jeff."

"That's enough," said Tom hotly. "I've heard all I'm going to about that thing, from friends or enemies."

"I ain't no way shore about that," said the horse-trader easily. "I was 'lottin' to say a few things, m'self."

Tom pulled the bay up short in the cart track.

"There's the road," he said, pointing. "You can have the front half or the back half — whichever you like."

Japheth's answer was a good-natured laugh and a tacit refusal to take either.

"You cayn't rile me thataway, boy," he said. "I've knowed you a heap too long. Git in the fu'ther rut and take your medicine like a man."

Since there appeared to be no help for it, Tom set his horse in motion again, and Japheth gave him a mile of silence in which to cool down.

"Now you listen at me, son," the horse-trader began again, when he judged the cooling process was sufficiently advanced. "I ain't goin' to tell no tales out o' school this here one time. But you got to let Nan alone, d'ye hear?"

"Oh, shut up!" was the irritable rejoinder. "I'll go where I please, and do what I please. You seem to forget that I'm not a boy any longer!"

"Ya-as, I do; that's the toler'ble straight fact," drawled the other. "But I ain't so much to blame; times you ack like a boy yit, Tom-Jeff."

Tom was silent again, turning a thing over in his mind. It was a time to bend all means to the one end, the trivial as well as the potent.

"Tell me something, Japhe," he said, changing front in the twinkling of an eye. "Is Nan coming back to the dog-keeper's cabin when the family leaves the hotel?"

"'Tain't goin' to make any difference to you if she does," said Pettigrass, wondering where he was to be hit next.

"It may, if you'll do me a favor. You'll be where you can see and hear. I want to know who visits her — besides Miss Ardea."

Brother Japheth's smile was more severe than the sharpest reproach.

"Still a-harpin' on that old string, are ye? Say, Tom-Jeff, I been erbout the best friend you've had, barrin' your daddy, for a right smart spell o' years. Don't you keep on tryin' to th'ow dust in my eyes."

"Call it what you please; I don't care what you think or say. But when you find a man hanging around Nan —"

"They's one right now," said the horse-trader casually.

Tom reined up as if he would ride back to Pine Knob forthwith.

"Who is it?" he demanded.

"Young fellow named Kincaid — jest back f'om out West, somewheres. Brother Bill Layne let on to me like maybe he'd overlook what cayn't be he'ped, and marry Nan anyhow. And that's another reason you got to keep away."

"Let up on that," said Tom, stiffening again. "If you had been where you could have used your ears as you did your eyes back yonder at Pine Knob, you'd know more than you seem to know now."

There was silence between them from this on until the horses were footing it cautiously down the bridle-path connecting the cart track with the Paradise pike. Then Pettigrass said:

"Allowin' ther' might be another man, Tom-Jeff, jest for the sake of argyment, what-all was you aimin' to do if you found him?"

It was drawing on to dusk, and the electric lights of Mountain View Avenue and the colonial houses were twinkling starlike in the blue-gray haze of the valley. They had reach the junction of the steep bridle-path with the wood road which edged the Dabney horse pasture and led directly to the Deer Trace paddocks, and when Japheth pulled his horse aside into the short cut, Tom drew rein to answer.

"It's nobody's business but mine, Japhe; but I'd just as soon tell you: it runs in my head that he needs killing mighty badly, and I've thought about it till I've come to the conclusion that I'm the appointed instrument. You turn off here? Well, so long."

Brother Japheth made the gesture of leave-taking with his riding-switch, and sent his mount at an easy amble down the wood road, apostrophizing great nature, as his habit was. "Lawzee! *how* we pore sinners do tempt the good Lord at every crook and elbow in the big road, *toe* be shore! Now ther's Tom-Jeff, braggin' how he'll be the one to kill the pappy o' Nan's chillern: he's a-ridin' a mighty shore-footed hawss, but hit do look like he'd be skeered the Lord might take him at his word and make that hawss stumble. Hit do, for a fact!"

XXX

THROUGH A GLASS DARKLY

On the night of the fire, Ardea had remained on the cliff's edge until the blaze died down and disappeared, which was some little time, she decided, before Tom could possibly have reached the foot of the mountain.

When there was nothing more to be seen she went back to the hotel and called up the Young-Dicksons, whose cottage commanded a short-range view of the Gordon plant. It was Mrs. Young-Dickson who answered the telephone. Yes; the fire was one of the foundry buildings — the office, she believed. Mr. Young-Dickson had gone over, and she would have him call up when he should return, if Miss Dabney wished.

Ardea said it did not matter, and having exhausted this small vein of distraction she returned to the music-room and the Bach fugue, as one, who has had a fall, rises and tries to go on as before, ignoring the shock and the bruisings. But the shock had been too severe. Tom Gordon had proved himself a wretch, beyond the power of speech to portray, and — she loved him! Not all the majestic harmonies of the inspired *Kapellmeister* could drown that terrible discord.

The next day it was worse. There was a goodly number of South Tredegar people summering at the Inn, and hence no lack of companionship. But the social distractions were powerless in the field where Bach and the piano had failed, and after luncheon Ardea shut herself in her room, desperately determined to try what solitude would do.

That failed, too, more pathetically than the other expedients. It was to no purpose that she went bravely into the torture chamber of opprobrium and did penance for the sudden lapse into the elemental. It was the passion of the base-born, she cried bitterly. He was unworthy, unworthy! Why had he come? Why had she not refused to see him — to speak to him?

Such agonizing questions flung themselves madly on the spear points of fact and were slain. He had come; she had spoken. Never would she forget the look in his eyes when he had said, "Good night, and — good-by;" nor could she pass over the half threat in the words that had gone before the leave-taking. To what deeper depth despicable could he plunge, having already sounded the deepest of them all — that of unfaith, of infidelity alike to the woman he had wronged and to the woman he professed to love?

At dinner-time she sent word to her grandfather and her

cousin that she was not feeling well, which was a mild para-
phrasing of the truth, and had a piece of toast and a cup of tea sent
to her room. The bare thought of going down to the great dining-
room and sitting through the hour-long dinner was insupport-
able. She made sure every eye would see the shame in her face.

With the toast and tea the servant brought the evening paper,
sent up by a doting Major Caspar, thoughtful always for her comfort. A marked item in the social gossip transfixed her as if it had
been an arrow. The Farleys had sailed from Southampton, and the
house renovators were already busy at Warwick Lodge.

After that the toast proved too dry to be eaten and the tea took
on the taste of bitter herbs. Vincent Farley was returning, coming
to claim the fulfilment of her promise. She had never loved him;
she knew it as she had not known it before; and that was dreadful
enough. But now there were a thousand added pangs to go with
the conviction. For in the interval love had been found — found
and lost in the same moment — and the solid earth was still
reeling at the shock.

Ardea of the strong heart and the calm inner vision had
always had a feeling bordering on contempt for women of the hys-
terical type; yet now she felt herself trembling and slipping on the
brink of the pit she had derided.

The third day brought surcease of a certain sort. In the Gallic
blood there is ever a trace of fatalism; the shrug is its expression. It
was generations back to the D'Aubignés, yet now and then some
remote ancestor would reach up out of the shadowy past to lay a
compelling finger on the latest daughter of his race. Her word was
passed, beyond honorable recall. Somewhere and in some way she
would find the courage to tell Vincent that she did not love him as
the wife should love the husband; and if he should still exact the
price, she would pay it. After all, it would be a refuge, of a kind.

Now it is human nature to assume finalities and to base conduct on the assumption. Conversely, it is not in human nature to
tighten one knot without loosening another. Having firmly
resolved to be unflinchingly just to a Vincent Farley, one could
afford to be humanely interested in the struggles shoreward or
seaward of a poor swimmer in the welter of the tideway. She did
not put it thus baldly, even in her secret thought. But the thing did
itself.

The opportunities for marking the struggles of the poor
swimmer were limited; but where is the woman who can not find
the way when desire drives? Ardea had something more than a
speaking acquaintance with Mr. Frederic Norman who, as
acting-manager of the foundry plant in Tom's absence, had generously thrown one of the buildings open for a series of Sunday

services for the workmen, promoted by Miss Dabney and the Reverend Francis Morelock. Since the warm nights had come, Norman had taken a room at the Inn, climbing the mountain from the Paradise side in time for dinner, and going down in the cool of the morning after an early breakfast.

Being first and last a man of business, he knew, or seemed to know, nothing of the valley gossip, or of the social sentence passed on his chief by the Mountain View Avenue court. When Ardea had assured herself of this, she utilized Norman freely as a source of information.

"You've known the boss a long time, haven't you, Miss Dabney?" asked the manager, one evening when Ardea had made room for him in a quiet corner of the veranda between the Major's chair and her own.

"Mr. Gordon? Oh, yes; a very long time, indeed. We were children together, you know."

"Well, I'd like to ask you one thing," said Frederic, the unfettered. "Did you ever get to know him well enough to guess what he'd do next? I thought I'd been pretty close to him, but once in a while he runs me up a tree so far that I get dizzy."

"As for example?" prompted Miss Ardea, leaving the personal question in the air.

"I mean his way of breaking out in a new spot every now and then. Last winter was one of the times, when he made up his mind between two minutes to chuck the pipe-making and go back to college. And now he's got another streak."

Miss Dabney made the necessary show of interest.

"What is it this time — too much business, or not enough?"

Norman rose and went to the edge of the veranda to flick his cigar ash into the flower border. When he came back he took a chair on that side of Miss Dabney farthest from the Major, who was dozing peacefully in a great flat-armed rocker.

"I declare I don't know, Miss Dabney; he's got me guessing harder than ever," he said, lowering his voice. "Since the night when the office burned he's been miles beyond me. While the carpenters were knocking together the shack we're in now, he put in the time wandering around the plant and looking as if he had lost something and forgotten what it was. Now that we've got into the new office, he shuts himself up for hours on end; won't see anybody — won't talk — scamps his meals half the time, and has actually got old Captain Caleb scared stiff."

"How singular!" said Ardea; but in her heart there was a great pity. "Do you suppose it was his loss in the fire?" she asked.

The manager shook his head.

"No; that was next to nothing, and we're doing a good business. It was something else; something that happened about the same time. If I can't find out what it is, I'll have to quit. He's freezing me out."

Ardea was inconsistent enough to oppose the alternative.

"No," she objected. "You mustn't do that, Mr. Norman. It is a friend's part to stand by at such times, don't you think?"

"Oh, I'm willing," was the generous reply. "Only I'm a little lonesome; that's all."

At another time Norman told her of the mysterious walking delegate, who was admitted to the private office when an anxious and zealous business manager was excluded. Later still, he made a half confidence. Caleb, in despair at the latest transformation in his son, had finally unfolded his doubts and fears, business-wise, to the manager. The Farleys were returning; a legal notice of a called meeting of the Chiawassee Consolidated had been published; and it was evident that Colonel Duxbury meant to take hold with his hands. And Tom seemed to have forgotten that there was a battle to be fought.

Norman's recounting of this to Miss Dabney was the merest unburdening of an overloaded soul, and he was careful to garble it so that the prospective daughter-in-law of Colonel Duxbury might not be hurt. But Ardea read between the lines. Could it be possible that Tom's lifelong enmity for the Farleys, father and son, had even a little justification in fact? She put the thought away, resolutely setting herself the task of disbelieving. Yet, in the conversation which followed, Mr. Frederic Norman was very thoroughly cross-questioned without his suspecting it. Ardea meant to cultivate the open mind, and she did not dream that it was the newly-discovered love which was prompting her to master the intricacies of the business affair.

Two days later the Farleys came home, and since Vincent went promptly into residence at Crestcliffe, the evenings with Norman were interrupted. But they had served their purpose; and when Vincent began to press for the naming of an early day in September for the wedding, Ardea found it quite feasible to be calmly indefinite. You see, she had still to tell him that it had become purely a matter of promise-keeping with her — a task easy only for the heartless.

It was in the third week in August, a full month, earlier than their original plans contemplated, that the Dabneys returned to Paradise and Deer Trace. Miss Euphrasia was led to believe that the Major had tired of the hotel and the mountain; and the Major thought the suggestion came first from Miss Euphrasia.

But the real reason for the sudden return lay in a brief note signed "Norman," and conveyed privately to Ardea's hands by a grimy-faced boy from the foundry.

"Mr. Tom was waylaid by two footpads at the Woodlawn gates Saturday night and half killed," it read. "He is delirious and asks continually for you. Could you come?"

XXXI

THE NET OF THE FOWLER

Which of the Cynic Fathers was it who defined virtue as an attitude of the mind toward externals? One may not always recall a pat quotation on the spur of the moment, but it sounds like Demonax or another of the later school, when the philosophy of cynicism had sunk to the level of a sneer at poor human nature.

To say that Mr. Duxbury Farley, returning to find Chiawassee Consolidated in some sense at the mercy of the new pipe plant, regarded himself as a benefactor whose confidence had been grossly abused, is only to take him at his word. What, pray tell us, was Caleb Gordon in the crude beginning of things? — a village blacksmith or little more, dabbling childishly in the back-wash of the great wave of industry and living poverty-stricken between four log walls. To whom did he owe the brick mansion on the Woodlawn knoll, the comforts and luxuries of civilized life, the higher education of his son?

In Mr. Farley's Index Anathema, ingratitude ranked with crime. He had trusted these Gordons, and in return they had despoiled him; crippled a great and growing industry by segregating the profitable half of it; cast doubt on the good name of its founder by reversing his business methods. Chiawassee had been making iron by the hundreds of tons: where were the profits? The query answered itself. They were in the credit account of Gordon and Gordon, every dollar of which justly belonged to the parent company. Was not the pipe-making invention perfected by a Chiawassee stock-holder, who was also a Chiawassee employee, on Chiawassee time, and with Chiawassee materials? Then why, in the name of justice, was it not to be considered a legitimate Chiawassee asset?

Mr. Duxbury Farley asked these questions pathetically and insistently; at the Cupola Club, in the Manufacturers' Association, in season and out of season, wherever there was a willing ear to hear or the smallest current of public sentiment to be diverted into the channel so patiently dug for it. Was his virtuous indignation merely the mental attitude of all the Duxbury Farleys toward things external? That bubble is too huge for this pen to prick; besides, its bursting might devastate a world.

But if we may not probe too deeply into primal causes, we may still be regardful of the effects. Mr. Farley's bid for public sympathy was not without results. True, there were those who hinted that the veteran promoter was only paving the way for a *coup de grâce* which should obliterate the Gordons, root and branch; but when the days and weeks passed, and Mr. Farley had done nothing more revolutionary than to reëlect himself president of Chiawassee Consolidated, and to resume, with Dyckman as his lieutenant, the direction of its affairs, these prophets of evil were discredited.

It was observed also that Caleb remained general manager at Gordonia, and still received the patronizing friendship of former times; and to Tom the full width of the pike was given — a distance which he kept scrupulously. But as for the younger Gordon, he knew it was the lull before the storm, and he was watching the horizon for the signs of its coming — when he was not searching for clues or brooding behind the closed door of his private office with the devil of homicide for a closet companion.

During this reproachful period Vincent Farley gave himself unreservedly, as it would seem, to the sentimental requirements, spending much time on the mountain top and linking his days to Ardea's in a way to give her a sinking of the heart at the thought that this was an earnest of all time to come.

Mountain View Avenue had understood that the wedding was to be in September; but as late as the final week in August the cards were not out, and Miss Euphrasia, the source and fountainhead of the Avenue's information, could only say that she supposed the young people were making up for the time lost by separation and absence, and were willing to prolong the delights sentimental of an acknowledged engagement.

But at the risk of cutting sentiment to the very bone, it must be admitted that, after the first ardent attempt to commit Ardea to a certain and early day, the delay was of Vincent's own making; and the motive was basely commercial. Through Major Dabney, who was not proof against Colonel Duxbury's blandishments at short range, however much he might distrust them at a distance, Tom's plan of reorganization, with the suggestion of the trusteeship for Ardea's third, had become known to the Farleys. Thereupon ensued a conference of two held in Vincent's room in the hotel, and sentence of extinction was passed on Tom and Caleb.

"The ungrateful cub!" was Colonel Duxbury's indignant comment. "To use his influence over Major Dabney to sequestrate, absolutely sequestrate, a full third of our property!"

"Forewarned is forearmed," said the son coolly. "It's up to us to break the slate."

"We'll do it, never fear. Just give me a little more time in which to win public sentiment over to our side, and don't press Ardea to name the exact day until I give the word," was the promoter's parting injunction to his son; and Vincent trimmed his sails accordingly, as we have seen.

Planting the good seed, which was a little later to yield an abundant harvest of public approbation sanctioning anything he might see fit to do to the Gordons, was a congenial task to Mr. Farley; but in the midst it was rather rudely interrupted by a belated unburdening on the part of his first lieutenant in the South Tredegar offices.

Dyckman held his peace as long as he dared; in point of fact he did not speak until he saw his superiors rushing blindly into the pit digged for their feet by the astute young tyrant of the pipe foundry. If they could have fallen without carrying him with them, it is conceivable that the bookkeeper might have remained dumb. But their immunity was doubly his, and the end of it was a bad quarter of an hour for him, two of them, to be precise: the first, in which he told the president and the treasurer the story of the missing cash-book and ledger pages and the extorted confession, and the other, during which he sat under a scathing fire of abuse poured on him by the younger of his two listeners. After it was over, he escaped to the welcome refuge of his own office while father and son took counsel together against this new and unsuspected peril.

"Anybody but an idiot like Dyckman would have found out long ago if those papers were burned in Gordon's safe," snapped Vincent, when the danger had been duly weighed and measured.

The president shook his head mournfully.

"Anybody but Dyckman would have burned them himself, you'd think. It was criminally careless in him not to do so."

"They are the key to the lock," summed up the younger man. "We've got to have them."

"Assuredly — if they are in existence."

"You needn't try to squeeze comfort out of that. I tell you, they went through the fire all right, and Tom has them."

"I am afraid you are right, Vincent; afraid, also, that Dyckman so far forgot himself as to set fire to Gordon's office in the hope of retrieving his own neglect. But how are we to regain them?" Mr. Farley's weapons were two, only: first persuasion, and when that failed, corruption.

Vincent's cold blue eyes were darkening. The little virtues interpose but a slight barrier to a sharp attack of the large vices.

"The fight has fallen into halves," he said briefly. "You go on with your part as if nothing had happened, and I'll do mine. Has the old iron-melter been taken in on it, do you think?"

"No; I don't believe Caleb knows."

"That's better. Are you going up the mountain tonight?"

"Yes, I had thought of it. Eva wants me to take her."

"All right; you go, and get Major Dabney to yourself for a quiet half hour. Tell him we are all ready to close the deal, and we're only waiting on the Gordons. I'll be up to dinner, and if anybody asks for me later, let it be understood that I have gone to my room to write letters."

This bomb-hurling of Dyckman's occurred on the Wednesday. That night, between the hours of nine and eleven, the new steel safe in Tom Gordon's private office was broken open and ransacked, though nothing was taken. On Thursday afternoon, while Martha Gordon was over at Deer Trace training the new growth on Ardea's roses, Tom's room at Woodlawn was thoroughly and systematically pillaged: drawers were pulled out and emptied on the floor, the closets were stripped of their contents, and even the bed mattresses were ripped open and destroyed.

Mrs. Martha was terrified, as so bold a daylight housebreaking gave her a right to be; and Caleb was for sending to the county workhouse for the bloodhounds. But Tom was apparently unmoved.

"It won't happen again," he said; and it did not. But on the Saturday evening, just before the late dinner-hour at Woodlawn, Japheth Pettigrass, who had been trying to halter a shy filly running loose in the field across the pike, saw a stirring little drama enacted at the Woodlawn gates; saw it, and played some small part in it.

It centered on Tom, who was late getting home. He never rode with his father now if he could avoid it, and Japheth saw him swinging along up the pike, with his head down and his hands in the pockets of his short coat. The Woodlawn entrance was a walled semicircle giving back from the roadway, with the carriage gates hinged to great stone pillars in the center, and a light iron grille at the side for foot-passengers. Tom's hand was on the latch of the little gate when two men darted from the shadow of the nearest pillar and flung themselves on him.

Japheth saw them first and gave a great yell of warning. Tom turned at the cry, and so was not taken entirely unawares. But the two had beaten him down and were busily searching him when Japheth dashed across the pike, shouting as he ran. The footpads persisted until the horse-trader came near enough to see that they were black men, or rather white men with blackened faces and hands. Then they sprang up and vanished in the gathering dusk.

Tom was conscious when Pettigrass got him on his feet and hastily bound a handkerchief over the ugly wound in his head. He was still conscious when Japheth walked him slowly up the path to the house, and was sanely concerned lest his mother should be frightened.

But after they got him to bed he sank into an inert sleep out of which he awoke the next morning wildly delirious. Ardea's name was oftenest on his lips in his ravings, and while his strength remained, his calling for her was monotonously insistent. He seemed to think she was at the great house across the lawns, and it took the united efforts of Japheth and Norman to hold him when he tried to get to the window to shout across for her.

Norman stood it until late Monday afternoon. Then, when Caleb had relieved him at Tom's bedside, he drove down to Gordonia and wrote the note to Miss Dabney, sending it up the mountain by one of the Helgerson boys with strict injunctions to give it to Miss Ardea herself.

The Dabneys came down from the mountain Tuesday morning, and Ardea was so far from disregarding her summons that she stopped the carriage at the Woodlawn gates and went directly to comfort Mrs. Martha and to offer her services in the sick-room. Tom was in one of his stubbornest paroxysms when she entered, but at the touch of her hand he became quiet, and a little later fell into a deep sleep, the first since the Saturday night of coma and stertorous breathings.

That same afternoon Crestcliffe Inn lost another guest, and the smoking-room at Warwick Lodge was lighted far into the night. Two men talked in low tones behind the carefully-shaded windows, one of them, the younger, lounging in the depths of an easy-chair, and the other pacing the floor in deepest abstraction.

"I only know what Ardea tells me," said the lounger, answering the final question put by the floor pacer. "He's out of his head — and out of the way, temporarily, at least. Now is your time to strike."

Mr. Duxbury Farley nodded his head slowly.

"It was providential for us, Vincent, this assault just at the critical moment. I have struck. I had an interview with Caleb this evening and made him an offer for the pipe plant. He is to give us his answer tomorrow morning."

Silence fell for a little time, and then the younger man in the wicker chair smote his palms together.

"Curse him!" he gritted vengefully, transferring his thought from Caleb Gordon to Caleb Gordon's son. "I hope he'll die!"

The elder man paused in his walk. "Why, Vincent, my son! What has come over you? It is merely a matter of business, and we mustn't be vindictive."

"Business be damned!" snarled the younger man. "Can't you see? She has promised to marry me — and she loves *him*. Are you going to bed? Well, I'm not. I've got something else to do first."

A few minutes later he let himself noiselessly out at the side door of the Lodge, and turned down the avenue in the direction of Deer Trace. But after crossing the bridge over the creek, he took a diagonal course through the stubble-fields and bore to the right. And when he finally reached and climbed the wall into the pike, it was at a point directly opposite the forking of the rough wood road which led off to the Pine Knob settlement.

As he leaped over into the highway, a man carrying a squirrel gun stepped from behind a tree.

"I was allowin' you'd done forgot," said the man, yawning sleepily.

"I never forget," was the short rejoinder. Then: "Come with me, and you shall hear with your own ears, since you won't take my word for it. Then, if you still want to sleep on your wrongs, it's your own affair."

XXXII

WHOSO DIGGETH A PIT

If Thomas Gordon, opening his eyes to consciousness on the mid-week morning, felt the surprise which might naturally grow out of the sight of Ardea sitting in a low rocker at his bedside, he did not evince it, possibly because there were other and more perplexing things for the tired brain to grapple with first.

For the moment he did not stir or try to speak. There was a long dream somewhere in the past in which he had been lost in the darkness, stumbling and groping and calling for her to come and lead him out to life and light. It must have been a dream, he argued, and perhaps this was only a continuation of it. Yet, no; she was there in visible presence, bending over a tiny embroidery frame; and they were alone together.

"Ardea!" he said tremulously.

She looked up, and her eyes were like cooling well-springs to quench the fever fires in his.

"You are better," she said, rising. "I'll go and call your mother."

"Wait a minute," he pleaded; then his hand found the bandage on his head. "What happened to me?"

"Don't you remember? Two men tried to rob you last Saturday evening as you were coming home. One of them struck you."

"Saturday? And this is —"

"This is Wednesday."

The cool preciseness of her replies cut him to the heart. He did not need to ask why she had come. It was mere neighborliness, and not for him, but for his mother. He remembered the Saturday evening quite clearly now: Japheth's shout; the two men springing on him; the instant just preceding the crash of the blow when he had recognized one of his assailants and guessed the identity of the other.

"It was no more than right that you should come," he said bitterly. "It was the least you could do, since your —"

She was moving toward the door, and his ungrateful outburst had the effect of stopping her. But she did not go back to him.

"I owe your mother anything she likes to ask," she affirmed, in the same colorless tone.

"And you owe me nothing at all, you would say. I might controvert that. But no matter; we have passed the Saturday and have come to the Wednesday. Where is Norman? Hasn't he been here?"

"He has been with you almost constantly from the first. He was here less than an hour ago."

"Where is he now?"

She hesitated. "There is urgency of some kind in your business affairs. Your father spent the night in South Tredegar; and a little while ago he telephoned for Mr. Norman — from the iron-works, I think." She had moved away again, and her hand was on the door-knob.

He raised himself on one elbow.

"You are in a desperate hurry, aren't you?" he gritted; though the teeth-grinding was from the pain it cost him to move. "Would you mind handing me that desk telephone before you go?"

She came back and tried it, but the wired cord was not long enough to reach to the bed.

"If you wish to speak to some one, perhaps I could do it for you," she suggested, quite in the trained-nurse tone.

His smile was a mere grimace of torture.

"If you could stretch your good-will to — to my mother — that far," he said. "Please call my office — number five-twenty-six G — and ask for Mr. Norman."

She complied, but with only a strange young-woman stenographer at the other end of the wire, a word of explanation was necessary. "This is Miss Dabney, at Woodlawn. Mr. Gordon is better, and he wishes to say — what did you want to say?" she asked, turning to him.

"Just ask what's going on; if it's Norman you've got, he'll know," said Tom, sinking back on the pillows.

What the stenographer had to say took some little time, and Ardea's color came and went in hot flashes and her eyes grew large and thoughtful as she listened. When she put the ear-piece down and spoke to the sick man, her tone was kinder.

"There is an important business meeting going on over at the furnace office, and Mr. Norman is there with your father," she said. "The stenographer wants me to ask you about some papers Mr. Norman thinks you may have, and —"

She stopped in deference to the yellow pallor that was creeping like a curious mask over the face of the man in the bed. Through all the strain of the last twenty hours she had held herself well in hand, doing for him only what she might have done for a sick and suffering stranger. But there were limits beyond which love refused to be driven.

"Tom!" she gasped, rising quickly to go to him.

"Wait," he muttered; "let me pull myself together. The papers — are — in —"

He seemed about to relapse into unconsciousness, and she

hastily poured out a spoonful of the stimulating medicine left by Doctor Williams and gave it to him. It strangled him, and she slipped her hand under the pillow and raised his head. It was the nearness of her that revived him.

"I — I'm weaker than a girl," he whispered. "Vince — I mean the thug, hit me a lot harder than he needed to. What was I saying? — oh, yes; the papers. Will you — will you go over there in the corner by the door and look behind the mopboard? You will find a piece of it sawed so it will come out. In the wall behind it there ought to be a package."

She found it readily, — a thick packet securely tied with heavy twine and a little charred at the corners.

"That's it," he said weakly. "Now one more last favor; please send Aunt 'Phrony up as you go down. Tell her I want my clothes."

Miss Dabney became the trained nurse again in the turning of a leaf.

"You are not going to get up?" she said.

"Yes, I must; I'm due this minute at that meeting down yonder."

"Indeed, you shall do no such insane thing!" she cried. "What are you thinking of!"

"Listen!" he commanded. "My father has worked hard all his life, and he's right old now, Ardea. If I should fail him — but I'm not going to. Please send Aunt 'Phrony."

"I'm going to call your mother," she said firmly.

"If you do, you'll regret it the longest day you live."

"Then let me take the papers down to Mr. Norman for you."

He considered the alternative for a moment — only a moment. What an exquisite revenge it would be to make her the messenger! But he found he did not hate her so bitterly as he had been trying to since that soul-torturing evening on the cliff's edge.

"No, I can't quite do that," he objected; and again he besought her to send the old negro housekeeper.

She consented finally, and as she was leaving him, she said:

"I hope your mother is still asleep. She was here with you all night, and Mr. Norman and I made her go to bed at daybreak. If you must go, get out of the house as quietly as you can, and I'll have Pete and the buggy waiting for you at the gate."

"God bless you!" said Tom fervently; and then he set his teeth hard and did that which came next.

The Dabney buggy was waiting for him when, after what seemed like a pilgrimage of endless miles, he had crept down to the gate. But it was Miss Dabney, and not Mammy Juliet's Pete, who was holding the reins.

"I couldn't find Pete, and Japheth has gone to town," she

explained. "Can you get in by yourself?"

He was holding on by the cut wheel, and the death-look was creeping over his face again.

"I can't let you," he panted; and she thought he was thinking of the disgrace for her.

"I am my own mistress," she said coldly. "If I choose to drive you when you are too sick to hold the reins, it is my own affair."

He shook his head impatiently.

"I wasn't thinking of that; but you must first know just what you're doing. My father stands to lose all he has got to — to the Farley's. That's what the meeting is for. Do you understand?"

She bit her lip and a far-away look came into her eyes. Then she turned on him with a little frown of determination gathering between her straight eyebrows — a frown that reminded him of the Major in his militant moods.

"I must take your word for it," she said, and the words seemed to cut the air like edged things. "Tell me the truth: is your cause entirely just? Your motive is not revenge?"

"As God is my witness," he said solemnly. "It is my father's cause, and none of mine; more than that, it is your grandfather's cause — and yours."

She pushed the buggy hood back with a quick arm sweep and gave him her free hand. "Step carefully," she cautioned; and a minute later they were speeding swiftly down the pike in a white dust cloud of their own making.

There was a sharp crisis to the fore in the old log-house office at the furnace. Caleb Gordon, haggard and tremulous, sat at one end of the trestle-board which served as a table, with Norman at his elbow; and flanking him on either side were the two Farleys, Dyckman, Trewhitt, acting general counsel for the company in the Farley interest, and Hanchett, representing the Gordons.

Having arranged the preliminaries to his entire satisfaction, Colonel Duxbury had struck true and hard. The pipe foundry might be taken into the parent company at a certain nominal figure payable in a new issue of Chiawassee Limited stock, or three several things were due to happen simultaneously: the furnace would be shut down indefinitely "for repairs," thus cutting off the iron supply and making a ruinous forfeiture of pipe contracts inevitable; suit would be brought to recover damages for the alleged mismanagement of Chiawassee Consolidated during the absence of the majority stock-holders; and the validity of the pipe-pit patents would be contested in the courts. This was the ultimatum.

The one-sided battle had been fought to a finish. Hanchett,

hewing away in the dark, had made every double and turn that keen legal acumen and a sharp wit could suggest to gain time. But Mr. Farley was inexorable. The business must be concluded at the present sitting; otherwise the papers in the two suits, which were already prepared, would be filed before noon. Hanchett took his principal into the laboratory for a private word.

"It's for you to decide, Mr. Gordon," he said. "If you want to follow them into the court, we'll do the best we can. But as a friend I can't advise you to take that course."

"If we could only make out to find out what Tom's holdin' over 'em!" groaned Caleb helplessly.

"Yes; but we can't," said the lawyer. "And whatever it may be, they are evidently not afraid of it."

"We'll never see a dollar's dividend out o' the stock, Cap'n Hanchett. I might as well give 'em the foundry free and clear."

"That's the chance you take, of course. But on the other hand, they can force you to the wall in a month and make you lose everything you have. I've been over the books with Norman: if you can't fill your pipe contracts, the forfeitures will ruin you. And you can't fill them unless you can have Chiawassee iron, and at the present price."

The old iron-master led the way back to the room of doom and took his place at the end of the trestle-board table.

"Give me the papers," he said gloomily; and the Farleys' attorney passed them across, with his fountain-pen.

There was a purring of wheels in the air and the staccato clatter of a horse's hoofs on the hard metaling of the pike. Vincent Farley rose quietly in his place and tiptoed to the door. He was in the act of snapping the catch of the spring-latch, when the door flew inward and he fell back with a smothered exclamation. Thereupon they all looked up, Caleb, the tremulous, with the pen still suspended over the signatures upon which the ink was still wet.

Tom was standing in the doorway, deathly sick and clinging to the jamb for support. In putting on his hat he had slipped the bandages, and the wound was bleeding afresh. Dyckman yelped like a stricken dog, overturning his chair as he leaped up and backed away into a corner. Only Mr. Duxbury Farley and his attorney were wholly unmoved. The lawyer had taken his fountain-pen from Caleb's shaking fingers and was carefully recapping it; and Mr. Farley was pocketing the agreement, by the terms of which the firm of Gordon and Gordon had ceased to exist.

Tom lurched into the room and threw himself feebly on the promoter, and Vincent made as if he would come between. But there was no need for intervention. Duxbury Farley had only to step aside, and Tom fell heavily, clutching the air as he went down.

The dusty office which had once been his mother's sitting-room was cleared of all save his father when Tom recovered consciousness and sat up, with Caleb's arm to help.

"There, now, Buddy; you ortn't to tried to get up and come down here," said the father soothingly. But Tom's blood was on fire.

"Tell me!" he raved: "have they got the foundry away from you?"

Caleb nodded gravely. "But don't you mind none about that, son. What I'm sweatin' about now is the fix you're in. My God! ain't Fred ever goin' to get back with Doc Williams!"

Tom struggled to his feet, tottering.

"I don't need any doctor, pappy; you couldn't kill me with a bullet — not till I've cut the heart out of these devils that have robbed you. Give me the pistol from that drawer, and drive me down to the station before their train comes. I'll do it, and by God, I'll do it now!"

But when old Longfellow, jigging vertically between the buggy shafts, picked his way out of the furnace yard, he was permitted to turn of his own accord in the homeward direction; and an hour later the sick man was back in bed, mingling horrible curses with his insistent calls for Ardea. And this time Miss Dabney did not come.

XXXIII

THE WINE-PRESS OF WRATH

There was more to that crazy outburst of Tom's about the cutting out of hearts, and the like, than would appear on the surface of things, to you who dwell in a land shadowed with wings, where law abides and a man sues his neighbor for defamation of character, if he is called a liar, I mean.

In the land unshadowed, where Polaris makes a somewhat sharper angle with the horizon, there is law, also, but much of it is unwritten. And one of the unwritten statutes is that which maintains the inherent right of a man to avenge his own quarrel with his own hand.

So, when the younger Gordon was up and about again, and was able to keep his seat soldierly on the back of the big bay, folk who knew the Gordon blood and temper looked for trouble, not of the plaintiff-and-defendant sort; and when it did not come, there were a few to lament the degeneracy of the times, and to say that old Caleb, for example, would never have so slept on his father's wrongs.

But Tom was not degenerate, even in the sense of those who thought he should have called out and shot the younger of the Farleys. It was in him to kill or be killed, quite in the traditional way: that grim gift is in the blood as the wine is in the grape — to stay unless you shall water it to extinction with many base inbreedings. Nor was the spur lacking. When the sweeping extent of the business *coup de grâce* was measured, Woodlawn was left, and there were a few thousands in bank; these and the three hundred and fifty shares of the reorganization stock which the Farleys might render worthless at will.

Tom's heart burned within him, and the race thirst — for vengeance that could be touched and seen and handled — parched his lips and swelled the veins in his forehead. Vincent Farley had it all: the business, the good repute, the love of the one woman. At such crises the wild beast in a man, if any there be, rattles the bars of its cage, and — well, you will see that the gnashing of teeth and that fierce talk of heart-cutting at the quickening moment were not inartistic.

Soberer second thought, less frenzied, was no less vengeful and vindictive. Tom had lived four formative years in a climate where the passions are colder — and more comprehensive. Also, he was of his own generation — which slays its enemy peacefully and without messing in bloody-angle details.

Riding up the pike one sun-shot afternoon in the golden September, Tom saw Ardea entering the open door of the Morwenstow church-copy, drew rein, flung himself out of the saddle and followed her. She saw him and stopped in the vestibule, quaking a little as she felt she must always quake until the impassable chasm of wedlock with another should be safely opened between them.

"Just a moment," he said abruptly. "There was a time when I said I would spare Vincent Farley and his kin for your sake. Do you remember it?"

She bowed her head without speaking. Her lips were dry.

"That was a year ago," he went on roughly. "Things have changed since then; I have changed. When my father is buried, I shall do my best to fill the mourners' carriages with those who have killed him."

"How is your father today?" she asked, not daring to trust speech otherwise.

"He is the same as he was yesterday and the day before; the same as he will always be from this on — a broken man."

"You will strike back?" She said it with infinite sadness in her voice and an upcasting of eyes that were swimming. "I don't question your right — but I pity you. The blow may be just — I don't know, but God knows — yet it will fall hardest on you in the end, Tom."

His smile was almost boyish in its frank anger. But there was a man's sneer in his words.

"Excuse me; I forgot for the moment that we are in a church. But I am taking consequences, these days."

She looked out from the cool, dark refuge of the vestibule when he mounted and rode on, and her heart was full. It was madness, vindictive madness and fell anger. But it was a generous wrath, large and manlike. It was not to be a blow in the dark or in the back, as some men struck; and he would not strike without first giving her warning. Ardea had been cross-questioning Japheth about the assault at the Woodlawn gates — to her own hurt. Japheth had evaded as he could, but she had guessed what he was keeping back — the identity of the two footpads blackened to look like negroes. It was a weary world, and life had lost much that had made it worth living.

After the incident of the church vestibule, Tom spent a week or more roaming the forests of Lebanon in rough shooting clothes, with the canvas hat pulled well over his eyes and a fowling-piece under his arm.

People said harsher things then. With old Caleb failing visibly from day to day, and his mother keeping her room for the greater part of the time, it was a shame that a great strong young giant like Tom should go loitering about on the mountain, deliberately shirking his duty. This was the elder Miss Harrison's wording of the censure; and it was kinder than Mrs. Henniker's, since it was the banker's wife who first asked, with uplifted brows and the accent accusative, if the unspeakable Bryerson woman were safely beyond tramping distance from Woodlawn.

They were both mistaken. For all Tom thought of her, Nancy Bryerson was as safe in her retreat at Pine Knob as were the squirrels he was supposed to be hunting; and they came and frisked unharmed on the branches of the tree under which he sat and munched his bit of bread and meat when the sun was at the meridian.

And he was not killing time. He was deep in an inventive trance, with vengeance for the prize to be won, and for the means to the end, iron-works and pipe plants and forgings — especially the forging of one particular thunderbolt which should shatter the Farley fortunes beyond repair. When this bolt was finally hammered into shape he came out of the wood and out of the inventive trance, had an hour's interview with Major Dabney, and took a train for New York.

I am not sure, but I think it was at Bristol, Tennessee, that the telegram from Norman, begging him to come back to South Tredegar at speed, overtook him. This is a detail, important only as a marker of time. For three days a gentleman with shrewd eyes and a hard-bitted jaw, registering at the Marlboro as "A. Dracott, New York," had been shut up with Mr. Duxbury Farley in the most private of the company's offices in the Coosa Building, and on the fourth day Norman had made shift to find out this gentleman's business. Whereupon the wire to Tom, already on his way to New York, and the prayer for returning haste.

Tom caught a slow train back, and was met at a station ten miles out of town by his energetic ex-lieutenant.

"Of course, I didn't dare do anything more than give him a hint," was the conclusion of Norman's exciting report. "I didn't know but he might give us away to Colonel Duxbury. So, without telling him much of anything, I got him to agree to meet you at his rooms in the Marlboro tonight after dinner. Then I was scared crazy for fear my wire to you would miss."

"You are a white man, Fred, and a friend to tie to," said Tom; which was more than he had ever said to Norman by way of praise in the days of master and man. Then, as the train was slowing into the South Tredegar station: "If this thing wins out, you'll come in for something bigger than you had with Gordon and Gordon; you can bet on that."

It was ordained that Gordon should anticipate his appointment by meeting his man at the dinner-table in the Marlboro café; and it was accident or design, as you like to believe, that Dyckman should be sitting two tables away, choking over his food and listening only by the road of the eye, since he was unhappily out of ear range. When the two had lighted their cigars and passed out to the elevator, the bookkeeper rose hastily and made for the nearest telephone. This, at least, was not accidental.

The conference in Suite 32 lasted until nearly midnight, with Dyckman painfully shadowing the corridor and sweating like a furnace laborer, though the night was more than autumn cool. The door was thick, the transom was closed, and the keyhole commanded nothing but a square of blank wall opposite in the electric-lighted sitting-room of the suite. Hence the bookkeeper could only guess what we may know.

"You have let in a flood of light on Mr. Farley's proposition, Mr. Gordon," said the representative of American Aqueduct, when the ground had been thoroughly gone over. "I don't mind telling you now that he made his first overtures to us on his arrival from Europe, giving us to understand that he owned or controlled the pipe-making patents absolutely."

"At that time he controlled nothing, as I have explained," said Tom, "not even his majority stock in Chiawassee Consolidated. Of course, he resumed control as soon as he reached home, and his next move was to have me quietly sandbagged while he froze my father out. But father did not transfer the patents, for the simple reason that he couldn't. They are my personal property, made over to me before the firm of Gordon and Gordon came into existence."

The pipe-trust promoter nodded.

"You are the man we'll have to do business with, Mr. Gordon," he said promptly. "Are you quite sure of your legal status in the case?"

"I have good advice. Hanchett, Goodloe and Tryson, Richmond Building, are my attorneys. They will put you in the way of finding out anything you'd like to know."

There was a pause while the New Yorker was making a memorandum of the address. Then he went straight to the point.

"As I have said, I'm here to do business. We don't need the plant. Will you sell us your patents?"

"Yes; on one condition."

"And that is — ?"

"That you first put us out of business. You'll have to smash Chiawassee Limited painstakingly and permanently before you can buy my holdings."

The shrewd-eyed gentleman who had unified practically all of the pipe foundries in the United States smiled a gentle negative.

"That would be rather out of our line. If Mr Farley owned the patents, and was disposed to fight us — as, indeed, he is not — we might try to convince him. But we are not out for vengeance — another man's vengeance, at that."

"Very well, then; you won't get what you've come after. The patents go with the plant. You can't have one without the other," said Tom, eyeing his opponent through half closed lids.

"But we can buy the plant tomorrow, at a very reasonable figure. Farley is anxious enough to come in out of the wet."

"Excuse me, Mr. Dracott, but you can't buy the plant at any price."

"Eh? Why can't we?"

"Because the majority of the stock will vote to fight you to a standstill."

"But, my dear sir! Mr. Farley controls sixty-five per cent. of the stock!"

"That is where you were lied to one more time," said Tom with great coolness. "The capital stock of Chiawassee Limited is divided into one thousand shares, all distributed. My father holds three hundred and fifty shares; Mr. Farley and his son together own four hundred and fifty; and the remaining two hundred are held in trust for Miss Ardea Dabney, to become her property in fee simple when she marries. Pending her marriage, which is currently supposed to be near at hand, the voting power of these two hundred shares resides in Miss Dabney's grandfather, *and my father holds his proxy.*"

This was the thunderbolt Tom had been forging during those quiet days spent on the mountain side; and there was another pause while one might count ten. After which the man from New York spoke his mind freely.

"Your row with these people must be pretty bitter, Mr. Gordon. Are you willing to see your father and these Dabneys go by the board for the sake of breaking the president and his son?"

"I know what I am doing," was the quiet reply. "Neither my father nor Miss Dabney will lose anything that is worth keeping."

"Have you figured that out, too? The field is too small for you down here, Mr. Gordon — much too small. You should come to New York."

Tom rose and took his hat.

"You will fight us?" he asked.

The short-circuiter of corporations laughed.

"We'll put you out of business, if you insist on it. Anything to oblige. Better light a fresh cigar before you go."

Tom helped himself from the box on the table.

"You have it to do, Mr. Dracott. On the day you have hammered Chiawassee Limited down to a dead proposition, you can have my pipe patents at the figure named. If you will meet me at the office of Hanchett, Goodloe and Tryson tomorrow morning at ten o'clock, we will put it in writing. Good night."

XXXIV

THE SMOKE OF THE FURNACE

Hoping always for the best, after the manner prescribed for optimistic gentlemen who successfully exploit their fellows, Mr. Duxbury Farley did not deem it necessary to confide fully in his son when the representative of American Aqueduct broke off negotiations abruptly and went back to New York.

It is a sad state of affairs, reached by respectably villainous fathers the world over, when the son demonstrates the mathematical law of progression by becoming a villain without regard for the respectabilities. Mr. Farley saw the growing outlaw in his son, was not a little disturbed thereby, and was beginning to crouch when it menaced.

Hence, when the comfortable arrangement with the pipe trust threatened to miscarry, all he did was to urge Vincent to hasten the day when Miss Dabney's stock could be utilized as a Farley asset. Pressed for particular reasons, he turned it off lightly. A young man in the fever of ante-nuptial expectancy was a mere pawn in the business game: let it be over and done with, so that the nominal treasurer of Chiawassee Limited could once more become the treasurer in fact.

Whereupon Vincent, who rode badly at best, bought a new saddle-horse and took his place at Miss Dabney's whip-hand in the early morning rides, the place formerly filled by Tom Gordon, — which was not the part of wisdom, one would say. Contrasts are pitiless things; and the wary woman-hunter will break new paths rather than traverse those already broken by his rival.

Tom, meanwhile, had apparently relapsed into his former condition of disinterest, and was once more spending his days on the mountain, seemingly bent on effacing himself socially, as he had been effaced business-wise by the Farley overturn.

A week or more after the relapse, as he was crossing the road leading over the mountain's shoulder, he came on the morning riders walking their horses toward Paradise, and saw trouble in Miss Dabney's eyes, and on Farley's impassive face a mask of sullen anger.

When they were out of sight and hearing, Tom sat on a flat stone by the roadside with his gun between his knees, thoughtfully speculative. Were the high gods invoked in the midnight conference at the Marlboro beginning to point the finger of fate at these two? He was malevolent enough to hope so, and in the comfort of the hope, walked many miles that day through the forests of crimson and gold showering with falling leaves.

Whatever their influence in the field of sentiment, undeniably in that of fact the high gods were imposing Sisyphean labors on Mr. Duxbury Farley.

With the negotiations for the sale to the trust so abruptly terminated, the promoter-president set instant and anxious inquiry afoot to determine the cause. It was soon revealed; and when Mr. Farley found that the pipe-pit patents had not been transferred with the Gordon plant, and that Major Dabney had given Caleb Gordon a power of attorney over Ardea's stock in the company, there were hard words said in the town offices of Messrs. Trewhitt and Slocumb, Chiawassee attorneys, and a torrent of persuasive ones poured into the Major's ear — the latter pointing to the crying necessity for the revocation of the power of attorney, summarily and at once.

The Major proved singularly obstinate and non-committal. "Mistah Caleb Gordon is my friend, suh, and I was mighty proud to do him this small faveh. What his object is makes no manneh of diffe'ence to me, suh; no manneh of diffe'ence, whateveh," was all an anxious promoter could get out of the old autocrat of Deer Trace. But Mr. Farley did not desist; neither did he fail to keep the telegraph wires to New York heated to incandescence with his appeals for a renewal of the negotiations for surrender.

When the wired appeals brought forth nothing but evasive replies, Mr. Farley began to look for trouble, and it came: first in a mysterious closing of the market against Chiawassee pipe, and next in an alarming advance of freight rates from Gordonia on the Great Southwestern.

Colonel Duxbury doubled his field force and gave his travelers a free hand on the price list. Persuasion and diplomacy having failed, a frenzy like that of one who finds himself slipping into the sharp-staked pitfall prepared for others seized on him. It was the madness of those who have seen the clock hands stop and begin to turn steadily backward on the dial of success.

Ten days later the freight rates went up another notch, and there began to be a painful dearth of cars in which to ship the few orders the salesmen were still able to place. Mr. Farley shut his eyes to the portents, put himself recklessly into Mr. Vancourt Henniker's hands as a borrower, and posted a notice of a slashing cut in wages at the works.

As a matter of course, the cut bred immediate and tumultuous trouble with the miners, and in the midst of it the president made a flying trip to New York; to the metropolis and to the offices of American Aqueduct to make a final appeal in person.

But the door was shut. Mr. Dracott was not to be seen, though his assistant was very affable. No; American Aqueduct was not trying to assimilate the smaller plants, or to crush out all competition, as the public seemed to believe. With fifty million dollars invested it could easily control a market for its own product, which was all the share-holders demanded. Was Mr. Farley in the city for some little time? and would he not dine with the assistant at the Waldorf-Astoria?

Mr. Farley took a fast train, south-bound, instead, and on reaching South Tredegar, wired his New York broker to test the market with a small block of Chiawassee Limited. There were no takers at the upset price; and the highest bid was less than half of the asking. Colonel Duxbury was writing letters at the Cupola when the broker's telegram was handed him, and he broke a rule which had held good for the better part of a cautious, self-contained lifetime: he went to the buffet and took a stiff drink of brandy — alone. The following morning the miners and all the white men employed in the furnace and foundries and coke yards at Gordonia went on strike.

"Whom the gods would destroy, they first make mad," has a wide application in the commercial world. Duxbury Farley had resources! a comfortable fortune as country fortunes go, amassed by far-seeing shrewdness, a calm contempt for the well-being of his business associates, and most of all by a crowning gift in the ability to recognize the psychological moment at which to let go.

But under pressure of the combined disasters he lost his head, quarreled with his colder-blooded son, and in spite of Vincent's angry protests, began the suicidal process of turning his available assets into ammunition for the fighting of a battle which could have but one possible outcome.

Strike-breakers were imported at fabulous expense. Armed guards under pay swarmed at the valley foot, and around the company's property elsewhere. By hook or crook the foundries were kept going, turning out water-pipe for which there was no market, and which, owing to the disturbances which were promptly made an excuse by the railway company, could not be moved out of the Chiawassee yard.

Later, when the striking workmen began to grow hungry, riot, arson and bloodshed were nightly occurrences. A charging of coal, mined under the greatest difficulties, was conveyed to the coke yards, only to be destroyed — and half of the ovens with it — by dynamite cunningly blackened and dropped into the chargings. For want of fuel, the furnace went out of blast, but with the small store of coke remaining in the foundry yards, the pipe pits were kept at work. By this time the promoter-president was little better than a madman, fighting like a berserker, and breeding a certain awed respect in the comment of those who had hitherto held him only as a shrewd schemer.

And Thomas Jefferson: how did this return to primordial chaos, brought about in no uncertain sense by his own premeditated act, affect him? Only a man quite lost to all promptings of the grace that saves and softens could look unmoved on the burnings and riotings, the cruel wastings and the bloodlettings, one would say.

When he was not galloping Saladin afar in the country roads to the landward side of Paradise, Tom Gordon was idling purposefully in the Lebanon forests, with the fowling-piece under his arm and Japheth Pettigrass's dog trotting soberly at heel, as carefree, to all appearances, as a school-boy home for a holiday.

The dog, a mongrel, liver-spotted cur with hound's ears, chose to be of this companionship, and he was always waiting at the orchard gate when Tom fared forth. For the unsympathetic analyst of dog motives there will be sufficient reason in expectation, since Tom never failed to share his noon-time snack of bread and meat with Cæsar. Yet Deer Trace set a good table, and there were bones with meat on them to be had without following a gunsman who never shot anything, miles on end on the mountain side.

Then there were children, — a brood of dusty-haired, bare-legged shynesses at a mountaineer's cabin in a cove far beyond the rock of the shadowing cedars, where Tom sometimes stopped to beg a drink of water from the cold spring under the dooryard oaks. They were not afraid of the strong-limbed, duck-clad stranger, whose manner was the manner of the town folk, but whose speech was the gentle drawl of the mountain motherland. Once he had eaten with them in the single room of the tumble-down cabin; and again he had made a grape-vine swing for the boys, and had ridden the littlest girl on his shoulder up to the steep-pitched corn patch where her father was plowing. We may bear this in mind, since it has been said that there is hope still for the man of whom children and dogs have no fear.

In these forest-roaming weeks, business, or the carking thought of it, seemed furthest from him; it is within belief that he heard the news of the rapidly succeeding tragedies at Gordonia only through the dinner-table monologues of his father, since his wanderings never by any chance took him within eye-or ear-shot of them.

Caleb's ailment based itself chiefly on broken habit and the lack of something to do, and in a manner the trouble at Gordonia was a tonic. What a man beloved of his kind, and loving it, could do toward damping the fierce fires of passion and hatred and law-lessness alight at the lower end of Paradise, he was doing daily, going where the armed guards and the sheriff's deputies dared not go, and striving manfully to do his duty as he saw it.

Tom was always a silent listener at the dinner-table recountings of the day's happenings; attentive, but only filially interested: willing to encourage his father to talk, but never commenting.

Why he was so indifferent, so little stirred by the tale of the tragedies, was the most perplexing of the puzzles he presented, and was always presenting, to Caleb, the simple-hearted. Thomas Jefferson, the small boy who had threatened to die if he should not be permitted to be in and of the struggle with the railway invaders, was completely and hopelessly lost in this quiet-eyed, reticent young athlete who ate heartily and slept soundly and went afield with his gun and the borrowed dog while Rome was burning. So said Caleb in his musings; which proves nothing more than that a father's sense of perspective may not be quite perfect.

But Tom's indifference was only apparent. In reality he was eagerly absorbing his father's daily report of the progress of the game of extinction — and triumphing hard-heartedly.

It was on an evening a fortnight after the furnace had gone out of blast for lack of fuel that Caleb filled his after-dinner pipe and followed his son out on the veranda. The Indian summer was still at its best, and since the first early frosts there had been a return of dry weather and mild temperatures, with warm, soft nights when the blue haze seemed to hold all objects in suspension.

Tom had pushed out a chair for his father and was lighting his own pipe when he suddenly became aware that the still air was once more thrumming and murmuring to the familiar sob and sigh of the great furnace blowing-engines. He started up quickly.

"What's that?" he demanded. "Surely they haven't blown in again?"

Caleb nodded assent.

"I reckon so. Colonel Duxbury allowed to me this mornin' that he was about out o' the woods — in spite of you, he said; as if you'd been the one that was doin' him up."

"But he can't be!" exclaimed Tom, so earnestly and definitely that the mask fell away and the father was no longer deceived.

"I'm only tellin' you what he allowed to me, son. I reckoned he was about all in, quite a spell ago; but you can't tell nothing by what you see — when it's Colonel Duxbury. He got two car-loads o' new men today, the Lord on'y knows where from; and he's shippin' Pocahontas coke, and gettin' it here, too."

Tom sat glooming over it for a time, shrouding himself in

tobacco smoke. Then he said:

"You feazed me a little at first; but I think I know now what has happened."

Caleb took time to let the remark sink in. It carried inferences.

"Buddy, I been suspectin' for a good while back that you know more about this sudden smash-up than you've let on. Do you?"

"I know all about it," was the quiet rejoinder.

"You do? What on top o' God's green earth —"

Tom held up his hand for silence. A man had let himself in at the roadway gate and was walking rapidly up the path to the house. It was Norman; and after a few hurried words in private with Tom, he went as he had come, declining Caleb's invitation to stay and smoke a pipe on the veranda.

When the gate latch clicked at Norman's outgoing, Tom had risen and was knocking the ash from his pipe and buttoning his coat.

"I was admitting that I knew," he said. "I can tell you more now than I could a moment ago, because the time for which I have been waiting has come. You remarked that you thought the Farleys were at the end of their rope. They were not until today, but today they are. Every piece of property they have, including Warwick Lodge, is mortgaged to the hilt, and this afternoon Colonel Duxbury put his Chiawassee stock into Henniker's hands as security for a final loan — so Norman tells me. Perhaps it would interest you a trifle to know something about the figure at which Henniker accepted it."

"It would, for a fact, Buddy."

"Well, he took it for less than the annual dividend that it earned the year we ran the plant; and between us two, he's scared to death, at that."

"Heavens and earth! Why, Buddy, son! we're plum' ruined — and so's old Major Dabney!"

Tom had finished buttoning his coat and was settling his soft hat on his head.

"Don't you worry, pappy," he said, with a touch of the old boyish assurance. "Our part, since Colonel Duxbury saw fit to freeze us out, is to say nothing and saw wood. If the Major comes to you, you can tell him that my word to him holds good: he can have par for Ardea's stock any time he wants it, and he could have it just the same if Chiawassee were wiped off of the map — as it's going to be."

"But Tom; tell me —"

"Not yet, pappy; be patient just a little while longer and you shall know all there is to tell. I'm leaving you with a clear conscience to say to any one who asks that you don't know."

Caleb had struggled up out of his chair, and now he laid a hand on his son's shoulder.

"I ain't askin', Buddy," he said, with a tremulous quaver in his voice; "I ain't askin' a livin' thing. I'm just a-hopin' — hopin' I'll wake up bime-by and find it's on'y a bad dream." Then, with sudden and agonizing emphasis: "My God, son! they been butcherin' one 'nother down yonder for four long weeks!"

"I can't help that!" was the savage response. "It's a battle to the death, and the smoke of it has got into my blood. If I believed in God, as I used to once, I'd be down on my knees to Him this minute, asking Him to let me live long enough to see these two hypocritical thieves, — thugs, — sandbaggers, — hit the bottom!"

He turned away, walked to the north end of the veranda, where the flare of the rekindled furnace was redly visible over the knolls, and presently came back.

"I said you should know after a little: you may as well know now. I planned this thing; I set out to break them; and, as it happened, I wasn't a moment too soon. In another week you and Major Dabney would have had a chance to sell out for little or nothing, or lose it all. Farley had it fixed to be swallowed by the trust, and this is how it was to be done. Farley stipulated that the stock transaction should figure as a forced sale at next to nothing, in which all the stock-holders should participate, and that the remainder of the purchase price, which would have been a fair figure for all the stock, should be paid to him and his son individually as a bonus!"

The old iron-master groaned. In spite of the hard teaching of all the years, he would have clung to some poor shadow of belief in Duxbury Farley if he could have done so.

"That's all," Tom went on stridently: "all but the turning of the trick that put them in the hole they were digging for you and the Major. Vint Farley had no notion of letting Ardea bring her money into the family of her own free will: he planned to rob her first and marry her afterward. Now, by God, I'm going down to tell them both what they're up against! Don't sit up for me."

He had taken a dozen strides down the graveled path when he saw some one coming hurriedly across the lawns from Deer Trace, and heard a voice — the voice of the woman he loved — calling to him softly in the stillness:

"Tom! O Tom!" it said, "please wait — just one minute!"

But there are lusts mightier, momentarily, than love, and the lust of vengeance is one. He made as if he did not see or hear; and lest she should overtake him, left the path to lose himself among the trees and to vault the low boundary wall into the pike at a point safely out of sight from the gate.

XXXV

A SOUL IN SHACKLES

The blue autumn night haze had almost the consistency of a cloud when Gordon leaped the wall and set his face toward the iron-works. Or rather it was like the depths of a translucent sea in which the distant electric lights of Mountain View Avenue shone as blurs of phosphorescent life on one hand, and the great dark bulk of Lebanon loomed as the massive foundations of a shadowy island on the other.

Farther on, the recurring flare from the tall vent of the blast-furnace lighted the haze depths weirdly, turning the mysterious sea bottom into fathomless abysses of dull-red incandescence for the few seconds of its duration — a slow lightning flash sub-merged and half extinguished.

Gordon was passing the country colony's church when one of the torch-like flares reddened on the night, and the glow picked out the gilt cross at the top of the sham Norman tower. He flung up a hand involuntarily, as if to put the emblem, and that for which it stood, out of his life. At the same instant a whiff of the acrid smoke from the distant furnace fires tingled in his nostrils, and he quickened his pace. The hour for which all other hours had been waiting had struck. Love had called, and religion had made its silent protest; but the smell in his nostrils was the smoky breath of Mammon, the breath which has maddened a world: he strode on doggedly, thinking only of his triumph and how he should presently compass it.

The two great poplar-trees, sentineling what had once been the gate of the old Gordon homestead, had been spared through all the industrial changes. When he would have opened the wicket to pass on to the log-house offices, an armed man stepped from behind one of the trees with an oath in his mouth and his gun-butt drawn up to strike. Before the blow could fall, the furnace flare blazed aloft like a mighty torch, and the man grounded his weapon.

"I beg your pardon, Mr. Gordon; I — I took ye for somebody else," he stammered; and Tom scanned his face sharply by the light of the burning gases.

"Whom? — for instance," he queried.

"Why-e-yeh — I reckon it don't make any diff'rence — my tellin' you; you'd ought to have it in for him, too. I was layin' for that houn'-dog 'at walks on his hind legs and calls hisself Vint Farley."

"Who are you?" Tom demanded.

"Kincaid's my name, and I'm s'posed to be one o' the strike guards; leastwise, that's what I hired out for a little spell ago. I couldn't think of nare' a better way o' gettin' at the damned —"

Gordon interrupted bruskly. "Cut out the curses and tell me what you owe Vint Farley. If your debt is bigger than mine, you shall have the first chance."

The gas-flash came again. There was black wrath in the man's eyes.

"You can tote it up for yourself, Tom-Jeff Gordon. Late yeste'day evening when me and Nan Bryerson drove to town for your Uncle Silas to marry us, she told me what I'd been mistrustin' for a month back — that Vint Farley was the daddy o' her chillern. He's done might' nigh ever'thing short o' killin' her to make her swear 'em on to you; and I allowed I'd jest put off goin' back West till I'd fixed his lyin' face so 'at no yuther woman'd ever look at it."

Gordon staggered and leaned against the fence palings, the red rage of murder boiling in his veins. Here, at last, was the key to all the mysteries; the source of all the cruel gossip; the foundation of the wall of separation that had been built up between his love and Ardea. When he could trust himself to speak he asked a question.

"Who knows this, besides yourself?"

"Your Uncle Silas, for one: he allowed he wouldn't marry us less'n she told him. I might' nigh b'lieve he had his suspicions, too. He let on like it was Farley that told him on you, years ago, when you was a boy."

"He did? Then Farley was one of the three men who saw us up yonder at the barrel-spring?"

"Yes; and I was another one of 'em. I was right hot at you that mornin'; I shore was."

"Well, who else knows about it?"

"Brother Bill Layne, and Aunt M'randy, and Japhe Pettigrass. They-all went in town to stan' up with me and Nan."

Then Tom remembered the figure coming swiftly across the lawns and the call of the voice he loved. Had Japheth told her, and was she hastening to make such reparation as she could? No matter, it was too late now. The fierce hatred of the wounded savage was astir in his heart and it would not be denied or silenced.

"Give me that gun, and you shall have your first chance," he conceded. "I make but one condition: if you kill him, I'll kill you."

Kincaid laughed and gave up his weapon.

"I was only allowin' to sp'ile his face some, and a rock'll do for that. You can have what's left o' him atter I get thoo — and it'll be enough to kill, I reckon."

At the moment of weapon-passing there came sounds audible above the sob and sigh of the blowing-engines — a clatter of horses' hoofs and the grinding of carriage wheels on the pike. Gordon signed quickly to Kincaid and drew back carefully behind the bole of the opposite poplar.

It was the Warwick Lodge surrey, and it stopped at the gate. Two men got out and went up the path, and an instant later, Kincaid followed stealthily.

Gordon waited for the next gas-flare, and by the light of it he threw the breech-block of the repeating rifle to make sure the cartridge was in place. Then he, too, passed through the wicket and went to stand in the shadow of the slab-floored porch, redolent of memories. He had forgotten the lesser vengeance in the thirst for the greater, — that he had come to fling their misfortunes into the faces of the father and the son, and to tell them that the work was his. He heard only the voice of the savage in his heart, and that was whispering "Kill! kill!"

It was close on midnight when the door giving on the porch opened and two men stood on the threshold. The younger of the two was speaking.

"It's quieter than usual tonight. That was a good move — getting Ludlow and the two Helgersons jailed. I was in hopes we could snaffle old Caleb with the others. He pretends to be peace-making, but as long as he is loose, these fools will hang to the idea that they're fighting his battle against us."

"It is already fought," said the older man dejectedly. "My luck has gone. When Henniker puts us to the wall, we shall be beggars."

The young man's rejoinder was an exclamation of contempt.

"You've lost your nerve. What you need most is to go to bed and sleep. Wait for me till I've made a round of the guards, and we'll go home. Better ring up the surrey right now."

He left the porch on the side nearest the furnace, and Gordon saw an active figure glide from the shelter of a flask-shed and go in pursuit. He followed at a distance. It was needful only that he should know where to find Farley when Kincaid should have squared his account.

The leisurely chase led the round of the great gates first, and thence through the deserted and ruined coke yard to the foot of the huge slag dump, cold now from the long shut-down.

Tom looked to see Farley turn back from the toe of the dump. There were no gates on that side of the yard, and consequently no guards.

But the short cut to the office was up the slope of the dump and along the railway track over which the drawings of molten slag were run out to be spilled down the face of the declivity. There had been no slag-drawing since the new "blow-in" earlier in the day; but while he was watching to keep Farley in sight in the intervals between the gas-flares, Gordon was conscious of the note of preparation behind him: the slackening of the blast, the rattle and clank of the dinkey locomotive pushing the dumping ladle into place under the furnace lip.

Farley had taken two or three scrambling steps up the rough-seamed declivity when the workmen tapped the furnace. There was a sputtering roar and the air was filled with coruscating sparks.

Then the stream of molten matter began to pour into the great ladle, a huge eight-foot pot swung on tilting trunnions and mounted on a skeleton flat-car; and for Gordon, standing at the corner of the ore shed with his back to the slag drawers, the red glow picked out the man scrambling up the miniature mountain of cooled scoria, — this man and another man running swiftly to overtake him.

He looked on coldly until he saw Kincaid head off the retreat and face his adversary. Instantly there was a spurt of fire from a pistol in Farley's right hand, a brief flash with the report swallowed up in the roar from the furnace lip. Then the two men closed and rolled together to the bottom of the slope, and Gordon turned his back.

When he looked again the trampling note of the big blast-engines had quickened to its normal beat, the blow-hole was plugged with its stopper of damp clay, and a red twilight born of the reflection from the surface of the great pot of seething slag had succeeded to the blinding glare. Where there had been two men locked in struggle there was now only one, and he was lying quietly with one leg doubled under him. Gordon set his teeth on an angry oath of disappointment. Had Kincaid broken his compact?

The first long-drawn exhaust of the dinkey engine moving the slag kettle out to its spilling place ripped the silence. Gordon heard — and he did not hear: he was watching the prone figure at the dump's toe. When it should rise, he meant to fire from where he stood under the eaves of the ore-shed. The murder-thought contemplated nothing picturesque or dramatic. It was merely the dry thirst for the blood of a mortal enemy, as it is wont to be off the stage or out of the pages of the romancers.

The puffing locomotive had pushed the slag-pot car halfway to the track-end before Farley sat up as one dazed and seemed to be trying to get on his feet. Twice and once again he essayed it, falling back each time upon the bent and doubled leg. Then he looked up and saw the slag-car coming; saw and cried out as men scream in the death agony. The end rails of the dumping track were fairly above him.

Gordon heard the yell of terror and witnessed the frenzied efforts of the doomed man to rise and get out of the path of the impending torrent. Whereupon the murder devil whispered in his ear again. Farley's foot was caught in one of the many scars or seams in the lava bed. It was only necessary to wait, to withhold the merciful bullet, to go away and leave the wretched man to his fate.

That fate was certain, lacking a miracle to avert it. There were no workmen in that part of the yard; and the two men in charge of the slag kettle were on the opposite side of the engine where the dumping mechanism was connected. Farley was screaming again, but now the safety-valve of the locomotive was blowing off steam with a din to drown all.

Gordon tossed the gun aside and turned away. It was better so. Possibly at the climaxing instant he might have lacked the firmness to aim and press the trigger. This was simpler, easier, more in keeping with Vincent Farley's deserts; more satisfying to the thirst for vengeance.

Was it? Like a bolt from the heavens, into the very midst of the cold-blooded, murderous triumph, came a long-neglected form of words, writing itself in flaming letters in his brain: *Thou shall do no murder.* And after it another: *But I say unto you, love your enemies, bless them that curse you, do good to them that hate you.*

He put his hands before his eyes, stumbled blindly and fell down, groveling in the yellow sand of the ore floor, as that one of old whom the possessing devils tore and rended. Hell and the furies! — was this to be the end of it? Did the old, time-worn fables planted in the lush and mellow soil of childhood wait only for the moment of superhuman trial to assert themselves truth of the very truth? God in Heaven! must he be flogged back into the ranks he had deserted when every drop of blood in his veins was crying out for shame?

Something gripped him and stood him on his feet, and before he realized what he was doing he was running, gasping, tripping and falling headlong, only to spring up and run again, with all thoughts trampled out and beaten down by one: would he still be in time?

There was something wrong with the dumping machinery of the slag-car, and two men were working with it on the side away from the spilling slope. Gordon had not breath wherewith to shout; moreover the safety-valve was still screeching to gulf all human cries. Farley was lying face down and motionless, with the twisted foot still held fast in a wedge-shaped crack in the cooled slag. Tom bent and lifted him; yelled, swore, tugged, strained, kicked fiercely at the imprisoned shoe-heel. Still the vise-grip held, and the great kettle on the height above was creaking and slowly careening under the winching of the engine crew. If the molten torrent should plunge down the slope now, there would be two human cinders instead of one.

Suddenly the frenzy, so alien to the Gordon blood, spent itself, leaving him cool and determined. Quite methodically he found his pocket-knife, and he remembered afterward that he had been collected enough to choose and open the sharper of the two blades. There was a quick, sure slash at the shoe-lacing and the crippled foot was freed. With another yell, this time of glad triumph, he snatched up his burden and backed away with it in the tilting half second when the deluge of slag, firing the very air with shriveling heat, was pouring down the slope.

Then he fell in a heap, with Farley under him, and fainted as a woman might — when the thing was done.

XXXVI

FREE AMONG THE DEAD

The skirmish-line rivulets of melted slag had crept to within a few feet of the two at the toe of the dump when the men of the engine crew ran with water to drench them.

Tom recovered consciousness under the dashing of the water, and was one of the bearers who carried Vincent Farley on a hastily improvised stretcher to the surrey waiting at the office gate.

Afterward, he went for Doctor Williams, deriding himself Homerically for playing the second act in the drama of the Good Samaritan, but playing it, none the less. And not to quit before he was quite through, he drove with the physician to Warwick Lodge, and sat in the buggy till the other Good Samaritan had performed his office.

"Nothing very serious, is it, Doctor?" he asked, when the old physician took the reins to drive his horse-holder home.

"H'm; he'll be rather badly scarred, and there is a chance that he will lose the sight of one eye," was the reply. Then: "It's none of my quarrel, Tom, but you hammered him pretty cruelly — with a stone, too, I should say."

"Did I?" grinned Tom. He was willing to bear the blame until Kincaid should have ample time to disappear.

"Yes; and with all due allowance for your provocation, it was a good bit beneath you, my boy."

The younger man laughed grimly. "Wait till you know the full size of the provocation, Doctor. I'm not half as bad as I might be. Another man would have left him to burn — here and hereafter."

The doctor said no more. It was not his province to make or meddle in the quarrel between the Gordons and the Farleys. And Tom also was silent, having many things to render him reflective.

When he was put down at Woodlawn it was after one o'clock. Yet he sat for an hour or more on the veranda, smoking many pipes and trying as he could to prefigure the future in the light of the night's happenings.

What an insufferable animal Farley was, to be sure! — with the love of a woman like Ardea Dabney failing to keep him on the hither side of common decency! Would Ardea break with him, now that she knew the truth? Tom shook his head. Not she; she would stand by him all the more stoutly, if not for love, then for pride's sake. That was the fine thing in her loyalty.

That thought led to another. When they were married, there would have to be a beginning in a new field. Chiawassee was gone, and the Farley fortune with it; and the new field would be a bald necessity. Tom decided that not even Ardea's pride and fortitude could face the looks askance of the Mountain View Avenue folk.

He measured the country colonists justly. They might have forgiven the moral lapse, though that was not the side they had turned toward him. Yet he fancied that when the business failure should be super-added, the Farley sins would become too multitudinous for the broadest mantle of charity to cover.

"Which brings on more talk," he mused, pulling thoughtfully at the pipe. "They can't start in the new diggings without money. Anyway, Vincent's no moneymaker; and if the look on a man's face counts for anything, old Colonel Duxbury has made his last flight from the promoting perch. O Lord!" — rising with a cavernous yawn and a mighty stretching of his arms overhead, — "I reckon it's up to me to go on doing all the things I don't want to do; that I didn't in the least mean to do. Somebody ought to write a book and call it *Saints Inveterate*. It would have simplified things a whole lot if I could have left him to be cremated after all."

Mr. Vancourt Henniker was not greatly surprised when Tom Gordon asked for a private interview on the morning following the final closing down of all the industries at Gordonia.

Without being in Gordon's confidence, or in that of American Aqueduct, the banker had been shrewdly putting two and two together and applying the result as a healing plaster to the stock he had taken as security for the final loan to Colonel Duxbury.

"I thought, perhaps, you might wish to buy this stock, Mr. Gordon," he said, when Tom had stated his business. "Of course, it can be arranged, with Mr. Farley's consent to our anticipating the maturity of his notes. But" — with a genial smile and a glance over his eye-glasses — "I'm not sure that we care to part with it. Perhaps some of us would like to hold it and bid it in."

Tom's smile matched the genial expansiveness of the president's.

"I reckon you don't want it, Mr. Henniker. You'll understand that it isn't worth the paper it is printed on when I tell you that I have sold my pipe-pit patents to American Aqueduct."

"Heavens and earth! Then the plant doesn't carry the patents? You've kept this mighty quiet, among you!"

"Haven't we!" said Tom fatuously. "I know just how you feel — like a man who has been looking over the edge of the bottomless pit without knowing it. You'll let me have the stock for the face of the loan, won't you?"

But the president was already pressing the button of the electric bell that summoned the cashier. There was no time like the present when the fate of a considerable bank asset hung on the notion of a smiling young man whose mind might change in the winking of an eye.

With the Farley stock in his pocket Tom took a room at the Marlboro and spent the remainder of that day, and all the days of the fortnight following, wrestling mightily with the lawyers in winding up the tangled skein of Chiawassee affairs. Propped in his bed at Warwick Lodge, the bed he had not left since the night of violence, Duxbury Farley signed everything that was offered to him, and the obstacles to a settlement were vanquished, one by one.

When it was all over, Tom began to draw checks on the small fortune realized from the sale of the patents. One was to Major Dabney, redeeming his two hundred shares of Chiawassee Limited at par. Another was to the order of Ardea Dabney, covering the Farley shares at a valuation based on the prosperous period before the crash of '93. With this check in his pocket he went home — for the first time in two weeks.

It was well beyond the Woodlawn dinner-hour before he could muster up the courage to cross the lawns to Deer Trace. No word had passed between him and Ardea since the September afternoon when he had overtaken her at the church door, — counting as nothing the effort she had made to speak to him on the night of vengeance.

How would she receive him? Not too coldly, he hoped. It was known that Vincent's assailant in the furnace yard was a stranger; a man who had taken service as a guard: also that Mr. Gordon — they gave him his courtesy title now — had saved Vincent from a terrible death. Tom thought the rescue should count for something with Ardea.

It did. She was sitting at the piano in the otherwise deserted music-room when he entered; and she broke a chord in the middle to give him both of her hands, and to say, with eyes shining, as if the rescue were a thing of yesterday:

"O Tom! I *knew* you had it in you! It was fine!"

"Hold on," he said, a bit unsteadily. "There must be no more misunderstandings. What happened that night three weeks ago, had to happen; and five minutes before it happened I was wondering if I could aim straight enough in the light from the slag-pot to hit him. And I fully meant to do it."

She shuddered.

"I — I was afraid," she faltered. "I knew, you know — Japheth had told me, in — in justice to you. That was why I ran across the lawn and called to you."

The sweet beauty of her laid hold on him and he felt his grip going. Another word and he would be trespassing again. To keep from saying it he crossed to the recessed window and sat down in the sleepy-hollow chair which was the Major's peculiar possession in the music-room.

After a little he said: "Play something, won't you? — something that will make me a little less sorry that I didn't kill him."

"The idea!" she said. But when he settled himself in the big easy-chair as a listener, lying back with his eyes closed and his hands locked over one knee, she turned to the piano and humored him. When the final chord of the *Wanderlied* had sung itself asleep, he sat up and nodded approvingly.

"I wonder if you appreciate your gift as you should? — to be able to make a man over in the moral part of him with the tips of your fingers? The devil is exorcised, for the moment, and I can tell you all about it now, if you care to know."

"Of course I care," she assented.

"Well, to begin with, I'm no better than I have been; a little less despicable than you've been thinking me, perhaps, but more wicked. I've hated these two men ever since I was old enough to know how; and to get square with them, I haven't scrupled to sink to their level. The smash at Gordonia is my smash, I'm responsible for everything that has happened."

"I know it," she said. "Mr. Norman has told me."

"Looking it all over, I don't see that there is much to choose between me and the men I've been hunting down. They went after the things they needed, without much compunction for other people; and so did I. On the night of the — on the night when you called to me and I wouldn't answer, I was going down to rub it in; to tell them they were in the hole and that I had put them there. I met a man at the gate who told me what Japheth told you. It made a devil of me, Ardea. I took the man's gun and followed Vincent around the yard. I meant to kill him."

She nodded complete intelligence.

"The provocation was very great," she said evenly. "Why didn't you do it, Tom?"

"Now you've cornered me: I don't know why I didn't. I had only to walk away and let him alone when the time came. The slag-spilling would have settled him. But I couldn't do it."

"Of course you couldn't," she agreed convincingly. "God wouldn't let you."

"He lets other men commit murder; one a day, or such a matter."

"Not one of those who have named His name, Tom — as you have."

He shook his head slowly. "I wish that appealed to me, as it ought. But it doesn't. Where is the proof?"

She rose from the piano seat and went to stand before him.

"Can you ask that, soberly and in earnest, after the wonderful experience you have had?"

"I have asked it," he insisted stubbornly. "You mustn't take anything for granted. Just at that moment I couldn't kill a man; but that is all the difference. I've done what I meant to do, or most of it."

She was holding him steadily with her eyes. "Are you glad, or sorry, Tom?"

He frowned up at her.

"I don't know. Now that it's all over, the taste of it is like sawdust in the mouth; I'll admit that much. I'm free; 'free among the dead, like the slain that lie in the grave,' as David put it when he had sounded all the depths. Is that being sorry?"

"No — I don't know," she confessed.

He was smiling now.

"You think I ought to go back to first principles: get down on my knees and agonize over it? Sometimes I wish I could be a boy long enough to do just that thing, Ardea. But I can't. The mill won't grind with the water that has passed."

"But the stream isn't dry," she asserted, taking up his figure. "What will you do now? That is the question: the only one that is ever worth asking."

He was frowning thoughtfully again, and the words came as an unconscious voicing of vague under-depths.

"They took to the woods, the waste places, the deserts — those men of old who didn't understand. Some of them went blind and crazy and died there; and some of them had their eyes opened and came back to make the world a little better for their having lived in it. I'm minded to try it."

She caught her breath in a little gasp which she was careful not to let him see.

"You are going away?" she asked.

"Yes; out to the 'beyond' in northern Arizona. There is a new iron field out there to be prospected, and Mr. Clarkson wants me to go and report on it. And that brings us back to business. May I talk business — cold money business — to you for a minute or two?"

"If you like," she permitted. "Only I think the other kind of talk is more profitable."

"Wait till you hear what I have to say in dollars and cents. That ought to interest you."

"Why should it — particularly?"

"Because you are going to marry a poor man, and —"

She turned away from him quickly and stood facing the window. But he went on with what he had to say.

"That's all right; I can say it to your back, just as well. You know, I suppose, that your — that the Farleys have lost out completely?"

"Yes," — to the window-pane.

"Well, a curious thing has come to pass — quite a miraculous thing, in fact. Chiawassee will pay the better part of its debts and — and redeem its stock; or some of it, at least." He rose and stood beside her. "Isn't it a thousand pities that Colonel Duxbury couldn't have held on to his shares just a little longer?"

"Yes; he is an old man and a broken one, now." There was a sob in her voice, or he thought there was. But it was only the great heart of compassion that missed no object of pity.

"True; but the next best thing is to have the young woman who marries into the family bring it back with her, don't you think? Here is a check for what Mr. Farley's stock would have sold for before the troubles began. It's made payable to you because — well, for obvious reasons; as I have said, he lost out."

She turned on him, and the blue eyes read him to his innermost depths.

"You are still the headlong, impulsive boy, aren't you?" she said, not altogether approvingly. "You are paying this out of your own money."

"Well, what if I am?"

"If you are, it is either a just restitution, or it is not. In either case, I can not be your go-between."

"Now look here," he argued; "you've got to be sensible about this. There'll be four of you, and at least two incompetents; and you've got to have money to live on. I made Colonel Duxbury lose it, and —"

She stopped him with the imperious little gesture he knew so well.

"Not another word, if you please. I can't do your errand in this, and I wouldn't if I could."

"You think I ought to be generous and give it to him, anyway, do you?"

"I don't presume to say," was the cool rejoinder. "When you have come fully to your right mind, you will know what to do, and how to go about it."

He crumpled the check, thrusting it into his pocket, and made two turns about the room before he said:

"I'll see them both hanged first!"

"Very well; that is your own affair."

He fell to walking again, and for a full minute the silence was broken only by the murmur of men's voices in the library adjoining. The Major had company, it seemed.

"This is 'good-by,' Ardea; I'm going tomorrow. Can't we part friends?" he said, when the silence had begun to rankle unbearably.

"You've hurt me," she declared, turning again to the window.

"You've hurt me, more than once," he retorted, raising his voice more than he meant to; and she faced about quickly, holding up a warning finger.

"Mr. Henniker and Mr. Young-Dickson are in the library with grandpa. They will hear you."

"I don't care. I came here tonight with a heart full of what few good things there are left in me, and you — you are so wrapped up in that beggar that I didn't kill —"

"Hush!" she commanded imperatively. "Grandfather has not heard: he knows nothing, and he must nev —"

The murmur of voices in the adjoining room had suddenly become a storm, with the smooth tones of Mr. Henniker trying vainly to allay it. In the thick of it the door of communication flew open and a white-haired, fierce-mustached figure of wrath appeared on the threshold. For a moment Tom's boyish awe of the old autocrat of Deer Trace came uppermost and he was tempted to run away. But the wrath was not directed at him. Indeed, the Major seemed not to see him.

"What's all this I'm hearing now for the ve'y first time about these heah low-down, schemin' scoundrels that want to mix thei-uh white-niggeh blood with ouhs?" he roared at Ardea, quite beside himself with passion. "Wasn't it enough that they should use my name and rob my good friend Caleb? No, by heavens! That snivelin' young houn'-dog must pay his cou't to you while he was keepin' his —"

The Major's face had been growing redder, and he choked in sheer poverty of speech. Moreover, Tom had come between; had taken Ardea in his arms protectingly and was fronting the firebrand Dabney like a man.

"That's enough, Major," he said definitely. "You mustn't say things you'll be sorry for after you cool down a bit. Miss Ardea is like the king: she can do no wrong."

There was a gasping pause, the sound of a big man breathing hard, followed by the slamming of the door, and they were alone together again, Ardea crying softly, with her face hidden on the shoulder of shielding.

"Oh, isn't it terrible?" she sobbed; and Tom held her the closer.

"Never mind," he comforted. "He was crazy-mad, as he had a good right to be. You know he will be heartbroken when he comes to himself. You are his one ewe lamb, Ardea."

"I know," she faltered; "but O Tom! it was so unnecessary; so wretchedly unnecessary! It's — it's more than two whole months since — since Vincent Farley broke the engagement, and —"

He held her at arm's length to look at her, but she hid her face in her hands.

"Broke the engagement!" he exclaimed, almost roughly. "Why did he do that?"

She stood before him with her hands clasped and the clear-welled eyes meeting his bravely.

"Because I told him I could not marry him without first telling him that I loved you, Tom; that I had been loving you always and in spite of everything," she said.

And what more she said I do not know.

XXXVII

WHOSE YESTERDAYS LOOK BACKWARD

"Tom, isn't this the same foot-log you made me walk that day when you were trying to convince me that you were the meanest boy that ever breathed?" asked Ardea, gathering her skirts preparatory to the stream crossing.

"It is. But you didn't walk it, as you may remember: you fell off. Wait a second and give me those azaleas. I'll go first and take your hand."

Tom Gordon, lately home from a full half year spent in the unfettered solitudes of the Carriso iron fields, to be married first, and afterward to start up — with Caleb for superintendent — the idle Chiawassee plant as a test and experimental shop for American Aqueduct, was indemnifying himself for the long exile.

On this Saturday evening in the lovers' month of June he had walked Ardea around and about through the fragrant summer wood of the upper creek valley, retracing, in part, the footsteps of the boy whose fishing had been spoiled and the little girl who was to be bullied into submission; and so rambling they had come at length to the old moss-grown foot-log which had been a newly-felled tree in the former time. Tom went first across the rustic bridge, holding the hand of ecstatic thrillings, and pausing in mid-passage that he might have excuse for holding it the longer. Ah me! we were all young once; and some of us are still young, — God grant, — in heart if not in years.

It was during the mid-passage pause, and while she was looking down on the swirling waters sometime of terrifying, that Miss Dabney said:

"How deep is it, Tom? Would I really have drowned if you and Hector had not pulled me out?"

He laughed.

"It's a thankless thing to spoil an idyl, isn't it? But that is the way with all the little playtime heroics we leave behind in childhood. You could have waded out."

She made the adorable little grimace which was one of the survivals of the yesterdays, and suffered him to lead her across.

"And I have always believed that I owed my life to you — and Hector!" she said reproachfully.

"You owe me much more than that," he affirmed broadly, when they had sat down to rest — they had often to do this, lest the way should prove shorter than the happy afternoon — on the end of the bridge log.

"Money?" — flippantly.

"No; love. If it hadn't been for me, you might never have known what love is."

His saying it was only an upbubbling of love's audacity, but she chose to take it seriously. She was gazing afar into the depths of the fresh-green forest darkening softly to the sunset, with her hands clasped around the tangle of late-blooming white azaleas in her lap.

"It is a high gift," she said soberly; "the highest of all for a woman. Once I thought I should live and die without knowing it, as many women do. I wish I might give you something as great."

"I am already overpaid," he asserted. "For a man there is nothing so great, no influence so nearly omnipotent, as the love of a good woman. It is the lever that moves the world — what little it does move — up the hill to the high planes."

"A lever?" she mused; "yes, perhaps. But levers are only links in the chain binding cause to effect."

His smile was lovingly tolerant.

"Is that what your religion has brought you to, Ardea — a full-grown belief in a Providence that takes cognizance of our little ant-wanderings up and down the human runways?"

"Yes, I think so," she said; but she said it without hesitancy or a shadow of doubt.

"I'm glad; glad you have attained," he rejoined quite unaffectedly.

"It was hardly attainment, in my case," she qualified; and, after a momentary pause, she added: "any more than it was in yours."

"You think I, too, have attained?" he smiled. "I am not so sure of that. Sometimes I think I am like my father, who is like Mahomet's coffin; hanging somewhere between Heaven and earth, unable to climb to one or to fall to the other. But I'm not as brash as I was a year or so ago; at least, I'm not so cock-sure that I know it all. That evening in the music-room at Deer Trace changed me — changed my point of view. You haven't heard me rail once at the world, or at the hypocrites in it, since I came home, have you?"

"No."

"Well, I don't feel like railing. I reckon the old world is good enough to live in — to work in; and certainly there are men in it who are better than I'm ever likely to be. I met one of them last winter out in the Carriso cow country; a 'Protestant' priest, he called himself, of your persuasion. He was the most hopeless bigot I've ever known, and by long odds the nearest masculine approach to true, gritty saintliness. There was nothing he wouldn't do, no hardship he wouldn't cheerfully undergo, to brother a man who was down, and the wickedest devil in all that God-forsaken country swore by him. Yet he would argue with me by the hour, splitting hairs over Apostolic Succession, or something of that sort."

She smiled in her turn. "Did he regard you as a heretic?" she asked.

"Oh, sure! though he admitted that I might escape at the last by virtue of my 'invincible ignorance.' Then I would laugh at him, telling him he was a lot better than his bigotry. But he got the best of me in other ways. I owned the one buckboard in the northern half of Apache County, and my broncos were harness-broken and fast. So, when there was a shoot-up at the Arroyo dance-hall, or any other job of swift brothering to be done, I had to drive Father Philip."

She was musing again. "You used to write me that you were on the edge of things out there: it was a mistake, Tom; you were in the very heart of them."

He shook his head.

"No; the heart of them was back yonder in the music-room. There were chaos and thick darkness to go before that day of days; and it was your woman's love that changed the world for me."

"No," she denied; "that was only an incident. When chaos and darkness fled away, it was God who said, 'Let there be light.' The dawn had come for you before our day of days, Tom."

He stretched himself luxuriously on the sward at her feet.

"You may put it that way if you please. But I shall go on revering you as my torch-bearer," he asserted.

"Tell me," she said quickly; "was it for my sake that you spared Vincent Farley when all you had to do was to turn your back and go away?"

He took time to consider, and his answer put love under the foot of truth.

"No, it wasn't. If you make me confess the bald fact, I was not thinking of you at all, just at that one moment."

"I know it," she rejoined. "And I am big enough to be glad. Neither was it for my sake that you instructed your lawyers to return good for evil by redeeming the Farleys' stock just before they left for Colorado, or that you made restitution to the families of the men at Gordonia for their losses during the strike."

But again he was shaking his head dubiously.

"I'm not so sure about that. It's in any man to play high when the good opinion of the one woman is the stake. I'm a *poseur*, like all the others."

She smiled down on him and the slate-blue eyes were reading

him to the latest-indited heart-line.

"You are posing now," she asseverated. "Don't I know? — don't I always and always know?" And, after a reflective moment: "It is a great comfort to be able to love the poses, and a still greater to be permitted to discern the true man under them."

"I am glad to believe that you don't see quite to the bottom of that well, Ardea, girl," he said with sudden gravity. "I get only occasional glimpses, myself, and they make me seasick. I don't believe any man alive could endure it to look long into the inner abysses of himself."

"'The heart knoweth his own bitterness,'" she quoted, speaking softly; and then — O rarest of women! — she did not enlarge on it. Instead —

Silence while she was gathering the sweet-smelling tangle in her lap into some more portable arrangement. And afterward, when they were drifting slowly homeward in the lengthening shadows, a small asking.

"Mr. Morelock is coming out tomorrow to hold service in St. John's, and I shall go to play for him. Will you go with me, Tom?"

He smiled out of the gold and sapphire depths of a lover's reverie.

"One week from the day after the day after tomorrow — and it will be the longest week-and-two-days of my life, dearest — your grandfather will take you to church, and I shall bring you away. Won't that be enough?"

She took him quite seriously.

"I shall never be a Felicita Young-Dickson, and drag you," she promised. "But, O Tom! I wish —"

"I know," he said gently. "You are thinking of the days to come; when the paths may diverge — yours and mine — ever so little; when there may be children to choose between their mother's faith and their father's indifference. But I am not indifferent. So far from it, I am only anxious now to prove what I was once so bent on disproving."

"You yourself are the strongest proof," she interposed. "You will see it, some day."

"Shall I? I hope so; and that is an honest hope. And really and truly, I think I have come up a bit — out of the wilderness, you know. I am willing to admit that this is the best of all possible worlds; and I want to do my part in making it a little better because I have lived in it. Also, I'd like to believe in something bigger and better than protoplasm."

Her smile was of the kind which stands halfway in the path to tears, but she spoke bravely to the doubt in his reply.

"You do believe, Tom, dear; you have never seen the moment

when you did not. It was the doubt that was unreal. When the supreme test came, it was God's hand that restrained you; you know it now — you knew it at the time. And afterward it was His grace that enabled you to do what was just and right. Haven't you admitted all this to yourself?"

They had crossed the white pike to the manor-house gates and were turning aside from the driveway into the winding lawn path when he said:

"To myself, and to one other." Then, very softly: "I sat at my mother's knee last night, Ardea, and told her all there was to tell."

Ardea's eyes were shining. "What did she say, Tom, dear — or is it more than I should ask?"

"There is nothing you may not ask. She said — it wasn't altogether true, I'm afraid — but she put her arms around my neck and cried and said: *For this my son was dead, and is alive again; he was lost, and is found.*"

She slipped her arm in his, and there was a little sob of pure joy at the catching of her breath. The moon was just rising above the Lebanon cliff-line, and the beauty of the glorious night-dawn possessed her utterly. Ah, it was a good world and a generous, bringing rich gifts to the steadfast! Instinctively she felt that Tom's little confession did not require an answer; that he was battling his way to the heights which must be taken alone.

So they came in the sacred hush of the young night to a great tulip-tree on the lawn, and where a curiously water-worn limestone boulder served as a rustic seat wide enough for two whose hearts are one they sat down together, still in the companionship that needs no speech. It was Tom who first broke the silence.

"I have been trying ever since that night last winter to feel my way out," he said slowly. "But what is to come of it? I can't go back to the boyhood yesterdays; in a way I have hopelessly outgrown them. Let us admit that religion has become real again; but Ardea, girl, it isn't Uncle Silas's religion, or — or my mother's, or even yours. And I don't know any other."

She laid a hand on one of his.

"It is all right, dear; there is only the one religion in all Christendom — perhaps in all the world, or in God's part of it. The difference is in people."

"But this thing that has been slowly happening to me — this thing I am trying to call convincement: shall I wake up some day and find it gone, with all the old doubts in the saddle again?" he asked it almost wistfully.

"Who can tell?" she said gently. "But it will make no difference; the immutable fact will be there just the same, whether you are asleep or waking. We can't always stand on the Mount of Certainty, any of us; and to some, perhaps, it is never given. But when one saves his enemy's life and forgives and forgets — O Tom, dear! don't you understand?"

But now his eyes are love-blinded, and the white-gowned figure beside him fills all horizons.

"I can't see past you, Ardea. Nevertheless, I'm going to believe that I feel the good old pike solid underfoot . . . and they say that the House Beautiful is somewhere at the mountain end of it. If you will hold my hand, I believe I can make out to walk in it; blindfolded, if I have to — and without thinking too much of the yesterdays."

"Ah, the yesterdays!" she said tenderly. "They are precious, too; for out of them, out of their hindrances no less than their helpings, comes today. Kiss me, twice, Tom; and then I must go in and read to Major Grandpa."

THE END